It begins with a dream of buried children.

It begins with a resurrected child.

It begins with human sacrifice.

It requires new blood.

Malcolm Coffey has buried his past, but it has scraped its way out of its grave to find him.

"Next time, it's going to be me coming for you, boy, and I'll be somebody you trust, and you'll forget you're afraid until it's too late. Do you know what it feels like to burn from the inside out? It's like maggots crawling under your skin, maggots with stingers and suckers boring through you, eating their way out, slow at first, real slow . . ."

There is a place where nightmares are born.

There is a town where the night is eternal.

There is a breeding ground for horror.

There is one man and one girl, strangers bound by the past.

What waits in the Goat Dance, waits for them.

GOAT DANCE

DOUGLAS
CLEGG

POCKET BOOKS
New York London Toronto Sydney Tokyo

An *Original* Publication of POCKET BOOKS

POCKET BOOKS, a division of Simon & Schuster Inc.
1230 Avenue of the Americas, New York, NY 10020

ISBN: 0-671-66425-5

First Pocket Books printing July 1989

10 9 8 7 6 5 4 3 2 1

Printed in the U.S.A.

FOR MY MOTHER AND FATHER, AND PETER, JOHN, MUFFIE, AND THE BOY-EATING SPIDER

With special thanks to Mary Connally for putting it in good hands, and to Tracy Farrell for getting it in the right hands. Also, thanks to my publisher, Irwyn Applebaum, and to Dana Isaacson who, through various drafts, provided encouragement and cautionary tales. But most of all, I want to thank my editor, Linda Marrow, for taking my book (and me) in hand and for showing me what kind of smoke I am.

GOAT DANCE

PROLOGUE

WHAT KIND OF SMOKE ARE YOU?

News item from *The Westbridge County* (Va.) *Sentinel,* January 3, 1985:

THE LITTLE GIRL WHO CAME BACK FROM THE DEAD

Her name is Theodora Amory, her friends call her Teddy, and the doctors at the Westbridge Medical Center are calling her a modern-day miracle.

Teddy, who is all of 7 years old, was ice skating with her older brother, Jake, late yesterday afternoon on Clear Lake, when the ice gave way beneath her. Teddy went through the ice, while her brother struggled in vain to reach her. Several Pontefract Preparatory School students witnessed the accident from the football field and went out onto the ice, forming a human chain to try and aid in Jake Amory's rescue attempts of his sister. But it was Teddy's own father, Riland "Riley" Amory, who arrived shortly upon the scene and dove into the icy water to bring the little girl out of the freezing water just as an emergency unit arrived.

According to Mr. Amory, his daughter was beneath the water's surface for the better part of forty minutes. "But she's an Amory, and her mama's a Houston," he is reported to have told one of the paramedics, "and that means, she'll come through." Teddy was presumed dead by many of the witnesses, but after she'd been covered in warm towels and laid in the back of the ambulance, Mr. Amory administered some good old mouth-to-mouth resuscitation and within seconds, she was breathing again.

Upon Teddy Amory's arrival at Westbridge Medical, Dr. Walter Scott told Mr. Amory, "There's nothing wrong with this little girl. What's she doing in Emergency?"

Teddy, who will remain at the medical center for observation until Tuesday, told the *Sentinel,* "It was kind of scary and real cold. You know, the kind of scary that gets inside you? I guess I drank a lot of water, too, and my mommy says it's good for you. Lots of water. Maybe scary's good for you, too. Because I guess I knew it would be okay. My daddy says it's in my blood. And maybe it is."

Her father, Riley, Director of Buildings and Grounds at the Pontefract School, added, "My little baby's something else, ain't she?"

Obituary from *The Westbridge County* (Va.) *Sentinel,* August 27, 1986:

RILAND "RILEY" AMORY

PONTEFRACT—Riland "Riley" Amory died August 21 in Pontefract.

A lifetime resident of Westbridge County, Riley was Director of Buildings and Grounds at the Pontefract Preparatory School for Boys.

He is survived by his wife, Odessa Houston Amory, and two children, Jacob and Theodora.

Services were held at Gethsemane Baptist Church on August 26.

But what the obituary didn't say:

A man by the name of Riley Amory, a family man, a man who loved his work, a man who once upon a time took his wife to the Gethsemane Baptist Annual Potluck Supper, took his son skeet shooting, in other words, a regular guy; this man found a clearing on a hillside a few miles outside his hometown. He put a shotgun into his mouth, stroking the barrel lightly against his tonsils, savoring that rusty coldness as the last thing he would ever feel. He shut his eyes and sent out a prayer for his family and squeezed the trigger.

If you could've been there to ask him, before he did it, he might've told you about the funny smell he noticed in the air. A smell that meant for most folks sweat, lakewater, dying fish, and the end of summer, but which for him was a terrible, sweet smell. One that he'd inhaled one winter with a couple of friends. It was a smell that had gotten him high that night, and he'd never felt that young or strong since. That night when all hell broke loose.

Riley might also tell you that one of those friends had come back. That friend was talking to him in his dreams, and recently, when he was awake, too. But always late at night.

That friend told Riley about his daughter.

The power she wielded.

What had crawled inside her underwater.

Riley's little girl.

Teddy.

Something inside her, the thing that was causing her epilepsy, as well as her communion.

But on that lone hillside there was no one for Riley Amory to tell all this to. The blast from his gun was probably not even heard—there was no one within a three-mile radius to listen for it. The last thing Riley saw were some sparrows in the oak tree that he leaned against as he squeezed that trigger.

In the next second, the birds would fly out of the oak's branches into the fair morning air.

PART ONE

DISTURBANCES IN THE FIELD

Can these bones live?

—Ezekiel 37:3

CHAPTER ONE

DEM BONES

December 2, 1986

1.

Something snapped inside Jake Amory that morning. He felt his brain flexing, cracking like a whip. Driving him on. He knew that it was all building to this night, this one night. All the digging, all the bones, all the shit he'd been putting up with all his life.

He stepped up onto the front porch of his mother's house. It was three A.M., his usual hour of arrival. Jake might've joked that he still managed to get his eight hours sleep a night because he always slept straight until noon. But he didn't joke about too many things and he didn't talk to too many people. And lately he had not been getting more than three hours sleep a night.

Jake was swinging a gas can in his left hand. The weight of the can felt good to him, and he liked the way the gas sloshed around inside it, splashing him like a light rain. They'd told him no fire, but he figured that he could do it his way, and if it worked that would be all that mattered. The muscles in his left arm ached and even that felt good. He set the can down on the splintery gray boards of the porch and fumbled in his pockets for his housekeys. As he pulled the keychain out of the back pocket of his jeans, he felt the heat rising in his hand. Like friction against blisters, the keychain burned and froze his palm at the same time.

And man, it hurts so good. Jake grinned.

It was his good luck charm that caused the weird glowing in his hand. He clutched his fist about it. The keys dangled out from the opening between his thumb and forefinger. It seemed to wriggle in his fist like a worm.

Jake relaxed his fist. He looked down at the thing in his hand.

The human-bone charm possessed a glowworm-like phosphorescence. Just as it had the day Teddy almost drowned two years before *(did drown, my man, and something else crawled inside her and came back just like the Creature From The Black Lagoon).* That day that Jake opened Teddy's fist while his father bent over her, and there was the bone. How it had shone then like a beacon in the darkness of his life. It was just a fragment of a bone, maybe a toebone, Jake didn't know; but he did know that it gave him power. He was invincible. And he knew that he would always keep that bone with him. He drilled a small hole at its thickest edge and looped his keychain through it.

And he was never separated from it.

Oh, de toebone connected to de footbone, and de footbone connected to de—what the hell was it connected to, anyway? He jingled the keys in his hand.

Jake sought out the housekey, but tried the doorknob first. If his mother had been drinking, she would have left the front door open. She was always doing stupid things like that when she hit the bottle. When he nudged the door with the back of his hand it slid open as if it were greased. Inviting him in. Jake wanted to laugh out loud; this was turning into quite an amusing morning.

What's it matter? Ma's gonna say. No Manson family living in the woods. Them schoolboys got a hell of a lot more money and nice things than us. And if somebody wants to break in, well, god help 'em if they can find anything worth taking, and no lock's been invented's gonna keep 'em out. That's just what she's gonna say.

Why lock your door in a town like this?

Who was even going to hear you scream?

Jake rarely laughed these days, but standing on his front porch like this, gas can at his feet, door open, he wanted to break out in the biggest hyena cackle he had in him. Instead, he blew an imaginary feather out from between the gap in his front teeth: *got to stay in control, man, chill out.* But he couldn't help thinking his ma shouldn't do that—shouldn't forget to lock her doors. *It was downright dangerous. Anybody could just walk right in. Anybody. Murderer. Rapist. Thief.*

Even her own son on a crazy winter morning after he'd spent the past three nights camping out in the field. Just doing some fieldwork, Ma, that's all. Talking with some old friends, if you know what I mean. De armbone connected to de shoulderbone. Having heart-to-hearts with the dead. The dead, he considered, over and over, awestruck that he himself had been chosen by them, *the beyond, the out there. The what-will-come. Picked me. Jake.*

Jake Amory was six feet tall, just turned sixteen, and skinny. He was skinny by default: he'd never found any food he particularly liked. He combed his hair back away from his forehead, greasing the thick red strands with Brylcreme where it fell over his ears. He liked his ears. They were pointy. *Devil ears,* his ma called them, and he took this as an indication of his being special. Marked. Born to some purpose.

And this was it.

He covered his bloodshot, yellowish eyes with sunglasses. Jake had become sensitive to light this winter, and just that thin shaft of lamplight sketched across the porch hurt his eyes. His shades were the coolest things going, the kind with mirrors so that any jerk looking at you only sees himself reflected back.

Jake knew how intimidating that could be. To only see yourself everytime you look at somebody.

It was like he'd told his girlfriend the other night when she met him at the cemetery. They were making out on top of a flat gravestone. It was freezing but it felt kind of good, the cold stone against his back. "You want to become me," he told her, and she looked at him like he was crazy, "I can see it, inside you, like The Man With The X-Ray Eyes." But he knew that Maggie wasn't listening. Nobody listened yet, but they would. *Not just another pretty face, oh-ho, my friends, not just another pretty face. I am the herald of the Pocket Lips, dig?*

They'd all listen, and very soon. Those assholes at that snotfaced prep school, too. Just because his pa had been some Bozo at Buildings and Grounds the tuition was free and Jake was forced to go to that private zoo called Pontefract Prep. PeePee.

But Jake Amory was not part of that prep school bullshit. Jake was a townie and proud of it, a rebel when you came right down to it. *Not a backwoodsman, either, like you, Pa,* although he respected the hell out of his old man for what he'd done. It was the best thing his father could've done given the way things were.

Jake was made of sterner stuff. Sure, everything was a slimy joke in this Virginia backwater, but Jake knew how to fix that. *Oh, yes. The end of the world is coming, the Apocalypse, what Teddy called the Pocket Lips. It's all coming, Soon to a Theater Near You!* And when that shining moment arrived, Jake Amory intended to be wired for sound. He could feel it. *Dem bones, dem bones, dem dry bones.*

All those preppies with their pretty boy smiles and shiny hair and Daddy's credit cards. Nasal southern accents. Jake could only stomach so much of those squirrels at school before he felt like puking his guts out all over them.

And that night, lying on the cold gravestone with Maggie McBean, he'd told her, "I don't just hate them, babe, you know, Ma, Teddy, the fucking school, prepdipshits. Hate ain't enough. I want them destroyed. Kiss 'em with my Pocket Lips." He dreamed of the sky raining fire and snowing fallout down on Pontefract. Anything would've been better than the way things were: dull, stagnant as a swamp, like a sewer. "They're all dead now, only nobody told 'em." Jake grunted as he dry-humped Maggie against the stone. As he continued his tirade against the town, punctuated by heavy breathing, Maggie gave him that look. The look that meant she knew he'd been dusting or speeding or snorting. That look meant she was scared of him, what he might do.

Jake loved that look.

But these days he was into heavier junk than you could get if you hopped a bus to Richmond once a month. Junk made him think more clearly, and it pushed his soul to the limit. It made him potent, focused him. Like a magnifying glass on an ant, frying that sucker to a crisp at high noon. But he didn't need the kind of junk you bought from some two-bit pusher in an alley. Now he had *dem bones dem bones dem dry bones.*

Jake wiped his nose as he ground his crotch into Maggie's. "It's gonna be judgment day, Mags, and they're gonna see. Who they are."

He squeezed Maggie's right breast through her Coors sweatshirt.

"Ow!" she cried out and slapped him, leaving a crimson handprint across his pale face. "Jeez, Jake, that hurt!"

He didn't even feel the slap. "You know I could do it to you right here, Mags. I did it to a stiff this morning, and I could do it to you, too. If you lie real still I can pretend that you're dead, too."

"You're gross, Jake, stop it, will ya?"

He continued bucking his denimed hips into her corduroyed thighs. "You know what this town is, babe? It's a scraping. A scraping from the asshole of hell." And Jake thought, *what a beautiful image, what a clear way of looking at things.* It turned him on.

But now Jake Amory stood on the front porch of his mother's house at three A.M. and heard the voices in his head. They were getting louder, more insistent, like hunters' drums driving the beast that was within him out into the front hall light.

The voices seemed to be just under the skin of the world. He felt like if he reached out and scratched the surface of things with his dirty fingernails, beneath would be the veins and arteries and the yellow fat of the world.

Just like when you skin a rabbit.

You ever skin a little girl, son? The voices curdled into this one voice, buzzing around his head. Now Jake could almost see his pa standing in the half-light of the front hallway. His pa looked none the worse for having shot half his face off, because it was like a mask had been pulled off to reveal another face behind the one Jake had grown up with. A face that sizzled with red tendons stretched across a shattered yellow skull, and skin torn back to his ears as if a wild animal had eaten into it. Jake might've wondered how he could speak at all, given that he had no lower jaw. But there he stood, clear as day now, in his bib overalls that he wore to work, his hands tucked tidily in his pockets, acting like he was just giving Jake another talk on the birds and the bees. *It ain't so hard a thing to do, you know. You just hang her upside down, heat yourself a good sharp blade. Your Boy Scout knife'll do. Then you start down at her ankle—it's real tender and thin there—and it's just like peeling potatoes. Only most potatoes don't scream, I guess, but it can't be helped. You got to ignore her screams. She's only tricking you. She's only after one thing and it's a blasted thing for a sister to want from her brother, you know, it, boy. But you always knew what she wanted from you, didn't you, boy? You was always a smart one. You know your shit, son, you ain't just another pretty face. You been kissed by the Pocket Lips. And now you just got to peel that skin off her so you can show the world what she really is.*

Somekindamonster. Somekindamonster.

She ain't your sister and she ain't no little girl. She ain't human. Why, you know your real sister drowned in that lake two years ago and what that water sent you up was this monster in your sister's skin. But it's just skin, son, and you got to remove it. She'll scream, boy, but don't you pay her no never mind. 'Cause under that skin it's just laughing its nasty little head off at you. You know what it really wants from you, dontcha?

But his pa stopped speaking as Jake entered the house. *We'll be waiting for you, Jake, and we will be waiting for the skin and the blood. We will be waiting for you, too, though, so don't fuck up. We don't take kindly to fuck ups.* The image of his pa burned away reminded Jake of the time he was at the movies and one of the picture frames got stuck and burned and bubbled on the screen. That was how his pa went—he just bubbled and blistered until all Jake saw was the staircase behind him. The voices were also gone.

Jake climbed the stairs. His left arm ached from carrying the gas can, so he changed it over to his right hand. Gasoline sloshed across his wrist. When he reached the landing he set the can down. He was sweating.

Jake reached up to wipe his hand across his forehead, careful not to knock his sunglasses off. He coughed from the smell of gasoline. He rubbed his bone keychain but felt no heat. He was on his own.

2.

Jake's sister Teddy sat up in bed.

She thought she'd heard a noise in the hallway.

She'd been dreaming of gas stations, of having to use the "facilities," which her mother kept telling her was more polite than "I gotta go to the can, man." In the dream a stranger was driving her somewhere in his car. They pulled over at a gas station. She got out of the car and went toward the restroom. The gassy smell grew stronger. She thought she might faint.

Teddy knew that if she passed out she'd be drowning in that cold blue water again, that clutching water where that thing had touched her, tried to get inside her; she had been dying, she even had wanted to die in that water, it was so peaceful, but that thing had grabbed her, tried to pull her back. And she knew that the thing in the water had been bad. The way the gas station smell was bad.

Teddy, in her dream, did not faint. She went into the restroom. She was determined not to give in to that weak feeling. And even as the gas grew more intense and smothering when she opened one of the toilet stall doors, she felt all the more powerful for not giving in to that collapsing feeling inside her. No, she would not faint.

That was her dream. And this was also her dream: *within the toilet stall of that gas station she knew she was safe. But just beyond its four walls she sensed its presence. The thing in the water. The thing that smelled of gas and swampy decay.*

Teddy awoke from this dream just as she relieved herself in her pajamas.

Wet the bed.

Whenever she dreamed of going to the bathroom, she usually did. As her mother would say with a disappointed look, "It came to pass."

It came to pass, she imagined Mommy whispering in the darkness, *and passing it draws near. The kiss of the Pocket Lips.*

Teddy shuddered, but knew that it was her imagination speaking to her in the blackness. It was only her imagination that pressed against the side of her face like her mother's lips kissing her goodnight.

Teddy was now wide awake. Her eyes began adjusting to the dark. She smelled something strange. Something besides the gas station smell and the odor from the damp yellow stain on her bed. She thought she smelled . . . something burning. But when she sniffed the air again, nothing.

Do dreams smell?

3.

Jake stood over his mother's bed and gazed curiously at the sleeping figure as if she were an alien. Through the purple darkness, Jake could see her dirty blond hair stuck greasily along her face with sweat, her flimsy nightgown barely covering her flabby body, her sagging breasts beneath the robe's sheer material, heaving with each snore, exhaling putrid air. He smelled the bourbon all around him. *Drunk as a skunk, just like every night since Pa bit the big one.* The sight and smell of her nauseated him.

Then Jake heard his pa's voice rise like a gust of wind in his head. *Her first, boy, and then the little monstergirl. But you be careful with that fire, hear?* The voice came and went with Jake's own deep breathing.

Jake lifted the gas can and began pouring its contents around the edge of the sleeping woman's bed. Like warmed-up Karo syrup on a stack of pancakes.

Odessa Amory stirred in her sleep. Her eyes remained closed as she sniffed dreamily at the air.

Jake reached into his breast pocket for the book of matches. Boy Scout motto was *Be Prepared.* Even though Jake was kicked out of the Scouts when he was still a Tenderfoot for painting swastikas on gravestones, he still went along with it. He was always prepared.

His mother's head twitched as if in a spasm. She smelled the gasoline. She smelled him.

"Who's there?" she whispered, slurring her words so that it became "Whooshere?" like wind escaping from a balloon.

Jake flipped open the matchbook. His hands were trembling. He hadn't expected her to wake up, not if she was on one of her drunks. He expected her to be like one of the corpses he'd been digging up—to just lie there and be still. To allow him to get his job done right. Jake plucked a match from the book and struck it against a bedpost.

The match gave off a brief puff of smoke and a spark. It did not catch fire.

"Jakey? Zhat you?" his ma asked. "Whatshallthish?" She rubbed her eyes. When she turned onto her side, trying to sit up, a bottle of Virginia Gentleman rolled out from the bed and thumped to the floor.

Maybe if you were cold sober you'd figure it out, stupid bitch. Jake tossed the bad match down on the bed. "Shit," he hissed. He tore another match from the pack and struck it against the bedroom wall, but it bent in two and he dropped that one, also. "Goddamn it, sucker, light up!"

Odessa Amory sat bolt upright in bed. She clutched her hands to her breasts, holding her robe together. "Jake?" Fear curdled in her voice.

He gave no response.

"What are you—ishat you, Jakey?" Her voice was meek and pleading, and he knew that she wanted him to answer, *yeah, Ma, just me, no Manson family in these woods, no boogeyman gonna jump out from under the bed, Ma, just your boy, and I got something here for you, too.*

His ma began coughing violently, her smoker's hack.

Jake reached down to touch her face. He slid his fingers from her earlobe down her cheek to the tip of her nose. His fingers left a slimy gasoline trail.

"Jake," she whimpered, sounding like a thick sponge being squeezed of water.

Jake jerked his hand back. Made a fist. Brought it down in a razor-fine arc. Across the bridge of her nose. He kept his eyes closed. He did not want to think about what he was doing.

When Odessa yelped an image formed in Jake's mind: he saw a bristling rat with blood-red eyes lying on his ma's bed. And he knew that if he was smart, if he wanted to make it through this night, he must hold that image.

Jake could open his eyes now. It was safe.

He saw the rat. *Blood spurting out of its snout. Its whiskers bristling as it gnashed its silver, dagger-like teeth. It shrieked in pain, its red eyes widening in feral terror. Dirty, dirty, filthy,* the words flooded through Jake as he lifted the gas can over his head, *you stuck your fucking whiskers in the wrong mousetrap, you dirty, dirty,* and brought it down full force on the rat, *oh god no Ma what am I . . .*

The rat did not shriek a second time.

Jake hit the rat across its forehead three more times. Each time the can came down, more gas splashed out on the bed.

The rat lay still.

He took a few deep breaths. The gas smell was beginning to make him sick. He reached down and touched the rat's muzzle. He opened its mouth. He poured gasoline down its throat. The rat made some choking noises, spitting up as much gas as went down its throat, but continued to lie very still.

It was beginning to look less like a rat and more like something human. Something familiar. Jake turned away quickly. He went over to his ma's dresser and switched on the lamp. He would not look back at the rat. He was afraid it would start bubbling and melting, that it would pull off its mask. That it would no longer be a rat.

"Yeah," Jake mumbled, as if answering a call within his brain, "got to burn the rat, my man." He opened the top dresser drawer. There among scarves and earrings were a couple of packs of Merit cigarettes and a Bic lighter.

Jake smiled. He lifted the lighter carefully out of the drawer. "Just want to flick my Bic," he said.

Then he returned to that bed where the rat lay unconscious.

4.

Teddy was in the hallway when she saw Jake come staggering toward her. He held a can in his hand. Like her dream, he smelled of gas stations.

He set the can down on the hall carpet.

He did not say anything. She could not see his face clearly in the dim light.

"Something's burning," she said to the dark figure.

She peered beyond him to her mother's bedroom. The door was shut; smoke curled out from beneath it.

"Mommy!" Teddy squealed, "Jake!"

Jake stepped closer to her. He seemed to relax when she cried out, tired, but still able to smile compassionately for his sister. He opened his arms wide to her.

Teddy took a step backwards.

Jake moved forward swiftly and touched her shoulder. A blue spark ricocheted between them; Teddy jerked back as if she'd been hit with a rock. The blue of that spark was like a flashbulb in her face. Jake's hand smelled of gas stations.

"It's under control, Teddy," Jake said, his voice raspy. He patted her on the head, his fingers lingering in her long strands of hair. He began stroking her hair, and she felt shivers inside her. A crackle of static electricity seemed to go through her.

"But, Jake, Mommy," she sobbed.

Jake grabbed her hair in bunches, pulling at her scalp. "Gimme kiss, Teddy, gimme kiss."

"Let me go!" She tried pulling her head back, but it hurt too much. Jake did not let up on his grip.

"C'mon, Teddy, you want it, you need it now—kiss of the

Pocket Lips, right? Here it comes, just for you, Teddaroo, the Pocket Lips," and with his free hand, Jake reached into his pocket and pulled something out. He held it up for Teddy to see, forcing her head back. "Behold, the kiss of the Pocket Lips!"

It was a knife.

"Kissy-kissy," Jake cackled.

Teddy screamed. As she cried out, striking at Jake with her arms and legs, she felt the heat rising under her skin. And she knew it was coming. It had been a flash of blue she'd seen, something was shortcircuiting her brain. Unlike in her dream, she would not be able to resist passing out. What her mom called a "gift from God," but what Teddy knew was a curse. What had begun two years ago beneath the ice of Clear Lake. What Dr. Scott called a seizure. Coming. On its way.

Not now, she thought, *not now!*

Teddy was losing consciousness. The world was becoming pinpoints of blackness. She felt a prickly heat along her arms and legs. She was not even aware of her older brother standing over her as she fell to the carpet; he was singing, "Kissy-kissy, time to dance, baby, dance for the Pocket Lips!"

Behind Teddy's eyes the world became a translucent ice that shattered as she fell into a cold, viscous blue darkness.

Excerpt from Dr. Prescott Nagle's *First Families of Pontefract, Including a Brief History of the Region* ($12.95, Lexington-Jackson Printers. All proceeds to go to The Pontefract Historical Society.):

> . . . One particularly bloodthirsty tribe was that of the Tenebro Indians who occupied for various periods modern day Rockbridge and Westbridge Counties. They are best known for having been wiped out by the Catawba on the eve of the French and Indian War. The Tenebro were mainly hunters, and lived for a while in

peace with fur traders who passed through this ridge of the valley. But they evidently had one habit that the other Indians of the time, the Senedos, Tuscarora, and Shawnee, found repulsive, and so when the Catawba massacred the tribe as they crossed the mountains to the west of the county, no tears were shed, either among the whites or among the Tenebro's Indian brothers.

The Tenebro celebrated a winter festival, when they felt the rebirth of some Great Spirit was imminent, either symbolically or in actuality. Many men died for sport during this festival, when the Shaman would perform his Ghost Dance for the tribe, and the bones of the dead were exhumed for their descendants to carry as they followed the Shaman in his dance. Thus came the nickname among tribes for the Tenebro: Men-Of-Bone. Less obvious is their totem, the maggots which they held sacred for the invertebrates' ability to clean the corpses after the exhumation. But at the end of this week-long dance and feast, the Shaman would choose a maiden and a brave to represent the twin aspects of the deity. It is presumed that a ceremony of sorts, perhaps a fertility rite, took place. A great cannibalistic bloodfeast would follow, in which prisoners, white men in particular, were torn limb-from-limb and eaten without benefit of fire. Of course, these stories come to us primarily through tales from such marginally reliable men as William Parsifal in his *1826 History of the Shenandoah,* and we must keep in mind he was writing seventy years after the Tenebro were wiped out completely. Other sources are perhaps even less reliable: supposed unnamed eyewitness accounts appear in the County Register of 1756, but hatred of the Indian was at an all-time high in that year because of the frequent unprovoked attacks upon townships (including the burning of our own first town of Pontefract, not two miles from the present location—an act of arson which apparently was committed by our forefathers themselves because of fear of an outbreak of some cholera-type plague from the use of tainted drinking water).

The Tenebro, and their mysterious rituals which even the most violent tribes feared, are gone from this earth. The present day excavation on the shores of Clear Lake, which was undertaken with a grant from the Virginia Society for Historical Preservation, has not only uncovered relics of the first town of Pontefract, but also evidence of a Tenebro burial mound . . .

CHAPTER TWO

CUP: THE PAST

1.

From *The Nightmare Book of Cup Coffey:*

What I remember of December 18, 1974, is not as vague as I'd like it to be. I would like to say I was younger then, only a child, but that is as weak an excuse as any. But I *was* younger then, and childhood had only visibly turned to adolescence—inside, in my heart of hearts, I was just a boy with a crush on a girl.

And I was willing to protect her from anything.

That winter at Pontefract Prep, before Christmas break, I tried. I know that's what I was doing: trying to protect her. But how foolish and gallant and tragic it became.

The night of my initiation.

You see, we had clubs, we called them tribes, sort of junior fraternities. We took the names of various Indian tribes of the region, and through them, formed our cliques. These were our forums for mild rebellions, getting seniors to buy beer, all the early male bonding rituals. The club I was in took its name from local Indians called the Tenebro, but we were just adolescent white boys out for a good time at a boarding school.

2.

"This winter would be unbearable without you," Lily told him, "but I'm not sure I like this initiation business, I mean, really, Cup, bones and bourbon. Don't you think you and your little friends should grow up?" She kept her voice to a whisper, and she patted the top of his head as if he were a puppy crouched down there behind the kitchen door, spying on the party.

Lily brushed her fingers through her shiny blond hair, and it crackled with static electricity. "That's what I get for rubbing your scalp—now I'll look like Medusa when I take the canapés out."

Cup grinned from where he huddled and winked at her. "Turn 'em to stone." His legs were beginning to cramp from that position and he wished she'd just get out there, grab the bottle and get back with it so he could get the hell out of the Marlowe-Houston House. If he were to be caught . . .

"What can you possibly see from down there, anyway? Women's panties?" Lily headed for the refrigerator. She opened it and pulled out a tray full of hors d'oeuvres, and then nudged the door shut.

"Come on, Lily," Cup whispered.

She put her finger to her lips to shush him and carried the tray into the living room. The kitchen door swung shut behind her. Cup had to push it forward a bit so he could see more than just the back of some teachers' pants as they huddled around the piano while someone, very drunk, played a rather original rendition of "Have Yourself A Merry Little Christmas."

But the music stopped suddenly when a snowball hit the front picture window with a loud *mush!* and then dropped into the snow-covered bushes below, out of view. Its icy, dirty imprint remained like that of a child's palm pressed against the glass.

Cup saw Gower Lowry, the head of the English Department, duck as if the snowball was meant for him, and then try to make it seem as if he were merely bending over to check his shoelaces. The other teachers around the piano continued their drinking and buzzing conversations. Dr. Cammack, Pontefract Prep's headmaster, raised his glass of sherry to the frosted window, "To the spirit of youth, shall we say?" This was followed by obligatory laughter from the faculty.

"One of those Indian clubs," someone suggested. "What do they call themselves? Tribes?"

"No, I think the Potomacs or Sioux or something," said a woman, who stood out of Cup's field of vision.

"Tuscarora, Catawba and Tenebro," Dr. Prescott Nagle corrected them, and although Cup could not see Dr. Nagle clearly, only a bit of his reflection in the picture window, he could tell from his voice that he was nervous—as though unsure of his own subject: history. "I believe the Tuscarora make up most of the lacrosse team. And the Tenebro—well, I suppose since the boys consider it their secret, I should leave it at that."

Cup heard Mr. Lowry whisper, "Old Bagel is an expert on everything these days. Always digging around," and a woman chuckled at this. Gower Lowry, whom Cup could see the most clearly, then wagged his head from side to side—although in his mid-fifties, he had already Grecian-formulaed his hair into a peculiar metallic red. He hunched his shoulders up and thrust his hands stiffly into the pockets of his herringbone tweed jacket. Now Cup could see him in profile, and for just an instant Lowry resembled a vulture sitting high on some craggy peak looking down upon a dying animal, waiting for his chance. "I think we know who's responsible for such . . . mischief." Then turning to nod almost defiantly at Dr. Nagle, he continued, "And who encourages it out of an unprofessional and desperate attempt at 'popularity.' This school needs a clean sweep, can't have rotten apples in the barrel, I always say. And inside those that appear shiny and edible lurks the worm of corruption. By that I mean one Mr. Coff—"

Dr. Cammack set his sherry glass down hard upon the

side table like a judge hammering his gavel for silence in the court.

Lowry pretended not to notice. "—ffey," he completed his statement, and Cup winced when he heard his own last name mentioned. Cup let the door shut completely and looked up at the ceiling, his eyes welling with tears. This confirmed his fears that the faculty talked about him, about what happened during semester finals. He felt doomed. He reached into the pocket of his jacket and touched the prize he'd wrestled from a dog that evening. No matter what they did to him after Christmas break, he still had this night, initiation.

He took a deep breath and opened the door a crack. He heard the tail end of what Dr. Cammack was saying, "and I think, Gower, you are, perhaps, violating the confidentiality of quite another matter."

Under his breath, Gower Lowry mumbled, "Headmasters should not play favorites." But this comment was lost among the clinking glasses, the intermittent chuckles and "ahems" that punctuated the several conversations going around the room.

From where Cup was crouching, he could only see a vertical rectangle of the Marlowe-Houston House's living room. The back of Dr. Cammack's head, Dr. Nagle's arm when it flailed out as he was telling a story, the back edge of the sleek black piano, five teachers gathered around the piano (he mainly only saw their trouser legs, they were so close to the kitchen door). But he could not see Lily at all. The plan had been that she would go directly to the bar, and when she saw that no one was looking, she'd grab the bottle and walk back to the kitchen with it.

Dr. Cammack looked to his left, out of Cup's range of vision. "Lily, could you bring out some clean glasses? I think we've run through here and Bob Reed seems to think he needs another sip."

Other voices, near the piano:

"I thought you said there'd be a major spread here. I skipped dinner for this hamster food?"

"There's your major spread."

"Cammack's daughter?"

"Odds on she's a virgin?"

"Not the way Lowry is going after her. Look at the way his eyes follow her."

"Don't be ridiculous—he's too busy planning to make the evening miserable for Pres Nagle, did you notice that snippy comment he made about teachers and popularity? Lowry does have it in for the old guy, doesn't he?"

"I saw you, the way you put your hand on that Cammack girl's shoulder . . ."

Cup could not make out who the teachers were that were saying all this, but it made him angry to think they'd talk about Lily the way they did.

Then Lily came back into view, heading toward the kitchen with a tray of empty glasses.

Cup sat back, allowing the kitchen door to shut all the way.

In another moment, Lily Cammack stepped back into the kitchen.

She set the tray with the glasses across a cutting board near the oven. Then she returned to where Cup sat and offered her hand to him; he took it, and repressing a groan, stood up. Neither of them spoke as she led him to the far side of the kitchen. "This is boring, and I can't get to the whiskey," she finally whispered.

"Did you hear Lowry?"

"How could I not? You mean about you, well, he's just an old goat who's always looking to butt heads. He always has it in for somebody, doesn't he?"

"Yeah, only it's my butt he'd like to butt right out of here."

"Keep your voice down. Poor baby," she whispered. She drew Cup's face toward her own. Her lips brushed across his and pressed against his cheek.

"Can we hurry this along?" Cup murmured, and felt suddenly intoxicated, not from the sherry she'd given him earlier, but by her jasmine perfume which seemed so unwinterish and yet fit her perfectly. "I'm—I'm going to be in hot water if—"

She gave him another peck on the cheek. "How hot can it get?" She brought her face back and her mood darkened. "It's this stupid Tenebro initiation. Don't you think your little clubs are silly? They aren't really fraternities, are they? Just excuses for getting drunk and acting juvenile. What's the point of going through with this if you might not even be here next semester?"

Cup shrugged. "Nothing to lose, I guess."

"Life and limb. Really, Cup, digging up bones and stealing liquor. How attractive. How mature. You owe me one. You still want the bottle?"

He glared sarcastically. "What do you think?"

"Well, Daddy will do his little toast number any minute, and then I'll grab it."

"So dramatic. Why can't you just get it now? I got to take a leak."

"Tie a knot in it," she said playfully. She went to the cupboard for clean sherry glasses and Cup helped her arrange them on a silver tray. "Was it your little gang that threw that snowball earlier, Cup? Or do I dare attribute it to your best friend, ha ha, Bart?"

3.

From *The Nightmare Book of Cup Coffey:*

I was only sixteen and I had never before cheated on a test—God's honest truth. May He strike me dead. I panicked so much over that damn chemistry test and I was caught cheating, stupidly, *stupidly,* my own mistake, poor execution, "dishonorably," as Lowry put it. Caught by that devil Bart Kinter.

I have a theory now, looking back on that cheating episode of December, 1974: those who get caught at anything only do so because someone is out to get them. A lot of people don't get caught. But I did.

I was aware that more than a few of my fellow students at

Pontefract Prep cheated. Constantly. I watched one of my former roommates scribbling notes for an upcoming English Lit. test onto the seat of his desk with a ballpoint pen. No, I take that back, he didn't just scribble, he *engraved.* I saw my Tenebro Blood Brother with crib notes for the French final. Thad Stamp, III, had even gone so far as to set a whole slew of three-by-five cards on his lap while he took the World History mid-term. He forgot those cards at the end of the test. He stood up from his desk. As he stood, those index cards filled with arcane doodlings about Huguenots and the Hundred Years War flew like a magician's white doves across the classroom. But Thad Stamp, III, was not turned in to the vicious and unyielding Honor Council. Oh, no. Old Bagel, as we called Dr. Nagle, was absorbed in one of his textbooks. He didn't notice those telltale cards scattered across the floor, even while Thad went around and collected them. Thad Stamp, III, aced the World History mid-term and destroyed all hopes the rest of us had for some kind of curve. All it would've taken was one, "J'accuse."

But there were no takers.

I, on the other hand, did get caught. Did get turned in.

What separated me from students like Thad Stamp, III?

What mark of Cain did I bear?

Someone had it in for me. As Lily used to say, *my best friend, ha ha, Bart Kinter.*

Bart Kinter was a senior, a towhead from the neighboring town of Cabelsville. He was only admitted to Pontefract Prep because he was somehow related to one of its founders (you know, all those backwoodsmen intermarried and created three-toed babies, albinos and the likes of Bart Kinter). He was what you call a legacy student. Wouldn't you know it? He was also "Chief" of the Catawba tribe, a campus club that boasted more bullies than Teddy Roosevelt. He was what guidance counselors politely referred to as a "disciplinary problem," because even teachers, you know, are afraid of some students.

He was the oldest senior the school had, weighing in at nineteen years old. But you'd never know it to talk to him.

And Bart Kinter had it in for me.

I think there are some people in a given lifetime who are natural born enemies. It might have something to do with an incompatible smell, or something rotten you detect in the other guy's eyes. Somehow you know when you meet that you will never get along.

Kinter and I were of this variety. There was nothing I did not loathe about him. Not his pug little nose that was eternally dripping, not his slit green eyes, not those warped apricot ears that burst with fur in the winter when he forgot to clip back the hair. That sniggering, adenoidal way of speaking. He reminded me of one of those little plastic trolls that girls play with and think are so adorable, when we all know they're as ugly as sin.

Oh, and permit me to mention one other thing Kinter possessed: the talent for inspiring fear. I can admit that now. Fear. Plain and simple, with no logic to back it up. Just fear.

Initially when I was just entering my freshman year at school I thought Bart Kinter disliked me because there really *was* something wrong with me (maybe I *did* smell bad—I only washed my socks every third week). But you can only believe something like that for so long before you've got to sit back and say, "Fuck it," and get on with life.

And admit if the truth be known, the guy's a creep.

This was a revelation to me.

How it happened, the cheating episode, involving my best friend, ha ha, Bart Kinter. This is as close to a play-by-play as I can come:

I'm in one of the three main examination rooms. A test is usually administered in one of the ordinary classrooms. But for the end-of-term exams, they really like to stick it to you, both physically and psychologically. Every piece of furniture in the designated exam room is dark, hard, wooden. You are forced to sit in the kind of chair that will, in later life, result in hemorrhoids. You are supervised not by teachers but by Proctors. A Proctor is usually a student-teacher from one of the local colleges who is incapable of answering questions that might arise while you take the exam.

Why is it that whenever you take a test, your senses sharpen like the tip of your Number 2 pencil, and you hear people in the world, laughing, perhaps out ice skating on the lake, or making a snowman near the footbridge? And dogs—do they only bark and race across campus during exams? You smell every hickory-smoke fire from every chimney in town. You take time to analyze, for sentence structure, the obscene graffiti about donkey genitalia on your desktop, and read the Braille of dried chewing gum on the desk's underside.

My real best friend, Whit, sits across from me and looks earnest and scholarly. He is prepared. Unlike me.

I scan the exam. It looks like a very bad recipe. Haiku in the original Japanese. Chemistry for me is when two people get together and make sparks: Bogie and Bacall, Catherine the Great and her unholy mule (back to donkey genitals). And Lab? Well, I like to think of Lab as a kind of furry, dark dog with a pleasant personality.

I glance over to Whit for help, but Whit is no cheater, no passer of notes. How could I expect him to be? Had I sunk so low that I would do that to my best friend? How could I even be a cheater, Malcolm Coffey, called "Cup" by one and all? I am an okay student, never honor roll material, but then, *hey, who needs it?*

No, I'm no cheater.

But I am up against some tough competition here, not only the other students, but also that invisible competition my parents often mention:

Getting into a good college.

I don't have the heart to get Whit to cheat on my behalf. I'd never ask a friend to risk that.

I'd much rather drag down a nodding acquaintance. Or an enemy.

So I look to my left and there is my best friend, ha ha, Bart Kinter. Looking like God's fool. Bart, nineteen years old and here he is in Junior Chemistry for another year. This year, I am sure, Bart has done his homework. He knows what he's doing.

Then, something like seduction occurs. I drop my pencil to the floor.

I wait for my classmates to look up and see what my next move is going to be.

I make no move.

I pretend that I haven't even noticed the missing pencil.

I am still reading the exam. I squint my eyes and drop my lower lip down, slightly, so that it looks like I am intent upon a particular question. Then I glance up to the ceiling as if the question I have just read needs to be rolled around in my brain until it hits something and then, *tilt!*

So. Now I am ready to answer this question. I reach for my pencil, which Not Two Seconds Ago rested upon the worn horizontal groove at the top edge of my desk.

I look around the desk for my pencil. Not there. Under the blue examination book? *Nope.* Maybe it's still in my pockets —not there, either. So I look down to my right and then to my left, and—there it is, on the floor!

I reach down for my Number 2 pencil. As I come up, in the arc of my ascent, I cock my head just a bit more to the left and gooseneck it out further to catch the tail end of some chemical equation Kinter has just written down.

I begin to write scrawl for jagged scrawl exactly what Kinter is writing. After two years in this course, he is a good chemistry student. He has even studied for this test.

I forget it is his paper I am looking at. As I copy his work, our papers become one.

Like I said, it's pure seduction.

Only I'm the one who gets screwed because Bart Kinter turns around. He is smiling. He puts two and two together. His curdled ears blaze crimson with delight. He raises his hand to get the Proctor's attention.

And after the wheels are set in motion I am given a stay of execution until after Christmas break.

What I remember most, after the Honor Trial, was that I cried a hell of a lot. Getting caught cheating probably meant no Good College, and worse, public humiliation. I was sure I'd be expelled. Pontefract Prep had a strict honor code. Lying, cheating, stealing. If you were caught, no questions asked.

But when I was done crying, I thought of Bart Kinter. The boy who found it in his evil heart to turn me in. To squeal.

I plotted in my feverish adolescent mind. What would be his punishment? What form of execution? It scares me now, thinking back on all this, retracing my footsteps to that night twelve years ago. Now I know the outcome, where things finally led. I know I planted the seeds that night just as surely as I'd taken that bone from a dog before the Tenebro initiation ritual. The night Lily stole a bottle of Jack Daniels from a faculty party.

What is it about an open field at night that frightens you? Could it be that someone, or something, is waiting in that field for you?

Back when I was sixteen, stealing bones and bourbon and getting myself royally expelled, I didn't worry too much about consequences. I didn't worry about things waiting for me in empty fields.

In those days, all I knew about was revenge.

4.

Cup was shivering behind the snow-covered boxwoods outside the Marlowe-Houston House while the faculty party continued inside. He was trying to keep in the shadows, out of the light from the veranda while he urinated in the snow. He tried to pee in the shape of a heart, but only succeeded in getting it all over his hand. He washed his hands in the fresh snow.

While he was zipping up and adjusting himself, Lily emerged from the back door. She waved the bottle in the air. As she came down the veranda steps, Cup noticed that her royal blue dress was hidden beneath an oversized men's jacket. "Gower Lowry," she said. When she mentioned the names of his teachers, Cup felt that she was a part of that adult world to which he could only spy upon through kitchen door cracks. Lily was twenty, but at times she seemed far more mature than any college girl he had ever met; she seemed comfortably worldly. "Very tweedy," she continued, raising the collar up around her neck. She gently tucked her shoulder-length blond hair into the back of the collar. "He couldn't wait to slip this over my shoulders." She laughed at this, and her delicate laughter created tiny clouds in the cold air.

Lily came over and handed him the bottle of bourbon. "Daddy didn't even notice when I grabbed it. I did my best Lauren Bacall for Gower, who became my unwitting accomplice. He cornered me, Cup, against the bar, like this—" Lily squared her shoulders and came as close to Cup as she could without touching him. The tweed jacket fell open revealing her royal blue dress, with just a suggestion of nipples beneath the fabric. Cup's eyes wandered up the pale skin of her neck, back to her face. His breathing became very slow. He could hear his own heartbeat and was afraid that she might hear it, also.

Her lips barely parted as she said softly, "He told me, 'My dear, you certainly are our winter's blossom, a rare flower indeed.'" Lily reached up with her right hand and began stroking the edge of Cup's face; he became painfully aware of the peach fuzz on his chin that had yet to be replaced by heavy beard. "'A rare flower that blooms in such a cold climate.'" Lily's warm palm remained against Cup's face. "So I picked this ice cube out of my glass and slipped it into his mouth like this . . ."

Lily's fingers were on Cup's lips, parting them. She scraped a fingernail along the bottom row of teeth, and his tongue licked her finger. ". . . And I said to him, 'Gower Lowry, you could melt ice, couldn't you?'"

She laughed and plucked her finger from Cup's mouth. She brought her hand back down and rubbed it with the other as if she'd bruised it. "That old masher."

Cup was praying she would not notice the erection that was straining against the inside of his trousers. He took a step backwards, embarrassed. He tried to pull his jacket further down so as to hide the lump.

But it was no good. She'd already seen the wet spot around his crotch. "Oh, Cup, did I make you do that?"

Cup unscrewed the cap to the Jack Daniels bottle and took a swig from it. His face was red.

"It must be difficult at times . . . being a boy. All that testosterone."

This made Cup feel even more self-conscious. He gulped down more bourbon.

Lily raised her chin and peered at Cup critically as he moved the bottle away from his face. "You better save some of that for your little pow-wow tonight. I don't think I can get away with swiping another bottle. Gower might want more than just an ice cube to help with that."

5.

From *The Nightmare Book of Cup Coffey:*

There I was, drinking from the bottle I was supposed to be saving for the Tenebro initiation ceremony, while Lily Cammack watched, back from her first year in college, no doubt fascinated by the alcoholic consumption of the average, or in my case below average, preppie. Sticking out from my down jacket's side pocket was some animal bone I'd wrestled away from one of the janitor's dogs, while another, more personal bone pressed against my khakis.

Lily told me that her older sister Clare was getting married and asked me what I thought of that. I told her I didn't think anything of it—Clare was four years older than Lily, and I had never met her. She lived in New York. What did I care about her marriage? But Lily insisted I think about it—not Clare, but the idea of always being there for someone. Not the marriage that ends with "Death do us part," but the marriage that will always be, in this world and the next.

"You know, true love, do you believe in it?" she asked. She had to repeat herself a few times before the question even registered on my drunken adolescent brain. Let's see, I'd had a beer with my friend Whit earlier in the evening, then three plastic cupfuls of sherry while hiding behind the kitchen door in the Marlowe-Houston House, and there, speaking with her in the backyard of the house, I had drunk the equivalent of at least three shots of bourbon. I had a right to fuzzy thinking.

She took my hand at some point. We began walking down to the chapel. If you've never been there, the way the campus is laid out: you've got your Marlowe-Houston House facing Campus Drive and Clear Lake, but behind it, Pontefract Prep just opens up like a flower. To the north, about fifty yards, are the academic buildings along a brief, but impressive colonnade; straight ahead, as you face away from the Marlowe-Houston House, is the new library, the alumni house and the dormitories; and due south is the chapel.

So we took that southern route to the chapel. Our shoes crunched in the snow. I took the bourbon bottle and swept it across the top of a row of boxwoods, with snow scattering like dust from the leaves.

I glanced back at the house where the party continued, half-expecting someone to be following us. I've always had that habit, looking over my shoulder. It is not a good one. You never get anywhere, just back where you started.

Lily wrapped her right arm casually about my waist as we walked, slipping her hand into my coat pocket. I'd like to tell you that my love for Lily, my enormous crush on her, was pristine and free of animal motivation. Because I did worship her. I was sixteen, clumsy and unpopular, and here was this beautiful girl who, at the very least, enjoyed my company. But at sixteen, my mind was still in the gutter when it came to girls and sex. I was a virgin and like most virgins I cherished any feeling that even came close to sex: my senses were not yet dulled by experience. When Lily slipped that hand into my pocket, I felt a sweatshop heat rising up in my loins. I was afraid that that would be all I needed to send me over the top.

When I glanced at Lily, her pale face and white hair glowed in the scrim darkness like luminescent white sand beneath an ocean wave.

Do you believe in true love? As if she had to ask me. *How could I not, Lily? Just looking at you, brushing against you like this. Every moment with you is a constant ecstasy.* These are a rough approximation of my thoughts then. I was so naive and romantic that just the touch of her hand made me believe that love could not only be true, but that it could last through all eternity. This meant constant, neverending sexual bliss.

But I said something blasé and non-committal. "I don't know, I think maybe, but who knows. Maybe when your sister gets married you can ask her."

Lily didn't pursue the subject of love any further.

"I guess," I continued with my non-sequiturs, "Bart Kinter's got teachers like Lowry on his side. That fucking brownnose."

"Oh, ha ha, your best friend," Lily said. "He's just—" but she gasped before she could finish her sentence. "Cup, do you have to hang on to that thing?" While we'd been talking, her hand, still in my pocket, had felt the old bone in my jacket.

"It's part of the ceremony, Lily."

"And you can't tell me about it."

I nodded.

At sixteen I thought it was pretty cool to have gotten hold of a bone of that size—all my blood brothers in the Tenebro would think I'd really gone out to one of the cemeteries in town and dug it up. But the truth was: I stole it from a dog. Since it was my second year in the tribe I knew I had to come up with something pretty unusual for initiation. Your first year you are an initiate, but the second year is crucial. You're either a Shaman or a Warrior, and almost every guy was just a Warrior. But a select few got to be Shaman. That's what I was shooting for. I have never been so ambitious since. Most Tenebro brought pigeon feathers and a six-pack of Pabst Blue Ribbon. One of the guys who made Shaman last year, during my initiation, brought a bottle of Cuervo Gold. Another brought what we figured out was a possum skull, but what he swore was a giant rat's skull. So, here was my chance. I had, not only a bottle of Jack Daniels, but also this huge bone, about as long as my arm from wrist to elbow. Not only that, I had bad karma on my side: I didn't just buy the booze and I didn't just find the bone. I swiped the bottle from the headmaster's party, and I dug the bone out of Christ Church cemetery.

But what really happened (and this is not the story I would tell my blood brothers) was I saw this mutt dragging a bone around in the snow. This was such a good omen I knew I had to get that bone. Who cared if I was going to be kicked out of school after Christmas for cheating? I would go down with flying colors. For the Tenebro initiation ceremony, it would be bones and bourbon all the way!

I had to really wrestle with that dog; the animal growled and shook its head violently. I almost lost my grip. I only was able to get the bone when the dog relaxed for an instant. I pulled as hard as I could, thought its teeth were going to come with it when the bone popped out of its mouth. The dog whimpered after that, and I felt bad. I am a sucker for dogs. I gave it a Baby Ruth bar that had been rotting in my pocket for a few weeks.

And the bone itself! It was the bone to end all bones. That bone even had some maggots on it! How authentic could you get? It never occurred to me to wonder where the dog could've found it.

Lily pulled the bone out of my jacket pocket. She held it with disdain. "Is it one of Bart's?" She swung it back and forth, almost dropping it. Then she slipped it back into my pocket. "What perverted things do you boys do with bones?"

"It's a secret."

"Yes, well, I can tell you what Freud would say about that bone, but I don't suppose you'd want to hear it. You're a lot more like Bart Kinter than you'd like to admit, Cup."

"Right," I said sarcastically, suddenly furious that she would even compare me to Bart. I wasn't anything like him. *No way.*

Lily hugged me closer. The chapel bells rang the hour: eleven o'clock.

I still wanted this to be a romantic scenario. I wanted it to lead to something. There she'd mentioned love a while back, and now we'd descended into bones and Bart Kinter.

As if reading my thoughts, she said, "No, you're really not like Bart, are you? Whenever he's around me he licks his lips. Like he's just waiting for his . . . moment. You're much more chivalrous, Cuppie. You'd be my knight in shining armor, wouldn't you?"

"Slay all your dragons," I whispered drunkenly.

Neither of us spoke for a few minutes. We continued trudging through the snow—it seemed to take forever to get to the chapel. When we reached the chapel steps, she asked me if I meant it about slaying her dragons. Not realizing what I was getting myself in for, I said yes.

"Sometimes, Cup, dragons are big monsters in stories, and sometimes . . ." Lily seemed very mysterious now, and for the first time since I'd met her when I was thirteen and she was seventeen, practically babysitting me, I realized that there were things about her I didn't know, things she was just now hinting at. It almost scared me to think that Lily Cammack was not just the image I had of her, but that she possessed a life independent of my knowledge. "Cup," she said, "let's play 'Smoke.'"

What Lily liked about this game, silly as it was, is that when you are It you can crawl into someone else's skin and see things through their eyes. Even though you make fun of them, you try to, momentarily, put yourself in their place. You could never just be yourself—the game required that you be the other person, answer as the other.

But all this is in hindsight. When I was sixteen I thought it was a stupid game, a little kids' game actually. But I did love Lily. How easy it is to write that now: I do love you, Lily. She didn't play "Smoke" with anyone else but me.

The way the game goes:

You ask the person who is It, What kind of smoke are you? and she tells you, and in answering this and other similar questions (what kind of animal, vegetable, mineral, fire, wind, water, etc.) she reveals something about the nature of the mysterious It.

And there were other questions if you were wrong with your first guess.

The last question, however, is set. When you ask it, it's a signal that the jig is up, the game is over, you are on to whomever the mysterious It is.

The last question: *What kind of monster are you?*

6.

The boxwoods that surrounded the front entrance of the small chapel in a precise semi-circle shook off their snow as if shivering from the cold. Wind blew from off the lake. Cup Coffey and Lily Cammack heard it whistle as it came through the trees near the Marlowe-Houston House.

But it wasn't the wind that caused the bushes around them to tremble. Cup first heard a low growling. The noise seemed to surround them. He wished that the chapel door hadn't been locked, initially because he was freezing, but now because of the lurking animal or animals in the hedge.

But Lily saw the dog and pointed it out to Cup. "Have you ever been dogfishing?" The dark, wet dog came lumbering out of the boxwoods, its tail wagging. It was a black labrador retriever, a clumsy, friendly dog Cup had often thrown sticks to. One of the janitor's dogs.

"Here, puppy," Lily coaxed the dog into the chapel floodlights. An aside, she whispered to Cup, "I've never been fond of these campus dogs. But I think it's because of their master."

"You think Riley owns every dog that runs around here?" Cup asked. Riley Amory was the new head janitor; he and his family lived off in the woods "with all the albinos," Lily would scoff.

Lily didn't respond. She picked up the half-empty Jack Daniels bottle that Cup had set down between them. She dipped the bottle down to the dog's level and snapped her fingers. "Come on, girl, that's a good doggie."

"Don't do that."

"Cup, this wasn't the dog you took that femur from?"

"You think it's a femur?"

"Femur, tibia, whatever." She shrugged.

Two other dogs also emerged from the bushes, sheepishly wagging their tails, heads down. "How many dogs does Riley own?"

"I see a certain resemblance to their master," Lily said. "Let's see if they get as drunk as Riley does." She tipped the bottle so that some bourbon splashed onto the lab's muzzle.

One of the dogs, a miniature collie mix, came up to Cup and began sniffing around his jacket. "This is the one," he said. He reached down to pat the dog, but it snarled and backed away.

"Vicious. I'll bet it was some struggle for that bone, Cup."

"Ha."

All three dogs began licking the bourbon-soaked snow.

"Hey." Cup reached over to take the Jack Daniels from Lily, but she was too quick. She pulled it behind her back. "I need some of that for later."

"Come and get it," she told him playfully.

He hesitated and looked into her translucent blue eyes. "Okay." He put his arms around her, pretending to reach for the bottle. Impulsively, he kissed her, and he tried to pry her lips apart with his tongue. No go. He pulled back. He brought his arms back from around her waist. "I should get back to the dorm. The guys are going to wonder . . . it looks like the bourbon's mostly gone, but I still have—"

Lily smiled, settling her left hand down upon his lap. "You still have that bone, don't you?"

Now she played aggressor. Lily brought her face against his and kissed him, licking his lips with her tongue, lightly, before kissing his cheek, his chin, his neck. Cup did not move. She pressed her lips against his ear. Her face seemed sticky, as if from sweat or tears. He felt her breath inside his ear. She exhaled into him. She whispered, "Why couldn't it have been you?"

He said nothing.

She said, "Ask me now."

The world went silent, no wind, no dogs thirstily lapping at the bourbon-stained snow, no strange crunch of branches that Cup might've heard if his senses had not been so totally focused on Lily. It was as if a needle had just been removed from a record. He didn't look at her when he asked.

"What kind of smoke are you?"

7.

She said, "I'll tell you what kind of monster I am."

Then she told him.

They held each other for what seemed like hours. Lily cried, and her breath was a mist surrounding them. He told her she was the most beautiful woman in the world. He swore undying love, he promised her he would slay all her dragons, now and forever.

Even as he said these words and inhaled the cold night and her jasmine perfume, they were jumped.

"I know what kind of monster I am!" came the high-pitched squeal.

The Jack Daniels Hounds barked and howled all around them.

This occurred one night, December 18, 1974, the night of Dr. Cammack's annual Christmas faculty party at the Marlowe-Houston House, and the night, two days before Christmas break, when certain so-called Indian Clubs held their initiation ceremonies. The boys called it Hell Night.

Just before midnight, a nineteen-year-old boy named Bartholomew Andrew Kinter, Jr., born in nearby Cabelsville, but pretty much a hometown boy in Pontefract, Virginia, fell down the cellar of the Marlowe-Houston House, breaking his neck. An electrical fire also started in that cellar as a result of faulty wiring. The fire was easily extinguished by the Pontefract Fire Department. The fire did not spread beyond the cellar.

The boy's body was burned beyond recognition.

Advertisement from *The Westbridge County* (Va.) *Sentinel,* September 18, 1985:

ODESSA HOUSTON AMORY ANNOUNCES
HER SERVICES AS SPIRITUAL ADVISOR
IN TANDEM WITH HER DAUGHTER
THEODORA LOUISE, MEDIUM.
CALLING HOURS:
8 TO 10 PM, M-F; NOON TO 8 PM, WKNDS.
BEREAVED?
CONTACT LOVED ONES, BE COMFORTED.
CHRISTIAN HOUSEHOLD.

Portion of transcript of conversation recorded between Dr. Prescott Nagle of the Pontefract Historical Society and Teddy Amory, February 12, 1986:

Prescott: Let me speak with Virginia now.
Teddy: My, how you do require a lot from this little girl, Dr. Nagle.
Prescott: Am I speaking with Virginia Houston?
Teddy: Yes.
Prescott: Virginia, may I ask you a few questions?
Teddy: Yes.
Prescott: Where are you?
Teddy: In the belly, Dr. Nagle, of the beast. We are all here. Your wife, too. She perverted her calling, you see, just as mine was also perverted.
Prescott: What was your calling?
Teddy: I was the chosen vessel. I was the door. My brother shut the door, Dr. Nagle, and he locked it. And in so doing sealed his own doom, and that of

our entire line. He had an unnatural love for me, Dr. Nagle, and that drove him to this desperate act.
Prescott: What desperate act?
Teddy: You know.
Prescott: No I don't, Virginia, please tell me.
Teddy: What your wife did to herself. A perversion of nature. She was not a suitable passage. But this one, this child, shall be.
Prescott: Who is the beast?
Teddy: My brother calls it by the name Goatman.
Prescott: And what do you call it, Virginia?
Teddy: (word is indecipherable—a series of moans and growls) It is ecstasy, its name is unspeakable by human tongue.
Prescott: What do you call it, Virginia?
Teddy: The Eater of Souls.

CHAPTER THREE

DEM BONES, II

December 2, 1986

1.

Behind Teddy's eyes the world became translucent ice that shattered as she fell into a viscous blue darkness.

Jake Amory watched his sister drop onto the carpet. She was going into one of her fits.

She's a monster, the words buzzed around in his head, *don't trust her for a minute, boy. She's laughing at you, too, boy, but on the inside. Just take your knife and open her up and you're gonna see for yourself. But don't cut deep, boy, 'cause you got to save something for the big day of the Pocket Lips, just skin her.*

Teddy was twisting, shaking, shivering like she was being hosed down with ice water, arching her back against the floor, slapping her hands up and down as if she were trying to swim. The irises of her eyes rolled up under the lids. She was swallowing air like it was liquid.

Jake held his Boy Scout knife high, as if this were a ritual he was about to perform. "Kissy-kissy," he said between clenched teeth. He brought the knife down in a clean slice through the smoky air; the blade flashed in front of his sister's contorted face as she continued to struggle against herself.

He heard the characteristic rumbling coming from Teddy's body, her muscles and bones fighting against the seizure. *Now, get her now, give her the kiss, Jake, fast, she's a rattlesnake, she can be anything she wants, she ain't human, she's a monster—*

"I got it under control!" Jake shouted, trying to shut out all the damn noise in his mind. He knew what he was doing. He didn't need all that buzzing around his ears, all that static. His head seemed like a jungle, full of howling, screaming things. He thought he was going to explode. Drool gushed down his chin, and he wiped it away. "Shit!" His mouth curled downward, and he said, "Okay, monsterbaby, it's time for the Pocket Lips," and he swung his arm down again, the knife whistling in the air, to his sister's squirming body.

But as he did this, and he was thinking of the sheer beauty of that one movement, his hand clutching the knife, his elbow bent, curving through the air, homing in on its destination—her left ankle, if he could keep her still long enough to peel that tender young skin away from the bone—just as the knife skimmed her foot, it flew out of his hand. It was as if someone had physically wrenched the knife from his fingers. He watched in angry disbelief as the knife sailed down the stairs, clattering to the floor below.

Nervous, just nervous, that's all, you can do it, you can get that fucking door open.

Jake clapped his hands together and laughed. "Under control, my man, still got it under control. Jake's your man, if he can't do it, nobody can!"

He knew what he would do.

He was going to set her on fire. Some vestige of the spirits of the dead he'd been rapping with down by the lake tickled his ear: *no, no fire. Mustn't use . . .* But he cut that voice off. *You didn't have to have gasoline for this monster, oh, no, you just use that long frizzy hair to get the inferno going.*

Now that voice was like a mosquito buzzing around his head: *not the fire, not her, it's not—*

But he swatted at the voices, overriding them with his own thoughts: *fire, fire, fire, fire.*

Teddy was coming down from her fit. Her eyes were closed. Her pajamas were soaking wet; her bathrobe had flown open beneath her like clipped angel's wings as she lay there, still.

Jake would have to act fast.

He reached into his breast pocket for the Bic lighter he'd used to torch the rat in the bedroom.

He flicked the thing on and a lovely, tiny spark erupted from its heart.

Jake knew one golden moment when he smelled victory through the fire that still raged in the bedroom down the hall, and saw it there in his helpless sister as she came down from her dance.

And then Jake Amory howled in pain as his entire hand burst into flame, while the thought shot through his head like a bullet:

Asshole, you used the wrong hand, you used the hand with all that fucking gas on it—

But even this thought did not seem to make any sense to him as he tumbled down the staircase, screaming, burning.

2.

Teddy Amory was out of the burning house, not even sure how she'd managed to get down the staircase through the smoke, around her brother's screaming, writhing body (she wanted to help him but he looked at her like he was going to throw her back into the flames), around the tongues of fire that shot out at her from all directions. It was something she'd never imagined in her worst dreams.

She ran out into the field that adjoined the house, as far as she could run, and then collapsed in the damp grass, sobbing. She closed her eyes tight, praying that when she opened them again the fire behind her would go away and the nightmare would fade.

But when she raised her head from the ground, opened her eyes and glanced back at the house, fire still vomited from the windows. Her brother was screaming even louder.

"Please God, let it be over, let it be over," she whimpered. Teddy rubbed her fists into her tear-filled eyes.

Then she heard the front door slam.

"Teddy! Teddy, get back here!" Jake yelled. "It's time for a bedtime kiss, it's the Pocket Lips comin' for ya!"

She ducked down and then peered through the tall grass. She watched her brother stomp stiff-legged around the porch, backlit by the inferno. He was clutching one of his hands.

Her first impulse was to run back home. Just to get it over with. It was Jake, and no matter how crazy he was acting, maybe that fall down the stairs had reawakened something human in him.

Because she knew. She knew what had gotten into him.

It was part of that gas station smell. She remembered it, how it snaked around her, pulling her back through the freezing water, trying to suck something out of her. But she had escaped it in the water. Her daddy had saved her.

And the thing was mad she'd gotten away. It wanted her for something. Because of what had gotten inside her, whatever it was that was causing the fits, the thing that she'd brought on herself and on her family.

But her daddy hadn't gotten away, and now her mother, too, was caught.

And Jake.

"You cunt, Teddy!" Jake boomed, his voice raking across the darkness of pre-dawn hours. "I know you're out there! It's just a matter of time, baby sister! Come on back and maybe I'll treat you nice, yeah, real nice!" As he shouted obscenities, Teddy noticed something bright and silver flashing in his hand.

A knife.

Teddy stifled a scream. She hoped her fits wouldn't come on.

From *The Diary of Worthy Houston,* Winter, 1801:

My sister, Virginia, grows weaker by the day and we pray for her recovery. But Father does not seem to notice her troubles. He bids me ignore her falling sickness, her depressions, her auguries of doom. He warns me that I must not mistake the door for the doorway, or the lock for the key. He is more concerned with his digging in the earth beneath our house.

What madness must have possessed him to build this house upon their graves?

We have heard him the whole evening long and into the dawn. In my dreams I can hear his shovel scraping against the rock and earth. He believes, I think, that he is planting them deeper as if in so doing he will allay his fears. As when he sows his fields, the further down in the soil he plants the seed, so shall the grain not rise up against him.

CHAPTER FOUR

CLARE

January 9, 1986

1.

The Winter Before Jake Amory Torched His House

FOUNDERS DAY

Clare Cammack Terry knew these things about herself: she had wavy black hair that could not be tamed with hairstyles or conditioners, her younger sister, Lily, had shoulder-length blond hair that sparkled. She had an olive complexion that no one envied, whereas Lily had that creamy skin that Clare equated with a tubercular condition but which everyone else thought was a sign of grace and purity. Lily was a woman who in her early thirties could still wear dresses that might be described as "frocks" and still looked as gorgeous as she had at seventeen; Clare was more of a Banana Republic kind of girl, getting most of her wardrobe out of catalogs rather than from the local stores—and she always felt she looked out of place in Pontefract, like Annie Hall in John-Boy Walton territory. Clare had failed in marriage and career (failed marriage: to David Terry, Manhattan ad agency man, who thought Clare should concentrate on her femininity more, and who himself concentrated on other women and the occasional accommodating man—but her first roommate had warned her to not get serious with a man who wore bikini underwear. Failed career: nursing, although, *ha-ha, as Lily would say,* she was certainly nursing her own father now). Lily was a success in marriage and had no desire for a career. But Clare was doing her darnedest to put the screws to her sister's marriage, *ha-ha.*

Oh, and I know this, too. My episodes. Vertigo, dizziness, call it what you like, I see things. Just these neurotic little dreams while I'm awake. How very New York of me. Hallucinations.

Like this one in front of me.

Clare Terry didn't immediately recognize the woman who gazed at her from the second-story Venetian window of the Marlowe-Houston House. But the woman evidently knew Clare, because she waved and seemed to be trying to say something to her from behind the glass. Then Clare began to understand what the woman was saying. Clare couldn't really hear her, but suddenly the woman's voice was in her head.

Clare felt her own blood turn to ice inside her.

The woman was saying, "Big kiss, Clare, Daddy wants to give you a big kiss, he's right here, with me," and the woman was no longer unfamiliar, with her auburn hair and high cheekbones. It was Clare's mother, Rose Cammack. "Big kiss," her mother repeated from behind the window. "You didn't have to come home," her mother continued, "he would've been fine without you. Nobody wants you here. But since you're here, he has a Big Kiss just for you."

Clare looked away from the window, tried to look away from the house, but she could not escape it. Every way she turned her head, there were its Greek Doric columns, there the white front steps, the molded brickwork, there the thick dead vines snaking about the trellis, all leading her like strands of a spider's web straight to the dark spider at its heart, her mother gazing at her from the window. And the words seemed to froth out of her mother's pincer-like mouth, "Big kiss, Clare, bigkiss—bigkiss—biggest . . ."

"I'm telling you," a more honeyed voice said.

Clare was standing in front of her Volkswagen Rabbit, the back door still open. She was staring at the empty, dark Venetian window supported by a false railing, crowned with an arch. It was just like any of a number of windows on houses in Pontefract, nothing special. When she'd been a little girl, she even looked out this particular window, pressed her face right up against the pane, pushing the sash aside. Her mother was dead. This was just the Marlowe-Houston House. No one was staring back at her.

Shelly Patterson, who leaned against the hood of the car, was saying, "The biggest tits yet. Miss Perky Boobs. I'm telling you, Clare, they get bigger every time I see her." Shelly had a round pudgy face that Clare found eternally pleasant, framed by those tight ringlets of carrot red hair. Even if she was overweight, she looked supremely comfortable in that body. *Not like me,* Clare thought, *not like me.*

Shelly wore an oversized black sweater and had drenched herself with imitation gold jewelry because she thought it minimized her weight. It didn't; Clare thought Shelly looked even heavier than usual. Shelly held her hands out in front of her as if carrying enormous sacks of groceries. "And I am also here to inform you that Cappie's tits were not like that yesterday. Oh, sure, they were big, but they weren't galaxies unto themselves."

Then Clare remembered. *All right, this vision from that upper window,* mother, *is just an episode. All is right with the world. Just another vision, and who are you to have visions, anyway? It's not like you're Joan of Arc, you're the most devout atheist on the face of this earth.*

Clare reached in her purse for her version of the double martini: a pack of Salems and a half-Valium, a habit she'd acquired in Manhattan before the divorce became final. She re-oriented herself. She'd just gotten out of her car when Shelly Patterson came down the front steps to help carry the four jugs of wine she'd brought for the luncheon. Shelly had begun gossiping about other people who were already inside: the First Families of Pontefract with their little cliques of whomever was most closely related to the town fathers. Then the dizziness had hit her, and she had clutched the car door for support. Not exactly dizzy; she felt like she was on a different magnetic frequency from the Marlowe-Houston House and had hit its invisible field.

Shelly hadn't noticed any of the signs of her episode.

Clare was getting so used to them that she had learned to disguise the sweating and trembling fairly well. Basically, Clare had taught herself not to freak whenever one of these came on.

Now, listening to Shelly go on and on about Cappie Hartstone's recent increase in breast size (". . . it's like she's trying out for Nursing Mother of the Year when everybody knows she's more like the Iron Maiden of Nuremberg . . .") and looking boldly up into that empty window, Clare felt in control. Stronger, that was it, she was stronger after her episodes.

"It's so cold," Clare said, "let's go inside."

Shelly, lifting one of the grocery bags with the wine in it, went on ahead. Clare stayed back a moment. She lit a cigarette, took several quick puffs, then dropped it in the gutter. She put it out with her heel. She decided against the half-Valium after all. *I'll be okay.* She took the other bag out of her Rabbit and pressed her back against the door to shut it. *I do feel stronger,* she told herself.

Yeah, I must be feeling pretty strong to go in there.

The Marlowe-Houston House had always intimidated Clare, even when she'd been a little girl. Because her father had been headmaster of Pontefract Prep, the family occupied the house for several years in the late '50s and early '60s. She never felt that it was home; she was relieved when, at twelve, her family moved into the old Federal-style brick house on Porter Street, while the descendants of the Houston family converted the Marlowe-Houston House into a museum of sorts as well as the site for various Town and Gown functions, like this snobby Founders Day Luncheon.

And Warren Whalen, mustn't forget Warren.

For it was within those walls of the Marlowe-Houston that she had first succumbed to his charms, had allowed him, as Shelly crudely put it, *to get into her panties.*

2.

Inside the Marlowe-Houston House

Clare made a mental note as she went through the living room: everyone in Pontefract, Virginia, was a First Family. Not that everyone in town was invited to this Invitation Only affair. The Town and Gown Society, which overlapped with the Christ Church Altar Guild to create a hybrid Junior League–cum–Episcopalian Coffee Hour, were very careful with their genealogical research: *no alien blood, please.* Bill Hartstone was already leaning against the bar, exchanging good-old-boy talk with Ken Stetson, whose son, Rick, was playing bartender and sneaking a swig when the others weren't looking. Another teenager, Tommy MacKenzie, sat in a corner rigidly, wearing a coat and tie, something Clare never saw the kid in when he came over to do yardwork in the summer; she barely recognized him. She felt a great deal of sympathy for him: like him, she didn't want to be here either. Tommy's father and mother stood near the picture window talking quietly among themselves. Mrs. MacKenzie always reminded Clare of a wounded bird, shying away from other people and helplessly gravitating to the safety of her own husband. Clare could not relate to wives like that; she didn't believe that any husband could be very safe.

Howie McCormick, possibly the last McCormick left in town since his parents died, tried to talk up a few of the golf set who stood near the piano. Howie was the same mailman who had handed Clare a letter from her ex-husband and at the same time told her pretty much what was in it. Thankfully, today he was not wearing his blue uniform and pith helmet. He wore a bright madras jacket and lime green pants, and he was drunk off his ass and leering at anything and everything female in the room.

Prescott Nagle was trying to plink out a tune on the piano, with Gower Lowry scowling at him from a corner of the room. Ever since she'd been a little girl, Clare had always known about, although never fully understood, the enmity between those two men. *But you'd think they'd have outgrown it by now.* Clare waved quickly to that group and prayed that Gower would not use the opportunity to come over and talk her up. He didn't. All the good Pontefract "Name" families were well represented, lounging on the sofas, dressed in their suits and overly extravagant gowns, and the conversation that filtered down to Clare as she passed through them centered upon the mild winter they were having, and a comparison of genealogical backgrounds. "It was my great-grandfather Campbell who built the Regency Row Arcade, but then it was just called the Row, and that was before they gutted it," or "When William, the first William in our family, married your great-aunt Jenny, he was able to," or "He took up arms with General Lee, and his wife had to run the farm by herself, even pulling the plow, yes, can you imagine."

Shelly came out of the kitchen's swinging door, and fluttered her eyebrows a la Groucho Marx. "With all this inbreeding I'm amazed you 'Firsts' aren't all twelve-fingered dwarves," Shelly said, reaching for the bag in Clare's arms.

"That's all right, Shelly, I'll get it." Clare didn't understand why Shelly was blocking her way to the kitchen.

"I don't know if I'd want to go in there if I were you," Shelly whispered. "I think you're the hot topic of the day."

"Why am I here?" Clare asked amusedly.

"People are wondering why you're not wearing a big fat scarlet 'A' across your boobs."

"Look," Clare said, indicating the people around the room with a shrewd glance, "I can't just stand here like this. Do you think I could make it out the front door?"

"You slut," Shelly laughed, "give me the wine." She held her hands out again to take the grocery bag. "You go into the dining room and admire the china. I'll find your sister and tell her you're not feeling well. Then we'll sneak you up the stairs to the roof. You can jump."

"I'll be damned if I'm going to give this place more grist for the mill."

"So you're going into the enemy camp?"

"Like Daniel into the lions' den."

"Those lions didn't have the teeth that Georgia Stetson's got, and they didn't know about Thursday night."

"They all know about Thursday night?"

Shelly nodded. "Maybe you'll want a drink before you go in there."

Everybody knows about Thursday night?

How could they? Clare didn't even know for sure about Thursday night.

"Cappie of the ballistic breasts will probably play compassionate and understanding, and the others will just glance at Georgia—who will be full of self-righteous indignation."

"Everybody knows?" Clare heard her own voice go wimpy and spineless. She'd only showed up for Lily's sake, and she should've known it would be a mistake.

"From Georgia the story of the howling dogs, and one married dog in particular, radiated out to the provinces. She broadcast it on the wire."

"Lily, too?"

Shelly shrugged. "I don't know. Who knows? Did you know when David cheated on you? Well, you were born suspicious, Clare, but I don't think the ice goddess—"

"I wish you wouldn't call her that."

"She may be your sister, Clare, but she sure ain't mine. I always thought pregnancy brought out some maternal instinct, but with her, she just gets a little higher and a little mightier . . ."

"That's mean, I wish you'd stop, this hasn't been easy for her, she's . . ." Clare searched for the right word.

But Shelly filled it in. "So sensitive, yeah, I know. That pale flower, Lily." Her voice was full of sarcasm.

"I'm going in there," Clare said.

Shelly stepped out of her path like a matador neatly avoiding being gored. "Your funeral."

Clare went on ahead and pushed the kitchen door open.

3.

Everybody Knows About Thursday Night

Last Thursday . . .

They'd gone to Shelly's house in the afternoon—Shelly condoned such things as extra-marital affairs. Clare and Warren Whalen, brother- and sister-in-law. They always went to Shelly's because it seemed less suspicious to go into that small house on Jessup Street than to risk a motel out on the highway. Up to the guest bedroom. "Do Not Disturb" sign on door so Shelly would know when she came back home. Clare left her guilt outside; those laws of fidelity and family loyalty had no bearing in that room. They were irrelevant details.

Even the thought of how her sister would react, with that big belly full of baby: *maybe Lily would be relieved to know that her husband was having an affair with her sister and not with some stranger.* Clare did a lot of wishful thinking.

But Thursday afternoon, before the notorious Thursday night, she and Warren went with the sole purpose of making love in Shelly Patterson's guest bedroom, and then Clare had done something unforgivably stupid knowing Warren Whalen's nature.

She told him to fuck off.

At the time it seemed like a reasonable thing to do given what led up to it. Aside from guilt and an oncoming episode, and oh yes, her period. Her period was really the jumping off point.

"I've got to tell you something," Clare murmured to him, clutching his dark locks of hair as he continued to kiss his way down from her breasts. His "mmmph?" reply indicated he'd heard her even as he was kissing the sallow skin of her stomach, licking around her navel like it was a Tootsie Pop.

Clare giggled because of his tickling and the essential

absurdity of her sister's husband being so avidly interested in her anatomy. "No stop, really," she said. Her feet were shackled in the jeans he had moments ago pulled down in his sudden passion. Her peach blouse lay across the floor where Warren had practically torn it off her; beside it were Warren's Brooks Brothers tie, shirt and blue chinos. When Warren looked up at her from her navel, she looked at the clothes. She blushed. There was something embarrassing about clothes on the floor. She felt the warmth of his face heading down in a beeline to what he crudely and charmingly referred to as *homeplate*—all this made her not want to tell him at all. *Maybe he won't even notice.*

And then she imagined: *a face, not his, and not her father's, but a man with no features, just an empty face, indentations where the eyes and nose would be, and a gaping, hungry mouth. Down there, between her legs. His mouth covered with her blood.*

The face flicked a worm-like tongue across its red-stained lips and said, "Oh, that's lovely my baby, my little blind Clare with no eye, a nice Big Kiss."

"Jesus, Clare, are you all right?" Warren asked, stroking her legs.

Clare was sweating, shaking. Terrified of that episode, which was the same episode she'd had since she was nine. She brought Warren's face up to her own and kissed him gently. "It's nothing."

"Honey, I thought you were in pain. Did it hurt that much?" Warren glanced back down at the small pink imprint on the inside of her thigh. "I didn't think I bit down all that hard."

Clare smiled weakly. "I thought hickeys went out in the eighth grade."

"Not leg hickeys," he winked. "Now let's get down to the good stuff."

Clare cupped his chin in her hand, forcing him to look into her eyes. He resembled a puppy getting all worked up about suppertime. He licked his lips. *So much like that faceless man, but no wormy tongue, or those teeth,* my god *the teeth!*

Then Clare just blurted it out: "Warren, I'm having my period."

He raised his bushy eyebrows and his hand began massaging her thigh, stealing *home.* "The old red river, huh?"

Clare winced at this description.

He continued speaking. "Now some guys have a motto that goes: I'll take a dip in the red river, but I won't take a drink from it. I, on the other hand, am willing to dive right in." He pushed his fingers up into her, and she just as quickly pulled back away from him.

"Look," she said, "just fuck off, will you?"

"Women and their periods."

"No, I mean it," and she pulled herself out of his grip, out of the tangle they'd gotten themselves into on the bed; standing, she pulled her jeans up and buttoned them. She bent over and picked up her peach blouse. "Fuck off, fuck off, get out of my life."

But Thursday night . . .

After Warren left, rather sheepishly like a little boy who was caught with his hands in the cookie jar, Clare took the longest, most scalding shower of her life. *To wash him away, off me.* Her skin was pink when she toweled off. *I am not unattractive, I could find someone who isn't married, isn't taboo, doesn't look like . . .* The steam began clearing from her medicine cabinet mirror, and she said aloud to her reflection:

"I am losing my mind."

She chain-smoked into the evening.

Clare met Shelly down at the Columns restaurant for their weekly Girls Night Out. Their third partner, Debbie Randolph, could not make it. Clare barely touched her food.

"Obviously you still haven't discovered the pleasures of eating as a recreational sport," Shelly said when she was mid-way through her third helping. Clare didn't talk much during the meal, but Shelly kept up a running monologue about the upcoming Founders Day luncheon for over an hour.

When they were through they went out the front door of

the restaurant. *Your first mistake.* At the time, Clare didn't notice the town gossip, Georgia Stetson, sitting at one of the window tables with her husband.

As soon as Clare opened the door to go out into the street, the singing began.

There were four very drunk men swaying, laughing, slapping each other on the back, singing.

The voice that was the loudest and the most off-key was none other than Warren Whalen's. His buddies were holding him up.

They were singing "Red River Valley," punctuated by howls and coyote yips. One of the drunks shouted: "Which one of you bitches is in heat, anyway?"

In Manhattan, Clare thought, *no one would bat an eye. But in this little backwater, where you were already a tramp if you were a divorcée, this was the capper. This was monumental. This would stoke the engines of all those gossipmongers for months to come.*

4.

In the Kitchen

FOUNDERS DAY

"Is Lily here yet?" Clare asked when she finally screwed up the courage to walk into the kitchen. *Definitely the enemy camp.* Georgia Stetson and Maude Dunwoody did not look up from the hams they were carving. Cappie Hartstone *did* look up for a second *(and yes, her breasts were definitely a few cups larger than normal—do women "stuff" after thirteen?).* Cappie offered a perky little half-smile before returning her attention to the range where she was stirring some kind of gravy.

Yes, I suppose we all know about Thursday night's little sing-along. How did it go, Georgia? Did you take the direct route or did you slip it in casually, something like, "And you'd think the Whore of Babylon wouldn't have the nerve to show up for a family-oriented gathering like this." Or was that too subtle for the Rona Barrett of Pontefract? Was it more like: "That little tramp stealing husbands couldn't even leave her own sister's husband alone, but she was always after what that younger girl had. Looks, happiness, love and now even a husband. You should have heard those men, ladies, howling like horny dogs after her, and I guess we all know that's as good as she deserves."

Cappie, still stirring the saucepan, said, "Lily's around somewhere I think, *Mrs.* Terry, although I wouldn't know."

"Thank you," Clare replied trying to sound sweet. Unruffled. "Is there anything I can do to help?" She was afraid of what kind of reply Georgia might give to this, but the women continued slicing ham.

Maude Dunwoody set her knife down and wiped sweat from her brow. She glared at Clare. *"Your own sister, how could you?" those eyes were saying.* But she said without emotion, "She might be in the cellar. Someone's down there, anyway."

Cappie acted as if she were about to say something to contradict the information that Maude had just volunteered, but her mouth remained clamped shut.

What the hell possessed me to come to this luncheon? Just to have an afternoon away from Daddy in exchange for this?

Clare moved cautiously between the women and their cutting boards on her way to the cellar door. Clare would not normally go down into the cellar by herself. She associated very bad things with that part of the house, she remembered that face that came at her out of the darkness, the face like her father's, the hands that touched her. But she'd only been a little girl, and she hadn't believed it was anything other than her imagination.

But on Founders Day, she felt that perhaps this was her only retreat, and if her younger sister were down there, maybe she would be able to talk about the baby-to-come, something, anything to take her mind off her troubles.

Clare opened the cellar door, and in spite of the stale, musty air that hit her as she took a tentative step down, she was happy to be out of firing range of these women. The light was on in the cellar, and she walked carefully down the old steps, clinging to the thin wooden banister with her left hand, her right hand feeling along the cold stone wall as she went into the bowels of the house. "Lily?" she asked as she went down, and it was after all just a cold cellar full of old junk.

Someone was lifting bags of ice from the corner near the steps on the far side of the cellar which led outside to the back yard. It was not Lily, but a man, and before he turned around, Clare recognized him and thought: *not my day.*

It was Warren.

"I was just leaving," she said, backing up the steps.

"Yeah, 'beam," Warren said, "you go right back into the clutches of those hometown harpies why don't you?"

"What do you mean?" She paused.

He held up his hands, splaying his fingers out. "See? They shoved bamboo shoots up my fingernails. I confessed to things I've never even fantasized about."

"Serves you right—you're a schmuck. I guess we're both schmucks. Where's Lily?"

Warren shrugged, lifting a bag of ice up from the floor. "Around. She said she wasn't feeling well—you want to give me a hand? I'm supposed to crush these for daiquiris or something."

"Does she know?" Clare figured: *What the hell?* and went back down the steps, finally sitting on the bottom one. Before Warren could answer she sniffed the air, wrinkling her nose. "Is there a gas leak or something?"

"Septic tank maybe." Warren pointed to a brick-lined shelf alongside the wall. "You lived here before, didn't you know about that old conduit under there?"

Clare ignored this question. "What about Lily?"

Warren's violet eyes locked into hers before she could glance away. As if even now, even after Thursday night, she was still his property. The thick dark wavy hair, the square set to the jaw (with that little dimple pressed into his chin), those deepset jeweled eyes. Clare realized she hated him for his good looks. *He's better looking than I am. Maybe better looking than any other man, woman, or child in this town.*

Except one.

"Lily," she said aloud.

"I think she's so out of it these last months of pregnancy she doesn't know what's going on with anything. She's been imagining a lot of things, anyway."

"Like her husband having affairs?"

"You know there's something between us, Clare, even now, some chemistry." Warren was doing his best matinee-idol rap. He smashed the bag of ice down on the shelf and several bricks fell off and broke on the floor.

That septic tank smell was getting to Clare, and the human septic tank who was standing in front of her smashing ice and leering was also making her feel a bit nauseated. She stood up from the bottom step, brushed herself off, and turned to go back up the stairs. "If you see Lily, tell her I'm looking for her," Clare said flatly. She was not going to put up with any more of Warren's guff.

"Okay, Moonbeam, I will do that," but even as he said this, and even as Clare turned to go, there was a creaking noise coming from the cellar doors that led to the outside of the Marlowe-Houston House. Clare turned around—that sound had been like someone tapping her on the shoulders, and the septic tank smell like a foul-sweet wind came up.

Coming down the steps of the other side of the cellar directly across from Clare was her sister, Lily.

Her belly full in her seventh month. Clutching her stomach with her hands as if the child inside was the only thing left for her to hang onto.

"You bastards," Lily moaned.

Looking back on that day, nearly a year afterward, Clare Terry could honestly say it was a bad day, that day. The Founders Day luncheon. The day her sister found out about her affair with Warren.

But that wasn't the worst day.

Because every progressive day became a worst of its kind.

Clare had an awful feeling that the worst day was still to come.

CHAPTER FIVE

DREAMERS

December 2, 1986

1.

After Midnight

Tommy MacKenzie, Jr., lay in bed and could not sleep. He had heard a noise in his closet. He was fifteen and no longer believed in the boy-eating spider. He did believe in the strength of his father's fist, and that his mother had pretty much given up on both him and his father. She spent too much time away.

In the morning, Tommy might discover that the noise in his closet had been a scarf falling down, or just the house settling again. Old houses were always supposed to be settling—that explained away a lot of his fears.

But after midnight, Tommy could think of no such rational explanations.

In that vivid darkness, the thing in his closet was the same thing that had scuttled through the nightmare he'd been having.

And it was the boy-eating spider.

2.

Before Sunrise

Sheriff George Connally woke up in a cold sweat, screaming. His wife, Rita, wrapped her arms around him. "Is it the same one?"

George pressed his face into her neck, closing his eyes. "Yes," he gasped.

"Want me to warm up some milk?"

"What time is it?"

"Almost four."

"Might as well just get up."

Rita stroked the side of his face. "You're working too hard. These dreams . . ."

"Just dreams," he said, drawing away from her. He got up out of bed and walked over to the bedroom window. George Connally looked out onto the dark streets of Pontefract. A dog was barking somewhere. He'd been sweating so much his boxer shorts clung to him.

"I'll put the coffee on," Rita said.

"Just dreams," he repeated.

Dreams, Rita, that you wouldn't understand, dreams that the goddamn state boys couldn't even figure out when they'd descended upon the town years ago. Dreams of . . . love.

It had been what old Frank Gaston wrote on the wall of his hunting cabin. In his own blood. "LOVE DID THIS." Could anything but love be so terrible? An old man whose wife is dying of bone cancer shoots her to lay her to rest and then turns the gun on himself. "Murder-suicide," the investigating detective from Roanoke had said, "happens every day." But the writing on the wall in blood.

George Connally, as he looked out the window of his house on Lakeview Drive, thought Clear Lake was, itself, turning to a bright blood red with splashes of amber. But it was only a reflection of what was to the north of the prep school, behind the football field, set back near the woods.

A house was on fire.

The Amory house.

3.

Sunrise

Teddy Amory fell asleep twice along the roadside. She dreamed of: nothing, and was happy for that. Each time she'd crawled back into the dead, high grass, trying to ignore the cold and damp. She knew it was early morning but did not feel any safer than she had in the dark night. Every few minutes she would hear her brother Jake wailing, fanning the fire with his monstrous tongue, but she knew it was only in her head. She wondered if she would freeze to death.

And she wondered if her seizures would come on again, the rumbling inside, the heat rising through her stomach and up to her heart, her arms and legs, shaking, tossing her up and down like a rag doll. The cold blue water. Under her skin. She wondered if Jake was going to find her. She did not wonder what he would do to her. She knew.

And Teddy Amory wondered if that was not such a bad idea after all. To let him get her. Maybe what she'd once heard her father tell her mother had been true: she should've drowned in the lake. Maybe she was meant to. If Jake caught her, maybe it would all be over soon, everything would be all right. *No illness, no more fever, no more chills. No pain. No nothing. No people staring, no kids laughing and yelling, "Hey, Freak!"*

Teddy lay on the cold earth, sheltered by tall stalks of dead yellow grass, gazing up at the hazy purple sky, trying to remember what it had been like before she went through the ice two winters before. She blinked, and in that split second a shadow came across the sky. She opened her eyes and saw a Hallowe'en monster towering above her.

Teddy Amory screamed.

4.

From *The Nightmare Book of Cup Coffey:*

AN INFORMAL TOURIST GUIDE

Pontefract, Virginia, is the kind of town you miss seeing because of the new overpass between Cabelsville and Newton, or the interstate that runs between the mountains to Charlottesville. Even so, it's the Westbridge County seat and means something to those who live in the county. It means history. And when you're worried about last month's bills, or what life means, or if you'll ever be happy—just remember, someday, you're going to be dust. Just like the song says, the worms will go in and they're going to come out, too. There's no way around it, we all end up six feet under. But history continues, above ground, in things that never die: buildings, traditions, books, even gossip. People who live in small towns know this. They know history is the only thing that lasts.

Folks in Pontefract, for instance.

Maybe you've heard of the school. Maybe you know someone who went to the Pontefract Preparatory School for Boys. Or you've heard of the hot springs over in Cabelsville, and you know that Pontefract is the last gas station stop before you head over the hills. Perhaps you drove through Pontefract and remarked to your spouse, "Looks like a great place to raise kids," or "Imagine the history, honey."

The name of the town means "Broken Bridges," or something close to it. There's an old Revolutionary War story about the footbridge that was torn down and this bridge was not resurrected until the 1920s, but nobody recollects that story the same way twice.

Dr. Prescott Nagle, when he delivers his Founders Day speech, refers to the town as "Point-of-Fact," and has a hundred different stories about it. He'd be sure and drop a few Scotch-Irish and German names into his anecdotes so that the original town's descendants would stand up taller and contribute a few extra dollars to the Historical Society.

Pontefract does have its historical interest. Point of fact: the Virginia Society For Historic Preservation partially funded an archeological excavation just to the north of the prep school. The prep school was built, in fact, on the site of the original settlement. Now the town is set directly across Clear Lake from Pontefract Prep. Dr. Nagle could tell you everything you'd ever want to know about that dig, the Scotch-Irish in the Shenandoah Valley of Virginia, and the military school that later became Pontefract Prep. He could even show you army uniform buttons and the bits and pieces of muskets from the 1700s he and his students found in the dig. Before he lost state and local funding.

If you drive that overpass, say on your way to Route 64, or south to Roanoke, you wouldn't even have to blink twice before you'd gone by Pontefract.

But if you caught a glimpse of it, you'd think this was just another picturesque Virginia town, with a whitewash of Southern genteel history, nestled, as the guidebook might say, in the Southwest Shenandoah Valley, three hours from Washington, D.C., two to Richmond. Someplace to pull in for gas or a bite to eat or a look-see.

A place where young people move away and old people remain to play out their last days.

CHAPTER SIX
THE CALL

1.

From *The Nightmare Book of Cup Coffey:*

END OF FALL TERM—ALMOST CHRISTMAS!

As far as I'm concerned, it's been a bad fall, to say nothing of the entire year.

Besides the usual bullshit, I've been having those dreams again. Dreams? More like nightmares. About the kids.

Last night's was a doozy. Unlike the series of dreams I was having back in August when I slept with the entire cast of the TV show "Dynasty." Those sexual dreams were something of a relief, actually, and good normal fodder for my therapist. He can handle non-violent dreams brought on by boob tube addiction, Oedipal struggles, sexual unfulfillment and couch potatoism.

In these recent dreams, though, the bad ones, the kids are buried up to their necks in this beautifully manicured lawn, perhaps half an acre or more of children's heads rising up to my ankle. Some of the kids are talking, while others are just looking at all the flowers that border their ears.

In the dream I go over each kid's head with a lawn mower. Power mower, in fact, the kind where you just flip a switch and the wheels move all by themselves.

I told my therapist some of this. You know, my basic theory about kids: they are monsters in children ziploc suits, which they discard when they go to school each day. Parents never fully realize this.

The first time I had this nightmare I woke up laughing at its absurdity.

Then, on my way to work, it began to seem eerily plausible. You actually could bury kids up to their necks and mow them down. I mean, I'd never want to do it, but it is physically possible. Reminds me of something I heard in college, to the effect that when you come across a potential vice, first you look at it and are repulsed, then it starts to seem attractive and okay, and finally, you embrace it. Since my college days—six years now—I could've screwed that expression up in my head, but that's how this dream starts coming to me. I am at first repulsed. Then, after a few evenings of head mowing, I start thinking it's kind of neat. In a very gross way, of course, and only in this dream. When I wake up I'm still disgusted with myself for having dreamed it. I've had this dream off and on for about three weeks now. Always with a slight variation on the basic theme.

For instance, one time the kids are all crying, another time some of these kids don't seem to care that their heads are being torn off. I write about this with the calm serenity of a madman, but let me tell you, when I think about the implications I am scared shitless. How many young boys' bodies did they finally dig up in John Wayne Gacy's backyard? And who knows, maybe old Johnnyboy had nightmares, too, and maybe he shuddered every time he saw someone mowing their lawn. But then *one day* . . . Yeah, and maybe he saw those bodies buried under the house before he ever dug that first grave. In his dreams.

I told most of this to my therapist. About this journal, too. God, I hope no enemy of mine ever gets a hold of this thing or I am in deep shit. He asked me just who I was writing this for, and I told him, "Posterity." I don't want to make his job any easier than it already is—not at sixty bucks a shot. The good doctor believes that all this journal-writing has served its purpose and will only remind me of bad things from here on in. But I am convinced there is a reason for these nightmares. It's this feeling of unfinished business. Somewhere inside these dreams is a key, to God only knows what, but it's there. And I hope, through this Nightmare Book, I will find that key.

Back to those dreams. The good doctor says these nightmares are a combination of many things: my own unfulfillment in terms of children, that I'm being pressured by society to marry and raise kids, and subconsciously I am rebelling. He also thinks I am cutting off my own childhood memories "at the head." Heh-heh. Pretty good joke from such a humorless man.

The one thing my sixty-buck-an-hour therapist can't make out is the essential symbol: the lawn mower. He did suggest that perhaps the mower is a symbol of my maleness. My phallus. My penis. But the good doctor actually put it another way. He said it represented my "member," as if there were a country club where all those members gather. Men, he explained to me, traditionally do yardwork. "So there we are," he said, closing his files for the afternoon, content with his summary.

Was that summary worth sixty bucks?

Doubtful.

But what I haven't even told my therapist, and I don't intend to, is that last night the worst thing happened in the nightmare.

What, you may ask, could be worse than mowing a lawn full of children's heads?

It was right after one of those miniseries episodes with Jane Seymour and Richard Chamberlain, I think, a costume epic where everyone has adulterous affairs, lots of people get killed, and no one seems to do anything for a living. Miniseries are great sleeping pills. Most TV has that effect on me. I always fall asleep in front of it. The week had been shot to hell anyway since over the weekend I saw Tess (my *sort of* girlfriend) with another guy. They were waiting in line for an Ingmar Bergman festival at the Circle Theater, and I was walking up H Street. The guy was some lawyerly-type in a blue pinstripe suit and a lemon tie. How could she go for a man like that? A lemon tie to go see *Cries and*

Whispers? So what if he was All-American good-looking, tall, broad-shouldered, had stylishly cut blond hair, probably made megabucks? A man who wears a lemon tie to a Bergman film just ain't all there. He probably saw Rambo and wondered if Stallone subscribed to the Stanislavsky method.

It seemed like the ultimate betrayal to see Tess with this yuppie. Although I don't know why I expect her to be faithful: I am no great shakes. I make very little money, and most of it goes to therapy. Believe me I am not proud of seeing the good doctor as often as I do, but with lawn mowing dreams and others, it quickly becomes a necessity. I stand about six-foot-one on a good day, have dark brown hair, and no visible scars. I have, as people who want something from you will inform you, a nice smile and deep brown eyes. I do not wear lemon ties, and occasionally my gut pushes up too much against my size-thirty-six-inch-waist slacks and I have to cut out the ice cream (never the beer). Oh, and I have recurring nightmares about chopping kids up with a lawn mower. There's my personal resumé, and looking over it I can see why Tess might be standing in line with Mr. Lemon Tie for a Bergman festival (and she hates Bergman, too).

In the eight months I've been seeing Tess our relationship has gone from potentially romantic to a user-friendly system: I'll scratch your back if you scratch mine. We have a lot of welts on our backs from all that scratching.

So, depressed, I sit in the evenings in front of the tube, begging it to occupy my mind with something other than Tess and Mr. Lemon Tie, and last night, the dream came.

In this dream, the kids are, naturally, buried up to their necks, some screaming, some apparently enjoying the situation, and a few who actually look like they belong there in the dirt. As if they just sprouted. Don't ask me how I know, but I do. Some of these kids are growing out of the ground like flowers. As if this head, above ground, is a blossom, with roots just beneath the earth. I push the mower over their heads and think: I'm doing the right thing. These kids are evil. They should be nipped in the bud.

I go about my business. I chop the heads off most of the

kids. It isn't quite that neat and easy, but why describe the gory technicolor spectacle? If you're reading this journal you already know I belong in a zoo.

In the dream I feel like I have been given a mandate, that I am restoring the natural order of things. When things are planted in the ground they need to be trimmed and pruned.

But the mower's blades jam when I come upon those kids who, like I said, give me this funny feeling that somehow they're growing up from seedlings. Their heads break the blades of the mower. I keep trying to go over these anklebiters, but nothing doing. It's like when you're vacuuming and you come upon this toothpick caught in the carpet. You keep going over and over it, and it never gets sucked up into the machinery. But do you simply reach down and pick the toothpick up? Oh, no, that would make it too easy, and I think people really don't like things to be too easy. So you keep going over and over with the vacuum cleaner. You are going to conquer this thing through sheer force of your will.

Well, these kids' heads are like that. I keep running over them with this mower, but the machine is not doing its job. So I turn off the mower and walk over to the toolshed. You know how dreams are—one second there's just a lawn full of kids' heads and the next, presto, there's a toolshed? In the shed, I find a large pair of pruning shears. Possibly the largest, sharpest pruning shears I have ever held in my hands.

I return to the lawn to finish the job the lawn mower had been unable to do.

But these kids' heads are no longer planted in the ground. The kids have emerged. They are somewhere in the yard. And I am terrified. I break out in a cold sweat. I jab the blades of the pruning shears into the empty holes where the heads had been a few seconds ago, thinking maybe they've just sunk further down.

I hear a whirring noise behind me. I do not want to turn around. I am doing everything I can not to turn around. I am trying to keep my eyes straight ahead on the lilies and roses. But that noise behind me is getting louder. It sounds like a swarm of wasps.

I finally give in to my own feeling of dread and I turn around.

Facing me are several kids. I recognize them as the ones that defeated the lawn mower. They each have what is popularly known as a "weedwhacker." This is a sort of mechanical golf club with a cutting edge at its base. And a blade that spins around. It is commonly used to, yes, whack weeds.

These kids, with their whackers on HIGH, start to close in on me. Watching me with a curious mixture of hatred and glee. And love—should I write that? Hatred, glee and love. Go figure.

I know then that I am the weed in the garden.

As in most horrible dreams, I wake up before the terrible whackers cut across my paralyzed throat and to the most prosaic of settings: my miniature living room, lying scrunched up on the old smelly sofa my Uncle Phil gave me when I moved into the apartment in Washington, D.C.

I glance at my alarm clock and it is already quarter to eight. My back is sore from the uncomfortable position on the couch, and I contemplate calling in sick to work.

But I am a teacher, after all, and Christmas break looms on the horizon. I feel a strange kind of loyalty to those rug-rats I teach at Hardy Elementary School. So I turn on the Mr. Coffee machine (no jokes, please, about it being named for me, Malcolm "Cup" Coffey of Woodley Park in Our Nation's Capital). I jump in and out of the shower, throw on some clothes and get the show on the road.

Teachers aren't a scarce commodity in the Washington, D.C., area, so it took four years to work my way into the public school system, finally ending up out in Arlington County rather than in the District itself. Last summer, I convinced the principal of Hardy Elementary, Mrs. Radisson (also more popularly known among faculty and students alike as "Mrs. Radish"), that I was the person to take over Language Arts (also known as Grammar and Reading) for the fourth through sixth grades. I never really wanted to be a teacher, but I knew when I got into it that there would be a lot of vacations and summers. Not too shabby a deal. What you don't get is good pay.

But it's almost Christmas break, and this morning I was thinking, *eleven whole days off.* No lesson plans to write up, no sentences to parse, no margins to check, no themes to grade, no halls to monitor.

No Billy Bates.

William Scott Bates, as his report card reads.

Or *Master Bates,* as he has been known to call himself.

Get it?

Because when I get off the subway, jog up the escalator, and shuffle out into the cool morning air to walk three blocks to school, I am not expecting that I will have such problems as Billy Bates. What would Billy have to gain by causing me problems right before Christmas vacation? Admittedly, he is probably the prototype for my lawn mower nightmares. I am not the only teacher at Hardy Elementary who feels that way, either.

I was warned about Billy Bates my first week of teaching. "Just plain bad," Liz Jackson, the math teacher across the hall, informed me, "I've known that boy since he was five and he's always been bad."

"Naughty?" I suggested, not yet having had any indication of the depths of his badness.

Liz shook her head. "Too precious a word for him. In second grade he poured glue in a girl's hair and almost blinded one of the McNutt boys with a pair of scissors. Maybe that was naughty. And when he poisoned the fourth-grade science project? They were raising mice and Billy fed them rat poison. When he was caught, he said he didn't think the mice would die because it was rat poison, not mouse poison. Call him mischievous for that. But when he tried to bury Mary Alice Seidman alive, well, it was just plain bad. That's too kind a word, but it certainly describes him. Just look how the other kids treat him."

I remarked that I hadn't noticed.

She smiled that kind of wry half-smile that means: you ain't seen nothing yet, kiddo. "They stay *away* from him."

But I learned fast enough to stay away from Billy Bates myself, more out of pity and incomprehension than anything. There's nothing a problem teacher will avoid more than a problem child. My first and biggest negative run-in with Billy Bates happened around Thanksgiving. He was in my homeroom class, and was pretty unobtrusive most of the time. He turned in his work on time and kept to himself. I was, and still am, a fairly unmotivated teacher. I think in those first months of the year I was waiting to catch fire, to suddenly find within myself some great vocational torch that would be fueled by the Arlington County public school system. It never happened. I found myself, instead, only calling on those students who would give me the least hassle, those who wrote in neat, legible rocker curves and raised their hands before I'd even finished asking the question. Until that day in November I didn't have much cause to worry about Billy Bates.

But that afternoon I was leading my class back from the library where we were working on our First Thanksgiving projects. I had confiscated a number of rubber bands and been hit in the back of the neck with at least one spitball, but all in all it had been a quiet day.

As we passed the hall bathroom, a few of the boys mentioned that they "gotta go." I lined the rest of the class up against the blue cinderblock wall and allowed those boys to go and do their duty. Billy Bates was among them.

A few moments later one of the boys came out of the bathroom, still buckling his belt, and told me that Billy Bates was going to kill Eric Ownby and that I'd better get in there quick.

I rushed into the boys' room. Two boys were holding a stall door open and when they saw me they whispered among themselves, wide-eyed, and then slipped past me as I took hold of the door. There behind the toilet stall door was Billy Bates being bad.

Billy had one foot on Eric Ownby's back, pushing the boy's face down into the toilet bowl, flushing it, keeping him down, snickering, "I think I hear your mommy calling for you down there, Eric!"

I pulled Billy off Eric and brought Eric's head out of the toilet. Eric was gasping, but he managed to tell me he was okay. I turned all my fury on Billy Bates. I really wanted to thrash that kid, beat some sense into him. I felt my skin turning red with anger. I took a few deep breaths. It was as if I had taken whatever wildness that had gotten loose inside me in that second and coaxed it back into its cage. Rule Number One in teaching, I had learned, is not to lose your temper in front of the kids.

Eric Ownby was still spitting out water and had begun crying. I cleared the other boys out of the bathroom and lined them back up in the hall. I helped Eric down to the nurse's office, but before I went I said to Billy, who was still crouched against the yellow tile next to the toilet bowl, "You stay put, Bates, and if I see you've moved one muscle you're in for it big time, you hear me?" I remember thinking: *Oh, God, I sound like my father.* It was the best threat I could come up with on such short notice.

When I returned from the nurse's office, Billy was still slumped down on the bathroom floor. Only now he was giggling and drooling. He told me, through the drool, that he had moved one muscle.

That was when I noticed what his hand was doing. In his lap. His fly was unzipped and he had taken out his member, as my therapist would say, and was stroking it.

I don't remember what kind of shocked thing I must've gasped—nothing in student teaching in college had prepared me for this moment. But Billy Bates curled his lips in a canine snarl and said, "Call me Master Bates! Masturbates! Get it get it get it?"

Later, in the teachers' lounge, everyone had a good laugh over my inaugural trauma with Billy Bates. One teacher even quipped that I could charm the pants off my students. Another suggested we call in an exorcist for Billy, and I wondered if that might not be a good idea. But then I found out about his file, and decided to look over it to check out his past history.

This kid has the fattest student file I've ever seen. It's about the size of your local community yellow pages. Mainly it's a listing of all Billy Bates' offenses since the age of five. The first that caught my eye was his notorious attempt at a live burial of Mary Alice Seidman. He pushed her in a gravel pit near the playground and started to keep her head down while he filled the pit in with dirt. Luckily, one of the school busdrivers was nearby and was able to stop him before it had gotten too serious for Mary Alice (who, I might add, is no longer at Hardy Elementary). The busdriver wrote in his report:

I asked Billy what he thought he was doing with Mary Alice. He told me in no uncertain terms that he was trying to plant her to see if she would come up again in the spring.

Another teacher wrote:

. . . It was an animal's heart and she was crying because she'd already taken a bite out of it. Susan Beauchamp told me that Billy Bates was the boy who'd put it into her baloney sandwich. I confronted Billy and he admitted this. He said it was his pet guinea pig's heart and he brought it in for Show and Tell. When I asked him why he had put the heart in Susan's sandwich, he told me it was because she is such a pig that she should have a pig's heart, too. This kind of cruel behavior is typical of Billy Bates. Suggest expulsion.

Many more entries like this: Billy dissected dead pregnant cats to see if the kittens were still alive, he opened all the milk cartons in the cafeteria and was caught spitting in each one, he hid in the girls' bathroom, he set fire to Annie Crowe's hair. But one entry explained it all for me:

I saw some bruises before yesterday, but I assumed Billy had fallen down somewhere. I know how he rough-houses. But this was a long yellow and blue mark that encircled his neck. Almost like a tattoo of a necklace. I asked him what happened. He told me that his father had taken his puppy to the Pound. He started crying as he told me. Billy got angry with his father and knocked a lamp over. His father undid his belt, wrapped it around Billy's neck, and started choking him. I know Billy has lied about some things, but I think he is telling the truth about this. Suggest we contact the authorities.

I stopped reading the file then and put it back in the cabinet. From that moment on I felt pity and sadness for Billy Bates, I could even understand his badness. So I treated him as I would any other student and he sat, quietly, through my classes for most of the fall.

2.

From *The Nightmare Book of Cup Coffey:*

So this morning, the morning of what shall from here on in be known as "Hell Day," I don't expect a Billy Bates problem. I arrive just two minutes before the bell rings for classes to begin, duck by the front office so that Mrs. Radish doesn't see me ("Late again!") and grab a quick cup of coffee in the teachers' lounge. I tell Lyndi Wright, the second-grade teacher, that I'm disappointed there are no doughnuts and she flashes me a grin and suggests that if I watch her class for a few minutes before recess, she'll make a Krispie Kreme run. There's a note in my mailslot from Mrs. Radish informing me that my lesson plans have not yet found their way to her desk and to please see her immediately. I crumple the note and toss it in the circular file on the way out of the lounge.

Then, down the hall to the classroom—thankfully, my room is as far away from the principal's office as possible. I've been daydreaming about summer a lot lately (and it's not even January!), the job interviews I will go on, how I'll visit my folks out in California in July and lie on the beach in Laguna, how I might finally apply to a graduate school; but mainly I am looking forward to sleeping in.

Just another week. One more week. I could count the hours. The minutes. Then Christmas break—made me feel like a kid.

* * *

When I walk in the room this morning, my bulletin board is in a cat-scratched shambles. I figure Mrs. Radish has done this in her zeal to kick me off my duff. All the tacks and pins are on the floor, and the kids' papers are littered across my desk, completely covering it. I never put things like this beyond Mrs. Radish's capabilities ever since I caught her snooping through my desk and trash can (possibly looking for one of the several notes that Liz and I pass back and forth to each other across the hall).

But then I see the words on the blackboard, and I know that even Mrs. Radish would not flip out so completely as to write them. The words make no sense.

In fluorescent blue chalk, written about twenty times, is the phrase *He says you cheat.*

I don't get it at all. I erase this cryptic message just as my homeroom files in, and in its place I write REMEMBER MARGINS! and SPELLING TEST, SECTION 11.4. Although the fifth-graders notice the tornado-hit quality of the bulletin board, no one says a word about it. We're all getting lazy and indifferent; the thought of vacation, so close (ten days away, but only eight school days), turns us into lotus-eaters.

I don't give my homeroom their spelling test until after lunch. I forget about the mess in my classroom and the blue chalk writing on the blackboard as the day progresses. When I get the fifth-graders back around 12:30, I read perfunctorily down the list of words from the spelling book. I don't even care that the students are whispering between words—in my mind I'm in Georgetown having a beer, or wondering if I should call the good doctor about last night's weedwhacker dream.

Nina Van Huyck, one of those precocious little girls who wears make-up by the time she's ten and is purported to have kissed every boy in the fifth grade before Christmas break, collects the tests. When she gets to Billy Bates' desk to pick up his test, she lets out a little squeal. It is more an ear-piercing shriek, like fingernails scraping against a blackboard.

I get up from my desk and glare at the two of them.

"Make him stop," she whines. She's standing right in front of his desk so I can't tell what he's doing.

Some of the boys seated near him start giggling, covering their mouths to hold in their snickers, and other students stare wide-eyed at Billy and gasp as if to clue me in that not only is Billy Bates being BAD but he is also going to get CAUGHT.

I'm thinking: *please, Billy, it's only a few more days, don't have your pants around your ankles.*

But his pants are on. His shirt is on. He is completely clothed. Thank God for small favors. I step away from my desk and walk wearily back to Billy's desk. "Take your seat, Nina," I say as I approach the two of them.

"Tell him to stop it," she says in that haughty little Daddy's princess voice, and I cringe to think I've encouraged her arrogant behavior all year just because she was willing to wash my blackboards in the afternoon.

Billy Bates is resting his head on the top of his desk.

"Are you all right, Billy?" I ask and reach down to feel his forehead.

It is cool. He doesn't have the flu or the plague.

He didn't look up. "Go away, Mr. Coffey."

"Excuse me, Billy?" I ask, and realize how asinine I sound.

"I'm playing dead, see?" He lifts his head up and I see that his face is smudged with blue. I touch his chin with my fingers and the color comes off in my hand. Blue fluorescent chalkdust.

He says you cheat, written in blue fluorescent chalk.

"But you aren't dead, Billy."

"He says I am. And he says you're going to be, too."

More nervous giggling from the other kids.

"All right, enough. Billy, put your desk in the hall and go sit there until class is over." This was my usual solution for the few times I suspected that Billy was about to get out of hand. *Park it, Mister,* I'd say, and he was usually content to sit out Language Arts in the hallway, just outside the door. This was a popular spot for him among my colleagues—it made up for our incompetence as instructors.

After I help Billy with his desk, amidst muffled giggles and whispers from the surrounding peanut gallery, I go over the spelling test with the rest of the class. Then we open our workbooks to the next session.

When class is almost over, I ask if there are any volunteers to go out to the hall and tell Billy he may return to class and line up with the rest of them. Of course, Nina Van Huyck's hand is the first up in the air.

"All right, Nina," I nod. Students always think that when they run errands for teachers and clap erasers that they are somehow part of a charmed circle. Nina is one of those.

She goes to the door, with some trepidation since she is probably wondering if Billy will still be playing possum for her benefit. But she opens the door, looks out into the hall, turns her head back to the classroom and says, "Mr. Coffey, he isn't here. His desk is here. But he isn't."

"Great," I whisper, and when an elementary school teacher says "great," what he is really saying is *"Oh, shit."*

The bell rings, I dismiss my kids. I walk out into the corridor amidst a sea of children as they pour into and out of all the classrooms. I go across the hall and ask Liz if she'll watch my next class for about five minutes while I go off in search of Billy Bates.

I nudge my way through the students, which is difficult to do when they only come up to your waist. It's like being mired in a bog among creepy-crawlies. I check the boys' room, the girls' room, the cafeteria, and even the principal's office. Then onto the library, and the whole way down the hall I am quizzing teachers and students: have they seen him? Finally I get the bright idea to check the playground.

There he is, standing near the jungle gym, talking to himself. I shout, "Billy Bates you get in here right this instant!"

Billy stops talking, and I think he is turning around to look my way. But it's more like he's cocking his head to one side trying to hear someone better. And it's not me he's listening to.

I march like a stormtrooper onto the blacktop. Billy finally notices me. His eyebrows knit on his brow. His lips are moving but I can't hear a word. I get right up next to him. Out of the corners of my eyes I notice that the entire school seems to be lined up at the windows facing out on the playground.

"I said get in that building right now, young man."

He looks confused. Frightened. He crosses his arms on his chest defensively. "He says No."

"I don't care what anyone says, I say, do it now!"

I grab his arm. He wriggles free and ducks under one of the bars of the jungle gym and then scrambles to the top of it. Aware that we are putting on some kind of show for half the school, I try to cool down. "Okay, Billy. Who says no?"

"Him. You know him. He says you go way back."

"When did he say this?"

Billy, clinging to the metal bars, glances to his left and then to his right, and whispers, "He *just* said it."

"Where is he? Tell him to come out. I'd like to meet him."

"You know where he is. He says you put him there."

"Billy!" My patience is wearing thin at this point. I'm positive that if I were a cartoon character, steam would be blowing out of my ears. "Did you write on the blackboard this morning?"

Billy shakes his head.

"Come on now, Billy. I know you did it. 'He says you cheat.' What was the meaning of that?"

He starts to sob, and wipes his nose with the sleeve of his shirt. "You know. He says you know."

"Who, Billy?"

"Him. Mr. Nobody. I dunno. He says it's true. You. You . . . cheat."

"Who?"

"You. You. You."

"Stop it. I am going to count to ten."

By the time I get to five, Billy jumps to the ground and tears off for the building. I watch him enter, and wave to those students and teachers who are still watching me. Then I walk as calmly as possible back to the school.

When I enter the building through the back double doors, Amy Meader, who teaches kindergarten, greets me with, "I think he went thataway," pointing to the janitor's door leading to the basement boiler room. "And I don't envy you the privilege, Cup. The Radish was out here a few minutes ago asking if I thought you had control of the situation."

"Fuck her," I say, and then notice a few five-year-olds standing in Amy's doorway. I pray that they don't go home and repeat this new word they learned today from the fifth-grade teacher.

I go down into the boiler room. "Billy?" The room is a charcoal gray—the only light filters in through three opaque glass windows. I switch on the overhead light. There, next to the furnace, sits Billy Bates, sucking his thumb and crying. "Are you all right?"

Billy catches his breath. He speaks in gasps, "He . . . says . . . you . . . killed . . . him."

"Who, Billy? Who says that?"

"Bah—Bah—" But he starts coughing before he can finish it. It's funny, but I don't even connect with what he is saying. I figure he's been watching too many "Amazing Stories" or "Twilight Zones."

"Whoever he is," I slowly move closer to him, trying not to alarm him, "he must be a liar."

"I dunno."

"Look . . ." I am close enough to reach down and offer him my hand. "Let's go back upstairs and talk this thing out, man-to-man. Everything'll be all right."

He shakes his head violently, and draws back from me like I am a rattlesnake coiled to strike. "He says you . . . you . . . you . . ."

"When did he say this?"

"Now."

"Is he here? Down here?"

Billy nods. He is calming down. His face is wet from tears. I'm thinking, *Jeez, I wonder if the old man took a belt or worse to him last night. What kind of hell do some kids have to live through?*

"We'll just go back upstairs."

He thinks about this for a moment. "Lemme go first."

So I step back, allowing him free access to the stairs. He goes around me, his eyes never leaving me. When he gets to the first step he turns around and flicks the light off. I can still see him, but it's through a hazy gray cloud. "Billy, turn it back on."

He does turn it on, then off, then on, then off. The effect is something like lightning flashes.

I move quickly to the stairs. "Stop it, right now." And as I get closer, I hear him whisper a chant, "He says you cheat, you cheat, you cheat." The strobe effect of the flashing light hurts my eyes. When I am standing right in front of him I grab him and shake him. "Just shut up."

The voice that comes back at me through that gauze darkness is not a little fifth-grader's, not Billy Bates' prepubescent soprano. This voice belongs to a much older boy. And I smell smoke. Who I think I hear and see is Bart Kinter who died when I was sixteen. "I know what kind of monster you are, Coffeyass," this voice says, and without thinking about what I'm doing, I draw my left hand back, still clutching a little boy by his collar with my right, and bring that hand down hard onto the side of his face; so hard that it practically whistles through the air, and when the palm of my left hand touches Billy's face it makes a loud *whack!*

Billy screams and cries, and I switch on the boiler room light. I throw my arms around him and I am crying, too, telling him how sorry I am, how I didn't mean to do it, not at all, I wasn't myself. He is pushing me away, crying, and I am hugging him tighter and tighter to me while he claws at the air for escape. I look at his face, and there is a giant red handprint across it like a scar. I hear some noise on the stairs and I look up to see Mrs. Radish, my boss, staring down at me and the fact of my losing my job, while implicit in her glance, is momentarily the least of my worries.

3.

From *The Nightmare Book of Cup Coffey:*

The next morning I am in Mrs. Radisson's office.

I can't even bring myself to look at her as I sit in a large, uncomfortable leather chair across the desk from her. My hands are trembling. I glance down at my lap—even my knees are knocking. I haven't slept all night. Afraid of those dreams.

She starts telling me that she's received several calls already from parents who heard about yesterday's incident. But, aside from that, there've been complaints since September concerning my lack of discipline in the classroom, my overall laziness. How she has asked to see my lesson plans every week, and I have not turned them in. She reminds me that there is only one week before vacation. She has already lined up a substitute to take over my classes. She is worried, she tells me, that Billy's parents might bring a lawsuit against the school. How my slapping Billy Bates dislodged one of his teeth, and even though it was a baby tooth . . .

I nod. God, I nod so much I feel like one of those dogs in the back windows of cars: up and down with the head, up and down. I agree with every last thing this woman I despise tells me. Because it is the truth. I feel right now like dirt under her feet.

I walk out of her office at ten o'clock in the morning, out of that school forever. I hop the Metro back to Foggy Bottom and from there, walk to Sign of the Whale, a bar on M Street. Just before noon on this lovely mild day in December, I order a beer.

After my sixth Heineken Dark (but who's counting?) I decide to give Tess a call. I forget about Mr. Lemon Tie at the Ingmar Bergman festival, and I tell the bartender what a sweet girl Tess is. "I don't blame her," I raise my bottle in a toast, "not after weedwhackers, and days like I've been having." The bartender agrees with me, and I go to the payphone and dial the number of the shop she manages in Georgetown.

"Hello, stranger," she says, and then whispers, "There's a customer in here right now, can't talk long."

"It's important." I'm thinking it would be funnier to say "It's impotent," but I'm afraid she won't see the humor in it.

"Where are you?"

"Sign of the Whale."

"Why aren't you at work?"

"Long story. Why don't you come by here?"

"It's getting busy. What are you calling about?"

"Ingmar Fucking Bergman."

"Look. We'll talk later. I don't have time to hold your hand right now."

I hang up the phone. I am at that wonderful drunken stage when you just want to say "To hell with it," and tell bawdy stories to the bartender.

But the bartender doesn't laugh at any of them and makes some excuse of not being himself today. "Well, who *are* you, then?" I finish off my beer and go out on the street to hail a cab.

When I walk in my apartment it dawns on me that I've forgotten to get in touch with the one person who might shed a little light on this depressed state of mind. My therapist. I dial his number. I'm going to tell him I need an emergency session. But that afternoon, the day after Hell Day, his secretary answers and informs me that the good doctor is out of the office for a few days and won't be in until Monday.

When you call your therapist's office and receive a message like that it seems like the ultimate rejection. I mean, you're paying this guy to listen to your problems: he should always be there! I say to his secretary, "Would you mind listening to me for a few minutes?"

She declines.

I hang up on her, the loudest, most phone splitting hang up I've ever done, as if everything that happened this week was entirely her fault and damn it, I want her to know it.

I pick the phone up again and slam it down hard into its cradle.

And again.

Finally, I lift the whole damn phone and throw it in the sink with the dirty dishes (but I unplug it first—I am angry, not stupid).

I look back across the kitchen counter for something else to demolish. What do I see but my answering machine, its belligerent red light blinking.

I push the play button. I am looking forward to listening to whatever message is on the tape. It's probably Tess offering her sympathy, but—too late! I am going to rip that microcassette out of there and shred that sucker.

"Hello, this is Cup. I can't come to the phone right now, but I'd like you to leave a message after the electronic beep. Thank you."

Beep.

I love those beeps. It gives your answering machine this Three Stooges touch, like you can have the most dignified message possible and there's Curly, Moe and Larry going "whoop-whoop-whoop" just at the end to throw the caller off.

At first I'm thinking whoever left this message is an obscene phone caller because I hear a lot of heavy breathing and faraway moans mixed with crackling static on the line.

A breathy female voice finally says, "Hello . . . Cup? Is it you? You'll die when you find out who this is."

4.

From *The Nightmare Book of Cup Coffey:*

AFTER HELL DAY

That same afternoon I'd gotten fired, dumped my girlfriend (or was dumped by her, I still don't know which), lost my therapist (good riddance), I played that answering machine message a dozen times. Over the next several days I played that message so many damn times the tape finally became garbled and I had to throw it out.

Each time I played that message, though, before it became unintelligible, I thought I caught subtle nuances of desperation and even love.

She said:

You'll die when you find out who this is.

But I did not die. In fact I felt more alive hearing that message than I had in twelve years.

I knew who the caller was immediately.

Lily Cammack.

"Remember?" she asked.

How could I have ever forgotten her? Lily haunted my waking hours. Every time a girl passed me on the street, no matter how lovely or self-possessed, that girl was nothing compared to my memory of Lily. Lily's graceful walk, her white-blond hair cut to her shoulders, those translucent blue eyes, beestung red lips, her breasts, slender waist, the way she used to turn her head to the side in mock-dramatic longing. The way her nose wrinkled just before she'd laugh. How many arguments could I then recall with Tess, ending with Tess saying, "Why don't you just go back to your goddamn goddess! Just ring up your old girlfriend!"

My old girlfriend. Lily Cammack was never my old girlfriend. We never dated. I only knew her for a few years, and in those few years I had imbedded her image in my mind forever, and those memories of my youth that include her are the ones I cherish above all others.

When I thought of Lily, I knew that Tess, and every other girl I'd ever been attracted to, was nothing to me. Tess was too coarse, she didn't have the ironic detachment from the world that Lily possessed, her hair was unkempt and Raggedy-Annish, while Lily's was always newly brushed, sparkling. Tess was too direct in her movements, she always had some place to go, a destination. But with Lily you had the feeling that there was no place to go, and so she moved almost dreamily, like a spirit, and wherever you were with her was destination enough.

No wonder Tess thought I was such a schmuck.

But the worst of all this, before Lily left that message on my machine, was that I could not just ring Lily up, as Tess had so archly suggested.

Because since that night, when I was sixteen, I'd had no contact whatsoever with Lily Cammack. After that night everything in my life changed. I underwent a kind of brainwashing by my parents. They wanted me to put all that behind me, and "all that" included Lily. "Bury it," they suggested. I spent the next semester in a school in Baltimore, Maryland, not speaking to any of my new classmates, feeling like a leper.

I pretended to forget about everything that happened that

night in Pontefract, Virginia. It seemed so far away from Baltimore that pretending was an easy thing to do. I even started telling lies about my past when anyone brought it up. I never told the truth to the new friends I eventually made.

And here was Lily again, December 18, 1986, her lovely voice captured on my answering machine:

"It's been a long time, Cup. Can I still call you 'Cup'? Too long a time. And things have happened . . ."

Then she seemed to brighten. "I'm still living down here in Pontefract, no matter how hard I try to leave, I can't. It's home forever. I'm married, Lily Whalen now, and living over on Howard Avenue, 4221 Howard, if you care. And I wanted . . . So funny talking to this machine . . ." Then, as if she realized she was being evasive, she said, in a desperate sounding succession of words, "I'm in a kind of trouble, Cup, and it's all about that night, you know what I mean, it's all coming back now, Cup, if I told you everything you'd think I was crazy, and I can't tell anyone down here, even my husband, because they're involved in these . . . things. Things that are happening here. Things I don't understand. About that night. You're going to hate me for this, Cup, but you just have to come down here, and you made a promise that night and it's mean of me, but I'm going to hold you to it. I need you to slay my dragons. If it wasn't a matter of life and death I wouldn't—"

And here her voice was cut off by the damn machine, because I'd only programmed it for a few minutes of message time. I called Information in Westbridge County, got her number (listed under Warren Whalen), called it, no answer, dialed her father's number, no answer, and finally fell asleep, again, on my old sofa in front of the television.

Throughout the Christmas holidays, I found myself more often than not in bars, either in downtown D.C. or in Georgetown. I called Tess once when I was very drunk, and she hung up on me. I slept off all the subsequent hangovers while the rest of the world caroled and shopped and shared in the holiday spirit.

But I was reveling in beer and long walks in the cold with my self-pitying loneliness. My Uncle Phil and Aunt Lisa invited me up to Silver Spring, Maryland, to spend Christmas Day with them and I went but did not talk much. I had about three hundred dollars in my bank account after setting aside January's rent. I didn't know if I would be working in the next few months, so I gave Phil a bottle of cologne I'd been given last Christmas and hadn't opened, and I gave Lisa some paperbacks I picked up at the drugstore. Phil, from the brilliant financially-successful side of the family, wrote me out a check for a thousand dollars to tide me over, he said, and to not worry about paying him back.

"Go visit your mom and dad," he commanded.

But I didn't intend to face my parents again until I was back on my feet. I had rarely experienced Shame in my life, if you don't count that other winter episode when I got caught cheating (*He says you cheat,* and how in hell could Billy Bates know that?), but getting fired from my teaching job, hitting a student, all that was pretty shameful business.

So Christmas came and went, a gloomy holiday for me as always. I sent three letters in quick succession to Lily both to her father's address, and to her more recent residence—no reply. I called her house several times, no one answered, and finally, in desperation, I called at two in the morning after returning from my nightly barhop. Her husband answered the phone (at least, I presumed it was her husband).

"May I please speak to Lily Whalen?"

"Who the hell is this?" His voice was edged with sleep, but he didn't sound angry, just surprised.

"If she's asleep, I'll call back," I said.

He started laughing, like I'd just told him the best joke in the world.

"Yeah, you do that, you just call back. I wouldn't want to wake up sleeping beauty right now, who knows what kind of fucking mood she'll be in." And then he slammed the receiver down.

The next day I called her father's house.

I recognized Dr. Cammack's voice immediately, bronchial, Southern, charming. "Why yes, she's right here," he said, and I felt a wave of relief go through me—I was afraid I would never locate her.

Then a woman's voice, "Hello?"

"Lily?" I asked.

Her voice turned very cold. "No, this is not. Just who is this anyway?"

But it was Lily, I was convinced it was her. Her voice had deepened a bit with age, did not sound quite so hesitant as it had when she'd left the message, but it was her voice.

"It's me, Cup."

"I'm sorry? Who is this?"

"Lily, it's me. You called a couple of weeks ago and I—"

"What kind of joke is this? I don't know anyone named Cup, and if you intend to make calls like this I will have to get in touch with the phone company."

I hung up the phone. Phones are miserable things to talk to people on, so exasperating. I didn't know what had gotten into Lily, but I knew that she had called me with a plea for help, and I had made a promise to her twelve years ago. I was out of work, out of shape, depressed, nowhere to turn, felt like I had no friends. If I wasn't afraid of pain as much as I am, I'm sure I would've considered suicide.

But instead, with that Christmas present from my Uncle Phil and nothing keeping me in Washington at the start of the New Year, I considered a trip to Pontefract. Because I felt somehow, in that weird, romantic way that only men who have not completely surrendered their adolescence feel, that Lily and I were destined to be together. To say that I had kept a torch burning for her would not be wrong.

New Year's Eve there were raucous parties up and down the streets of my neighborhood. I fell asleep with the help of TV and only one beer (I knew I had to start cutting back). I did not even make it to the countdown in Times Square, did not know that the New Year had definitely arrived until nine o'clock the next morning. I spent all of New Year's Day washing my clothes, unsuccessfully trying to reach Lily by phone, and then calling various motels in the area for a room. They were all too expensive or too far from town, so I finally settled on Campbell's Boarding House, a place I thought I'd never end up.

That last night in my apartment in Washington: no kids, no lawn mowers, no weedwhackers, no Billy Bates, no dreams.

Early on January 2, I got on a bus headed south.

CHAPTER SEVEN

PONTEFRACT, VIRGINIA: A DAY IN THE LIFE

1.

From *The Nightmare Book of Cup Coffey:*

The busride was long and uneventful—I left Washington, D.C., at 8 A.M. on a bus that I swear was filled with nuns, drunks and screaming babies, all smoking cigars. That bus pulled into every town on the map in its zigzag route down through western Virginia, finally setting me down in Pontefract at 3 P.M. I called what turned out to be the only cab service in town and waited for my driver.

My memory of this town has faded. Pontefract doesn't seem to be a chest full of my greatest terrors. I am a different person. An adult. They say that in a seven-year period, you shed your old skin entirely and replace it with a new "coat." I had not set foot in this town for twelve years—my skin was already nearly twice-removed from Pontefract's dust.

When I was in my teens, the surface of this town had always held my deepest loathing—the sunshiny, All-American streets, the good-old-boy way of greeting, old men chewing tobacco in front of the drugstore, beehive hairdos, a decadent charm that evoked for me black-and-white movies from the '50s about small Southern towns.

But when the taxi came, a Ford station wagon, I settled

into the back seat determined to see the town for what it is: innocent, untouched by the cosmopolitanism that is overtaking every other small town in Virginia. It still reminds me of all those things, beehive hairdos, "The Andy Griffith Show," chewing tobacco, '50s movies. But I think I can appreciate that—such a relief from all the noise in Washington, all the rush, all the bother over politics and fashion. Pontefract feels like a last refuge, and I realize my initial reaction is tinged with a nostalgia for what might have been had that night twelve years ago not occurred. I feel that somewhere in this town is the key to my own innocence, which was lost that one night.

We drove through the portals of town—the Henchman Lounge and an abandoned Mobil Gas Station, set diagonally across from each other on Main Street like dance partners frozen in a do-si-do. I can't believe that the Henchman is still here. It was a dive back when I was a teenager and snuck in with some friends to try and order beer (we were kicked out). The Henchman Lounge is still the very model of a dive, one of its windows broken, the other bearing the legend scrawled in dust: WASH ME.

The young, greasy-haired girl driving the cab scrutinized me through the rearview mirror and said, "'Course we shoulda stopped for gas back at the depot. I'm runnin' kinda low." She grinned a young hag's grin. "You a former student of old Peepee?"

I'd forgotten the school's notorious nickname. Peepee, Pontefract Prep. "Show us your peepees!" the redneck townies would shout as we walked down the street. This also became a term of endearment among the townies: if you were a student you might be referred to as peepeebrain, or peepeebutt, or even the more visually interesting peepeeface.

I laughed when my cab driver reminded me of this. "Yes," I replied, "I was a peepee in the olden days."

She was apparently no older than seventeen, so my reference to the olden days seemed entirely plausible. She smacked her chewing gum. "Yah, well, my boyfriend used to go there, too."

"It's a fine school."

"Bullshit," she said, smacking the gum again in punctuation. She honked the horn twice as we drove by a cemetery. "Good luck," she informed me, "when you pass boneyards ya either gotta hold your breath or honk your horn."

The girl steered with the careless abandon of one who invites accidents. We narrowly avoided hitting an old dog as it crossed the road ("Fifty points if I was to get him," she said) and a few squirrels.

The town was comatose along Main Street. What has changed about it is there are more stoplights. That's about the extent of the damage. The combination of Federal-style and Greek-revival buildings (even with gutted interiors which were now dime stores and specialty shops) gives the small town an almost patrician flavor, as if indicating that this was once a town of some prosperity. We passed all the same shops I remembered from before, the old barber shop with its twirling pole and leather shaving strop hanging in the window, the Regency Row Arcade, the Tobacconist Shop, the Kountry Kitchen Bakery, Dunwoody's Ham Biscuit Haven, the Key Theater, Fauquier's Five'N'Dime, Fisher's Drugstore (old men in baseball caps, plaid hunting jackets, standing around the jumbo bags of coal in front, waving to me as if we were all old friends), Hotchkiss Market . . . On the sides of some of the old red buildings are still stenciled COCA-COLA logos from the '30s, and from even earlier times, MILLER'S FEED & SUPPLY and CHAS. HOUSTON BUGGY WHIPS. The cool, blue mountains just beyond Pontefract give the illusion that this is a doll-sized town, and that at any moment a giant child's hand will reach over one of the distant peaks and smash his angry fist down on this setting.

We drove around to the east of town, alongside Clear Lake, which was not yet completely frozen—some teenagers were standing along the edges, testing the ice and then backing up to shore again. The lake is much smaller than I remembered it. Although I suppose the greatest disappointments in life come from realizing that things are never as great as they seemed when you were a child. Clear Lake is almost a perfect circle. On one side is Pontefract, on the other, the school. Almost as if they, the town and school, are staring at each other. On the shore opposite from where we drove, dense woods lead into foothills, while from our southern approach, homes litter a mostly empty plain as the road curves up to the entrance to the school.

"Could we stop for a second?" I asked my driver.

"Your money," she shrugged and pulled the car over alongside the curb. "You want to get out and stretch?"

"No, I just want to look. It's so . . . pretty," I said, for lack of a better word.

"I guess," she said, rolling her eyes.

Pontefract Prep, with its columns and old bricks, gray stones, elm, oak, boxwood mazes, the white chapel, spread out in front of us like a welcoming hand. I have never since felt such a flood of emotion as I did then. Here it was, the place I had been so terrified of, the place where I buried my childhood. And it was so beautiful, so timeless.

In the distance I saw the Marlowe-Houston House, its Georgian facade like the entrance of a mausoleum. The house made my heart skip a beat. But this is just guilt by association. The fact that I spent many happy afternoons talking with Lily on its veranda, or sneaking in through a half-open window in the spring to gawk at its treasures (old photographs of the Shenandoah Valley adorned the walls; Civil War souvenirs and ancient diaries were encased in glass; portraits of middle-aged Houston heiresses dripping with jewels and guarding the artifacts beneath their gilt frames)—none of this mattered to me when I arrived, age 28, to gaze upon the exterior of that old house. Instead I imagined it was somehow at fault with regards to the accidental death of Bart Kinter, and a conspirator in the destruction of my relationship with Lily Cammack. I turned away from it.

"All right," I told my cabbie.

She started the car again, but it died quickly. She turned the key in the ignition, at the same time pumping the accelerator. "Old shitkicker," she muttered. The taxi gave a few sputtering responses. We began to move slowly, shaking every few seconds, until the car stopped altogether and the engine gave up the spirit.

"Motherfucker," she said, under her breath. The girl bowed her head slightly, and all I could see was the stringy black hair and back of her neck. "Those assholes back at the office, those assholes meanin' my sister and her shithead husband, Sweeney, they was supposed to fill up the fuckin' tank this mornin'."

She rested her head down against the wheel with her arms wrapped about its rim.

"No sweat," I said.

"I'm sorry, Mister," she whispered, head still down. Then she jerked her head up and looked in the rearview mirror at me. "Sherry's such an asshole, 'xcuse me, but she is, and I get so damn angry I could blow up. I'm gonna get some kinda ulcer before I'm twenty!" She continued to rant and rave, explaining what perfect assholes, "excuse me but they are," her sister Sherry and brother-in-law Sweeney were.

I began to laugh. She must've thought I was nuts. I felt cured by the chilled country air, by the wounded sway and lurch of the station wagon as she tried to slam it to life. This was the kind of problem people had in towns like this. Car won't start. All of a sudden I suspected that when I finally did get hold of Lily, her problems would seem to be nothing compared to mine. She was considering divorce, or her father was ill, or she'd had an affair—in a town like this, those problems were monumental, but where I was from they were the ordinary business of life. Even when I was sixteen and she, twenty, we had blown her predicament up, because in a town of this size, you were not dwarfed by buildings or corporations or the indifference of the masses. In a town the size of Pontefract, Virginia, you were only made to feel small by gossips and the leanings of your own conscience. And cars that simply refuse to start.

"You okay, Mister?" the cabbie asked.

"Yeah."

"It's only a quarter mile to Campbell's. It's gonna be a half hour before Sweeney gets out here with the gas . . ." She let her voice trail off, leaving me to catch her drift.

I decided to walk it.

I grabbed my minimal amount of luggage, paid her my fare and said goodbye. I began walking up East Campus Drive, leading away from the school, and could just make out the pink house ahead and the white sign out front:

CAMPBELL'S BOARDING HOUSE
Reasonable Rates

2.

From *The Nightmare Book of Cup Coffey:*

Patsy Campbell is that woman whom Blanche Dubois would've become had she been released from the mental home, taken a fancy to chocolate moonpies, gained the inevitable 100 pounds that accompany such fancies, and grown a faint moustache on her upper lip barely camouflaged by bleach. Oh, and the glasses she wore—those thick round kind, giving her steely blue eyes an owl-like quality. When I was in my early teens, Mrs. Campbell's Boarding House had been the debutante capital of town, particularly during the big weekends like the prom and homecoming. If you brought Patsy a moonpie and an RC Cola, she might let you sit in the parlor with your date, and if you were from a First Family of Virginia, or were quarterback of the football team, or if your daddy was someone of rare distinction, she might even serve tea and butter biscuits and play the imitation 16th-century virginal that had been in her family since before the War Between the States. I only heard about this from friends; I never had a date when I attended Pontefract. I'd only seen the inside of her house once when I was caught red-handed, or in actual fact, pink-and-lace-handed, in the middle of a panty raid during my sophomore year.

I hesitated before knocking on the door of Campbell's Boarding House, wondering if Patsy would look the same, if chocolate would outline her lips, if the bug-eyed glasses would be replaced by contact lenses, if she'd have lost that frail catch in her voice that was so affectedly Southern.

One thing hadn't changed: the place was in need of repair. Everything about the house sagged, every pink board was warped. Even the doorbell didn't work. The front door was slightly ajar, which seemed odd considering how cold it was, but it allowed me to peer through the screen door and into the front hall—completely gray.

I gave the edge of the screen door three solid raps.

"Just a meenit," I heard her singsong voice come from one of the upstairs windows. Then, a padding of slippered feet down the stairs, and she emerged from the gray of the front hall truly larger than life. She had not changed a bit. Her hair was entangled in a bramble of pink plastic curlers, and she was draped like a Valkyrie in a baby-blue chenille bathrobe.

I nodded a greeting. "Hello, Mrs. Campbell? I'm Malcolm Coffey. I called from Washington? About a room."

She reached into one of the many folds in her robe and withdrew those orb-like eyeglasses, propping them across the bridge of her doughy nose. "Why good afternoon, Mr. Coffey-did-you-say? Yes, yes," she said, "I do believe your room is prepared." When she spoke, she tugged at vowel sounds, and stretched consonants into extended vowels, so "prepared" became "preepayaahd." "Just call me Patsy, honey."

She opened the screen door, her arm lifting up and out against the doorframe. I was forced to bend down and tunnel beneath her buttressing arm just to get inside the house.

Patsy Campbell apparently didn't recognize me, and of course my appearance was much different than when I was sixteen—I had lost most of the baby fat, my hair had darkened and thinned a bit, I stood straighter, was not quite as sloppy as I had once been.

I guess it helped that when I introduced myself I didn't use the name I was popularly called when I'd been a student at Pontefract Prep. The nickname Lily gave me, the one that stuck even with my family: Cup. Perhaps I should've used it. Maybe she would've taken one good bloated look at me and turned me out while she had the chance. I was sure that if there was any one name Patsy Campbell would remember it would be Cup. She might not even know my last name at all. All she would know was "Cup."

Patsy Campbell once had a nephew by the name of Bart Kinter.

3.

Lily Has Not Been By to See Her Father

4 P.M.

Clare Terry drew back the curtain in her father's bedroom. Late afternoon sunlight flooded the room, and the old man held his hands up to shade his eyes. "So dark and cold, people will think I keep you in the dungeon." This was how she'd found him, in his pajamas, standing in front of the television set, staring down at the blank screen. His bedroom, like hers and Lily's, had remained exactly as it had been for as long as she could remember. Tankards of men's cologne lined up on his dresser, while large bottles of L'Air du Temps and Shalimar sat like sentries upon her mother's dresser, as if expecting that at any moment Rose Cammack would come over to them, choose one, and dab a bit of the chosen perfume on her wrist. Clare wanted to change the room entirely, but her father, even as out of it as he often was, went into a rage when she tried. After nearly two years of living with him again, she was getting used to his sudden fits of temper. It was understandable, because he knew, even if the onset of Alzheimer's Disease made him forget things, he knew what was happening to him and he felt helpless.

The master bedroom was not terribly large. A king-sized bed took up most of the room. In spite of the fact that the maid had just been in that morning, it was an absolute wreck, the sheets tangled into the down comforter, the quilt practically threadbare, half on the Oriental carpet. Clare would have to make the bed for perhaps the second time today. The baby portraits of her and Lily hung next to each other above the bed. Even then, Lily had that pale cool beauty that Clare envied; and there was Clare, less than two years old, with that unruly dark curly hair, looking vaguely Italian, and who knew what gene that had come from? Their father had always said that Clare was the mystery child and teased her, saying that a gypsy woman left her on the porch.

While Lily, he would say proudly, *has the Cammack looks through and through, the porcelain skin, the white blond hair, the high cheekbones. By God,* he would say between puffs on his cigar, *she is a blueblood Cammack, and a McCammack before that.*

"Lily, Lily, child . . ." Brian Cammack said to the blank television screen.

"Daddy, it's me, Clare. Were you dreaming?"

"Has Lily been by yet?" He finally turned his gaze to Clare who was still standing nearby the window. She could not get over how much he had aged in the past year—his face was a pasty gray, there seemed to be no color in his eyes, and his skin had taken on the translucent quality of rice paper. At times she was afraid to look at him for fear that she might see the veins and bones beneath his skin. He had lost nearly twenty-five pounds in the past year, and his flannel pajamas hung on him as though made for a man twice his size.

"It's very cold today, Daddy, you shouldn't walk around in your bare feet." She went to the armoire and opened it. His shoes were stacked neatly. Clare pulled out his lime green duck shoes and held them up for him to see. "How about these? And the wool socks in your bottom drawer?" She nodded in the direction of his dresser.

"Je ne comprenez-vous." He threw his hands up in despair. Her father often lapsed into French when he was confused. His knowledge of the language was very basic, learned when he was in Paris just after World War II.

"Ah, pourquois pas, mon pére?" Clare said, uncertain of her pronunciation.

"They call her the little white dove, isn't that right?"

"Yes, Daddy," Clare replied, happy that they had returned to the familiar territory of English.

"That woman I saw before . . . before . . . she was lovely. Not like your mother. Rose was . . . my Rose . . ."

"No, not like Mother. Would you like a walk in the garden? Daddy, you can stay in your pajamas if we just get something on your feet and throw a nice warm coat over you."

"Yes," he said testily, clenching his fists and beating at the air like a trapped bird, "and I can dress myself, thank you. I've been to war, got lost in Paris one night, too, and I . . . do you know Pound? 'The apparition of these faces in a crowd' . . . I can dress myself, *ça va?"* He went over to the dresser, opened the top drawer and poked around. "No socks here."

"The bottom one," Clare said patiently.

He bent down, opened the bottom drawer and pulled out a pair of socks. Then he sat down on the edge of the unkempt bed and put one of them on. He glanced up at Clare and smiled. For a moment, she felt happy. He hadn't smiled much in the past year. But that brief moment of happiness passed as she heard him say, "Give Daddy a big kiss, sweetheart, you're the only girl for me, Rose. Big kiss."

Clare tried to remain composed. "Stop it, Daddy, I'm not Rose. Rose is gone."

"A fine woman, Rose Cammack. She gave me two lovely girls, and she is always behind me one hundred percent. Make that one-fifty." He was having trouble getting the other sock around his left foot.

"Daddy," Clare said, moving toward him, "let me help you."

Brian Cammack smiled again at his daughter and shrugged his shoulders, giving up on the sock. He shook his head slowly. "You've become a fine young lady. Your father is quite proud of you, Lily."

Before Clare could correct him again, the phone rang.

4.

From *The Nightmare Book of Cup Coffey:*

The first thing I did was ask Patsy Campbell if I could use her phone. "If it's local," she said firmly. She offered me an RC Cola, which I accepted, needing both the sugar and the caffeine (I was dog-tired from the busride), but there was no offer of a moonpie. Patsy undid the wrapping on one of the round chocolate pies and began eating it even while she spoke. "Eight dollars a day, Mr. Coffey, and no female guests, you understand," she said. Then she led me to the hall phone. "Your room is on the top floor, first one on the left. Bathroom is on the second floor, and I'd appreciate your wiping down the tub after making use of it."

I watched her pad down the stairs in her fluffy mohair slippers. I dialed Dr. Cammack's number, hoping to catch Lily there.

Dr. Cammack answered the phone.

"Hello, Dr. Cammack," I began, "is Lily by any chance there?"

"You, too, eh?" he said, coughing into the phone. "No, I'm afraid she hasn't been by today, not yet. You might try her at her home. Have you tried there? If you do reach her, ask her to give her father a call, will you?"

I said goodbye, hung up, and rang up Lily's house over on Howard Avenue. Just like the last time I'd called at two in the morning, her husband answered.

"She can't come to the phone right now," he told me.

"Could I leave a message?"

"Sure, I don't know when she'll be available. Hell, I don't even know where she went. I've been calling all over the house for her. I know she's here somewhere, but that's the trick, isn't it? May I ask to whom I'm speaking?"

"Oh, forgive me, Mr. Whalen, my name is Malcolm Coffey. We haven't met, but I'm an old friend of your wife's."

He paused on the line and I heard him whispering my name over and over. "Oh, I know you. She calls you 'Cup,' isn't that right? I feel like I know you very well—she's always talking about you."

I was happy to hear it. "Really?"

"Don't you live in Maryland?"

"Well, actually, I'm here in town right now."

"She'll like that. Very much. When she sees you, and I know she'll want to see you." There was an undercurrent of trembling to his voice.

"Well, I'd appreciate it if you'd tell her that I'm staying over at Campbell's Boarding House."

"Lily's really going to like this."

But as soon as he said this, he hung up the phone.

Having made no headway in terms of Lily, and exhausted, I carried my bags up to my room.

My room was larger than I had expected, and contained a rocking chair, a queen-sized bed and a dresser. Most of the space in the room was already occupied, however, by several other tenants: Patsy was evidently using this room as a storage area for her empty RC bottles. There seemed to be hundreds of them, all stacked neatly in their cardboard cartons. I wondered if the other rooms were similarly occupied. But for 8 bucks a night, I could live with it.

I fell down on the lumpy patchwork-quilted bed. I didn't even bother taking off my jacket or shoes. I felt emotionally and physically drained. It was great to lie down on a bed after what felt like a long day.

I tried falling asleep, but could not. Images of Lily kept flooding through my mind every time I closed my eyes. I lay on the bed watching the late afternoon sunlight begin to dim. From my window at Campbell's Boarding House I could see the top story of the Marlowe-Houston House beyond the chapel bell tower. In the fading light the house, although I suppose it would be more accurately described as a mansion, was a dried blood color, and its windows were dark. Looking at it from my window in Patsy Campbell's top floor room, the Marlowe-Houston House didn't seem as intimidating as it had when I caught my first glimpse of it on my cab-ride. It was just a house that bordered a prep school and an empty field. There were probably hundreds like it in the Shenandoah Valley. I could almost put what happened that night twelve years ago in perspective: it was all an accident. This old house by the lake was just that, nothing more.

At some point I fell asleep, and awoke not more than twenty minutes later. It had grown very dark outside. I went down to the bathroom, washed up with Patsy's Lavender Soap (even this bore traces of moonpie smudge). As I came downstairs into the parlor, I heard an "I Love Lucy" rerun on TV, and saw only the back of Patsy's becurlered head as she sat on the butterfly-print sofa watching the tube. "I hope everything is satisfactory," she said sweetly. She did not turn her head around.

I told her it was, and mentioned I was going out to wander around before it got too dark.

"Well, we do have some exquisite homes and gardens here in Pontefract, may I call you Malcolm? But you might try the Historical Society over on Green Street, in the town proper, they might be closed for the day but there are always brochures and literature available." Now that Patsy was no longer gobbling moonpies, I noticed she had a delicate gossamer way of speaking, and if you closed your eyes you might even imagine a lovely young debutante. I wondered if that was how she felt on the inside, like a Southern Belle trapped inside a body which ran on RCs and moonpies. "Dr. Prescott Nagle is the head of our Historical Society, he lectures quite a bit, perhaps you've heard of him?"

I told her I'd be back in a few hours, and she mentioned that if I was any later to use the key under the porch swing.

It was 5 P.M. when I walked out into the brisk evening, and the houses and trees along East Campus Drive stood out like black cut-outs against a deep purple sky. I passed a young couple jogging along. They waved and I returned the greeting. I heard dinner bells, and children calling out to each other in the distance, but children are always calling each other on crisp winter evenings when the light begins to fade.

5.

Rush Hour in Pontefract

Cup Coffey was just walking across the footbridge that led from the prep school side of town across Clear Lake to what Patsy Campbell referred to as "town proper," when rush hour began.

Streetlamps blinked on up and down Main Street, which, in spite of its stodgy patrician redbrick buildings, took on a yellow-green cast in the evening. The Regency Row Arcade shops were closing down, the Law Offices of Grady, Virginius and Dabney were being hastily vacated by the three men and their one secretary; Maude Dunwoody's cook, Billy Fine, was molding biscuit dough in the cool white fluorescence of the restaurant's front window; like moths around a light bulb, several of the good old boys, eternally dressed in plaid flannel, ear-flapped hats and baseball caps, sought their enlightenment in front of Fisher's Drugstore before heading off to the Henchman Lounge for some suds.

Eight cars constituted the rush hour traffic going east; twelve going west. The westbound traffic was held up at the intersection of Main and Jessup for ten minutes by an eight-wheeler rumbling slowly through town on its way to the interstate.

Other shops remained open for another half hour—no business would be transacted in that time, but these shopkeepers disliked getting caught in what little traffic there was. But every one had pretty much called it a day: Friday, January 2, 1987. TGIF.

6.

From *The Nightmare Book of Cup Coffey:*

It took me nearly twenty minutes to walk from Campbell's Boarding House to Howard Avenue—4221 Howard Avenue, to be precise. The house that Lily and her husband lived in was a two-story Victorian, painted a pale blue (although on my first visit it was too dark to tell), with a semi-circular driveway, and a giant magnolia tree set right in front, blocking a street view of the house.

I marched up the front stone steps like a man with a mission. The porch light was off. In fact, the entire house was dark. I knocked lightly, and when that failed to bring anyone running, I slammed the knocker hard against the heavy oak door several times.

I could swear I heard someone coming to the door, but very quietly, as if on tiptoe. The footsteps stopped just on the other side of the door.

"Hello?" I asked. "Anybody home?" I felt stupid standing there in the dark talking to a door.

That was evidently what I was doing, too, because no one answered. I knocked again and waited. I walked back out to the street, stood under the streetlight and wrote out a note on the back of one of my bank deposit slips I always keep in my wallet for just such emergencies: LILY, IT'S ME, AT P. CAMPBELL'S. CALL SOON, CUP.

I folded the deposit slip over again, and wrote Lily's name in large block letters across it. Then I went back up to the front door and slipped the note between the round brass knocker and the door.

7.

Warren Whalen peered through the peephole at the man walking away from the house. He waited until he'd seen him go on up the street, and turn left onto Main. Warren unbolted the door and slowly eased it open. The porch was completely enveloped in blackness. Warren reached back inside and flicked on the overhead lantern. The paper the man had written on fell out of the door knocker and floated down; Warren managed to grab it before it touched ground. He opened it, read it.

Warren Whalen had a three-day growth of beard. His jet black hair shone with grease. His skin was pale, as if he'd been sitting in a dark closet for the past few weeks. He was wearing his favorite suit, a vanilla suit. It was wrinkled, and spotted where he'd spilled food on it. His violet eyes possessed a feral intensity as he read the note. He wadded the note up and stuffed it in his pocket.

Warren went back in the house, shutting the door behind

him. He turned the porch light off. He pressed his back against the door. He glanced up the dark staircase.

Warren Whalen began giggling softly. "This is just too much," he said to the darkness.

8.

From *The Nightmare Book of Cup Coffey:*

After getting lost down a few side streets, I was about to give up my search for the Historical Society. Main Street was the only well-lit area, and I was tired. I kept my hands pushed deep into the pockets of my coat. I finally decided I'd better call a cab or walk back to Patsy Campbell's when I found the street she'd mentioned, Green Street. Like the other streets, it was poorly lit, and I decided that if the Historical Society wasn't among the first few buildings I would give up my search.

I figured Dr. Nagle would probably have gone home for the evening, but I could at least leave a note for him, as I had done at Lily's house. He might remember me. I trusted that he'd be one of the few Peepee teachers who would think of me in a favorable light.

I found the building almost immediately, and as I approached the door, a man was just locking it up. I startled him. He almost jumped.

"I'm sorry," I said, and then recognized him even in the shadows, his silhouette as prominent as Alfred Hitchcock's. "Dr. Nagle . . ."

"No, I'm sorry, you startled me," he said, extending a hand out of the shadows.

"You probably don't remember me, sir, but I used to go to school here."

"Always glad to see alums return home," he said, cheerfully. If I could not see him very well, then it was obvious I was also just a silhouette to him.

"My name's Coffey, Cup Coffey," I said.

He moved closer to me, stretched his arms out and grabbed me by the shoulders, trying to peer through the darkness to see me better. He sounded regretful when he said, "Of course I remember you, Cup. I was rather afraid, for your sake, that you'd be coming back this winter."

CHAPTER EIGHT

EVERYBODY'S GOT TO EAT

1.

From *The Nightmare Book of Cup Coffey:*

Other than his increased girth, Dr. Nagle had barely changed at all in the past twelve years. The first thing you noticed about him besides his salt-and-pepper hair, which still remained thick as uncut wheat despite his age, was the ruddy glow of his face. He had an Irish face, shiny cheeks that were sponged a burgundy shade, twinkling Santa Claus eyes. His face seemed less that of a man than of a large baby. He still propped his round, professorial spectacles upon his slight nose. He wore an old gray threadbare suit, his slacks reaching too far down over his scuffed shoes. I think if he'd been more circumspect in his manner of dress I would not have enjoyed his company so much. He looked comfortably, unabashedly unkempt.

After some initial hedging and anecdote-dropping while we walked to his car, he invited me to have dinner with him. I protested, saying that I didn't want to intrude, but he wouldn't take no for an answer. "Everybody's got to eat, and besides," he said as he opened the car door for me, "I cook enough for two. You might as well help me out or it all goes down the disposal."

* * *

Dr. Nagle lives in an old red barn out near the overpass. The barn had been converted into a two-bedroom house with a large workshop which had once been stables. He calls it his "barnhouse." From the front he has a perfect view of downtown Pontefract, if it could safely be called that, Clear Lake, and the tops of some of Pontefract Prep's buildings. He stopped his car on the way up the gravel road to his house and pointed off toward the lake. "I have no doubt that this is the spot where Fenton and Trump saw the first settlement burning, which helped precipitate the Great Indian Massacre of 1755. Of course, we dabblers in history now know that it was the early settlers themselves who set their own town on fire. But in those days, it was any excuse to drive the Indians out of the valley."

"Point-of-fact," I said, and we both laughed remembering all those lectures he used to give in and out of class.

For all Nagle's dithering, his elderly hesitation, I felt a warm glow in his presence. All the boys in school had loved him the way you love and respect someone who is kind and good and possesses just a touch of craziness. He was one of us, a kid in an old man's suit, and we could laugh both with him and at him. He was one of the few teachers who befriended students, took them on field trips, coached the debate team, spoke seriously with fifteen-year-olds about the state of the world. I truly believe that he looked upon all of us, students past, present and future, as somehow lost and eternally young. It was his duty to round us up, make something of us, being so lost and eternally young himself.

"Point-of-fact," he said, "I chose this old barn for my home twenty years ago because I felt the same stability here that I had with my dear wife when she was alive. Out of that muddle of town."

"Good vibes?" I asked.

He seemed to consider this offhand remark seriously, saying, "Well, *vibes,* at any rate."

Dr. Nagle parked the car next to what had been the old stable. Before we got out of the car, he turned to me. He looked at me directly, just like I was once again a student and he, my teacher, and this was a final exam. His chin trebled as he pushed it back against his neck. "You can tell me the truth, Cup, but you must tell me."

"Sir?"

"Whatever possessed you to return?"

2.

Howie McCormick Sniffs a Letter

Howie McCormick, first cousin to Sheriff George Connally, and employee of the U.S. Post Office, sniffed the letter.

He pulled out his broken-down sofa-bed, propped himself up with some pillows and opened himself a Michelob. He held three purple envelopes in one hand, and with the other took a swallow from the beer bottle.

"Oh, boy," he said, anticipation like an itchy humidity crawling across his skin. A grin spread across his face, ear-to-ear.

He'd been keeping ahold of Betty Henderson's love letters all week, just saving them up for this night. It was a perk he took advantage of as an employee of the United States Post Office in Pontefract. "The secrets of the human heart," he said in hushed tones. Howie didn't notice that he spoke aloud to himself anymore.

"Kinda new, kinda wow, Charlie," he sang when he finally recognized the fragrance that was sprayed across the envelopes. It happened to be Howie's favorite women's perfume.

He rubbed the letter across his lips.

He flicked his tongue like a snake over her initials, scrawled with a flourish at the top left corner of each envelope. "E.D.H.—Elizabeth Doreen Henderson."

Howie tugged unselfconsciously at his groin.

He was stretched across the unmade mattress of the sofa-bed, wearing a sweat-stained white Fruit-of-the-Loom T-shirt and his candycane-striped boxer shorts. He kept the heat up high in his apartment.

For the moment, he set the envelopes down on his bedside table. He reached beyond them for the phone and dialed a number.

Someone on the other end picked up. "Shaw's Pizzeria, can I help you?"

"Hey, Gonzo, is it you?"

"Yassuh," the man replied.

"Good buddy Howie Mc-Cee here, and I'm ready for a Friday Night Massacre," Howie said.

"That's one Massacre . . . Anything else, Howie?"

Howie thought for a second, putting his hand over the mouthpiece in case he was thinking aloud.

"Got everything else I need, Gonzo, my man, but hold those onions, willya? Maybe put on some extra anchovies, I love them little fish."

After he hung up the phone, Howie picked up one of the purple envelopes again. "The envelope, please," he said. He tore into it like a rabid animal. But when he unfolded the letter, he treated it delicately, like he would a moth's wing if he wanted to keep the dust from rubbing off.

He read the letter aloud to the four walls of his studio apartment:

"Darling,

I truly enjoyed our recent night of passion. I am itching for another weekend alone with you. When I think of you, your hard-muscled body, the way you hold me, how you drive me over the edge . . ."

Howie paused, feeling heat rising in his loins. "Good Lord, Betty, what you do to me, if only you could see!"

He continued reading:

". . . like a wild animal in heat." ("Owee!" Howie whistled.) *"No one else can do what you do to me, what I want you to do to me. I am writing this letter wearing nothing but that special peekaboo bra you like, and your favorite flavor candy panties: Mango. I wish you were here to take me like this, right here, right now. Please*

call soon, because I don't know if I can stand the agonizing wait until we're together again.

Sex and Passion,
Betts."

With a groan and a stiffening of his legs, his toes curling, Howie came across his candycane boxers. "Whew, Betty, Betty . . ."

He put the letter down with the two others he'd been sniffing.

Howie McCormick reached for the phone and dialed a number.

Betty Henderson's number.

3.

8 P.M.

The two main hang-outs in town were coming alive. Folks had been home from work, showered, maybe caught a little shut-eye, reapplied make-up, shaved away that five o'clock shadow, and hit the streets. Pontefract's class divisions could best be seen through those two places, the Henchman Lounge and the Columns. The Henchman Lounge was the place you went to get stone drunk, to play Patsy Cline on the jukebox, to start a fight with somebody, or to hustle a drink. The Columns was more of a restaurant, round wooden tables covered with red-checkered tablecloths, the menu written on a blackboard as you entered, soft Muzak playing in the background. You could still get stone drunk there, but you did so with the implicit understanding that all fights and vomiting must be done out back in the alley. The dress codes said it all: in the Henchman you could wear just about any unwashed thing you owned, whereas the Columns at times looked like a spread from *Town & Country* magazine.

When you entered the Columns you were reminded of

genteel Southern living. When you strode into the Henchman you might wonder if you were going to get out of there alive.

In the Henchman Lounge, Friday night:

Warren Whalen had, within his first ten minutes of arrival, polished off three shots of Johnny Walker Red with beer chasers. He hunched over the bar, trying to get a look down Francie Jarrett's amply filled blouse. "Dolly Parton's got nothing on you, Francie," he said. Warren snapped his fingers several times. "Hey, baby, how about just selling me the bottle." He pointed to the end of the mirrored wall behind the bar. "I'll take that one."

Francie flashed her infamous grin of gold-capped teeth. "Mr. Whalen, for a man who is a disciplinary counselor at Peepee, you sure do lack discipline yourself."

"Oh, Miss J., why don't you come on over and discipline me? Whip me, honey, beat me, make me write bad checks." Warren aimed his fingers at her like a gun and pulled his thumb-trigger back between his teeth. "Bang-bang."

"I think," she said, sliding the bottle of scotch in front of him, "that's the only way you're ever going to bang me."

Some guy was laughing down at the end of the bar. "Good one, Francie."

Warren glanced down the bar, around the two redheaded girls giggling and the man with the long black beard. A man leaned against the rail, lifted his glass to Warren, smiling. He wore a cowboy hat and a string tie, his shirt was a shiny robin's egg blue. "Cowboys in Virginia?" Warren asked sarcastically. "What'll they think up next? Feel a little out of place, Cisco?"

The cowboy's grin faded. "Look in the mirror, jackass."

Warren, feeling warm and agreeable, faced front and stared into the mirror at himself. He looked like hell, his white suit was a mess, his face looked like he'd slept on it funny, and his dark hair was a greasy bird's nest. "You win, Destry." He took a swig from the bottle; much of the whiskey ran down his chin. Warren began singing "Oh, Bury Me Not on the Lone Prairie," but he didn't know the words after the first line, so this faded to a hum.

Then he called the barmaid over to him again. Reluctantly, she went over and leaned across the bar. "Yeah?"

Warren's voice shrank to a whisper, and she had to strain to hear him. "If my wife comes in here looking for me tonight, don't let her know I'm here, okay? I'm just going to get one of those booths in the back, and sit down and enjoy this bottle in silence, okay?"

"Mr. Whalen . . ." Francie was about to say something else, but sighed when she saw him wink at her.

"Just a little ha-ha," Warren said.

Francie smirked, and, raising her eyebrows, whispered to him, "You be careful tonight, you hear? And if you need a ride home, I'll just get Jim to run you back. And I'd watch what you say to the man in the hat, Mr. Whalen, he's a trucker from out of state and I heard him talking like he was just itching for a fight."

"Gotcha," Warren winked. He picked up the bottle, got off the barstool, and headed for the red booths back near the pool table. As he passed the cowboy, he said, "Francie and I have this bet going, and I think I'm going to win."

The cowboy grinned again, pushing his hat to the back of his head. "I might like in on that bet, dude."

Warren, swinging the bottle carelessly, splashing it across a couple necking while they slow danced to "I Can't Help It If I'm Still in Love with You," kept walking by. "Well, she says you're a steer and I say you're a heifer, and, like I said, I think I'm going to win."

The first fight of the evening broke out at the Henchman Lounge shortly after eight o'clock.

In the Columns, Friday night:

Shelly Patterson said, "I've been starving myself all day on this Ultimate Diet." She sat at the table furthest from the door, her red hair brushed back from her face, dark circles under her eyes, and when she spoke her large front teeth caught the light from the little candle in the center of the table. Clare Terry sat across from her, while Debbie Randolph was on her right.

"Diets like that can't be healthy," Debbie said, fingering

her silverware. She wiped waterspots off her knife with her red napkin.

"No, really," Shelly said, looking for the waitress, "a doctor wrote the book."

"Hah, doctors are a dime a dozen when it comes to diet books. As far as I'm concerned the only ultimate diet is cancer. Which reminds me . . . " Debbie set her fork back down, leaned to the side and fished around in her purse. She brought out her cigarette case and said, "Anyone for coffin nails?"

Shelly gasped. "Oh, Debbie, I don't think you should talk like that, 'cause, you know, it could happen to you—cancer—like I had this cousin who always made fun of bald men, and when she turned thirty, she started losing her hair. Just like bad karma."

Debbie laughed and lit her cigarette; she passed the cigarette case to Clare who seemed eager for a smoke. "Well, if what goes around comes around, all three of us are in big trouble." Both she and Shelly laughed; Shelly kept repeating, "Oh, Debbie, you are just so—just so—"

But when Shelly stopped laughing, she noticed Clare had remained quiet. "You okay?" she asked her.

Clare attempted a smile, but her mouth became a horizontal line. "I was just thinking of Daddy and his sitter tonight. And . . . do you think that's true? What goes around, you know, comes around?"

Debbie caught the waitress's attention. The girl came over, and the three women ordered. "And a big carafe of chablis," Debbie added.

"It really bothers me," Clare said. She had a faraway look, and Debbie rolled her eyes for Shelly's benefit: *here she goes again.*

"What does?"

"Things going around, coming around."

Debbie tamped her cigarette out in the ashtray. "You've been listening to your dad too much. Could we get off this topic? It's getting spooky."

"I know," Shelly said, slapping the table, "let's see a movie after dinner."

"Our choice within a thirty mile radius is either one of those Friday the 13th movies or a Disney cartoon."

"I'll see either one," Shelly said. The carafe of wine arrived, and Debbie poured out three glasses. "Or we could take a drive over the hills and cruise Roanoke."

Debbie sipped her wine. "Shelly, really, *Roanoke.*"

"It's Friday night and I'm closing in on the amniocentesis years, let's have some fun." Shelly looked over to Clare for her reaction.

"That scares me," Clare said.

"Amniocentesis or Roanoke?" Debbie asked dryly.

"No, I mean what goes around, coming around . . . coming back. It really gets to me . . . like the way my father always talks about . . ."

Debbie lit another cigarette. "Just where is dinner?"

Clare thought Debbie had said: *Just what are you afraid of?* But when she looked at them, Shelly and Debbie, they were chatting away about the slow service tonight, about the new store opening up in the mall in Newton, about maybe renting a video.

And if she were to answer that questioning voice, she knew that the answer would be: *I am afraid of everything. But I am mostly afraid that when they put you in a box and bury you six-feet-down it is not always enough to keep you there. That there are ways out, avenues of escape. There, I've thought it. I don't have to believe it, but I will allow that thought.*

What goes around, comes around.

4.

While Clare excused herself from the table she shared with Debbie and Shelly, saying that she was worried about her father and should get home, and while the first punch of the evening was swung at the Henchman Lounge, and while Cup Coffey sat down to dinner with Dr. Prescott Nagle, Howie McCormick had dialed a number and hung up the phone six times. For a while the woman he was calling took her phone off the hook. But now, less than forty minutes after first calling her, the phone was ringing at the other end again. Howie held the phone to his ear in anticipation.

Finally, she answered. "Yallo." Betty Henderson sounded tired and annoyed.

Howie remained silent.

"Who is this, anyway?"

Howie didn't say anything. Not a word.

"Joe?"

Howie bit his lower lip, trying to contain himself.

"Is it you, Joe? Who is this? Dammit, what kind of asshole pervert is doing this? You want a thrill, whoever the hell you are? Okay, you got your little wiener in your hand, sonny? Picture me sucking on it, you'd like that, wouldn't you? You hot? Huh? Does that get you hot?"

Howie was. He felt his body temperature was up to a hundred and five. No woman had ever talked to him like this before.

"Yah," he said, trying to disguise his voice, making it vaguely foreign.

"Good, that's a good little boy, because now, picture this: I am biting down on your goddamn prick and tearing it out at its roots! Now fuck off!"

Howie hung up the phone. He felt like a thousand volt shock had gone through him. Like he'd just stuck his penis in a garbage disposal and turned it on. "Oh, m'God," he said, clutching himself down there to make sure everything was still in working order.

It had withered like a worm on a hotplate.

But it was still there, twitching.

He heaved a sigh of relief.

That Betty Henderson is some wildcat.

A girl who wrote letters like the ones he'd been reading every Friday, to all her boyfriends (Joe, Stan, Josh, Luke, Randy and three different Steves), you'd think that kind of girl wouldn't mind helping a guy get off over the phone once in a while.

"Well, Betty, you can go straight to hell," he muttered.

Howie frantically tore up all the other letters. "These'll never get where they're suppose to go."

He glanced over at his clock—it was almost 9 and Gonzo still hadn't shown up with the pizza. Howie got up off the sofa-bed and went over to his TV. There on top of the VCR were the movies he'd checked out from the video store in Cabelsville. *Eat Me Raw, I Got Something for You,* and the sequel, *I Got Something for You, Too,* and *Skin Dance.* Although Howie knew he could've found those videos here in town, he was too embarrassed to go back into the adult section of the video store on Main Street. What if somebody saw him? He picked up *I Got Something for You* and looked at the cover. A pretty blonde named Norma Vincent Peel pouted at him from the picture, and beneath it was a quote: "Norma's got a soft spot for men. If you ask, maybe she'll show it to you."

"Hot dog," Howie grinned.

5.

From *The Nightmare Book of Cup Coffey:*

Dr. Nagle prepared a wonderful dinner of southern fried chicken, mashed potatoes with gravy, green peas, spoonbread and apple brown betty for dessert. By the time we'd shoveled our ways through all that, we'd acquired what Nagle referred to as "Dunlaps disease."

"That's when your stomach dunlaps over your belt," he chuckled.

I'd never been inside his place before. When you're a sixteen-year-old kid, professors have very little to do with you after school hours. And with good reason. When I was a student and just getting involved with the Tenebro, we all set our alarms for 3 A.M. one night and snuck out of the dorms with as much toilet paper as we could carry. The seniors drove us out to Nagle's barn. We proceeded to teepee the place.

I mentioned the episode to him after dinner.

"I remember the night well, Coffey. I was coming down with the flu, and it was in the middle of a grading period. Work was piled up and I was tired all the time. This strange noise outside my bedroom window woke me up. Like the Huns descending."

Dr. Nagle and I were drinking sherry in what he called his "clubroom." This consisted of three large comfortable chairs with high, plush backs that you could sink right into and that made rather embarrassing noises when you moved around too much in them. There was a wall shelf lined with dusty, arcane-looking books, above a Danish modern coffee table, also dusty. This was buried in magazines: *Smithsonian, National Geographic, Virginia Country, American Heritage.* The clubroom looked the way I assumed Nagle was on the inside: dusty, intelligent, comfortable. It was all him, and smelled of hickory smoke.

Nagle continued talking about that teepeeing episode. ". . . I figured it was either a comet or God trying to punish me for my wanton ways. I went outside the next morning assuming I'd find a burnt meteor in my tomato patch, but of course, all I found was enough Charmin to last me a lifetime. Not wanting to waste it, I spent most of the day, even with the flu, rolling up toilet paper. More sherry, Cup?"

I nodded and held my glass out while he poured. "We only did it because we liked you."

"Liked me? Old Bagel?"

I was surprised that he knew his nickname.

Nagle smiled, patting his stomach. "We teachers are never as slow as you boys think. Mind if I light up?" He picked up a mahogany-red pipe from beside the sherry. He cupped the pipe bowl in his hands as if it were a delicate baby bird. He brought out a tobacco pouch from his jacket pocket. Then he began patting his various pockets, looking for something else. I felt like I was watching a Japanese Tea Ceremony. "I can never find my whatchacallit, you know, pipe thing, the thing." He snapped his fingers as if that would help him recall what a whatchacallit was.

"Lighter?" I volunteered.

"Quite right, Cup, lighter. The way my memory is going it's as if my mind is leaking." He finally found that he was sitting on it. He lit his pipe and heaved smoke. The room filled with a delicious aroma. "Remind you of anything?"

I tried to identify the scent. "Hershey Bars?"

He nodded, his eyes widening with a child-like delight. "Chocolate-flavored tobacco," he informed me as if this were one of the great secret luxuries of the universe.

I felt mildly high from the huge dinner and all the sherry I'd been drinking. The room seemed to possess a warm, fireplace-like glow. That's about the point I realized I was getting drunk and feeling very anti-social. Alcohol has the unique effect of bringing out all my inhibitions.

"Now, Coffey," Dr. Nagle said, sinking back into his chair, puffing like a steam engine on his pipe, "let's stop being so evasive about why you're here. You've told me you were fired, that you might like a teaching position, you need advice. Both you and I know what kind of rubbish that is."

I felt very self-conscious, what my therapist called "incentered." I pretty much clammed up. "And *you* told me you knew—were afraid—I'd be back this winter."

Nagle nodded his head and said, "Fair enough. I'll lay my cards on the table, if you will follow suit." He tamped his pipe into the ashtray that sat precariously on the arm of his chair. "It's Lily Cammack, isn't it?"

This took me somewhat aback. I'm not sure if my eyes popped out of my head or if my tongue suddenly dried up in my mouth. I could not find my voice. I had no idea that Dr. Nagle knew anything that would connect her to me. After several moments, I finally managed a thin, "Yes."

"Good lord, good lord," Nagle sighed, a worried look crossing his face, as if he had briefly hoped that Lily was not the reason I had returned to town. "Not exactly after-dinner conversation, is this, Coffey?"

6.

Howie McCormick Blows Bubbles

His pizza had finally arrived.

Howie munched on the thick pizza crust while he fast-forwarded the video tape to the first sexy part. This one was called *Eat Me Raw* and featured the bountiful Veronica Lay. Howie was drunk and sleepy, but he just had to see what this girl could do. He'd already watched Norma Vincent Peel perform pelvic tricks for the U.S. Marines, and Lana Turnover on her knees for some garage mechanics in *Skin Dance.* Now he wanted to see what Veronica could do.

"How do you think they get those girls to do that?" Howie asked the video store owner in Cabelsville when he'd gone in to get the films.

"Look," the man said, "it's Hollywood. All those pretty young girls going out there thinking they're gonna be the next Sally Fielding or Mariel Streep, and they just don't know the ropes. You never heard of the casting couch? Don't you watch 'Benny Hill'?"

Veronica Lay was quite a gal. She wanted it so bad. She talked in that video like Betty Henderson had in her letters and over the phone (except for that last part, where Howie had wished he owned a steel jockstrap).

Veronica looked at the camera and licked her lips. Howie noticed that these girls licked their lips a lot. "I have this problem, Doc."

Off-camera, a man's deep voice boomed, "Tell me about it, Veronica."

"Well," she said, and Howie thought she seemed rather sweet, "I haven't been getting any lately. I think I need a shot of something sticky and warm."

"And what kind of shot would that be, Veronica?" the man asked.

("I know! Oh, I know!" Howie shouted at his TV.)

Veronica began inching her bright lollipop red panties down her legs. She said, "I need it now, Doc, I need it now."

Howie was close again as he watched Veronica's fingers glide down her belly, but he thought he'd better hold off until he'd seen the whole movie. He liked to decide which was the best scene for the old Lustometer and then rerun that scene and really get into it.

The man in the movie, called Dr. Long, walked into the picture and began fondling Veronica's big breasts. She oohed and ahhed and licked her lips some more. This went on for a while; Howie belched in between oohs and ahhs.

Veronica reached for the man's crotch.

A close-up of the man grinning.

"C'mon, c'mon, show me whatcha doin', Veronica!" Howie shouted, spilling his beer all across his bed. "I need it now, Veronica!"

Then the camera pulled back, as if hearing Howie's plea. What Howie expected to see was Veronica doing some sexy thing with her tongue like spinning it on the guy's dong or something, but instead what he saw was:

Veronica Lay gnawing on what looked like a piece of raw, torn steak hanging between the guy's legs. The man in the video was screaming. And for the barest instant, Howie thought that it was himself in the video, with Betty Henderson down on her knees chewing hungrily on his penis. Her eyes burned lasciviously. She was enjoying her meal.

Then, her mouth full of bloody meat, she turned and stared into the camera, and said hungrily, "You next, Howie."

Howie felt his Friday Night Massacre pizza with extra anchovies gurgling up through his stomach.

He ran into the bathroom, leaned over the toilet (he always left the seat up) and vomited into the porcelain bowl. What hit the water now really did look like a Friday Night Massacre.

"Holy mother of Jesus," Howie gasped. He wiped his mouth, gasping with the sour aftertaste. He felt a fever burning inside him. Tears blistered from his eyes. He reached up from his kneeling position and pulled down on the toilet lever.

It didn't flush.

Again, pull!

Again, nothing.

"You sonofabitch," he muttered. Howie reached up for the third time and practically tore the metal lever from the toilet.

The toilet made a glup sound. It went *ga-lung, ga-lung.*

The bowl began to overflow. Pepperoni, mushroom, semi-digested cheese, anchovies all rinsed across Howie's shirt and pants.

He began gagging again. He lowered his head back down into the bowl, a half-inch from the polluted water. He felt a surge inside, like a wave coming from far off to break upon a shore.

That was when he felt pressure on the back of his head.

Someone was standing over him, pushing his head down into the toilet.

Howie McCormick screamed bubbles into the murky water.

7.

Clare felt drunk as she stumbled up Main Street toward her VW Rabbit, which she'd parked in front of the Key Theater. Her head was aching, and the few sips of wine she'd had, mixed with the Valium she took in the ladies' room at the Columns restaurant, gave her the feeling that her feet were not even touching the ground. As she approached her car, wondering if she should drive it at all, she noticed a woman staring at her from the alley by the movie theater. A woman in a blue dress, dressed for summer. A tall woman with blonde hair who should've been shivering with the icy chill, but instead she leaned comfortably against the brick wall. Staring.

Lily, Clare gasped, but when she looked again, it was just the movie theater poster for *Walt Disney's Sleeping Beauty,* and the blonde in the picture was a cartoon character, and next to that poster, another advertising the Midnight Show, *Dawn of the Dead.*

Clare felt her legs turning to jelly, and knew that in a moment she would be falling down. She wondered if she would crack her skull on the sidewalk. *What a silly way to die,* she thought as she leaned against the glassed-in movie poster. She rested there a few seconds, taking deep breaths.

"Lady, are you all right?" a teenaged boy asked. She hadn't seen him come around from inside the ticket booth in front of the Key Theater, and when she didn't answer, he handed her a large cup of Coke. "Here. It's on the house, only don't tell my dad or he'll put me back in there scraping Raisinettes off the floor."

"Thank you." Clare accepted the cup and took a sip. She still felt unsure of her balance, and the teenager, sensing this, offered her his arm to lean on. "I just had a bit of a fright."

"You're Dr. Cammack's daughter, right?" the boy asked. "Remember me? I mow your dad's lawn in the summers."

Clare hadn't really looked at the boy carefully, working hard to focus her eyes. He looked to be about fifteen or sixteen, clear blue eyes, light brown hair, a few of the obligatory adolescent pimples, and he was neatly dressed in a white button-down shirt, a blue crewneck sweater and dark pants. "Clare Terry. But still Dr. Cammack's daughter underneath all that. And you're Tommy MacKenzie? I barely recognized you—you've really gotten taller since August. Is this your, uh, winter job?" She had never really spoken to the boy before, just paid him his eight dollars for lawnwork. Clare felt so confused at this moment that she hoped he only thought she was drunk and not crazy.

"Dad runs the Key . . . Theater. I'm just the hired help. You want some more Coke?"

"No, this is fine, thank you. Do you go to the school?" Clare cringed at the snobby sound of this, something she detested in other people associated with Pontefract Prep like herself: they called it The School, as if the public schools in the area weren't worth considering.

Tommy MacKenzie nodded. "I'm a sophomore. School starts up again in a week. Dad figures I can put this time to good use in here."

Clare took his arm, feeling a bit like a feeble old woman,

but that still felt better than a woozy, neurotic, feeble *young* woman; Tommy made her feel better. She directed him to her car, but clutched hard enough onto his sleeve and then onto the car door to realize she was in no condition to drive.

"I can walk you home, Mrs. Terry," he volunteered.

Clare was about to refuse the offer. "What about your work?"

"Nobody buys popcorn at this hour, anyway." Tommy MacKenzie shrugged his shoulders. They walked up Main Street, Clare leaning against him, tripping slightly every few steps. "Can you smell that?" he asked her. Clare was afraid he'd meant her breath, and then tried to remember if she'd had *more* than just a few glasses of wine. *The last thing I need is a reputation as the town drunk as well as everything else.* But his head was back, his eyes closed, nostrils flared. Clare inhaled, smelling nothing. "It's the way the sky smells just before it rains. It's a clean kind of smell now, but I can guarantee that just before the rain starts coming down, there's going to be that kind of trashcan smell when the dust blows down Main Street. You'd never know a town this small would have that much dust, Mrs. Terry. It's all there just waiting for times like this, though—all that dust. But I'll get you home before the rain sweeps through. We still have a few minutes before this clean smell goes away."

8.

You might not recognize Jake Amory as he stood in Howie McCormick's bathroom, gazing down on the mailman who had just drowned in his own vomit. He still wore the dark glasses, but his skin was pale white, even his hair seemed to have blanched. Perspiration beaded his drawn face. He looked a lot like a worm in a leather jacket and jeans. He was covered with dirt and slime as if he'd been crawling through sewers—which he had been doing a lot of lately. His left hand was shriveled in on itself from his having accidentally set it on fire in December; it looked like a fried won-ton, with plump meat in the middle.

He was looking at Howie McCormick funny. Howie's head bobbed on the overflowing surface of the bowl.

Howie was a big man; Jake, even at six foot, was weak. Had become weak. He'd been losing some blood over the past month—not much. His dead friends who were taking care of him only took out enough to feed themselves for a short while. They left enough in him to get around without feeling *too* dizzy.

But he'd told them he'd bring them one of the people they wanted, and they could feed off him.

Now Jake had to figure out how to lift the dead man and get him in the Hefty trash bag he'd brought with him. And after that, just the thought of lifting fat Howie McCormick and having to carry him through the shadows back to the house—Jake groaned imagining it.

But *they* were hungry, and if not Howie, then it would be Jake they would dine upon.

Jake held the Hefty trash bag up, looked at the corpse and said: "Okay, sucker, time for the kiss of the Pocket Lips." Jake went to the kitchen of Howie's efficiency apartment, found a large cutting knife, then returned to the bathroom.

Jake figured it would be easier to carry a corpse back to them if it was divided into several pieces. Unfortunately, the blade was dull, and it took some hacking for Jake to complete his piecemeal work.

9.

From *The Nightmare Book of Cup Coffey:*

I don't know exactly what to make of what Nagle told me that first night in Pontefract. I'm not even sure what led up to it. What kind of prank is going on, what kind of elaborate lie is being spun. What kind of sick mind is at work.

Or is it my own sick mind? Have all the power lawn mowers in my dreams really been going over my head all this time instead of those dream children's?

Once Lily's name was brought up, and I explained that I

was in town on her behalf, his apparent openness, his gregarious nature, all seemed to cease—as if a dam had been closed suddenly, and not a drop could penetrate it. He changed the subject several times, talked about his archeological dig, talked about an old diary he was transcribing for the Historical Society, talked about a funeral he had to attend on Saturday.

Finally, we heard the chapel bells from campus and I mentioned that it seemed unusual to hear them so far away. "The water carries the sound," he said, and then, more seriously, "at least, I hope that's what carries it."

I suggested that I'd better be getting back to the boarding house, that I'd have to sneak in the back way as it was.

Dr. Nagle drove me back to Patsy Campbell's. On the way he pointed out some of the newer buildings in town. As he did this, I was beginning to wonder if, in my state of near-drunkenness from all the sherry we'd consumed, I had made some awful gaffe. There was one point in our after-dinner conversation when he began talking about his late wife, Cassie, and my attention waned as he went on about her. She'd died long before I'd even enrolled at Pontefract Prep; I had no frame of reference with regard to Cassie Nagle, so my mind wandered. Perhaps I made some innocent but insensitive remark—I just don't know.

That's the trouble with becoming reacquainted with someone: you go away unsure as to whether or not you got along at all. I sat in the car next to Dr. Nagle wondering if he thought I was the biggest jerk he'd ever had the displeasure to invite to dinner.

As Nagle pointed out the gutted buildings along Main Street that had been filled like Patsy Campbell's chocolate moonpies with the marshmallow of boutiques and hair salons, he kept interjecting in his monologue, "Perhaps this is why it's happening now."

"You're not telling me something," I finally interrupted.

We turned on that part of Lakeview Drive that eventually swings into Campus Drive, and he took his foot off the accelerator—we'd been going progressively faster as we went along, although this was still not too speedy since we'd begun our drive at a slow crawl of 15 mph.

"Yes, you're right, I'm not telling you something," he aid.

"About Lily. She's in some kind of trouble, isn't she?"

"Coffey," he began, but then hesitated. It was after nidnight and droplets of rain were beginning to hit the vindshield. Within a few seconds, it became a steady lrizzle. "No one predicted rain." Nagle reached over and lipped on the wipers.

We turned right onto East Campus Drive. The stoplight at he first intersection was flashing yellow, and as our car pproached it, Dr. Nagle slammed on the brakes. A hot rod ped by in front of us, honking its horn. Some teenagers eaned out one of its back windows and shouted, "Hey, ramps!"

Dr. Nagle kept his foot on the brake. The rain quickly ecame a torrent. The windshield was dripping amber, eflected off the stoplight, with the wipers coming up and licing into the rain, momentarily cleaning it off. "I am an ld man, Cup, like those kids just yelled. And because of hat I've been afraid to tell anyone anything about this, ecause if I were wrong I would lose my job. Senility. They're looking for a way to get rid of the older teachers iow. Right now only Mr. Lowry and I are left of the ld-timers. And he has already begun throwing dirt around o the Board of Governors concerning my suitability as a eacher. You know they've made him Acting Headmaster ince Dr. Cammack's retirement?" He said this as if it were he tragedy of the century; and if my memory of Gower owry served me correctly, I heartily agreed with that nood.

"I'm very sorry to hear that," I said, "but I still don't nderstand . . ."

He glanced out the window; the rain transformed the car's vindows into perfect mirrors, and what I saw reflected when e tried to look out through his was a man haunted by omething. "It has to do with history," he whispered, "and ou're somehow tied up with it. And I am, too. And there re others, in this town . . ."

"I don't get it, first Lily calls me and leaves a message, and hen I talk to—"

"She called you?" Dr. Nagle's face was alternately a brigh yellow and then a deep purple from the flashing stoplight "My God, my God," his voice was hoarse, defeated, "then i isn't just me after all. It's you, too." He said this as i confirming something, answering a question in his head.

"Lily's all right, isn't she?"

"Good lord, Cup, you talk about her as if . . ."

"As if what?" I was impatient. Whatever the worst was, wanted to hear. She'd gone crazy, she'd killed someone, sh was a whore, she set fire to buildings, she walked nake down Main Street; she was in the hospital, a victim of th mad rapist. I don't know if it was my drunkenness or hi own lack of clarity, but with the stoplight flashing and th rain shooting down against the car like bullets, I felt like I' been blindfolded and someone was spinning me around in circle.

"As if," he finally finished his sentence, his hands cover ing his face, "she were still alive."

PART TWO

THE TAINT

. . . ye shall scent out all the places—whether in church, bedchamber, street, field, or forest—where crime has been committed, and shall exult to behold the whole earth one stain of guilt, one mighty blood spot.

—Nathaniel Hawthorne,
Young Goodman Brown

CHAPTER NINE

TORCH

1.

A Brief Return to the Early Morning Hours of December 2, 1986: Teddy Amory Meets a Monster

The monster looked as frightened as Teddy herself did. He glanced about the roadside, then back down to the little girl. He mumbled something; she didn't understand him.

Teddy felt as if she were frozen to the ground. Her hair seemed to be filled with icicles from the damp grass she'd laid down in, and her arms and legs felt stiff. "Please don't hurt me," she said, tears welling in her eyes.

The monster dropped to his knees beside her. He reached out with his hands; when he touched her face, she flinched. He drew his mittened hands back and then laughed. His face was covered with dirty rags, and he wore a pair of jockey shorts between his gray hat and his head like it was his hair. His pants were filthy with large holes up and down the legs—but wherever there was a hole, it was stuffed with another rag. His coat was similarly shredded and patched. She noticed there was not an inch of him, other than his eyes, over which he wore sunglasses, that was not covered with rags. He smelled like B.O.

"Are you what got into Jake?" she asked, less afraid than curious.

The monster shook his head. He struggled out of his coat and offered it to Teddy. When she didn't move, he laid the coat gently down upon her.

As he bent over her, folding his coat around her legs, Teddy reached up to take his sunglasses off so she could see his eyes more clearly, but he flinched. She brought her hand back down in front of her face to defend herself. But he just reached up, took the sunglasses off, and revealed his eyes to her there on that cold morning.

His eyes were pinkish-red.

She felt a kinship to him then, that they were somehow marked in similar ways: her, with her cursed seizures, and he, with his beautiful red eyes.

But this occurred nearly a month before Cup Coffey arrived on a bus in Pontefract, and this good monster allowed Teddy to see his face for the first time the morning of January 3rd when he brought her the dead cat he'd found in an alley.

2.

He had forgotten his own name, it had been so many years since he'd last heard it. Call him Torch, like everyone else who called him anything did. It was a cruel nickname, considering the reason. He almost died in a fire back in '72. Burned seventy percent of his body, although it looked like a hundred. But as Georgia Stetson said to her husband Ken when she saw Torch rummaging through their trash cans on Tuesday mornings, "Maybe he looks better under all that with the scars—those people are frightening enough as they are, getting burnt could only be an improvement." By "those people" she meant albinos. There were many in the county, living up in the cabins in the woods, with the scattered hill folk. They said that if you hiked up the Cawmack Trail to Steeple Ridge, you'd see their shacks. You never noticed them most of the year, because you were too busy with your own life. But in the winter you tended to notice them: they might come into town on a snowy day, wearing their sunglasses, looking pale and worm-like, making the boys in front of Fisher's Drugstore feel uncomfortable. It was as if they burrowed in the ground and only emerged in the cold weather. Not that there were dozens of them, just a handful, but even one stood out like an inverted advertisement for genetic engineering.

Probably what bothered the Georgia Stetsons of this world the most was the possibility that they were related to each other. That Georgia, who was from the Houstons and the McCormicks and the Connally lines back to the mid-1700s, might have a cousin among those pigmentless people. Or worse, that if she ever had another child, or if her son, Rick, married a girl from town, the offspring might have those fierce red eyes.

Torch was one of the few who lived in town. And it had cost him. He did not come out much during the daytime, both because the sun bothered his eyes, but also because of the abuse. Teenagers tended to chase him down alleys and beat him up, while their parents didn't even seem to notice. He was Pontefract's invisible man.

The story of his burning goes like this: Torch is looking for food in a dumpster back in '72. Some kids are heading down the alley toward him, so, out of fear, he jumps in the Dempsey Dumpster. The kids see this, and one of them gets the bright idea to 'smoke' him out. He drops a lit match into the trash, and the thing practically explodes. Torch, afire, leaps out of there and runs down the alley, out into the street.

Now, probably, if he'd just stopped and rolled around in the mud, he might've been okay. But this guy Torch was positive that if he stopped running, he would die. Often he wished he had. He was put in the medical center for two months (at county expense), and then released back on the streets. He tried getting a job at the Kountry Kitchen Bakery, and then at Maude Dunwoody's Ham Biscuit Haven, but was told that he would scare away too many customers.

It seems he gave everyone in town the creeps.

The big joke around town was to take a burning match

and, holding it upright, move it along a table. Then you say, "What's this?" and when nobody knows, you say, "It's Torch celebrating his anniversary." Gets big laughs down at the Henchman Lounge. Another good one is if you see Torch around town, and he doesn't seem to come out much these days, you yell across the street to him, "Hey, how about cooking up a nice Torchburger?" or another, "I heard your favorite song is 'Come On Baby, Light My Fire'!"

Torch had a lot more things burning up inside him than any fire that got him on the outside. He would've liked to have told those guys off who beat him up outside the Henchman Lounge one night and then gave him a bottle of booze. "This is so's you won't talk!" one of the men shouted at him, and all the others slapped him on the back because it was such a good joke. Because Torch couldn't speak anymore—in fact his throat probably got burned worse than anything.

He would also tell them that there were compensations, if he could. Compensations for losing your voice. For losing most of your smooth skin to scar tissue. Compensations like being able to smell things. Not just things like coffee, or flowers, or dogshit after you stepped in it.

Torch could smell things like *Evil,* as well as *Good.* He would've liked to have told those guys who beat him up that he smelled them coming a mile away. That they stank to high heaven with their evil intentions. And he would've liked to tell the little girl he'd found by the road on the way into town that he smelled her, too, but that she smelled *Good,* that her smell was strong, like honeysuckle in the summer, that her scent made him feel warm even in the middle of winter.

He would also tell them about that other smell, the one coming out of the sewers in Pontefract, the one coming out of the frozen lake like dead fish to its surface. The foul odor of corruption that was, like a magnet, seeking out the girl's own power.

And Torch knew the many uses of fire.

3.

Up-to-Date: January 2, 1987

"Is it you?" Teddy asked. The knocking at the door had awakened her from a dream where she was not sick. But now, sitting up in bed, hoping it was Torch, she shivered with the fever and chills. She wrapped the blanket around her shoulders, dragging it on the floor as she rose and went to the door.

They had been living in a large cold place, surrounded by that gas station smell of her dreams, but she knew she was safe. Torch had promised her they would be safe, and when the time was right, he would get help.

From the other side of the door she heard a faint mumbling. She didn't know what time it was—she never did anymore, it always seemed dark in the room. When she heard Torch's characteristic scraping on the door, she did as he had instructed her to. She first went and got the oil-lamp from her bedside. Then she turned the fire in the lamp up as high as it would go—being careful, he had shown her, not to get too close to the flame. He'd written DON'T END UP LIKE ME on the Etch A Sketch he communicated on, always in a squiggly script. When he had jokingly warned her about the oil-lamp, she reached up and tugged his hat down further over his forehead. "I don't have enough clothes," she said, giggling, "to end up like you."

Teddy brought the lamp over to the door, carefully removing the hurricane glass that enclosed the flame. She set the glass chimney down on the floor. She remained crouched there by the door, and held the lamp by its base. She brought it close to the crack between the bottom of the door and the floor. Then she rolled the large rubber tires away from the door; they were heavy, and it took all her strength sometimes. Teddy picked up the lamp again and held it steadily in front of her.

Teddy didn't understand this ritual he made her go through every time he was out. Or why he surrounded their living quarters with candles. She didn't understand a lot of things that he wrote to her on the Etch A Sketch. But she did understand that he had saved her life that night in December, and that he was protecting her from what got inside Jake, what wanted to get inside her and open her up.

The door opened, and as instructed, Teddy held the lamp up in front of her. FIRE PROTECTS, Torch had written.

Torch stood there, swaddled in his rags, and attempted a few words, but as always, the sounds came out like an animal being tortured. He held a plastic bag up in one hand, and a small paper sack up in the other. "Rhoo," he whined, "rhoo."

"Food," she said, and took the small paper bag from him. He came into the room and set the large plastic bag down on the floor. Then he turned and bolted the door. He pulled one of his mittens off and felt her forehead. It was hot and damp. "Heh," he said, pointing to the bed, which consisted of an old mattress covered with moldy blankets.

"No, really, I feel better, honest," Teddy lied. Her face was pale white, and her hair stuck to her scalp with sweat.

Teddy impatiently tore into the paper sack. She pulled out a round package of bologna, a small jar of peanut butter, a half-pint of milk, a double-pack of Twinkies and a Coke. At the very bottom of the bag were two cans of Purina Cat Chow. "Cat food?" She wrinkled her nose. "You got cat food? I'm not that hungry, you know." She held one of the cans up like it was diseased. She took the groceries over to a low metal table, spreading them out as if she were preparing a banquet. "I'll make sandwiches," she said. She reached under the table for a cardboard box. Inside the box were plastic forks and knives, and half a loaf of Wonder Bread. Her back to him, spreading peanut butter on the bread, she said, "You've been gone a long time, I was getting worried."

Torch made a moaning sound from the corner of the dark room near her bed.

Teddy turned to look.

Torch was holding up the black plastic trash bag.

"More food?" she asked.

He shook his head violently. He motioned for her to come and sit beside him on the bed.

Teddy went over and tried to peek in the bag, but Torch kept it shut tight. "Okay, you win. What is it?"

Torch reached into the plastic bag. He kept his arm inside it for a while to tease her. "Oh, come on," she said, her eyes wide with curiosity.

Finally he brought the dead cat out.

He laid it across his lap, smoothing its fur.

"Deh," he said.

"I know," she said solemnly. "Poor baby. Poor little kitty."

Torch reached to the floor for the Etch A Sketch. He fiddled with the dials and showed Teddy the gray screen. Written on it was: FOR YOU.

Teddy stroked the dead cat's fur. She was crying. "Poor kitty," she said under her breath.

Torch wrote: MAKE U STRONG.

"You don't know that. You just think that. You think because you can smell what's inside me, that it's good, but I think it's bad. It's all just bad. And it doesn't make me stronger. I just get sicker. What I have is all about dead people, not like this." She saw that her words had no effect on him. "Besides, you don't even know if I can do it."

Torch wrote: SEE MY FACE. Then: IF U DO IT.

Teddy looked at him, surprised. "You will, you really will?"

Torch wrote: PROMISE.

And then: MAKE U STRONG. WELL.

But Teddy didn't believe it. She took the dead animal in her arms, stroked its fur. She didn't like to do this. Jake had made her do it, and even if she felt stronger, she hated doing it. She hated when her mother had made her go into her fit, and she especially had hated it when Jake had forced her to hold a dead rat, with all the maggots spilling out of it.

Teddy was playing last November in the woods, and Jake showed her the rat he'd caught in the basement and slam-dunked on the concrete floor. Its brains had smushed out of it. Then he'd buried it for a few days to see how quickly the worms ate into it, and then Jake had dug it up. "Everybody knows how you got dead people coming out your wazoo," Jake said, and Teddy laughed because he was being funny. She liked it when he was funny; no one else ever made jokes about her seizures. She still remembered the times before the fits, when things were normal at home, and Jake took her for rides on the handlebars of his two-wheeler, or brought her candy from town. But all that had changed when she fell through the ice two years ago. Jake seemed that way on the autumn day when he'd brought the dead rat to her. "I hear you can take the ghosts out of your body and put them back into theirs. Like this rat. You can make this rat live again, I know you can." At first she had refused, but he scared her by telling her what he would do to her if she didn't. Naughty things she didn't even like to think about.

"But I don't like to do it," she told him.

Jake had smiled then, wagging the dead rat by its tail in front of her face. Some of the maggots that clung tenaciously to its viscera lost their grip and fell into her hair. Jake helped her get the worms out—he said he didn't mean that to happen. He seemed so nice, even with that ugly gross rat, that she began the fit herself by gazing up into the blue sky long and hard. It took a while before she felt the first tremors within her—the pale blue of the sky was no match for the brilliant blue bug zapper her mother used in the seances. But if Teddy imagined the blue of blue, the blue water, she knew she would black out.

When Teddy came out of her fit, she watched the rat, its brain still exposed, scamper around by the woodpile. Teddy felt a surge of power, as if she had batteries that were recharged while she was out. She even felt happy that the rat was alive again.

Then Jake took a rock and slammed it down on the creature, killing it a second time. He turned back to her, smiling.

Jake should never have made her do it. Because while she felt stronger afterwards, she knew that that other thing, that thing that had touched her in the water, felt stronger, too, whenever she did it.

* * *

As Torch held the hurricane lamp above her face, Teddy petted the cat's fur. Reluctantly, she looked into the blue heart of the flame, concentrating on it, imagining a blazing pyramid of blue. She felt the fit coming on, could practically taste the blue water . . .

She didn't know how long the seizure lasted. Teddy awoke with a sharp pain in her arms—the black cat that had moments ago been dead was clawing at her, frantically trying to get away. "Don't be scared, kitty," Teddy said, and she realized that the fever had passed. She felt cool and dry. She let the cat jump to the floor and watched as it stood still in front of her, sniffing the room.

Torch wrote on the Etch A Sketch: BETTER?

Teddy was a little sleepy, and yawned. She nodded her head. "But it's evil, isn't it? Like what got into Jake."

Torch shook his head. "Naah," he bleated. He wrote: U GOOD.

He pointed to the cat. He wrote: NAME?

"How about 'Torchy'?"

He wrote: HA.

"You promised," Teddy said as she reached up to his face and parted the rags around his eyes. "I get to finally see what you look like."

He wrote: DONT B SCARED.

"I won't be," she said.

4.

After she saw his face, she got back under the covers. She thought he was crying, but she couldn't be sure because he'd quickly covered his scarred face as soon as she finished looking. "I love you, Torch," she said. Teddy watched the black cat go cautiously about the room, occasionally meowing, dipping her head down to the floor to sniff. "And now I know why you got the cat food . . . you didn't steal it, did you?"

Torch was about to write something on the Etch A Sketch but didn't.

"Oh, I don't like it when you steal. It makes me feel bad."

Torch drew an angry face on the Etch A Sketch.

"Yeah, that's how I feel on the inside," she said, and then reaching over to the dials, added a moustache and horns to the face.

Torch shook the Etch A Sketch to erase this.

"How do you feel on the inside?"

Torch bowed his head. Then he drew a picture of a hurricane lamp like the one Teddy kept by her bed.

When she'd seen the picture, he erased it and wrote: SAFE-LANTERN-FIRE.

"The kitty belongs to somebody," Teddy said, sadly. "After we feed it, we should let it go so it can go home."

Torch nodded.

Teddy turned her head away from him and looked at the stone gray wall. "Someday you're going to have to let me go, too, Torch. Because someday what got Jake is going to get me."

CHAPTER TEN

TALES TOLD OUT OF SCHOOL

1.

Saturday Morning in Pontefract

Howie McCormick didn't show up for work down at the Post Office, but nobody really missed him. Jodie Gale took his mail route without realizing that for the next several days he would still be subbing for Howie. Perhaps sometime in the following week somebody would wonder what the hell happened to Howie, but until then nobody really cared. His porno videos would remain unreturned to the video store in Cabelsville.

Georgia Stetson was gossiping with her husband Ken while she squeezed (just barely) into the dark purple dress she'd chosen to wear. "It's not like you're the widow," Ken chortled when he noticed her somber clothing, and Georgia remarked, "Don't I wish."

Sheriff George Connally sat in front of the television set and watched "Pee-Wee's Playhouse," but did not scream when the secret word was spoken on screen. He didn't even notice when his wife, Rita, came into the living room and turned off the set.

"Why don't we take a drive over the hills," she said, trying to get his mind off yet another nightmare he'd had in the early morning. George had awakened her at three, she'd gone through the usual routine of warming him some milk, and then listening to him describe bits and pieces of the nightmare.

He'd told her, "It was just another Frank and Louise dream, honey, nothing new. They just told me they loved me like a son, that's all." But what he hadn't told Rita was that she was in the dream, also. Nothing frightening there, though, nope, just Rita Connally pushing her husband away from her as he tried to hug her. And when she opened her mouth to speak, just a gargling sound.

"Yeah, a drive over the hills." George combed his hand through his waxy golden hair and aimed for a smile but ended up grimacing. "You think my job's getting to me?"

"I think you take the world on your shoulders." Rita tried to look him in the eyes but could not. She was exhausted from being awakened every other morning before sunrise with his screaming. "And I think this town is *not* the world. You can't even find a decent bowl of grits in the dang place."

"A drive over the hills, good." George nodded and attempted to rise from the couch; but pushing his hands into the cushions, he just sank lower.

"It's Saturday," Rita said, "today you belong to me, not Pontefract."

Cappie Hartstone was up at the crack of dawn with her Jane Fonda Workout tape going full blast downstairs in the family room. The room had flooded in the night when one of the pipes burst, and the fuzzy blue carpet where she exercised her buns off was damp and stunk to high heaven; it squished when her knees came down from doing fire hydrants. Bill had put electric fans in the corners of the room to try and dry the carpet out. Cappie was positive she would catch pneumonia. And of all days for this to happen, when she and Bill were hosting the calling hours for her Uncle Arthur's funeral. *When it rains,* she thought, *it certainly does pour.*

But nothing, not even these acts of God like pipes that burst in January, would keep her from her morning aerobic routine.

Saturdays were never good days for Cappie. The Altar Guild usually took up the better part of the day—she was always down at Christ Church organizing potluck suppers, or ironing palls, as she had to yesterday, or arranging flowers on the altar. And then her little angels, Heather, Jennifer and Jason, needed to be driven to scouts or ballet class or to piano lessons. Thankfully Cappie could count on her husband Bill to be out of sight most Saturdays, over at the club in Newton vegetating in front of a giant video screen with his sports cronies. And today, she'd managed to borrow Georgia Stetson's maid to get the living room tidy and to serve food and drinks after the funeral.

Saturday was rarely ever Cappie Hartstone's piece of the pie.

She wrote in her Day Runner Book:

This is the morning I will work on me, before the church obligations, before the reception. To become the best me I can be.

Beneath this, she outlined her goals for the following week:

1. *To be a better wife, the best wife. The kind of wife Bill will want to be a better husband for.*
2. *To accentuate the positive.*
3. *To love and cherish those around me. Not to nag.*
4. *To be free to be me.*
5. *To lose ten pounds by Founders Day so I can fit in my Von Furstenberg.*

Alongside this, in the margin, she scribbled:

If life gives you a lemon, squeeze it and make lemonade!

Cappie, who was 38 and in the kind of shape that is somewhere between aerobics instructor and refugee from the Scarsdale Diet, still could not rid herself of the cellulite on her thighs. Her husband had made another comment last night when she was doing her before-bed stretches and lunges. These usually turned him on.

"How come you've got those bumps on your ass and you

say you're keeping in shape?" Bill asked. "I don't see Jessica Lange with bumps like that. And your pal Hanoi Jane doesn't have them, either."

"Her name is Jane Fonda, Bill, and they are movie stars, so of course you don't see cellulite on them. They have good lighting, and all I've got is a ten dollar lamp from K-Mart." She refrained from mentioning his beergut, his lardass, his puffy, beer-stoked face. He was President of Westbridge Savings and Loan. Bill worked hard for anything he'd ever gotten, including Cappie, how often had he told her this?

While she was doing her Jane Fonda tape, squishing into the damp carpet, Cappie pretended it was Bill's face that her knees were hitting down on.

The big event in town this particular Saturday morning would be Arthur Abbott's funeral. Just about everyone in town was related to Arthur in one way or another, because Arthur's mother was a MacKenzie, and his maternal grandmother was a Connally, and his paternal grandmother was a Houston, and if you went far back enough with anyone who was still hanging around Pontefract, you'd find they'd all practically sprung from the same seed. Dr. Prescott Nagle called this the Sins-of-the-Father syndrome that was the curse of small, out-of-the-way towns like Pontefract. This kind of inbreeding worried Prescott when he ran through the genealogical charts he worked on at the Historical Society. There was just too much old blood walking around Main Street. But this morning, that was the furthest thing from Prescott's mind as he sat in Maude Dunwoody's front window table, eating creamed chipped beef and hush puppies; even Arthur Abbott's funeral (which would take place in an hour) was not occupying his thoughts.

Prescott Nagle was worried about a woman who had died in the storm of 1941. And, as if his memory was not cloudy enough, he was also wondering about a former student of his who was probably still asleep over at Patsy Campbell's Boarding House.

2.

From *The Nightmare Book of Cup Coffey:*

JANUARY 3, 1987, SAT.

I don't want to write much here. I'd like to forget I've ever come back down to this place. I don't like thinking about this. I really don't. But I've got to tell somebody, and you, fearless reader of forbidden diaries (even Nightmare Books!), are as good a father-confessor as any.

I didn't sleep at all last night. Every time I closed my eyes I saw her, Lily, or thought I heard her calling me.

I wrote several pages in this book, but I've torn them all out. Just trying to piece together . . .

It is five A.M. when I'm writing this. It is pitch black out. As good a time as any to try to put it together—not that phone message—not even what I thought I heard Billy Bates say up at Hardy Elementary School—but what happened. What actually happened that night.

Dr. Nagle asked me, when he dropped me off last night, how could I have not known what happened to Lily? Wasn't I close to her family? If I was going to come all the way down here based on one phone message, didn't I keep in touch? He was there, at the Founders Day luncheon at the Marlowe-Houston, and while she was dying, she mentioned my name. A dying woman doesn't just mention anyone's name—there must've been some significance.

I cried in his car when he told me this. Lily and I had not spoken to each other since that night twelve years ago, eleven years before her death.

That word—death. Sticks in my craw, as they say. There was a horror movie I once saw called *Picture Mommy Dead,* which is possibly one of the best titles for a scary movie, and here I am thinking, Picture Lily Dead. Picture her dying. And I could not.

This morning I've been thinking maybe old Nagle is senile, or doddering. It reminded me for a second of how I felt with Billy Bates, Jesus, a fifth-grader, and I wanted to hit him, I did hit Billy; I just wanted to strike out at Nagle, shut him up. To not hear what he was trying to tell me.

And how could I not know about Lily?

Who was there in all Pontefract, or Westbridge County, or the Western Shenandoah Valley, or even south of the Potomac River to tell me, to send me the newspaper clipping in the local paper: Lillian Cammack Whalen, wife of Warren Whalen, daughter of Dr. Brian Cammack and the late Rosalynn Cammack . . . is that what the obit would say?

No one in the world would've thought to inform me of her death. I never met her older sister, and her father probably forgot students as soon as they left the school. Although, given what happened that night, I might've been in the blessedly forgotten-on-purpose category. I was at best a bad memory to anyone who knew me at the school, except, as it turns out, Dr. Nagle who at the present moment seems less than reliable. Anyone who would possibly remember me would associate me with that incident over at the Marlowe-Houston, that thing with the good old hometown boy and the fire. *But,* someone might add, *was it really an accident?*

And if Lily is dead, what kind of sick twisted mind left that message on my machine? Had someone in this boring town waited twelve years to play a bad joke on me? Or am I just losing the old marbles? Did I begin losing them that night twelve years ago, when a 16-year-old boy gave his heart and soul to the woman he would always love, and in so doing, inadvertently killed another boy? Does love demand sacrifices like that? Well, I should tear this book up—if anybody ever reads it they will lock me up.

I've worked overtime trying to forget that night—as if it could ever be forgotten. Every time I feel that memory coming on, I swallow it like a sour taste in my mouth. My parents buried it in the garden of my childhood. I still don't know for sure what happened that night, what really happened, if there is an absolute reality—and I am an eyewitess. That night I got hold of a bottle of Jack Daniels and tole a bone from a mongrel; the night of my tribal initia-ion, which I never even made it to. The night of the faculty hristmas party, when Lily and I played "Smoke" for the ery last time.

The night the most beautiful woman in the world whis-ered in my ear what kind of monster she was.

"The kind who kills her own children," and it is not pecifically her own voice I hear replayed in memory, but ne I've fabricated over the years, the way I imagine Lily's rown-up voice would be. A voice that just two seconds efore possessed rare sparkling gems in its tone, but now ook on the quality of crushed opals: all turned to sand, a ired voice.

But how many children? I had asked her. She was twenty. 'd never seen her pregnant and I saw her all the time. I lidn't even know she had a boyfriend. I remember it felt like dagger thrust deep into my heart when she told me this.

"Abortions, Cup, do you understand? Two. Abortions." As she whispered this word *abortion,* her delicate fingers haped curves and helixes in the crisp winter air. I think my eaction to the word, the concept of abortion, was very iberal, what I thought was sophisticated. I blurted out, 'Well, it doesn't make you a monster, it's not like you killed hem."

Lily seemed to me then, as we sat on the steps of the hapel, freezing, like a pale crushed flower, exactly what Gower Lowry had called her: a rare blossom. But she felt as f she'd done the worst thing you could ever do.

I tried to laugh. "But you can't get pregnant when you're a rofessional virgin."

"It's the truth," she said.

When I drew her face back to mine with my hand, she was rying. I reached my arm around her shoulders. I kissed her. Her lips were trembling. I remember her sweet warm breath ntruding into my mouth and how I didn't care if she had ex with another boy, I didn't care because I knew that our ove for each other was purer than that.

"I love you," I said.

Lily didn't reply.

I told her she was beautiful. I told her I would always be there for her. Always love her.

I didn't hear the dogs again until it was too late, until Bart Kinter and his cronies tackled us as we sat there, embracing.

3.

From *The Nightmare Book of Cup Coffey:*

"I know what kind of monster I am!" Bart Kinter mimicked her in a high-pitched falsetto. Our attacker had come out of the snow-frosted boxwood hedge.

"You fucking tramp!" Kinter shouted with glee. He looked like a demon, painted with bright red lines across his face, feather stuck in his white hair, naked from the waist up even with it being as cold as it was. His buddies had me in a half-nelson; I felt like I was being strangled. I didn't know who was holding me down.

Kinter had Lily by the wrist and was twisting it, while another boy, whom I recognized as another school bully, held tight to her other arm.

"Get your hands off me," Lily whimpered. She was sobbing; her face had turned a deep red.

"I'll bet Daddy would just love to hear about what his little girl is doing in college these days, don't you?" Kinter sneered.

Whoever was holding me down pushed his knee hard into my back. I couldn't utter a word; probably the worst physical pain was the bone in my coat pocket which now felt like a crowbar thrust into my gut. The boy on top of me shoved my face into the snow, telling me to eat it. I tried kicking him, and the hand on the back of my head pushed harder. I began coughing into the snow.

"Shit," the boy spat out, "this douchebag's kicking me like a girl."

Kinter snarled, "Well, kick the motherfucker back." I glanced to the side and saw Kinter glaring at me with eyes like red embers. He pointed at me with his free hand. "And when I'm finished fucking little Miss Slutburger, I'm gonna cut your fuckin' balls off, jizzface."

Lily let out a scream—one boy had cupped his hand over her mouth to keep her from doing just that, but he had stupidly moved it for a second.

"You cunt," Kinter snarled and smacked her across the face with his fist. "They say that debutantes like you need a good fuck, bitch, so boys, hold her down—"

While the boy held both her arms, Bart Kinter undid the snap on his jeans.

I found new strength—in fact, strength I didn't know I had. Adrenaline was pumping through me. I began to rise from my attackers. "You son-of-a-bitch!" I was able to get out, and then the world went to blackness, and it was like I'd gotten a shot of morphine and was going under.

When I came to, I knew it had not been anything as pleasant as morphine. The back of my head felt like a train had just run through it, and I tasted blood in my mouth. Whoever hit me had hit me hard, with that damn Jack Daniels bottle. I am surprised now that I didn't need more than the stitches I later received. I also felt pains in my side, along ribs I didn't know existed. I was lying in Lily's lap, looking up at her tear-streaked face.

"You're all right?" I asked. "They didn't . . . ?" I couldn't bring myself to say the word: *rape.*

"No," she shook her head, "they didn't." But to Lily Cammack, what those boys were going to do would be as bad for her as if they *had* raped her.

Kinter and his buddies were going up to the Marlowe-Houston House. They were going to break in on the party and tell them everything.

"No way," I mumbled, "they just said that to scare you."

"Daddy will die," Lily repeated over and over, sobbing, "he will die."

"They're not going to even get as far as that house." I felt heroic as I said this. It was my time to shine. To set right the balance that had been forever destroyed by that devil Kinter. I would slay all of Lily's dragons.

And the wasp of revenge must've been buzzing there in the back of my mind. It was just as though my enemy were being delivered right into my hands.

I ignored the throbbing pain in my head and sides. I just got up and started running toward the house. The Jack Daniels hounds were barking up ahead, running alongside Kinter and his drunken crew.

What I remember of those last moments before it happened:

Those dogs barking, howling, the shadow-gray footsteps in the crunchy snow, several boys running ahead of me, some turning to laugh as I ran after them. One fell down in the snow, so drunk he couldn't continue on. I passed him by—it wasn't some toadie I was after. I wanted Kinter. The boy shouted out to me as I ran by, "Don't get pissy, fartface, he isn't really gonna go through with it!"

But I kept running.

One of the big oafs was out of breath as he reached the back porch of the Marlowe-Houston House. "Hey, weenie, you ain't gettin' in this way," he said, swinging the bottle that I'd already been bludgeoned with. In my hurry, I slid into a slushy puddle of melting snow and I heard laughter all around me.

Standing above me was Bart Kinter. His hands on his hips. He whispered, "After this, Coffey, your fuckin' balls."

One of the teachers opened the kitchen window and shouted, "What in God's name is going on out here?"

Kinter flipped me the bird, and went over to the cellar doors of the house. These two wooden doors were thrust open as if to welcome him.

"Never!" I cried out as he took the first step down. The entire party must've heard me shout, but I didn't care. I got to my feet and rushed to the cellar doors.

I unsheathed the only weapon I had on me.

The bone.

Things started to go in slow motion, but perhaps this is just my memory trying to dissect the actual moves, what happened, who put whose foot where, whose hand went for the light, the bone as I swung it at Bart. The loud crack as the bone hit the wall, missing Bart. His turning around, twisting his ankle. The look of shock in his eyes. How he was reaching out to grab the bone. To hit me with. But no—that can't be, because he was going to fall—he was trying to grab the bone to balance himself. To keep from falling.

And I let go of the bone.

The whoosh of air escaping his lips. The water from the melting snow on the stone floor. I fell. My chin hitting the bottom step. Holding those slatted wood steps for dear life. Looking up. Kinter's scream. Turning, reaching, in mid-air; grasping the light cord. The whole light fixture tearing from the wall with his weight. Kinter falling. Flying. Across the cellar. Hitting the cement floor with a loud smack. Sparks. That wet snap.

I lost consciousness. I dreamed of fire.

Beautiful, sudden fire like a million suns bursting across that cellar, through rows of dusty bottles and spiderweb-covered books. And in the dream, that towhead boy was dancing a crazy, electric dance. "I know what kind of monster you are!" he shouted. When I awoke from that dream I was coughing smoke. Pains running through my entire body. Covered in a soft blanket. Firemen above me, hosing down the cellar.

Now I've told so many twisted versions of that story to myself, lies upon lies. This present version perhaps just being a variation on that theme. I'm not even sure sometimes whether I lived it or dreamed it.

Because there was something else in that fire dream, the Mother of all my Nightmares.

Something other than bursting flames, barking dogs, melting glass bottles and burning books.

There was a monster in that fire. It was someone I knew, but he had lost all semblance of humanity in the conflagration. (Bart Kinter I can tell myself from the safe distance of twelve years, and I know it was him and it wasn't him.) It was simply faceless. It was angry for burning, but the kind of annoyed anger of one who doesn't much enjoy being awakened only to be told to go back to sleep again.

Next time, the steaming mouth gasped, *next time, it's going to be me coming for you, boy, not some townie, some horny country moron, and I'll be somebody you trust, and you'll forget you're afraid until it's too late. Do you know what it feels like to burn from the inside out? It's like maggots crawling under your skin, maggots with stingers and suckers boring through you, eating their way out, slow at first, real slow, but then*

But that faceless voice dried like parchment and the monster's body folded in on itself, shriveling into the heart of the fire.

That is all that I experienced that night.

But the next afternoon, when I discovered that I was not as badly hurt as I would've liked to have believed, I learned the actual facts.

Bart Kinter died from his fall, breaking his neck.

The fire originated from the light switch; the electric current that had gone through Kinter couldn't have even killed a dog. I must've seen the fire all wrong, because it was isolated to a small area of the cellar, part of an old septic tank.

I also learned that Lily had lied about what had happened, and I understood. If she had told the truth, everything would've come out. She would have admitted what kind of monster she was. In the story she told, the boys had jumped me while we were walking back to the dorms. That was all.

But one of Kinter's cronies swore on a stack of Bibles that I had taken a stick or something, and hit Bart Kinter hard across the back of the neck, causing him to fall.

As my parents drove me out of Pontefract the following day, we passed the Marlowe-Houston House and I realized that neither Lily nor I had even said goodbye.

4.

From *The Nightmare Book of Cup Coffey:*

JANUARY 3, 1987

So, before noon I got dressed and walked back into town to the churchyard where Lily was buried.

When I arrived at Christ Church, having walked all the way imagining the morning chill would revive my spirits, I went around back. This part of the church was shaded by a half-dozen oak and elm trees, and felt fifteen degrees colder than the rest of the world. Scaffolding entwined like dying vines around the back of the church spire and bell tower. I narrowly avoided getting my ankle caught amongst the tangle of 100-year-old bricks and thick, gnarly roots, with mud puddles all around.

The lichen-kissed markers were like well-positioned dominoes that had frozen in mid-fall. Some of the older slabs leaned against a few of the newer ones that had been erected between the rows. I scanned the various tombstones. The names that were engraved upon them were all good old Pontefract names: Cavendar, Campbell, MacKenzie, Houston, McCormick, Connally.

I will admit to a love of graveyards. Their quiet and calm, partial shading always reminding me of a charcoal sketch. Tall, dead grass around the gray and white tombstones, here a marker's legend washed out with too many rains, there, a sober angel whose face is turned eternally skyward, with the inscription, "Commend My Soul," with all else indecipherable.

Then I came upon the McCammack family plots, some dating back as far as 1787. Gradually, as I moved up-to-date, the name became Cammack, and I found Lily's grave.

LILLIAN CAMMACK WHALEN, BELOVED

The plain white marker didn't say anything else, beloved wife, beloved daughter, nothing but the dates:

APRIL 2, 1953–JANUARY 8, 1986

Then, in small gothic lettering at the base of the marker next to hers, was the inscription:

MALCOLM BRIAN WHALEN
JANUARY 8, 1986
"WHOSOEVER SHALL NOT RECEIVE THE KINGDOM OF GOD
AS A LITTLE CHILD
SHALL NOT ENTER THEREIN."

The coolness of the day, the dull thudding in my head of caffeine and sleeplessness, my own confusion over this mystery, and the silence, the damn silence of people who die—it all conspired against me. I began crying.

I was down on my hands and knees reading the fine print of Lily's baby's gravestone. I felt, as I never before had, the loss of a good friend, someone who I wished I had kept up with, someone who had not forgotten me.

Someone who thought enough about me to have my name on her lips as she died; how many baby names had she and her husband fought over before deciding on "Malcolm"? My own name.

I felt like I had lost my soulmate.

I began talking to the grave as if it would hear me.

"Lily," I said, "come back to me."

As if to answer, someone standing behind me said, "You see, it's true."

I turned around to see Dr. Nagle, dressed in a dark and somber suit, shoes caked with mud. He looked as if he hadn't slept all night: circles beneath his eyes, lips drawn tight in a thin string, his skin the color of dirty dishwater.

5.

Prescott Gives Cup a Ride

"I guess I knew it was true last night," Cup said.

"But you still needed convincing . . . seeing is believing, isn't it? Aren't you worried about the mud?" Prescott pointed to the puddles that surrounded the gravestones.

"How did you know I'd be here?"

"I told you last night, my old friend Arthur Abbott was being buried today. I saw you through the stained glass," Prescott turned and pointed to one of the arched windows of Christ Church, "but even if I hadn't, I knew you'd be coming out here sometime soon. And I probably would've stayed around, hoping to catch you."

"Look, about last night . . ."

"I know what you're about to say, Coffey. Something rather polite, thank me for what information I've given you, and then mention that you have an appointment, or that you're just on your way to . . . It's the way most young people treat people over sixty, and those of us who've hit seventy even worse, and it's a damn shame. You think I'm some kind of crackpot, but I assure you I am not."

"I wouldn't say that."

"I know, I'm sorry. I don't mean to sound so harsh—you've had a big shock and I'm just thinking about the time and how little there is left."

"Until what?"

Using his black umbrella as a pointer, Prescott tapped Lily's gravestone.

"January 8th, Coffey, Founders Day."

"What do you mean?"

"The date your friend Lily died, Coffey, it's not some arbitrary date. There was some intent behind it. I would even be so bold as to say there's an intelligence. Something 'beyond our ken.' "

"I'm not following you."

"And that is precisely what I ask of you right now, Coffey. Follow me a little ways. Can I give you a ride back to Mrs. Campbell's?"

6.

Prescott drove uptown, turning off onto the Old Carriage Road where it began just above the Main Street–Walnut Road intersection which headed out to the highway.

"We're going the wrong way."

"I've lived here all my life, you think I don't know where I'm going?"

"I didn't say that. Shouldn't we be going down to Lakeview Drive?"

"Actually, Coffey, I am going to kidnap you for a bit, I hope you're amenable."

"Well, I am kind of tired, sir, perhaps another time."

"Let's stop that schoolboy routine, shall we? You may call me 'Prescott' or 'Pres,' but not 'sir.'"

"Then maybe you should stop with the authoritarian-professor - who - keeps - his - students - at - bay - by - calling - them - by - their - last - names. I've heard that people do that as a sign of contempt. You may call me 'Cup.'"

"Touché, Cup, and—oh, you're joking, well, I've certainly been hoisted by my own petard, as it were. But I'm quite serious about kidnapping you for the afternoon."

"And I am very tired."

"I've packed a lunch for myself in back, some of Maude Dunwoody's ham biscuits and a couple of Cokes. You know me, there's enough for two or three. Some food might revive your spirits. I guarantee, Coff—Cup, you will find what I have to tell you very interesting, especially with regards to the phone call from your friend, Lily."

Prescott was driving his car along the stretch of Old Carriage Road that came down to the edge of Clear Lake. There was a sheen of ice on the water, and some boys were ice skating on the town side. "They should be careful,"

Prescott said. He pointed out a few local sites of morbid interest as they drove out of sight of the lake and into a tree-enshrouded section of the road. There was an old hanging tree which was known to have been used as late as 1926 for the impromptu lynching of a fellow accused of raping some of the town fathers' wives. "I was about ten years old then," Prescott said, "but I remember the furor it caused. None of the authorities made an attempt to stop the lynching. The boy that was killed wasn't much over seventeen, and he had been a source of pride in Westbridge County, up until the alleged rapes. But I don't think any woman in town really was raped. I think the people in this town saw something in that boy. He was beginning to make a name in the area as a tent revival preacher."

Then they passed the remains of a house, with nothing but a blackened chimney and the foundation left. The ground around it was black. "A more recent tragedy," Prescott said, "someone set fire to it in early December. A rather disturbed family lived there . . ." He hesitated, slowing the car.

"But somehow it fits," Cup said.

"How so?"

"In this grove of trees, with a glimpse of the lake over there, it gives this area the feeling that people shouldn't live here. There's something quite beautiful in it—like a warning to keep out."

"A haunt . . ." Prescott said. "You're very perceptive, Cup. And look, over there." He pointed toward the lake. As they came around the Old Carriage Road, the lake was once again in full view like the moon coming out from behind a cloud, and there was the indomitable Marlowe-Houston House, looming like a giant over the campus buildings of Pontefract Prep. "People used to make pilgrimages from all of Southern Virginia to this lake, even when I was a child."

"What was it, a spa?"

"Not quite a spa, but those who wanted to take the Cure as it were, more often than not came here if the Hot Sulphur Springs over the hills didn't do the trick. Came here for everything from constipation to TB."

"No one comes anymore?"

Prescott shook his head. "It's just a lake, Cup, it couldn't compete with doctors and faith healers and mineral waters. More recently county health officials have discovered a problem with sewage, some of which goes right into the lake." Prescott said this almost sadly.

"And that house."

"Yes, that house. It does seem to dwarf even the foothills, doesn't it?"

The Old Carriage Road ended abruptly about a quarter mile from the Marlowe-Houston House, which marked the beginning of the campus. There was the football field set off the left, with the two tennis courts just at the foot of the first rise. Before them was an overgrown field, dead grass tamped down by the previous night's rain—the sunlight glinted off this, revealing sparkling diamonds among the weeds and grass.

"The Old Carriage Road continues, just on the other side of that hill, but was cut off here when the town was rerouted on the other side of the lake. This field before us has gone through several incarnations, Cup. Most recently, the school is turning it into a soccer field, thus," and Prescott pointed across the field where a big yellow bulldozer sat empty, "but it will never happen."

"Not enough funds?"

Prescott began laughing. "No, the school never has that problem. Now, I have had my problems with funding, but not this school. No, this field will never become anything other than a field for the simple reason that it is intrinsically a field. Sounds rather Zen, doesn't it?"

Cup found himself staring at the field.

"Is something the matter, Cup?"

"No, not really. But there's something . . ."

"Yes, it draws you, like you were saying about that wooded area with the burnt chimney back there—'it fits'?"

"Not that. No. Just the opposite. What is it about an empty field?"

"Perhaps like the concept of an abyss, there is really no such thing as an empty field. Nature is supposed to abhor a vacuum, after all, so no field is ever truly empty; the emptiness is in us. There, *that* sounds suitably pompous!"

He shifted into neutral and turned the key off in the ignition. The car trembled to a complete stop. "What say we stretch our legs, Cup?"

7.

"This was the site of an archeological dig I managed to get some funding for. But it was only temporary funding, Cup, a grant from the state, which is the Fairy Godmother of our local chapter. So I set about researching and digging, using the slave labor of my students to get most of the dirty work done. Now, I'm not the popular voice in Pontefract, I'm an old man with no money who lives in a barn. That's how they see me here. But I wanted to give them history, Cup, history, which is everything to me. History as it really was. But they want it their own way.

"Now, you and I know that Virginians take to history like a dog to a fire hydrant. But Pontefractors didn't want their cake—they wanted somebody else's. They want a past where Robert E. Lee waltzed with Aunt Bessie, or where Thomas Jefferson kept their great-great-grandmothers well-stocked in diapers. They don't want their own history, that of the Scotch-Irish backwoodsman who made this part of the country great. The real pathfinders, the explorers, settlers. People in this town would like to bury all that. And I am afraid that some things just can't be buried."

Prescott shook his head wearily. "Well, we may as well start lunch—the biscuits and sodas are in the white bag in the back seat. Would you mind getting them?"

When Cup returned to the edge of the field with the lunch bag, Prescott led him across a thin path, strewn with Coke bottles, crushed beer cans, old condoms ("A popular spot," Cup said), and cigarette butts. There was a broad flat boulder near the bulldozer, which Prescott sat upon and, patting the portion of rock next to him, offered a seat to Cup.

Cup set the bag between them as he sat down. Prescott

opened the bag and pulled out a ham biscuit wrapped in wax paper. "Maude makes the most delicious ham biscuits," he said, "and I've packed enough for an army."

"I'm not all that hungry."

Prescott's voice became gentle. "It's been quite a trip for you so far, hasn't it?"

Cup nodded. His eyes were dark encircled.

"Are you cold?"

"Not too."

"Do you know what this area, from here all the way down to the Marlowe-Houston, used to be called?"

Cup shook his head.

"It was called a 'goat dance' and it has quite an interesting history."

8.

From *The Nightmare Book of Cup Coffey:*

As Dr. Nagle spoke, telling me the history of this place, I felt a million miles away from the rest of the world. What I didn't tell him when I looked at that field, that empty field, was that I thought I smelled perfume, that jasmine perfume that Lily wore. Even in the dead of winter, that scent of flowers, and I thought if I closed my eyes and opened them again, I would be pressing my lips against Lily's sweat-moistened neck.

9.

When Prescott finished the first ham biscuit and took a swig from the Coca-Cola bottle, he began speaking again. He noticed that Cup seemed to be listening to him with one ear, and to, or for, something else with the other.

"It all has to do with the original settlement, Cup. Where we are now. Back in the long ago, the lake would've been a bit further away, and not so much a lake as two disconnected streams that crossed here and then forked off in opposite directions again. You know the town was built here? Yes, on the school side of the lake—of course, there was no school then 1748. This field was even then a field, but held in with a kind of stockade, a pen and grazing area for the livestock. The town, which properly began over where the football field is, and down to the colonnade, was inhabited by about a hundred people, not many more. And of those hundred, perhaps only a handful of names emerge: MacKenzie, Campbell, Connally, Cavendar, McCammack, Houston, McCormick and Carson. A lot of 'C' names, interestingly enough. English, Scotch, and one German, although one of the Houston descendants, Mr. Lowry, would dispute my claim.

"Of those eight families, Cup, one no longer exists. And through my research, and the dig I embarked upon, I discovered why. I also discovered why descendants of those early families seem lazily against my digging around down here, why they are so happy to let the school just smooth it over into a soccer field.

"Do you understand the concept of a 'taint'?

"Let me clarify: the lake, for instance, like I said, was once considered a place of miracle waters. Even at the turn of the century, there were country quacks filling bottles with the water and selling it for two bits. But the lake acquired a 'taint.' Not through any rational means—today we could mention the sewage trouble, but not so then. There are places that become tainted just through associations—and so the lake became associated with accidents, drownings. Never more than a body of water might normally have—there will always be someone to get drunk and drive a car on the ice, or get a cramp when they're swimming. But these stories about the lake stuck, until Clear Lake became connected to something that wasn't good in folks' minds.

"So, also, this field has acquired a taint over the years. It is not a place to go digging around in, evidently.

"I believe there is a good reason for this, and white men first encountered it just over two hundred years ago.

"Imagine yourself in those first settlers' shoes. And some of them didn't have much in the way of shoes. They were poor. They came from families who had never had much, and suddenly they arrive in this area and are landowners with huge acreages, and the only things keeping them from more and more land is the labor and time it takes to clear the forests and the Indians.

"All this meant possibilities for them, for their children, their grandchildren. They owned property. They lived on the edge of a vast wilderness. They could organize their own governing bodies with very little intervention from the Augusta County officials, miles away.

"It was a life of struggle and hardship, but also of great hope. And these eight families came to this wilderness, cut trees, built homes, stockades, raised crops, animals, families.

"In the first three winters, twenty children died from various ailments. If you lived to see eighteen years you were probably strong enough to last another forty. Twenty children, however, out of a hundred people is a sizable chunk. These people were tough, though, survivors, but to have all these children die in such a short period of time, it must've been sobering for the community. Don't forget, children weren't the economic liability they are perceived as today; in the mid-18th century, your sons would help run the farm, daughters helped in the house. But most important, in a population of eighty or so settlers, a fear existed which we can't appreciate today: the fear that your name might die out, that the work you've begun will not be continued into the next generation.

"Which makes what happened in that fourth winter even more horrifying."

10.

"I hope I'm not boring you, Cup," Prescott said, interrupting his story.

Cup was finishing a ham biscuit, and Prescott was happy to see that the young man had found his appetite. "No, really, if I had known that history was so fascinating I wouldn't have skipped it so much."

Prescott laughed. "If only our local residents shared your sentiments. But, again, it's not what they want to hear about. There's a diary, kept by one Worthy Houston; Gower Lowry donated it to the Historical Society, not realizing what subversive material it contained. That diary was a godsend as far as my research went. Worthy Houston lived on this side of the lake—in the Marlowe-Houston. He was writing in the early 1800s. His father had been brought up in the old settlement and told his son stories. Worthy's father called the stories 'visions' and in his sixtieth year, his father blinded himself to keep from seeing any more of these visions."

"Getting kind of gothic," Cup said.

"Yes, rather. Worthy, bless his heart, recorded his father's stories as well as other eccentricities of the family. When I discussed the diary with the Society, which interestingly enough is composed of the descendants of those founding families, it was rejected as 'the wild imaginings of a mental defective,' and this from Worthy's own great-great-great-ad nauseam-grandson, the eminent Mr. Lowry who thought the diary such a grand contribution to begin with. And perhaps that was correct—perhaps Worthy Houston was mentally ill; he was certainly mentally depressed, any amateur psychologist could tell you that from reading the Edgar Allan Poe–ish sorts of things he jotted down. You see, Cup, when I first sat down to read his diary I thought he was making a crude attempt at some fantastical fiction. I thought he was a deluded teller of tales. What he wrote, frankly, was unbelievable."

Prescott reached into his coat pocket and pulled out his pipe. "Man needs a pipe on a day like this." He tapped the pipe against his knee and filled it with tobacco from a small plastic pouch. "I hope I didn't forget my whatchacallit." He patted various pockets in search of his lighter.

But he had not; it was in the breast pocket of his shirt. "You're sure you're not too cold?"

Cup smiled; it was the first time Prescott had seen him smile since he'd told him about Lily Whalen's death. Prescott also smiled. "You're a terrific liar," Prescott said, "has anyone ever told you that? I'm freezing my derriere off." He lit his pipe and puffed away.

11.

According to Worthy's diary, the reason for the community's move from this side of the lake to the other had little to do with an Indian attack and the yearly flooding of this area. Why would these people move their families, uproot them from perfectly good land, to move less than a mile away, and the swampy side of the area? Even if the Indians had set the settlement on fire, as is still alleged to this day, why move to an area that was no better protected? It seems an illogical, arbitrary move, and has always disturbed me. It was illogical to Worthy's father, too, who felt a strong enough guilt to remain with his own family on this side of the lake.

The settlement's move was precipitated by that fire, but it wasn't the local Indians who set it. This fire that was set in the middle of winter.

The fire was set by the town's own inhabitants.

It was a cleansing, Cup.

You see, that winter, that fourth winter, more children died. If we are to trust Worthy Houston's account.

Eighteen children died that one winter, all before New Year's.

None of them died of natural causes.

In late November, some of the children were missing from their homes, and soon families were forming search parties. The snow in these hills gets bad—you remember the storm of '75? People of my generation talk in awed tones about the storm of '41, how people actually froze to death in the hills. But in 1754, these men searched for days, in one of the worst blizzards they had ever faced. They did not return with their children.

Now, that autumn something else happened. Tabitha Carson, the wife of Nathaniel Carson, died in childbirth. It would've been her eighth child. Nathaniel went mad with grief—quite literally. His neighbors had to restrain him one night when he went out into the snow half-naked "like a savage," Worthy wrote, and slaughtered more than a dozen of the domestic animals in this stockade. It was called the goat dance, but it contained more than just goats, it was their version of the community jackpot where all the horses, pigs and chickens were corralled during the long winter. There was even a stable of sorts over there.

Worthy wrote a twisted tale about the name, goat dance, actually being derived from an Indian source, a name known when trappers lived like nomads in the valley, cohabiting areas peacefully with the Indians. This field bounded by the Marlowe-Houston House was a sacred place, indicated by the forking of the streams. It was called the Ghost Dance, and it was where the Indians buried their dead in the belief that they became one with the Great Spirit. These were the Tenebro Indians—I believe you belonged to their namesake club? They were considered a fierce tribe, and would partake of a cannibalistic feast in the winter in which the spirits of the dead spoke through those who consumed their flesh. It was their Shaman test—those who survived the ordeal became men of great wisdom and religious power. At the end of the festival, the Tenebro built a great fire and cast living human beings, usually prisoners-of-war, into it. Of course, many such abominations have been attributed to Indians so that we white folks can feel a little less guilty. But even the Tenebro abandoned this place; for them, also, it acquired a taint. Something more than just the coming of the white man. Soon after, the Tenebro were hunted by colonists and the southern Indians, into extinction.

But back to those settlers. In the New Year, 1755, what is now called a False Spring occurred—but back then, it was called an Indian Summer. An Indian Summer wasn't then the wonderful hangover of summer that we see it as. An Indian Summer was a time of fear. Summer was considered a season of hard labor for people back in the 1700s, and also a time when the Indian attacks occurred. And when these bizarre changes in temperature came on, it meant that there was the possibility of Indian attacks on the homes.

The snow melted within a week in January; water flooded the settlement.

I suppose if it hadn't been for this unusual turn in the weather, the outcome might've been different. The settlers might have cooled down; their fears rose with the temperature. They might not have acted so rashly. But that is a small-town historian's hindsight, isn't it?

The waters from this flood poured into the goat dance, and to save the livestock, men went in and brought the animals out of the enclosure to the higher ground. The place was filled with mud, and the earth gave up something in the water. Something very horrifying indeed.

Eleven children's bodies emerged. Their faces looking upward. They had only been buried a few feet beneath the ground. The water brought them right to the top.

Someone had murdered every single one of those children. And it had not been an Indian. It had been one of the town's own men.

Within the hour, according to Worthy, townsfolk pointed the guilty finger at Nathaniel Carson. He was the most obvious lunatic after the animal slaughter in the fall, and small towns don't change much over the years, we all tend to look for a convenient scapegoat. He was also a sick man, physically, although the cause is unknown. Worthy believed he carried some plague, but perhaps by this he meant cholera. I suppose whether or not Nathaniel was guilty of murder doesn't really matter now. Within the hour, he was hanging from a tree.

But this didn't satisfy the people. They wanted more blood.

Carson was dead, his wife had died.

What about his children?

You must remember, Cup, that just about every family in this settlement felt they had lost at least one child to Carson's savage brutality, and then others to illnesses. Assuming that it was Carson. So, now these people are wondering: what about his own children? Why should Nathaniel Carson's name be allowed to trickle down through the years, when other names were almost snuffed out?

Several of the men from the leading families went to the house where the seven Carson children were being held while their father was hanged. Worthy says that according to his father, the settlers used the excuse of disease, that Nathaniel Carson had brought some sort of infestation upon the settlement, that all his children must have it, therefore. If there *was* a disease I have no doubt it was a result of "sepsis." A kind of poisoning of the local water through the occasional emptying into it of some kind of pathological microorganisms—the beginnings of the taint of Clear Lake. But it's only a guess on my part—based simply on the fact that an old underground septic tunnel, one of the town's first sewers, really, collided with a stream that feeds into the present lake.

But in that first settlement, the taint was clearly on the Carson family themselves.

They gathered up the children and put them in the shack that served as a stable at the edge of the goat dance. They tied their hands behind their backs. They locked them in. The ground was still wet, but the townsfolk threw dry cords of wood all around the shack. They blocked up the entrances and windows with hay.

And those people . . .

They set it on fire.

With those children inside, ages three to twelve. All crying for help, screaming, Worthy Houston describes the scene almost sadistically. He keeps claiming in his diary that his writing is word for word the way his father described the event—his father was a little boy when it happened.

The oldest Carson boy, Andrew, ran through the burning hay into the mob, his entire body on fire, trying to make it to safety.

But, Worthy's own grandfather, Cyrus, beat Andrew Carson over the head with a club and the boy died.

The Carson name died that night in Pontefract, the Old Pontefract.

And before dawn, the entire village was on fire, and that fire was blamed on the Indians—there had been attacks on other towns in the valley, so the settlers attributed this destruction to the various warring tribes. That spring, the Indian Massacre of 1755 was launched in southwestern Virginia. This coincided nicely with the French and Indian War that was brewing over the hills. Scapegoats were plentiful then.

But of course, it was guilt that set that fire—guilt over what an entire community had done to those Carson children. They must've been out of their minds from finding their own children dead.

I believe they set their own homes on fire as a means of absolution.

This place, this side of the lake, had acquired a "taint."

12.

Prescott caught his breath. "I hope this talk hasn't ruined forever your enjoyment of Maude Dunwoody's ham biscuits, Cup."

"My God, Dr. Nagle—Prescott, that's the most bizarre story I've ever heard. It tops any horror movie I've seen," Cup gasped.

"The past is often terrifying. Now you can see why those

narrow-minded biddies at the Historical Society don't like this idea of the archeological dig, never did like it. George Washington didn't sleep here, only the boogeyman slept here. Nobody wants to find out how bad it really was. Better to make it a soccer field for the school."

"But you think there's more than just history, don't you?"

Prescott nodded. "I found something here, in the field. Something that for the moment will have to remain a secret between you and I. You may have assumed that I found nothing but an old musket, some arrowheads and broken chips from some plates. Those are all set in the glass cases at the Marlowe-Houston House. Trinkets from two centuries ago, but nothing substantial. But it was right here I found something, something that gave me a good strong shock, something that when I touched it was like sticking my hand down into a nest of copperheads."

"What was it?"

"Bones, Cup. Charred bones. Dozens of them. A burial mound. And something happened, Cup, when I touched them." The old man shivered, and it was from his thoughts as much as from the weather. "But, it's getting late, and I have quite a bit to consider." Prescott did seem very tired; Cup noticed that his skin, in the dimming light, was sallow and painted a look of defeat across his round face. The old man seemed on the verge of a terrible revelation, but was holding himself back. Cup decided not to push. "If I am even half-right in my assumptions, Cup . . ." Then, wiping his eyes beneath his spectacles, Prescott said: "Forgive me if I'm incoherent. I was thinking about things; when you get to be my age you think about how things might've been too much." He looked off across the lake. The chilling wind came up. "You and I are in a similar boat right now, Cup. You see, I must be going crazy because after years of research on this area, I think there is something to this taint, and not just the lake, but this field, and the land that the house occupies. I'm still not sure how or why. And I think your phone call from Lily is connected, too. Because I don't think it was some prank, or your imagination. I think it was Lily Cammack who has been buried for the past year. I knew you'd be coming back," he sighed, as if admitting a secret he'd kept well-hidden for a long time, "because a little girl named Teddy Amory told me in October that you'd be here this winter. And God help us all, she was right."

13.

Teddy Amory awoke, shivering. Salty tears stung her eyes. Torch was gone; he often left her when she was sleeping so he could get some food and things to keep them both warm here. She had been dreaming again, dreaming the happy dreams of her family before the nightmare world had begun. She was dreaming that she was six years old and her daddy was twirling her around like a windmill; her mommy was shouting at Jake to get his blessed hair cut, and Jake was turning his boombox up loud so that Iron Maiden was drowning her out. Through shimmering woods, summer bare, the lake blinded her every time her daddy swung her that way. Teddy's stomach felt funny, and she heard someone's cat meowing, saw the cat scratching at the car—*now why is the kitty scratching at the car tires?*

Then Teddy woke up, because she knew it was not her daddy's car, or his tires, but the tires that were lined up against the door in the dark place where she lived with Torch. The black cat that she had helped bring back from the dead was scratching at the old, bald tires that blocked the way to the outside. To freedom.

"You want to go home, don't you, Kitty?" Teddy asked. Her voice had become weak in the past month. Whenever she awoke from sleep, Teddy felt sticky and soaked with sweat; she didn't like to wake up anymore to this constantly candlelit, achy world. She felt like she had the flu, and she brought the hood up on the oversized sweatshirt that Torch had found for her.

"Torch?" Teddy called out. "Torch?" Her throat was scratchy and dry.

The cat now began yowling; it attacked the tires as if it would dig its way out.

"Wait," Teddy said, "I'll let you out." She pushed herself up from the rag-covered mattress. Standing, she wobbled and had to clutch the edge of a table. Teddy took a few deep breaths. She told herself that she would not feel sick, that she would not cry. The kitty had a home and its own family, and she should let it go. It wasn't right to keep the kitty here in this dungeon. *I am going to be strong just this once. I am not going to let the fit come on, I am not going to barf, I am not going to start crying again.* Teddy looked up and caught her reflection in the paint-blackened windows. She barely recognized the little girl who stared hollow-eyed back at her. The wavy blond-brown hair draped greasily down from beneath the sweatshirt hood. There was only a trembling straight line where her lips had been, and her eyes were smudged with fever and sleeplessness.

Teddy thought she was looking at a ghost.

The cat yowled.

I am dying. Torch. I am dying. I am dying.

Teddy lifted a hurricane lantern up. *Good. I am dying. I was supposed to drown in the lake. Good. Let me just die. And maybe all these Bad Things will die with me.*

Teddy went to the small door in the back of the dark place where Torch kept her. The cat came over to her and rubbed against her ankles.

"We're going back home," Teddy told the cat.

14.

"Hey!" Rick Stetson shouted down the alley, his voice echoing through the chilling afternoon wind. "Save some for the roaches, man!"

"Shut up, Stets," Tommy MacKenzie said. The boys had been walking past the alley when Rick had spotted the guy near the overturned garbage cans. The guy had ripped into one of the Hefty trash bags and had some gunk in his hands.

"Don't you know who the fuck that is, man?"

"Stets, leave him alone, okay?" Tommy tugged at his friend's army jacket. He knew that the best way to handle

Rick when he was in one of his "moods" was to joke around and pretend that Rick was being silly. "C'mon, if we don't haul buns I won't make it back in time for the second show."

"Fuck your second show," Rick laughed. He reached down and patted some snow into a ball and tossed it hard down at the guy. It missed him, but just barely as it whizzed over his underwear-covered head. The guy didn't even flinch. "We got our own show here, don't you know who the fuck that is, man?"

Tommy sighed. "Leave him alone, okay?"

"Hey, Torch!" Rick yelled. "You just burn me up! You know that? You just fuckin' burn me up!"

15.

Torch sniffed the air. His nostrils froze with the effort; a headache stung him just behind the eyes. It wasn't those boys who were yelling at him, and it wasn't the trash he was going through looking for food, and it wasn't even that gassy smell that meant *They* were near.

"Tehh-ee," he bleated.

16.

Teddy watched the black cat run down the alley.

As if it was still her dream, Teddy walked barefoot down the alley in the same direction as the cat. Ice bit at her toes, and she stretched the red sweatshirt down over her knees. She felt like she was walking on a tightrope, and she was going to fall, but not if she rushed fast enough across the rope and reached the platform on the other side. And then she felt less dizzy. The cold fresh air slapped at her, and she felt blood rushing to her face as she moved faster toward the street, faster toward the black cat as the cat ran toward the street, faster and faster until it was no longer a tightrope but a long tunnel out of her nightmares to her home, faster and faster, her blood was turning to a runny snow cone as she chased the black cat to Main Street.

17.

"All right, that's it, Stets," Tommy said, "let's just go."

"Wimp. Woose. Pussy." Rick huffed. "Hey, Torch! I got some lighter fluid at home! You thirsty?"

"You're not even funny," Tommy whispered. But Tommy didn't move. Torch was not running down the alleyway toward them, and for a second Tommy was afraid because this guy was supposed to be looney tunes or something, and there was Stetson probably triggering some psychotic response in the guy. Tommy tugged again at Rick's sleeve. "Jesus, let's get the hell out of here before—"

"Let go, *faggot,*" Rick snarled, "I want to see a burn victim up close!" Rick was laughing, and Tommy wished now that they hadn't snuck the six-pack of beer out of the Stetsons' refrigerator *(but, hell, if my dad hadn't hit Mom like that I wouldn't need to have a couple of beers to get through the day today).* When Rick had any alcohol in him, even if it was just a sip, he started to get belligerent and argumentative. And this afternoon, Rick had drunk four beers in the space of ten minutes.

Torch was half-limping, half-running, calling out something that Tommy couldn't make out, and then Tommy noticed that Torch was not even interested in attacking the two of them *(thank you, God, I will never have a beer again until I'm legal age, I promise, thank you, thank you).*

But Rick was not satisfied with this.

As Torch ran alongside the wall, near the boys, Rick leaped and tackled the raggedy man, shoving his face in the snow.

18.

Teddy's head throbbed with the cold, with the air that seemed so clean, like her mother's laundry when she used to hang it out to dry in the summer and Teddy would smell it on the dogwood-scented breeze, the cat ran into the street and Teddy would join the cat there, too, in a second, as she dashed out of the alley, frozen, but alive for a moment, alive, and wanted to die so badly she could *feel* it.

19.

"Tell me what's it like to burn in hell?" Rick said as he pushed Torch's face into the melting snow.

"You fucking asshole!" Tommy screamed. Bending down, he gave Rick a heavy blow to his back. Rick kicked back with his legs, landing a shot right into Tommy's crotch. Tommy slipped on the ice and fell on to the cold concrete, clutching himself and groaning. "You *asshole,"* he moaned.

"I ain't gonna hurt this fucker, woossy, I just want to see his *face!"* And with one move, Rick reached across Torch's head and ripped off the bandana and rags.

"Tehh-ee," Torch moaned.

20.

Teddy screamed when she heard the car brakes squealing, and for just a second she thought it was her own self running across Main Street, rolling under the car as it skidded to a stop.

But it was her kitty, the one that she had brought back from the dead, only to send it back again in a shower of red across its black fur.

21.

"Jesus Fucking Christ!" Rick gasped, half-laughing, partly in awe. He rolled off Torch, and the man crawled onwards, and then up to his full height, still limp-running, now down the street as if the incident with the boys had not even occurred.

"You fucking asshole," Tommy groaned, brushing himself off, still wincing from the pain shooting through his groin. "Sometimes I wonder why I hang around you."

"Did you *see* that?" Rick asked. "I never seen anything so *re*pulsive in all my life! Jeez, it was just like one of your dad's horror movies!"

"Asshole," was all Tommy could bring himself to say, and he unfortunately was as curious about Torch's face as Rick had been, and he would've liked to kick himself again in the balls just for wanting to *see.* He stood up, feeling sore *down there,* and hobbled after Torch.

"Where you goin', pussface?"

"I'm going to make sure he's okay," Tommy said.

"Yeah, sure, you just want to get a peek for yourself!" Rick yelled.

22.

When Teddy screamed, something swooped down in a blurred rush and picked her up from alongside the curb and carried her back into the alley.

"Tehh-ee," Torch said as he cradled her in his arms and began hobbling down the alley to their hiding place. He heard footsteps behind him, and even though he couldn't

smell the Bad Ones who wanted Teddy and the Power she had, he wasn't taking any chances.

Behind him he heard a boy's voice cry out, "Hey! You okay?"

23.

Tommy thought for just a second he knew that little girl that Torch was holding: *Teddy Amory, the weird chick who supposedly burned up or else ran away with her brother, Jake, another creepozoid.*

But, heck, if that girl was still in town, wouldn't everybody already know about her?

Tommy pulled the corners of his jacket together because it seemed particularly cold. *Maybe it was just some other albino kid that Torch was protecting from the likes of Rick Stetson. Maybe it's just the Pabst Blue Ribbon clouding my brain.* Then Tommy MacKenzie remembered that his father would be really pissed off if he didn't show up soon to work the concession stand at the Key Theater in time for the next showing of *Sleeping Beauty.* In a life like his, Tommy knew why he hung around with creeps like Rick Stetson: *because everyone else seems worse.*

24.

Safely back in the dimly lit, concrete room, Torch wrote angrily on the Etch A Sketch: NEVER. EVER. DO. THAT.

"The kitty," Teddy said, but had no more tears to offer. She lay on her mattress and wished with all her heart that it had been her lying dead in the street and not the black cat. "I'm afraid," she whispered, but she didn't tell Torch what she was truly afraid of.

Herself.

She was afraid that everything she loved would die like

that cat. The way her mother had, the way her father had.

And Torch. She was afraid that Torch would die, because she loved him so much.

"Please," she whimpered, gazing steadily into his red eyes, *"kill me."*

CHAPTER ELEVEN

WARREN

1.

Clare pressed her back into the door to open it—her arms were loaded down with groceries. The door swung wide with the effort and slammed back into the wall. "Damn it," Clare muttered; she was holding two paper grocery bags in her arms, and dragging a third by the tips of her aching fingers. She wasn't sure if she would make it all the way to the kitchen with it and let the bag drop the few inches to the floor. "Daddy, I'm home!"

She heard his gruff greeting that was always more "ahem" than "hello." She carried the other bags into the kitchen and then came back out for the third. When she lifted it, the sack broke and cans of soup went rolling across the oak floor. "Shit."

After she picked up all the cans and stacked them in the pantry, she took one of the Swiss Miss tapioca puddings from the refrigerator. Then she got a spoon and some paper towels and went back toward the den. "I got your favorite pudding," she said as she entered the room.

"For me?" Warren said. He was stretched out on the couch where she'd let him sleep last night. It looked like he hadn't moved at all. Dr. Cammack was sitting in an armchair near the fireplace. Clare shot Warren an angry look and took the small cup of pudding over to her father.

"Here, Daddy, it's your favorite."

"What is it?" He looked at the plastic container skeptically. His hands trembled as he took the spoon from her. Clare laid the paper towels across his lap.

"Tapioca."

The old man wrinkled his nose and turned the container of pudding upside down—nothing spilled out. "This stuff is for babies." Dr. Cammack set the pudding down on the arm of his chair.

"You love tapioca," Clare said firmly.

"Now *I* love tapioca," Warren volunteered, "toss it here, Doc." Warren held his hands up for a catch. Dr. Cammack picked up the pudding and was about to toss it, but Clare took it and the spoon from his hands and brought them both over to Warren.

"If you're going to steal food from my father, you could at least sit up when you eat."

"Okey-dokey." Warren sat up and began eating the tapioca. "We were watching 'Soul Train.' Have you ever noticed that if you take a nap in front of the TV on Saturdays, no matter what time you wake up, 'Soul Train' is always on?"

Clare glanced at the TV screen; a basketball game was on. "That's not 'Soul Train.' "

"You be civil to my son-in-law," Dr. Cammack said, but was now engrossed in the game.

"What are you still here for?" Clare asked.

"Doc and I were having an interesting conversation. I mixed a few martinis, which I drank, while Doc had a tall glass of milk."

"Is there a point to this?"

"As a matter of fact there is. Patience has never been your hallmark, Moonbeam."

"Stop it, Warren."

"You be civil, do you hear me, girl?" her father growled. He began coughing, and Clare made a move to go get his medicine, but the coughing subsided.

"Seems Doc's been talking to my wife again."

"Warren."

"But not just talking, 'beam, nosiree. Seems she paid him a visit after you dropped him off from this funeral today.

She came out of his closet. Isn't that just like her? Don't you tell me to shut up, you heed your daddy and be civil. Lily just came right out of Doc's closet, isn't that right, Doc?"

Dr. Cammack nodded. "Lily's always liked surprises, why when she was only six years old she hid under the bed and spoke to Rose and me, pretending that the room was haunted."

"See?" Warren said, his mouth full of tapioca. "Doc remembers things. At least what's important."

Clare tensed. "Warren, why don't we discuss this in the kitchen? You can tell me all about it while I get dinner ready."

Warren ignored her. "What else do you remember about today, Doc? When she came out of the closet?"

"The party. Just like old times. She's throwing a party over at the old house, just like we used to have."

"That's right, Doc, and we're all invited, aren't we?"

"She said it's a come-as-you-are party. She's always been full of surprises. I remember when I took her to the convention in Richmond, just to show off my beautiful girl, and they all gathered around her, those old goats, but she wouldn't have any of them, no sir, she would only dance with her daddy."

2.

In the Kitchen

"You heard what Doc said, 'beam."

"Warren Whalen, you are not welcome in this house anymore." Times like these Clare wondered how she could ever have become involved with this disheveled loser standing before her.

"I think my father-in-law might disagree with you. And I'm not really what's at issue, am I? Me, I'm just sleeping late, enjoying my nightmares, letting my beard grow and wearing the same suit for two weeks in a row. Occasionally thinking I see a ghost. Generally losing my mind. Nothing new there. Look at you, you haven't had a decent night's sleep in over a year—you're popping Valiums like they were Life Savers, good God, Clare, it's like we've both aged ten years in the past twelve months—"

"Don't," Clare said, clutching the handle on one of the kitchen drawers. "Just stop it." The drawer was stuck and she had to tug hard at it; finally the entire drawer came out, and the stainless steel forks, knives and spoons went flying. They landed on the linoleum with a metallic clatter.

"Shit." Clare began sobbing, low at first, as if the weeping was deep inside her, gradually coming up to the surface. She dropped to the floor like a rag doll. On her knees, she began reaching around and picking up the silverware that was scattered. She kept her head down, eyes on the floor. "Now, look what you made me do," she said through her tears, and then laughed, "I'll have to wash these in the sink now. Shit, shit, shit."

Warren crouched down, and picked up a few spoons. "I'm not talking ghosts anymore, Clare."

"Oh, you've given up your 'the dead haunt the living' routine? Then what are you talking, Warren?" she said with sudden fury, looking him in the face. Her hand was raised in a fist that clenched around several forks. "What exactly are you talking?"

"Blackmail, Moonbeam, pure and simple."

Clare sat back on the floor. Her arms hugged her knees as she brought them up to her chin. "Oh, hahaha, really, Warren. That's rich, really, blackmail."

Warren calmly picked up the rest of the silverware and set it in the sink. "I think the man in the next room might be interested to hear about his daughter's lover. Or was it his daughter's husband? I always get those two confused. How about you?"

"Don't . . ."

"Look. What if this guy who's been calling, who's right here in town now, obviously has some scheme that he thinks is worth something. Who the hell knows what it is? Maybe he thinks it will look bad for the school if the whole story were to come out—who knows if this joker even knows what the whole story is?"

"No one in this entire county was spared the details of . . ."

"Look, it makes more sense to me than spooks, okay? And that's what I was beginning to believe, myself."

"Warren, do you believe . . ."

"I don't believe in anything I can't see with these two eyes. Now I don't know what kind of game this Cup fellow has lined up for us out at the old house, but I intend to be there for the kick-off. I think whoever it is he got to dress up like Lily and chat with Doc will be out there, too, and I'd like to shake her hand for doing such a first-rate job on the old man. Doc said Lily invited us for cocktails at seven, and that gives me about forty minutes to get there. You coming? This could be interesting."

"Warren . . ." Clare didn't know what to say; and when she looked at Warren's face, she realized that he understood that she was badly frightened. *I'm scared, I don't know what the hell is going on, I never really loved you, but I like you. I don't want you to get hurt. I don't want anyone to get hurt, because there's something there, it may not be a ghost, but it probably isn't some idiot blackmailer.* But Clare did not know what it was, just that phrase: what goes around, comes around. Finally, she said, "I'm staying here with Daddy. Even if what you think is correct, that somebody wants to go digging up skeletons, what's the point in going there? Why not just call the police?"

"Honey, as they say down at the Henchman, 'T'aint no cause.' I'm just doing my usual brilliant guesswork. But I do have a little itsy-bitsy microcassette on me so we can save whatever enlightening conversation occurs there for Sheriff Connally and his boys in blue. Now, it's getting late—howsabout a kiss for luck?"

"No."

"Just like your sister."

She slapped him hard. Twice.

3.

When Warren pulled his Audi in front of the Marlowe-Houston House, he reached underneath the front seat and pulled out a can of Coors. He popped the top, letting the foam spray out across the dashboard. "Shit—" he said, and then glanced down at the cassette recorder next to him on the seat. "I am now drinking a Diet Pepsi, for the benefit of you Mothers Against Drunk Drivers." He laughed and tapped the machine. "You on? I guess I should do that testing-one-two-three routine bullshit. All right, testing, one-two-three." He propped the beer between his knees. He picked up the cassette recorder and played back what he had just recorded. Then he drank some beer. He looked out across the lake, away from the house. "I never noticed how we've got a skyline here in Pontefract," he held the cassette up to his lips, "all those houses, and Steeple Ridge back there. The lake's so dark and all the lights are sparkling off the water. Is there a moon out? Well, there are a lot of clouds, anyway." He set the recorder down on one of his knees and finished drinking the beer. He glanced at his watch: 7:10 P.M.

"It's after seven, seven-ten to be precise, on Saturday, January 3rd, 1987. I am about to enter the Marlowe-Houston House to meet with—" he let out a laugh, "I don't know, my dead wife. She's throwing a party here tonight. I am arriving fashionably late. Look"—he tapped on the recorder's condenser mike—"I don't know who the hell is doing this, but whoever's behind these shenanigans is in this house and I will be talking with him, or them, shortly." Warren switched the machine off. He stuck it in the breast pocket of his jacket.

He tossed the empty beer can into the back seat. He got out of the car and stretched. The lake carried sounds of trucks rumbling out on the overpass. Warren picked up some gravel from the road and threw it toward the lake.

He knew what he was avoiding. He was avoiding looking at the house. *"How can you even stand to go back to the old house?" Clare asked as he walked out the door that evening, and the question seemed to reverberate in the highway noise from over the hills.*

"Because," he had told her, "it's just that. An old house."

As he turned to look at the house, he kept telling himself that.

The house itself didn't bother him much. It didn't look much different than all the other old mansions that speckled the area. The Georgian-style front, like most of the prep school's campus, the columns, the porch that ran the whole way around the house. Warren preferred his own Victorian-style home.

"That's a lie," he said aloud, reaching into his breast pocket and turning the tape recorder back on, "you know why you don't want to go in there."

As if shaking off the cold breeze, Warren shuddered and walked around his car, talking into the tape recorder. He went up the front steps of the house, bringing his hand up to knock on the door. With his fist in midair, he began laughing. "I've got the key," he said, and fished in his pockets until he found it.

After he opened the front door and stepped across the threshold, a peculiar odor assaulted him. "Jesus, it smells like shit in here, who died?" He reached over and flicked on the foyer light. The strong pungent odor was enough to send him out of the house; he made a sour face. "Sure could use some air freshener. Hello? Anybody home?"

Warren whistled "As Time Goes By," as he headed into the living room. He scanned the glass display cases filled with local Indian and pre–twentieth century artifacts. "I am walking through the Marlowe-Houston House now," he said, checking to make sure the tape recorder was still on. "Doesn't look like my host is throwing much of a party. Hey, this is interesting, what is this," he pressed his fingers against one of the glass panes, "some chip from an Indian burial urn? Part of some ancient tablet? No, looky here, it's just a piece of china from somebody's tea set."

The living room furniture was covered with broadcloth

dustcovers, and Warren drew one of the cloths back and sat on the edge of a red velveteen settee. The back of the settee was up against the pink-and-green flower patterned drapes of the front picture window; Warren poked his hand through the split in the drapes and looked out into the dark night. He let the drapes go. "Gad, this place looks like the anteroom for a French brothel. It wasn't like this last year. Or was it? Who the hell is the interior decorator for the Historical Society?" Then, in a louder voice, "If whoever invited me here doesn't show up in five minutes I am leaving!"

After a few minutes of finger tapping on the arm of the settee, he said, "This is the longest fucking five minutes . . . Time to go exploring."

4.

But exploring the upstairs rooms in the house brought nothing. "Well, gee, I like this," he said as he opened the upstairs bathroom door and saw the ornate tub with the four clawed feet, "how wonderfully creepy." He glanced in the bathroom mirror, wiping away the dust on its surface. "You look like death warmed over, Mr. Warren Whalen." He combed his fingers through his sticky, greasy hair. He spied a pimple on his chin, amongst the three-day-old whiskers. "Ah, the last vestiges of a misspent youth. And you thought you were too old a guy to get zits," he said as he reached up and popped it between his fingers. "Christ, you're a loser," he said to his reflection, "just another dissolute skirt-chaser gone sour. What the hell did Lily ever see in you?" He turned on the faucet, but the water that came out was a rusty brown. He waited for it to clear, but after a minute it apparently would not, so he splashed some of it on his face. He looked back in the mirror, feeling better with the ice cold water drying on his face. His violet eyes had dark circles beneath them and the lids were puffy; he hadn't been shaving and most of his face appeared stained with the wiry stubble. "Once beauty," he said, pursing his lips in a kiss to his mirror-image, "now, the beast."

That was when he heard the sounds of the piano from downstairs in the living room and he identified the tune as "I'll Be Around," which had been on one of the Billie Holiday records he and Lily used to dance to. She would put her feet on top of his, and he would lead her around the living room and jokingly groan about his "toe bones."

Warren turned off the running water. He said to his tape recorder: "You hear that? A musician, yet. This guy's talented."

He went downstairs.

When Warren returned to the living room, he saw the woman seated at the piano.

She struck a rather regal pose, in an emerald green silk dress, her auburn hair tucked neatly back with a comb, her skin pale white. She reminded him of a John Singer Sargent portrait, that quiet, authoritative beauty, poised, flattered by the light of the room—and then he noticed her muddy bare feet as she pressed them down on the pedals. She stopped playing suddenly, and turned to face him. "You're here for the party." She said this flatly, a statement of fact. Her eyes were small and sad, her lips thin and a dark carnelian shade that stood out in stark contrast to her paleness. Her nose all but vanished in the surrounding whiteness of her face; two dark nostrils were its only indication.

"You part of all this, too?" Warren asked, and then remembered his tape recorder. He said, sotto voce, "I've never seen this chick before. Looks like we're involved in some elaborate set-up."

The woman swiveled around on the piano bench, and stood up, all of this girlishly flirtatious. As she stood, she gathered her dress up above her calves, revealing that not only her bare feet were splattered with mud, but so were her legs. "The rain last night," she said, offering no other explanation.

"So, tell me, who the hell are you?" Warren asked, loudly, in hopes that this would bring her own voice up loud enough to be recorded on tape.

But her voice remained soft and sweet, demure. "Let's just say I'm a friend of a friend. You are here for the party, but didn't you bring a guest? A special friend?" She stepped closer to him, and there was that smell that had first hit him when he entered the house, the one he'd just gotten used to, striking him again as she approached. It was an odor that reminded him of an incident from childhood, when he and a friend had opened an old refrigerator in a junkyard, and inside had been a dead possum that must've gotten stuck in there who knew how long. Just that: opening that refrigerator door and getting this whiff of rottenness, making his friend vomit there among the rubbish, and making Warren gag, his eyes tear up. It was a smell so strong and offensive that it made him imagine that he'd been eating that foul thing that had been dead for days.

Warren groaned, and began breathing through his mouth. The woman was standing less than a foot away. He brought his hand up and covered his mouth. His eyes were filled with tears. "Jesus," he gasped, coughing.

"The party's downstairs in the cellar. Shall we?" She held her arm out, her pale hand dangling, almost daintily, from the wrist. She barely touched his own hand with the tips of her fingers. He felt a crackling of static electricity in the air; the hair on the back of his hand stood on end. He drew his hand back from the shock, and glanced down at the woman's hand. Small, feminine. Warren became spellbound, looking at that small hand of hers, dangling, dangling, hanging as if by a thread from her wrist. Thrust out for him to take hold of, to escort this woman downstairs to the cellar for this party. *Dangling. A few tendons seemed to be its only support and connection to the woman's arm, and her arm ended in this bloody red meat stump with the hint of gray bone poking out, ragged, at the end.*

But when he blinked, it was just a normal small-wristed hand, with a silver and ruby bracelet where just seconds before he'd seen the red stump. "Who are you?"

She smiled; her smile was dazzling, her lips all but eclipsed by brilliant white teeth and the border of pink gums. He noticed when she smiled her eyes seemed to flash from a cloudy gray to a pale green. "Like I said . . ."

Warren began breathing through his nostrils again—the rotten meat smell was no longer so smothering. It was almost becoming attractive, seductive. "Oh, right, a friend of a friend. Who is this friend?"

"You know. She's downstairs, our hostess, and I think it's rude to keep her waiting for so long." The woman in the emerald green dress kept her arm extended.

"Okay, it's your game, let's play ball," Warren said.

He offered her his arm, and she took it.

5.

Clare over that weekend: she didn't think much about Warren not returning that Saturday night—she hoped he just went home to his own house. She was getting sick and tired of his clobbering her with every paranoid scheme he could dream up. But Clare Terry was worried, that what went around had finally boomeranged back around, that what her father said was at least partially true. *I will at least admit that to myself, that all these nightmares, these daymares, these episodes, add up to something, and either I am going crazy or there is something out there.*

When she hadn't heard from Warren by Sunday evening, she called his house repeatedly, and, on her way back from the Jump 'N' Save out by the highway, stopped at Warren's house on Howard Avenue. His Audi was not in the driveway. There were no lights on in the house, and she honked her horn a few times to see if he might look out one of the darkened windows, but there was no sign of him.

She did not want to go over to the Marlowe-Houston House.

Since Lily died last year, Clare had never ventured to that side of Clear Lake—all that was there were bad memories. She did not even like taking her father down to the town side of the lake for one of his cherished walks along the sidewalk on Lakeview Drive, the old house perched on the other side like some wild animal, waiting. When the Marlowe-Houston House had been the headmaster's house, she had spent her first nine years of life there, but her memories of the place were vague, and she felt an indifference to her childhood, those few years she considered "innocent," before the trouble had started; her "episodes" where she saw things that just weren't there. Like the time she was nine and in the cellar. Her mother was angry with her for pouting, but it seemed to Clare that her little sister got everything. Clare hugged her Ted E. Bear to her and cried. Her mother, impatient, told her to go down in the cellar and just sit until she decided to behave like a lady. And that is when the first episode had come; sitting in that cellar. Her father, but it could not have been her father (he had taken Lily into town with him that day), sitting down there in the dark. Touching her in places she didn't like being touched. She had plucked out the eyes of Ted E. Bear because he wasn't supposed to see that, what she saw, and what she knew wasn't real but just an "episode" like what was on television. None of those episodes were real. *"Big kiss, Clare, come give Daddy a big kiss . . ."*

No, that never happened, you imagined that just like you are imagining all this. And what would a psychiatrist say about a little girl who was scared that her daddy might touch her the wrong way? I know perfectly well—yuck.

When Clare had driven around the block, slowly going by Warren's house three times, hoping to catch a light just switched on, she decided to go on home and see if he'd called while she was out.

He had. When Clare came in the door, Irene Rowe, her father's sitter, was reading the headlines from the *Sentinel* to Dr. Cammack. "Mr. Whalen called," she said, indicating a message on the coffee table. Irene, her reading glasses propped uncertainly on her nose, continued reading the paper aloud: " 'Storm Front Moving To Valley From East,' now, how do you like that, Brian? Who's going to shovel my walk when this blizzard comes?"

Clare read the note silently:

Mr. Whalen says that he is over at the old house and not to worry that they are all having a wonderful time.

Irene looked up from the paper. Her glasses fell off her nose with the sudden movement, but did not go far; the chain kept them conveniently around her neck. "Well, don't look so surprised, Brian, whatever storm is heading our way can't be worse than the storm of '41." Dr. Cammack's memories of the storm of '41 that knocked down all the powerlines were among his most cherished, and the older people in town brought that storm up often; Irene, who was herself pushing 66, mentioned to Clare once that her father seemed to remember things from forty years ago with greater clarity than what happened last week. "There's really no difference between his memory and mine," Irene had added, "it's just that he isn't as deceitful about forgetting as I am."

"I remember the storm of '41," Dr. Cammack said now, raising his hand up as if to emphasize the veracity of his statement. "Men froze to death in that blizzard. They were up in the hills, the fools, anybody who goes hunting in five feet of snow deserves to die, I say. But there was a woman and her three babies who froze to death back in the woods, too, in a log cabin, and the pity of it was the phones were down, so no one knew she was trapped. When someone finally found her, she was holding her babies and they were all frozen solid. I think another woman froze up on Steeple Ridge—women always freeze in blizzards, don't they?"

"Mrs. Rowe," Clare said; the hand that held the note was trembling so much she had to finally set the note back down on the coffee table.

"Yes, dear?"

"This message . . ."

"He seemed in very good spirits when he called."

When Irene Rowe noticed how badly shaken Clare seemed, she volunteered to fix dinner for her father and made Clare a cup of herb tea, suggesting she go lie down. "Or I could run you a hot bath, you'd like that, wouldn't you?"

"Oh, that's not necessary, really," Clare said, recovering somewhat. She lit a cigarette and began taking long drags on it as if she were inhaling pure oxygen.

"I insist. There's nothing in this world better on a cold

night like this than a steaming hot bubble bath," Irene said, and Dr. Cammack nodded in agreement.

When the bath was prepared, Clare heard a soft tapping at her bedroom door. "Bath's ready," Irene said.

Clare was just falling asleep on her bed when the woman's voice woke her. *It's some kind of Murphy's Law that you can only sleep when you don't want to, and only stay awake when you'd like to sleep.* "Thanks," she called out, groggily. The one-and-a-half Valiums she'd swallowed several minutes before were taking effect. She sat up and took her clothes off, letting her skirt remain where it fell next to the bed, tossing her blouse at the closet door. As she went out into the hall, only casually checking to see if Mrs. Rowe had gone back downstairs, she dropped her hose (gingerly stepping out of it), panties and brassiere in a snaky trail behind her. By the time she reached the bathroom she was completely naked, and the slight chill felt good on her skin.

The bathroom was steamed over, and it zapped her of all her energy and will as she walked through it. She tested the waters with her foot—boiling hot. Sat on the edge of the tub for a few minutes until she decided she would just have to lower herself in. Which she did, feeling awkward, like a lobster going into a bubbling pot.

But once she was in the water a tremendous sigh escaped her lips. She relaxed, resting her head against the porcelain back of the tub, while she turned the cold water dial on with her toes to bring down the temperature a bit. Then she turned it off and felt comfortably drowsy. She put her hands behind her head and shut her eyes for a moment—the tension headache she'd had when she read Warren's confusing phone message had vanished with the double whammy of Valium and hot bath.

And she dreamed, and knew she was dreaming. And dreaming, she remembered.

She was standing in the cellar of the Marlowe-Houston, again, Founders Day, 1986. Clare realized her own mouth was open in a silent scream, and she was frozen to the spot as she watched her younger sister, Lily, collapse to the floor. Warren was there, too, but he had taken on a canine aspect, he seemed to be growling at her, as if he were guarding Lily. Lily, clutching her stomach, still calling out, "You bastards," mixed with "My baby, oh, God, help me, my little baby," kicking her legs out, blood streaming from between her legs. Clare felt the wind being sucked out of her throat as she watched helplessly.

Lily began scratching at her stomach, which seemed to erupt as the head of the bloody child emerged from between her legs, tearing through the dress as if this baby were eating its way out of its mother. "God help me," Lily gasped, and then was lost in the pain that overtook her.

Clare tried to move, tried to change the course of things, but she did, in this dream, just what she'd done in real life: she stood still, trying to breathe, trying to make a move to help Lily. You were trained as a nurse, damn it, do some fucking thing. *The others were coming down the stairs from the kitchen: Georgia Stetson, Cappie Hartstone, Maud Dunwoody, Howie McCormick, Prescott Nagle, others that Clare could not identify. Someone shook Clare, she couldn't see who. Clare felt like it was her blood coming out of her own body, that she was watching her own death, the red milky fluid gushing down from between her legs, the squirming half-dead child, who, with his mother, Lily, would be dead in just a few seconds.*

In fact, it was all over in a few seconds, the screams, the pain, the blood that washed up against Clare's shoes.

*But in this dream (*I am dreaming, I am dreaming, I am dreaming*) those few seconds seemed to last for hours, the blood flowing from between Lily's legs, washing the dead child,* Malcolm was the name they'd picked if it was a boy and it was a boy, *down a river of blood, emptying into an old toilet in the cellar, washing Warren, who had been crouching near Lily, down against that shelf, into that toilet, and now the red tide was pushing against Clare, also. Clare resisted, but she was feeling weak, and now the townspeople gathered around her were trying to pry her from her spot and drown her in that blood that was washing down that drain, a drain that began to gurgle and spit and hiss just like a garbage disposal turned on. They were forcing her toward it, the whole town* *all the First Families of Pontefract, and the undertow from Lily's blood.*

Clare finally was able to scream when Lily's baby grabbed her around the ankles with his mitten hands, and licked at her with a wormy tongue. The baby was making sucking noises as he lapped up a trickle of blood that was sliding down Clare's leg.

Clare was screaming underwater, when someone reached in and brought her up for air. Her eyes stung, and she clawed at the air. She felt a washcloth being wiped across her face, around her eyes.

"Clare," Mrs. Rowe said, apparently as terrified as Clare. Clare was finally able to focus her eyes on the woman. She coughed water out of her mouth, sitting up in the tub.

"I'm—I'm all right, thank—" Clare managed to sputter, bringing her knees up to her chest and hugging them with her arms.

"I was afraid you'd fallen asleep, it's been nearly an hour." Irene dropped her gaze to the water in the tub, gasping, then turned away, embarrassed.

Clare looked down at the water, also, and there were droplets of red floating among the dissipating soap bubbles.

6.

Clare took the sheet off her bed that night and slept naked, wrapped in a ragged comforter. She tucked an old white T-shirt of Warren's up between her legs—she was classically out of Tampax, and too sleepy to run out to the Jump 'N' Save again. Clare believed, always futilely, that if she didn't stock up ahead of time on Tampax, maybe her period wouldn't arrive so soon after the last one. She felt like she'd just finished with her cycle a couple of weeks before. One thing she had always envied about pregnant women was the blessed ability to go nine months without a period.

Her lower back seemed rife with aches and sudden twinges. No amount of twisting and turning on the mattress lessened the frequent stabs of the cramps. At some point in the night, she'd managed to toss her two eiderdown pillows to the floor, and roll across her Ted E. Bear that had no eyes ("Just like you, Clare," her father had said when she'd plucked the round plastic pieces out of the bear's sockets, "you're our little blind Clare, you have no 'i' like other Clares. You're C-L-A-R-E, not C-L-A-I-R-E." And Clare crying, rubbing her eyes to make sure they really were there, not quite understanding what her father was saying, replied, "But Lily has an 'i.'" "Yes," her father said, "so the two of you have one eye between you.")

What the hell does it take to get away from all those damn insecurities of childhood?

Clare stared up at the canopy over her bed and when dawn came she did not think she'd gotten more than an hour of sleep. She was thinking about her nightmare in the bathtub, what it meant, if she had really spent the last year trying to kill herself: Valium, sleeping pills, thoughts while she was driving *(if I just spin the wheel around at this turn)*, the terrible, overwhelming longing for endless sleep. To-night in the tub.

"I don't want to die," she said to Ted E. Bear, as ragged a bed companion as any woman of 36 held onto—and still more faithful than most. She hugged it to her, feeling not much more grown up or less frightened than that little girl who had lived in the Marlowe-Houston House and plucked out this bear's eyes because she didn't want it to see what it could see. *The bear went over the mountain, the song went, to see what it could see.*

On Monday morning, January 5, 1987, Clare was sweat-soaked, and Warren's white T-shirt had a large brownish-red blotch where his neck would go. My scarlet letter, Clare thought as she threw the shirt into the wastebasket.

She called Warren's house again, with no answer.

Then Clare called George Connally, Sheriff of Pontefract, Virginia.

7.

From *The Nightmare Book of Cup Coffey:*

SATURDAY NIGHT/SUNDAY
JANUARY 3–4, 1987

Been doing the only thing I can do after Saturday's peculiar outing with Nagle.

Got drunk.

Well, Nagle threw me for a loop. Either the guy's cracked or something—I already know I'm cracked, so maybe I should just accept his theories about dead people. It feels pretty good to be drunk. This has been one hell of a weekend. We got a little girl who gives good seance, but who is now missing. We got some dead people running around making long-distance calls (who does AT&T bill to?). We got an empty field which isn't really empty—lots of Injun bones. We got a bunch of kids set on fire a couple of centuries back. We got this drunk guy named Cup Coffey who wonders if this is all going to be here tomorrow morning, or if he's going to wake up in front of his distorted-image TV set back in his lousy Washington apartment.

So everything goes on hold: last night, went out to Henchman Lounge and drank seven beers in quick succession, wanted to cry to the barmaid, but she had blue hair and gold teeth and I just couldn't bring myself to cry when I saw that. Pilfered some moonpies from Patsy's fridge when I got in. How I made it home I'll never know. Message from Nagle today, but I can't bring myself to call him. This is crazy. Beer for lunch. In and out of the bathroom while I'm writing this.

Tomorrow morning I guess I'll head back to D.C. Nothing keeping me here. Hope the hangover doesn't hit too hard.

8.

Monday morning, Cup awoke to Patsy's call: "It's quarter t nine, Mr. Coffey, rise and shine!" She went ahead an pushed his door open a crack. Her pie-shaped face wa covered with some kind of white cream. She kept her bab blue chenille robe closed tight with one hand and with th other, sprayed some kind of room deodorizer around Finally, all he saw of her was a disembodied hand and tha aerosol can spewing out its mist. The room suddenl smelled of lilacs. Cup began coughing. He fanned the ai when the spray ceased.

As Patsy padded down the hall, her fluffy slippers makin a piffle-piffle-piffle sound, she called back, "With the win dows closed all winter long the place starts to get a bit stale and a breath of spring is in order."

Cup's head ached, and he tasted the sour beer on hi tongue, mixed now with lilac spray. He sat up, looked at th clock, reached for the bottle of aspirin in his shaving kit b the bed. He tried opening the child-proof cap, but with n luck. He got up, set the aspirin bottle down on the floor grabbed the ashtray from the dresser and brought it dow hard on the plastic bottle, cracking it. Aspirin, much of i smashed, poured like sand out of the cracks. Cup grabbe the few whole ones and popped them in his mouth. H chewed them. They tasted about as good as the lilac an stale beer combo.

After he showered, he got started packing: he thre everything in the American Tourister suitcase. He sat on th lid to close it. He picked up the black notebook that la under his pillow.

No nightmares last night. He didn't think there'd ever b any again. He opened the book to its last page. He wrote i it:

Monday, January 5, 1987

Doesn't look like there's much else to put in this. Its whole purpose is used up. It was my link. My connection. But over and out. Goodbye to all that. Here's to no more nightmares. Damn the neuroses and full speed ahead!

He tossed the notebook into the trash, and then thought better of it. If Patsy decided to go snooping in the trash can she might get a rude shock. He laughed to himself. He picked the notebook up and set it on top of his suitcase.

After he called for the cab to take him to the bus station, Cup watched from the bedroom window for that taxi service's green station wagon. Patsy invited him to wait downstairs in the parlor, but he didn't really feel like listening to her chatter. He was through with this town. He was through with the bad memories. No more bullshit, no more grasping to some adolescent fantasy. Lily Cammack Whalen, the blond goddess of his dreams, was dead and buried. It was over. He had an overactive imagination. Someone had made a prank call. Dr. Nagle was about seventy. Old men always had theories. Old men worried about death. Old men wanted so badly to believe that the shadows that the fire cast were shadows of something. But Cup believed then, as he gazed out the window, almost fearlessly at the Marlowe-Houston House, that the shadows he had a glimpse of were shadows and nothing more.

Just a house, and just a field. Anything that happened there was gone, a canceled check. Just as he'd told his students once, that when spring follows winter, those are not the same leaves on the tree, not the same petals on the flower in bloom. *It is a different leaf, a different petal, and it is only our misinterpretation of natural phenomena that leads us to believe in the continuity of existence.* He'd certainly gotten enough angry parents on his back after sharing that little tidbit with the fifth grade.

Or, as Cup's successful Uncle Phil had told him on several occasions, "Life's a bitch and then you die."

A car did pull up in front of Campbell's Boarding House, but it was a black-and-white police car. A policeman got out of the car and disappeared from Cup's sight under the porch roof.

A few moments later, Patsy called up the stairs, "Oh, Mr. Coffey, you have a visitor!"

9.

"How do you do, Mr. Coffey, I'm George Connally, Sheriff here in Pontefract." The sheriff was a handsome man but with a scruffy look. Cup guessed he was probably in his early forties. He had thick hair the color of a golden retriever's, and a broad smile that was somewhat lessened by a tightness to his face and sad hazel eyes. Newly planted worries furrowed his brow.

"Hello," Cup said warily.

"There's been a kind of accident nearby, Mr. Coffey."

Patsy Campbell hovered like a spy satellite, watering potted plants around the windowsill, and George Connally suggested to Cup that it might be better if they took a little walk down East Campus Drive.

Walking out into the street, George turned to Cup and said bluntly, "A man died the other night, last night or the night before. Although we won't be sure until the county coroner takes a look. Mr. Coffey, there are some unusual circumstances surrounding this man's death. His name was Warren Whalen, and your name was mentioned in connection with him."

10.

Cup was down at the courthouse for three hours, mainly waiting, not really understanding the point of all the questions that the sheriff and a state detective were firing at him. After his interview with the detective named Firestone ("like the tire," the detective kept repeating, feeling that he had not exhausted the comparison completely by the fourth go-round), Cup walked out into the sheriff's main office. The young blond girl they called Bonnie offered him some coffee. Another woman was sitting near this girl's desk. He hadn't noticed her until just then, and she was quite striking—sitting there, her shoulders squared as if prepared for an onslaught, her eyes like dark almonds. She kept her coat on, even though the heat was turned up in the office. Her dark hair curled up against the back of her neck. It looked soft, fragrant. Pretty, rather vulnerable looking even with her defensive posture. But her eyes—intelligent and bright. Hiding something with their lids drawn halfway down.

"I'd rather you didn't stare," the woman said.

The voice caught Cup by surprise. He recognized it. "Do I know you?"

Bonnie, pouring coffee from a percolator into a styrofoam cup, chirped, "Mr. Coffey, this is Mrs. Terry."

At the mention of his name, Mrs. Terry stood up and said she needed to use the ladies' room. Bonnie directed her down the hall.

"That was Lily Cammack's sister, wasn't it?" Cup asked when the dark-haired woman had left.

Bonnie nodded and brought him the steaming cup. Bonnie was pretty, and Cup didn't think she was much over twenty. She had a way of sashaying toward him when she brought the coffee; it was refreshing to have a young pretty girl flirt with him. But then he saw the ring on her left hand. "You're married," he said, matter-of-factly.

Bonnie wrinkled her nose. "Isn't everybody?"

"I'm not."

Her eyes widened a bit. Bonnie Holroyd had what Cup would call alpine breasts, their peaks and slopes pushing against her fuzzy sweater. These were the advanced ski slopes. "You're cute. I heard you were from Washington." Bonnie sat on the edge of her desk, her skirt hiked up to expose her white thigh. She swung her legs back and forth like a little girl. "I've never even been to Richmond. Furthest west I've ever been is Covington. I'll bet it's pretty wild up in Washington."

"Like Rome in its last days."

"You have any weed?"

"Excuse me?"

"You know, weed, dope, grass." She winked.

"Sorry, not part of my diet. Anyway, that's illegal and you work for the sheriff."

"My husband works for the sheriff, and he is my connection. See, he whattayoucallsits, confiscates it from kids, you know, and then he brings it home and we party. You like to party?"

Lyle Holroyd walked into the office then, and Bonnie shut up immediately. Lyle looked sternly at Cup. "You trying to get a peek up my wife's dress, Mister?"

Cup was taken aback, but Lyle began laughing, as did Bonnie, who jumped girlishly from the desk and went back around it.

"This is your husband?" Cup asked.

Bonnie cracked a half-smile and muttered to Lyle, "Introduce yourself to the man, Godzilla."

But while Lyle Holroyd introduced himself, Cup's mind went back to Lily's sister, Clare. She had not come back from the bathroom a few minutes later when Sheriff Connally came back out of the room with the detective and told Cup he was free and clear. "Where'd Mrs. Terry go, Bonnie?" George asked the girl.

Bonnie shrugged. "Far as I know, George, she's still camping out in the john. You want me to go knock?"

"No, I'm sure she'll be back in a bit," George said, nodding to Cup.

As Cup went out the office door, Bonnie called out, "Goodbye, Mr. Washington-DeeCee."

Cup walked down the hallway to the restrooms.

He stood in front of the ladies' room, thinking of knocking on the door, and then decided it would be a dumb thing to do. What would he say to her, anyway? *Sorry about your sister, and sorry about your brother-in-law, and oh, yeah, did you by any chance call me up in Washington a couple of weeks ago and pretend you were your sister, because, lady, you sound just like her.*

Cup was just about to walk back down the hall and leave the courthouse, when the restroom door swung open. Clare Terry came out, stopping dead in her tracks when she saw him.

"You," she said flatly, as if he were a headache that had just come on, but not without some warning.

"We've never met," Cup said, extending his hand.

"Yes we have, Bonnie Holroyd introduced us." She stood in front of him, her back against the restroom door, her arms crossed. She squinted her dark eyes fiercely at Cup. He could tell that she had been crying in the bathroom—they were rimmed with pink, bloodshot, and the lids around them were puffy.

"I was a friend of your sister's."

She regarded him in such a way that he thought it best to shut up. She seemed to be staring through him. "My sister is dead. What are you doing here, Mr. Coffey?"

"I'm not sure."

"Well, I know all about you." Her lips were set thin and tight; his eyes were drawn to them as she spoke. He felt drained, defenseless. "And I want to tell you that I am on to you. Do you understand me? I am on to you. And I suggest you leave Pontefract as soon as possible with this—this disease you've brought with you—" Her speech became slow and clumsy. Her lips lost their firmness and began trembling. She turned away from him so that he could not see the tears in her eyes.

"Look, lady, if I have a disease, let me tell you, I caught it right here in this town. If you were half the woman your sister was—"

Before Cup could finish this last sentence, Clare Terry, her face red with anger, turned to face him again. She slapped him. The smacking sound echoed down the hall.

Cup's cheek stung, and Clare was crying. "I'm sorry, I'm sorry," he said. He raised his hands as much in defense against future slaps as in supplication.

Clare, wiping her eyes with a handkerchief, walked swiftly back down the hall to the sheriff's office.

11.

"You're what?" Prescott said when he opened the door to the Historical Society office.

Cup entered the room, rubbing his hands together, shivering from the cold outside. His face was a glowing pink, and his brown hair stuck out in feathery wings where the wind had blown it.

"I said looks like I'm stuck. Here in Pontefract. At least for a few more days. I was just down at the sheriff's office talking with some police detective from Roanoke or Richmond or someplace."

"I know," Prescott said, bringing a chair around from behind a long wooden table, "here, sit down. I've spoken with Sheriff Connally myself."

"I felt like they wanted me to confess to the Lindbergh kidnapping. So I told him about the phone message up in D.C. and most of the other stuff, the calls down to Dr. Cammack's and with Lily's husband. I've never been given the third degree like that before."

"Sounds like an unpleasant day."

"I'm exaggerating. I was treated pretty well—I got the impression that this detective didn't really suspect any foul play, and when I went out into the office I passed a woman who turned out to be Lily's sister, but she was introduced to me as Mrs. Terry. But she's Clare Cammack—I just didn't think that she might be married."

"Yes—well, divorced, I believe. Lived up in New York for a while."

"Well, she sounded just like Lily. Threw me for a loop. Didn't look much like her, but when I heard that voice . . . I kind of think she might have made that call to me in Washington. Oh, and she's a great slapper." Cup pointed to the dark bruise forming just beneath his right eye.

"I imagine so."

"Something funny is going on. I asked if it was okay to get the hell out of Dodge, and the sheriff asks me why, and then laughs and says something like 'Oh, yeah, who would want to hang around Pontefract in the dead of winter?' What happened with Whalen, anyway?"

"They didn't tell you?"

"Well, to be honest, I felt sort of weird asking, this sheriff was so on edge I didn't want to seem overly curious. I felt like the word *suspect* was already stamped on my forehead."

"You know, Cup, you're not stuck here at all. You can leave, and I think if you're smart you'll get on the next bus out of town."

"First you want me to stay and help you with some bizarre research, and now—you know, the sheriff was like that. Early in the day he suggested I stay until Wednesday, but when I left his office an hour ago I got the feeling he never wanted to see my face again—in a friendly way, like he was looking out for me. What gives?"

"I wish I had the answer to that. I was never terribly fond of Warren Whalen. Brian Cammack only hired him as Disciplinary Counselor because he didn't want his son-in-law to take his prize daughter elsewhere to live. He wasn't particularly good at the job, and he had the morals of an alley cat. But I wouldn't wish on my worst enemy the kind of death that man faced."

"Drop the other shoe, please. Nobody told me a thing."

"I spoke with George Connally this morning, just after he'd spoken with you at Patsy Campbell's—you mentioned my name, and he wanted to hear some good word about you. It didn't take him long to remember your name from twelve years ago, Cup. He was a deputy then. I reminded him that the Kinter death was just an accident, and he let slip that what happened to Warren Whalen was nothing that neat. Warren was found dead in the Marlowe-Houston's cellar. He had scratched himself to death, Cup."

12.

Warren's Tape

Sheriff George Connally sat at his desk and sucked on an ice cube while he listened to the cassette tape they'd found near Warren Whalen's body.

"... Take me to your leader, sweetheart. I didn't catch your name ..." Whalen said. "Cassie? Cassie what?" There was a sound on the tape like wind blowing, and George figured it was the material of whatever pocket Whalen had stuck the tape recorder into.

After a few seconds, there was the sound of a door creaking. "Weeelll, all this for me?" Whalen asked. "Your fearless leader, whoever he is, has certainly— Jesus, that smell, what the hell is that ... Yes, yes ... Oh, Christ! No, no, I just thought I saw something when you touched me ... How did you fit all these people down here? Who's the guest of honor ... Oh, yeah? This is one weird little surprise party, who put you up to this, anyway?"

Warren Whalen acted just as if someone was talking to him and he was listening for their responses and then continuing. His monologue seemed indecipherable. He kept up this one-sided conversation as he went down the stairs of the cellar, which acted as an echo chamber and his voice became booming. As he spoke, he described what sounded like a party gathering, people he didn't recognize for the most part. He introduced himself around, with no one responding.

George fast-forwarded the tape. There was something there he would come back to, but not yet.

Then he started the tape again. "Oh my God," Whalen said, "where am I? Who are you people—lord, Lily ... No, it can't be—Get it off me, get it the fuck off me, don't you touch me, don't—" His voice became frantic, pleading, then broke into a stop-start series of sobs and gasps. "Oh, God, my God, what is it, oh, God help me, Christ—" His voice erupted into a falsetto scream, and then the scratching sound began. His clothes being torn as if a wild animal were attacking him, the cassette recorder crashing to the floor, but still running. Still recording. The sounds of Whalen thrashing about, sounds gurgling up from his throat like something caught in a bear trap, and that constant scratching sound, echoing in that cellar where he lay dying. "Lily—no—no—get them off me—Jesus, it's inside me—fuck—oh, god-god-god-god-god—" until this last word, *god,* became just a series of hard *g*'s melting into each other.

George pushed the stop button on the tape recorder. He couldn't stand to listen to it anymore. Just imagining that poor man's body. The way he was found. His suit, which had once been white, now blood-red, ripped apart and in tatters. And beneath that suit, his skin torn off in strips like bacon, covered in blood from his neck down to his stomach, the fingers of his left hand still embedded in his ribs—even in his last moment, he was trying to pry more skin from his bones.

But what bothered George the most, what paralyzed him with fear, was located in the middle of the tape, when Whalen referred to somebody by name. Somebody George knew.

George had not mentioned this to the detective, Hank Firestone, nor to Lyle when they first listened to the tape. The reference hadn't clicked with Lyle, and George was wondering if maybe there was nothing to click. If this was not just a crazy man gibbering to himself before taking his own life.

George rewound the tape back to that middle section, when Whalen was introducing himself to his mute acquaintances.

"Say," Whalen was saying, "don't I know you from some place?" Then he paused, listening. "What kind of message?" A pause. "How sweet," he said, into the condenser mike, "a message of love. Gad, I feel like a DJ. And here's a message of love going out to whom it may concern, from Frank and Louise, who are doing this because of love . . . Any other messages from you folks?"

George turned off the tape recorder. He covered his face with his hands, rubbing the skin as if doing so would change things, would obliterate his memory of nearly eight winters back. A memory that continued to haunt him.

But George remembered without wanting to.

Frank and Louise Gaston, who had been like second parents to him, who had funded his education at the University of Virginia, had loaned him money for the house when he and Rita were newlyweds; Frank and Louise lying dead in the old hunting cabin in the woods near the west side of the lake. Frank had shot Louise and then himself. A couple in their late seventies, with their brains blown out. And some time after killing his wife, before putting the gun to his own head, Frank had written on the wall in blood: LOVE DID THIS.

To whom it may concern, George thought angrily, *that concerns me.*

George Connally pounded his metal desk with his fist.

At last, the sadness he had been holding onto like a precious stone came out. He began crying softly.

13.

Prescott's Tape

"I want you to hear this, Cup—it won't convince you of anything, but it certainly will open your eyes, I think," Prescott said, setting up the reel-to-reel in the claustrophobic cubicle at the Historical Society. As he threaded the tape through the player he explained: "The girl's mother gave me permission—I suppose she thought since I have a Ph.D. that somehow this was scientific research. I watched Teddy Amory go into one of her seizures—an unpleasant experience, which I might compare to witnessing a rape and being unable to make a move to stop it. And the guilt, Cup, afterwards, of knowing you should've stopped it. But I was fascinated by it. This girl seemed authentic. She went into . . . ecstasy. Ecstasy, Cup, a little girl. Her dull empty face took on a new aspect. It was like watching someone literally come alive. From a shy, quiet little girl to this—radiant and terrified creature—completely out-of-control . . . but listen."

He pressed the button, and the wheels began turning.

Cup closed his eyes and listened.

He heard a gasping, choking sound, and a noise like a bird's wings fanning the air. "It's coming over her," Prescott said, but then settled back in his desk chair and lit his pipe.

The tape played with no further interruptions.

Prescott: Who are you?

Teddy: You know.

Prescott: No, I don't—I—

(The girl made some more choking noises, as if she were trying to keep food down. When she spoke again, her voice was lighter, but with a mature resonance.)

Teddy: Scotty—

Prescott: Oh, my, God . . .

Teddy: It's so cold here, Scotty, so cold. I'm freezing, why aren't you here with me? Scotty, it's so cold—this is the coldest night—and the horses, Scotty, the horses . . .

Prescott: Cass? Cassie?

Teddy: Oh, Scotty, you do still love me, don't you? Am I still first in your heart?

Prescott: Cassie, I—

Teddy: We'll be together soon, Scotty, he says we will. He says that we'll all go riding, all three of us, you, me and—

Prescott: Stop it, Jesus, stop this, whoever you are—this is not—

Teddy: Scotty, you've upset the balance . . .

Prescott: How have I upset the balance?

Teddy: Lady Day, Lady Day.

Prescott: Who am I speaking with? Who the hell are you?

Teddy: Why don't you just come by for a visit, Scotty, you seem to know where we are . . .

(The voice changed, and Cup gasped as he recognized Lily's voice.)

. . . You've found the door, Dr. Nagle, but now you need a key, don't you? You're on the edge of a great mystery, the adventure to end all adventures. Well, very soon it will be the Last of the First. All of us, bound by blood and love. The sins of our fathers. And dreams, Dr. Nagle, don't forget dreams. I have a friend who is even now disturbed by his dreams, what they show him. But we'll be calling him back this winter, rest assured, to show him that dreams sometimes really do come true. You remember my friend Cup Coffey?

Cup opened his eyes as Prescott reached over and shut the tape player off. Cup looked over at the older man, confused.

Prescott was blinking his eyes, and turned his face away from Cup. "There are some things I want you to look over. My own research on this matter. You see, you are involved in this—I don't understand how or why. But I absolutely believe that there is something supernatural occurring here in Pontefract. Something more dangerous than I at first imagined. Now that Warren Whalen is dead."

CHAPTER TWELVE

THE DEAR DEPARTED

1.

From *The Nightmare Book of Cup Coffey:*

MONDAY, JANUARY 5, 1987

Everything—too bizarre for words. I can't even begin to describe . . . I don't know what I believe and what I don't. It's like everything rational I've ever had drummed into my head has just flown out the window. I didn't even think I'd be picking this book up again to write in it. But here I am. The nightmares don't end just 'cause you want 'em to.

Prescott and I (since we are on a first-name basis now) sat around his office at the Historical Society, each of us trying to put together pieces of this puzzle in our own very different ways. Everytime he mentioned the field he calls the goat dance, as if that name has a particular significance, I kept thinking "bullshit, bullshit." I tried to convince him that maybe this sister of Lily's had made that phone call to me, and even murdered her husband. But I couldn't convince him because, to be honest, I couldn't even convince myself.

My feelings on Clare Terry: she struck me (pardon the pun) as someone who is so afraid of something that she is willing to punish herself rather than face that fear. A lot like me. I knew when I met her that I only wanted to believe that she'd made that phone call up to D.C. and pretended she was Lily. Had she also rigged my run-in with Billy Bates? I am sure—yes, now I know it was Bart Kinter there in the darkness, somehow pulling the strings, not Billy Bates' strings, but mine, pushing me over the edge? Clare Terry is a bystander, like myself. But not innocent—no. I know that look. Guilty bystander. And that something that I saw in her mysterious, brooding eyes was a vulnerable guilt, like putty just waiting for someone to make their imprint on it. I see it in my own eyes when I look in the mirror sometimes. It's the quality that makes both of us, her and me, ideal victims. We believe in our own badness. Just as Billy Bates believed in his badness. It is reinforced by everything around us.

This could be bullshit, too—I mean, I only really got one good look at Clare, and maybe I saw too much of my own reflection in those eyes. I do that a lot—sometimes I think my ego knows no bounds.

Meanwhile, back at the ranch . . . Listened to tape of Teddy Amory "seance," in which Prescott is fairly sure he spoke with his late wife, Cassie. Then Lily's voice. Prescott showed me the copied pages from this diary he had. Looked like a crazy man's handwriting, this guy Worthy Houston, and he basically wrote what Prescott had said. About the ghosts of these kids coming back, the ones that were bumped off in a fire back in the 1750s. I didn't believe a word of it, but it did give me a strong case of the shivers. In one part of it, Worthy's father, Stephen, kept digging up these bones and burying them in different places, all around the field, and it was pretty gruesome the way the charred bones of these kids were described in loving, almost lascivious detail by Worthy. Eventually, Stephen Houston buried the "infested remains" beneath the Marlowe-Houston House itself. The coup de grace comes in this diary when Stephen takes one of the ribcages, if you can imagine this, and without my being excessively morbid, has spare ribs one evening. Well, actually, he grinds some of the bones up and then eats the powder. He died that night—Worthy describes his father rolling around on the ground, scratching at himself as if he were covered with ants.

"An unusual death," Prescott said, "but not that much different than the one this past weekend."

It got late, so Prescott brought out what I guess he considers further proof, and we copied some of them right there in the office so that I could spend time alone reading them. Newspaper clippings from the local paper.

More about Teddy Amory, a nine-year-old who was crowned with such epithets as: THE LITTLE GIRL WHO CAME BACK FROM THE DEAD, TELEPHONE TO THE SPIRITS? and THE VOICE OF THE BEYOND.

I've only skimmed the articles, but I know now that I'll be up all night reading them.

Because, as they say in that old time religion, I have seen the light. I am converted. I am a believer.

And Jesus, I am scared to death.

I collect all this stuff from Prescott tonight, all these clippings and this diary; he sticks it in an old beat-up accordion file folder, and ties it neatly with a string. He says to me, "You think it's a load of horse manure, I know, but just read this, and let's talk some more tomorrow." Then he offers me a ride back to Patsy Campbell's, and I politely refuse. I tell him I need a long walk in the cold air. I feel like I've been spun around in circles with a blindfold on.

When I walk outside it's snowing. Like a kid, I catch a few flakes on my tongue. Now, up in Washington you can't do this anymore because the snow is gray before it even touches the ground. But in Pontefract, the air is still clean, and the snow when it falls is still white and pure. It has been a long day; I don't know the time as I walk down Main Street, but I figure it's somewhere around eight or nine o'clock. I've been in one stuffy office after another, with only one meal between, a greasy burger and fries at the Columns (which still has this huge portrait of Jefferson Davis up over the bar and I ask the owner if the Confederates won the war, and she looks at me funny like it's no joke). So, anyway, it's nice to get out in the open air.

The wind picks up, and I raise the hood of my jacket. I pass a few people heading up the street. Some are parking their cars. The streetlamps have a soft, warm glow. Pontefract looks a lot like one of those towns in the glass ball filled with water, and someone has just shaken it so that the snow falls. Peaceful, quiet snow. Everything seems so normal, so in order. I am even looking forward to reading all this fiction that Prescott has handed me.

I take Lakeview Drive down to the footbridge. Patsy Campbell informed me over the weekend that this is the longest unsuspended footbridge in the world. I didn't believe her, but now as I start across it in the dark, it appears to be miles long. The lake is a black bottomless pit below me as I walk. I start thinking about what I am going to do next: getting back to D.C., asking Uncle Phil for another loan, retyping my resumé. Getting into some major psychotherapy . . .

As I am walking, about the halfway point, I hear footsteps behind me. I stop, figuring they might just be the echoes of my own footsteps. But I still hear them. Getting closer. I clutch the folder with the diary and clipping copies, and start to walk faster. The whole day has been pretty spooky, and who doesn't worry when they hear someone following them? The footsteps are also coming faster. This is classic fear escalation at work. My heart's beating a hundred miles a minute, and so to prove to myself that it's just some kid behind me, or a lady out walking her dog, I turn around.

And see nothing.

This is worse than anything my brain could cook up. Because even while I'm looking behind me on the shadowy bridge, with dappled illumination from the sky and the streetlights on both shores, I can still hear the footsteps coming closer and closer and closer, now almost on tip-toe.

Then I know.

Whoever has been walking just behind me is standing directly beneath me now. Under the bridge. Walking on the ice.

I hear his breathing.

I don't know why I do it, but I try to look down between the slats to see whoever is down there.

And then something that looks like a crab shoots out from beneath the bridge and attaches itself to my ankle. It is a hand. And attached to that hand, a wrist. And, I suppose, an arm, and then a body. I don't have to see the body to know whose it is. Not when he starts speaking. "I fuck her every night, Coffeybutt." Bart Kinter's nasal Southern twang is like a razor slicing metal. His grip is as cold as ice. "We do it down in the cellar doggystyle. She loves it. Your friend Lily's got the whitest ass I've ever seen."

I can't move. I feel like a thousand volts of electricity are going through me, and I am manacled, unable to resist. I can't even adequately describe the feeling of helplessness, of hopelessness. Of imminent death.

Then he pulls on my ankle. He is trying to bring me down there with him, trying to drag me under the bridge. My knees buckle, and I fall onto the wood. His hand, at first cold, now is burning into my skin—flesh feels like it's bubbling and blistering where he is touching it. "I've been waiting a long time for this," he hisses, "I've got something for you, something I know you're gonna want, asswipe."

The whole time I'm screaming, "Jesus Christ! Somebody help me!"

To keep myself from going over the edge of the bridge, I grab onto one of the siderails with both hands. It feels like my arms are going to burst, but I grip the rails and pull with all my might, trying to get further away, so that he will have to let go. I hear a stretching sound, and I think it's my leg about to tear apart at the ankle. My breathing is rapid, and I just want this to end, I just want it to end, I'll die but I'll die up here on top of the bridge, I don't need to see what's beneath it. With every ounce of strength I pull myself forward, away from that hand.

I hear a rending sound, like an elastic band about to snap, and it does. The wet pop. I expect to feel a searing pain down at my ankle. But there is none. I look back, and there is his hand, lying on the boards beside me. Torn off at the wrist. Fingers still wriggling. Then the hand crawls on its fingers and drops down between the slats. I hear him laughing beneath the bridge, laughing, and saying: "It's you, Coffeybreath, I'm in your blood." Then the sound of his running away. At the far end of the bridge, on the side of the town, I see the sillhouette of a figure scrambling from under the bridge and running across the ice, up on shore. Back into the shadows along the street.

I pick the folder up and make it back to Patsy Campbell's half-running, half-limping, trying to convince myself that a) I am crazy, b) it never happened, and c) I died and this is Hell.

I'm still hoping one of these is true.

Called Prescott as soon as I got in. All I could bring myself to say was, sort of a guess what? I've seen a ghost, with a few nervous chuckles thrown in for good measure in case he was about to tell me that it was all a practical joke, and he'd hired an impressionist to do Lily Cammack and Bart Kinter, and that hand, oh, yeah, Cup, that hand was rubber and had a little battery in it to keep the fingers wiggling around.

But all he said was, "Are you all right?"

I told him I was in one piece, if that's what he meant.

"I can come get you, you could stay in my spare room for the night," he said.

"Oh, this place is okay for tonight," I lied. For some strange reason I felt breezy—why is that? Why, when something reaches out and grabs you, as Bart Kinter has tonight, when fear incarnate does its song-and-dance routine, do you suddenly feel free? I felt as if I had been living under the misconception that the past cannot catch up with you. And now I knew the truth: it can and does. Somehow Bart Kinter had found me in an elementary school, and brought me back to the place where my nightmares began. Lily, too, was somehow involved. And knowing this kind of thinking isn't just crazy, but crazier than crazy. Crazy is murdering people on the advice of your pet dog; crazy is going apeshit for Jodie Foster and trying to bump off the President to prove it; crazy is walking into a McDonald's and gunning down people while they're scarfing Big Macs.

Those things are crazy because you can't understand them.

Now ghosts, ghosts is just plain folks.

But ghosts have something that separates them from the rest of us. They have a reason; we don't. Ghosts want something when they come back. They want something very, very badly.

Well, I'm writing this and it's getting late. I have a lot of reading to do before morning. Prescott said he'd be by to pick me up in the A.M. and after breakfast we'd go find out about the infamous missing pages from Worthy Houston's Diary. I don't know if I believe all this stuff Dr. Nagle is onto, but after tonight I am . . . open to the experience.

I laughed when I locked my windows and pushed a chair up against my door. How do you keep the dead out? If they want you, they'll find a way.

2.

From *The Westbridge County* (Va.) *Sentinel,* September 12, 1986:

TELEPHONE TO THE SPIRITS?

> PONTEFRACT—Table-rapping is passe, Ouija boards are out, the rage in Pontefract this year is a nine-year-old girl named Teddy Amory who has developed a reputation for herself as a medium. And her only prop is a sofa so she can lie down comfortably during the proceedings. "I don't know what happens," Teddy told this reporter. "It just comes over me. It's like someone's making a phone call through me." Her mother, Odessa, tells us, "My daughter is a natural medium. It is a gift, like speaking in tongues, and comes direct from the Holy Spirit."
>
> Thelma Kidd traveled all the way from Lookout Mountain, Ga., to have an audience with Teddy Amory. "My sister over in Covington wrote me about how this girl was the genuine article. I am a firm believer that the spirits are all around us, even now, as we speak." And what was Thelma's verdict about her visit with Teddy? "She is a doorway from the other side to this. When my grandfather Marshall spoke through

her, there was no doubt in my mind. She is blessed, that girl."

Cappie Hartstone, married to William Hartstone, the President of Westbridge Savings and Loan, said of her own experience with the half-pint psychic: "It was just like when I read Shirley MacLaine's book. Past lives and a New Age. Teddy Amory spoke directly to me, I felt 'connected.' Isn't it wonderful to be living in America where these things seem to be happening?"

The Edgar Cayce Foundation has yet to give Teddy Amory their seal of approval. Nor have a half a dozen other such institutions for exploration into so-called "paranormal" activities. In spite of queries sent to the Amory household, Odessa Amory, who was recently widowed, prefers not to subject her daughter to any kind of testing.

In spite of numerous seances in which several of the dear-departed have been summoned, there still remain those who are skeptical. According to Dr. Walter Scott from Westbridge Medical Center, Mrs. Amory "should be seeking proper medical treatment for her daughter rather than turning her into a side-show. She has a form of epilepsy the like of which I have never before witnessed or read of in any medical journal."

To which Odessa Amory replies, on her daughter's behalf, "If the Lord Jesus came down from heaven and went to Dr. Scott, the doctor would take one look at Him and ask Him if someone was treating those wounds. That is the extent of his understanding of things that are not of this earth."

Beside this article was a photograph of the mother and daughter. Teddy, plain, her face blank, no emotion showing. Her hair pouring wildly down her shoulders as if in conflict with this blankness. Small, deepset eyes like two buttons pushed into the fabric of her skin. Dressed in a smock that looked as if it should be worn by a girl four years younger. Her hand was clutching part of her mother's sweater. Odessa Amory, obviously enjoying this minor-league celebrity, smiling, her hair cut short and held back with a plastic hairband, again a little girlish touch as if the mother wanted to keep herself and her daughter within the age range from four to twelve.

From *The Richmond Times-Dispatch,* October 31, 1986:

THINGS THAT GO
BUMP IN THE NIGHT

PONTEFRACT, VA.—For a surefire case of the heebie-jeebies this Hallowe'en, the place to be is a picturesque town in the Shenandoah Valley called Pontefract. Hardly a ghost town, Pontefract is best known for the Pontefract Preparatory School, one of this state's premier private institutions, a rival for such schools as Christchurch and St. Christopher's. But in the near future, Pontefract may best be known as the place where the spiritualism craze is reborn. All because of a nine-year-old girl named Theodora Amory.

Teddy, as she is called by just about everyone in this town, with a population of 3000, is just your ordinary kid most of the time. She likes to watch *Moonlighting* and says she wants to be just like Maddie Hayes when she grows up. Her favorite singer is Madonna, although her mother won't let her buy any of her records. And she absolutely hates piano lessons.

One other thing. She is a medium on the side, and will call up your great-grandmother who died last year or your uncle who kicked off and didn't put you in his will. While other children her age will be attending parties, bobbing for apples and counting up trick-or-treat candy, Teddy will be summoning spirits in the family's living room.

Tonight, from 7 p.m. to midnight, she will be "in session," as her mother, Odessa Amory, told the Times-Dispatch. The fee is Teddy's standard $20 a head, reservations required. Groups of more than three at a time are discouraged. Although Teddy was taking her afternoon nap and unavailable for comment at press-time, her mother told us that "the spirits should be out in force tonight. As the winter comes on, they seem to grow stronger."

From *The Westbridge County* (Va.) *Sentinel,* December 3, 1986:

> PONTEFRACT—Teddy Amory, 9, known locally as the little girl who came back from the dead because of a near-drowning episode a few years ago, has been reported missing along with her brother, Jake, 16, after a fire destroyed their house located in the western section of Pontefract, Virginia. If anyone has any knowledge of the whereabouts of either brother or sister, they are requested to contact the Pontefract Sheriff's Office immediately.

Accompanying this brief article were two school photographs. One of Teddy Amory, again with that blank expression, as if anything that might vaguely be termed personality had been washed out of her, and those shiny button eyes. Her brother looked sinister, glaring into the camera, his hair greased back, his lips thick and pouty, the requisite teenage acne sprouting across his face. He looked like trouble.

3.

Excerpts from Worthy Houston's Diary, 1801–1802:

> —Since Mother's death, we only see our father at twilight when he leaves his bed and comes to supper. His eyes are like glowing embers, he gnashes his teeth like a madman. He has left his field to grow wild, and will not suffer any one of the slaves to till the soil. He tears at his hair at sunset, and smites his breast. He will not stand much human intercourse, and as the dark comes, Father goes down to the root cellar to dig. My sister has confided her fears to me. Virginia is afraid that he is digging his own grave—

—Our neighbor has brought our father in this morning, early before cock's crow, waking my sister and disturbing both of us greatly. He found Father in the field, the old goat dance, on all fours like a beast, eating the grass and digging in the clay. We are afraid now that our father's madness will be known to the community—

—"Spirits of the dark earth," he tells me, "they will not leave until they are given their due." Giles, Olivia, Andrew, Thomas, Matthew, Anne, Nathaniel—the children of that madman Nathaniel Carson, who brought so much sorrow to Pontefract, the innocents slain by our grandfather and the other townfolk. Father believes that they call for him at night, calling for us all. He believes that they have become one single demon upon their deaths, he calls this spirit the Goatman, and he is afraid this Goatman will come for his immortal soul—

—He has at last shown me the treasure which he buries deep each fortnight. The infested remains of the children. Our house is become unclean with those bones and our father's madness. I have entreated him to turn his eyes to God, and away from this heathen obsession. To repent him of his sins. Like a devil he laughs and tells me God has forsaken him and all his seed . . . He bids me touch the bones . . . The bones sing, and their song wreaks discord upon the mind, and the children of the bones bind my fingers to them and bid me: behold, your soul is damned—

—We have heard the sounds in the night. As if the pit of Hell lies directly beneath our house, and its legion of damned spirits clamber the labyrinthine tunnels Father has carved throughout this earth—

—Oh, God, would that these children were never so basely murdered by the hands of our forefathers. The stain of that sin finds no absolution. Our father speaks truthfully of demons, but the demons in our town of Pontefract have been within the cages of our own mortal souls, and we have loosed the door. The evil we have sown is risen. And though, after my skin, worms destroy my body, yet in my flesh shall I see God—

—They have taken Virginia. Oh, dear Lord, deliver us from evil, from evil . . . yea, though I walk through the shadow . . . the shadow . . . of the valley of the valley, death, death, death . . . Virginia—

—I will find her, I will not allow their corruption to invade my sister further. If this be the Indian Devil, or the spirit seeking righteous revenge, I will bring her back from perdition, I will save her from this infestation, Oh, Lord, make my flesh strong, turn not thy divine mercy from me—

4.

The nightmares came riding in that night, Monday, January 5, 1987, to Pontefract.

Members of the Altar Guild are dreaming:

Georgia Stetson, popularly known as the Rona Barrett of Pontefract, had been on the phone all evening with Patsy Campbell discussing Warren Whalen's death and Patsy's new boarder. "Of course I'm upset," Georgia said, but the glee was apparent in her voice. Her husband Ken, lying next to her in bed, glanced up from his *Wall Street Journal* and raised his eyebrows doubtfully at her. She wrinkled her nose at him. The phone cord was stretched across him, and he tugged at it playfully. Georgia continued, "I counted Mr. Whalen as one of my friends—remember the time he brought the college catalogs over for Ricky to look at? And Ricky being in public school, too . . . Yes, I should say, Patsy, I should say . . ."

Ken groaned and folded his paper down. He caught his wife's attention again and pointed to his watch; it was 11 P.M. She swatted at him as if he were a fly. He took the telephone out of her hands ("Oh, you!" she exclaimed), and said into the mouthpiece, "I'm sorry, Patsy, but Georgia is signing off now." And then he hung up the phone.

Georgia clucked her tongue against the roof of her mouth. "You're so rude, Kenny. Do you know that George Connally himself came to get the man staying at Patsy's?"

"No, but if you hum a few bars . . ." Ken reached up and turned off the lamp.

"Very funny. But it's got me thinking. Here this man comes to town and another man gets killed. Mr. Whalen."

"Are you going to play Miss Marple again like you did when that white trash Amory family burned up?"

"Now, you know they never found those children. They could be right here in town somewhere, right under our noses."

"Maybe they're the ones who killed the teacher."

"Very funny, Ken. But I'll have you know Warren Whalen died in a very mysterious way. I heard from Bonnie Holroyd that he had scratched himself, clean into his skin and bones. Over at the Marlowe-Houston House. A one-man bloodbath, she called it. They found slivers of his own flesh between his fingernails . . . did you hear that?"

"What?"

"I thought I heard something at the door . . . Ken, go see what's out there?"

Ken turned the lamp back on, sighing. "It was probably just the wind. You're scaring yourself with your own damn gossip." But Ken got out of bed and stomped over to the door. When he opened it, he laughed.

"Well, what is it?" his wife asked.

"Just Ricky, who at this very moment is tiptoeing down the stairs so I won't know it's him. Hey, son, just go on to bed, will you?"

From downstairs came a muffled, "Okay."

When Ken returned to bed and the lamp was out, Georgia began repeating a name aloud. "Coffey, Coffey, Coffey . . ."

Ken poked her. "Can't a man get to sleep in his own bed?"

"It's the man staying with Patsy. I know that name from somewhere, Ken, and I am not sleeping until I remember."

"The name will still be there in the morning."

Georgia ignored him, but brought her chanting down to a whisper, "Coffey, Coffey, Coffey . . ."

But she did fall asleep, and dreamed. In her dream, her father, Virgil McDonald, who had been dead sixteen years, was dressed in his Sunday best, covered from head to foot with dirt as if he'd just dug himself out of his own grave. "Daddy, I miss you," she said. Her father, his white hair scraggly and down to his shoulders, his fingernails yellow, long and twisted, reached out to hold her, and she went to him.

In the dream, Virgil tore into his daughter, Georgia, and his fingers were like straight razors slashing her.

She awoke screaming, her hands clawing at the thing in the dark that was holding her.

"For God sake!" her husband shouted; she calmed down. He switched the lamp on and she saw she was back in her bedroom. Ken was holding her arms firmly in his hands. There were gouges along his arm, tiny bloodmarks where she'd scratched him with her own fingernails.

Georgia looked at Ken and said meekly, "I did that?"

Cappie Hartstone recruited her husband, Bill, and the children, Heather, Jennifer and Jason, to help her with a church mailing. She was keeping the kids up late, until nearly midnight, but they were in their last week of Christmas vacation, so she didn't see any harm in it. They would just sleep late into the morning. Only Bill grumbled about helping out. "You do more things for that damn Altar Guild . . ." he complained.

But Cappie, who had been head cheerleader of Newton High, class of '66, got everyone organized as usual. Heather was in charge of the stamps, while Jason and Jennifer wetted the envelopes and stuffed them. "Daddy here is going to do the honors," Cappie said, and handed the letters to Bill for folding.

"What the hell do I do with these?" he muttered.

"Well, honey, you just fold them over. No, dear, not like

that, like this." She turned one of the letters over and creased it in two places. "See, it's plain and simple. I'm sure you can handle it."

"I don't see why I have to sit down at this table and do this ragpicker bullshit when I have to get up in six hours and put in a full day."

Cappie riffled through the box of envelopes. "Heather-Jason-Jennifer, you don't remember any of these words your daddy's saying, hear?"

"Hey, Mommy," Jennifer said, "Jason's getting jelly all over everything."

"Am not, for crying out loud!" Jason whined, and licked his fingers.

"If you don't watch out," Jennifer said to her brother, "the psycho's gonna get you!"

"Enough of that kind of talk," Cappie said, clapping her hands in punctuation.

Bill pushed his chair back and stood up. He slapped an envelope down on the table. "That's it, I'm through with this bullshit, I'm going to bed."

Cappie pointed both index fingers at Bill as if she were laying a curse on him. "You promised me you'd help, William."

"Yeah, well, I seem to remember a promise you made to me a few years back about honoring and obeying. And I say, it's time for bed!" He raised his hand as if to slap her, but stopped himself.

Cappie knew why he had taken control of himself. It wasn't because the kids were there. The kids were used to seeing Bill hit her when he thought she was getting out of line. No. The reason he did not go ahead and take a swing at her was because of the look in her eyes just then. They flashed like lightning at him. In that moment she knew she hated her husband with all her heart and all her soul.

Cappie Hartstone wrote in her Day Runner before she went up to bed an hour after Bill had:

No more. That's it. He has hurt and humiliated me for the last time. He just had to cause some kind of scene tonight to show who's boss. I know it is un-Christian of me to hate him, but I do.

Did forty leg-lifts tonight.

Finish Guild mailing in the a.m.

Call all Altar Guild members for contributions.

No more chocolate chip cookies, and this time I mean it.

An additional note, scrawled in a corner of the page:

Fuck you, William Hartstone!

Cappie's nightmare that night concerned her uncle, Arthur Abbott, whom they had just held services for the past weekend. It did not immediately seem unusual to see him: Cappie had been dreaming about him since his death the previous week, as if he hadn't died. They were standing in the upstairs hall of her house. She went toward him, and stood very close because she knew how hard-of-hearing her uncle was.

"You've always been such a handsome gentleman," Cappie told him in this dream. And he was: dressed in a shiny black dinner jacket, his sparse gray hair neatly combed back across his forehead to disguise his bald spot. Uncle Arthur smiled pleasantly. "They said I died peacefully in my sleep, Cappie. But don't you believe them. I was in pain, my dear, excruciating pain, they vivisected me in that hospital."

Cappie shook her head, unbelieving. "No, Uncle Arthur, in your sleep."

"They put me in a vise, my dear, and they sliced me up like some animal for study." As if to prove it to her, Arthur Abbott unbuttoned his dinner jacket, pulled several of the brass studs out of the pressed white shirt, and tore the shirt open. Long scars crisscrossed his chest and stomach. "Touch them," he said.

Without really wanting to, Cappie reached over and laid both hands against his chest, feeling the moist furrows of the cuts. Arthur brought his hands over hers. His hands felt clammy, and she tried to pull away, but he was strong. And then, his hands crushing hers, he pulled his own skin from his chest and ribcage, plunging her trembling fingers into the steamy, viscous cavity where his sternum had been cut away.

Rita Connally, realizing that her husband George was putting in yet another late night down at the courthouse, went to bed before eleven. Just herself in that king-size bed. The wind rattled through the eaves of the house, which made her nervous, so she lay awake in the dark for a long time before she dropped off to sleep.

George had been home for dinner, briefly, barely putting in a performance, and then all they did was argue about everything. She had gone to the trouble of following Julia Child's recipe for steak au poivre, with a garden salad, stuffed mushroom caps and a bottle of Pouilly-Fumé, harboring the thin hope that after a good dinner and a few glasses of wine, George would be too full and sleepy to return to his office. But he barely touched his plate, and would not have a single glass of the white wine.

"I've got too much to deal with," he said, pushing himself away from the dining room table. Rita had set up the long red candles she had purchased on her recent trip to Williamsburg, and in the flickering candlelight, the lines on George's face were like intersecting canals. He looked like he had aged ten years in just one afternoon.

As he stood up, George pushed his chair back into the table. Noticing his wife's disappointed expression, he went over to where she sat, chin in her hands, elbows on the edge of the mahogany table; George leaned over, and wrapped his arms around Rita from behind. He pressed his face into her neck and kissed her. "There's just so much to figure out," he told her.

"I thought you said some detective was taking care of that." She pulled away from him, and he also pulled back. Like boxers going to their separate corners of the ring, George went to the kitchen doorway, while Rita went into the veiled shadows of the living room, sat down, lit a cigarette.

"There's something more to this case than I think Firestone is aware of," George said. "I don't quite get it myself."

"Well, you don't really have to worry about it anyway, do you, George?" Rita lashed out unexpectedly. "Leave it to the state police if you think it's something bigger than suicide, it's what they're trained for. Let them figure it out."

"But I'm sheriff, honey, don't you understand—"

"What I understand is what everyone else in this town understands, George, but what you don't seem to get. When Cal Holroyd was sheriff, he understood. It's just you. You're the one who doesn't understand, George!" And then she said it, what was on her mind, had been on her mind for the past year, something that might never have come up had Warren Whalen not been found dead in the Marlowe-Houston House. "You're just a small-town cop, George, with a fat title. You don't have to let every damn thing that happens here get under your skin."

"Rita. We're both upset, and I have to go back to work. We'll talk this out tomorrow morning."

"You know what they say, George, tomorrow and tomorrow and tomorrow. I talked to Lyle about your obsession," she said that word as if she were biting into it, "with the Gaston case, how you aren't sleeping nights, though God knows, maybe you're finding someone else you can sleep with—"

"Damn it, Rita, but that tongue of yours is going to get you in trouble some day!"

"Can't you just leave it alone, George? Can't you let the pros handle this—if there's anything to handle? Can't you just do your job, come home, and be a husband, for one damn night, just one damn night?" She wanted him to come to her, hug her, smother her with kisses, promise to make everything better. But George turned and went out through the kitchen. The back door slammed shut. Rita left the plates on the dining room table. She blew out the candles. She found a half-empty bag of Doritos in the pantry and finished it off.

Lying in bed, listening to the wind outside, she only regretted having eaten all those tortilla chips. She was happy that she'd finally spoken her mind. He'd be mad for a while, he might even pout, but what she had said might finally sink in. George had been appointed sheriff because he was Mr. Nice Guy, and all anyone expected him to do was to keep the drunks off the street, enforce the speed limit and keep the barroom brawls to a minimum. He didn't have to be the blue knight who concerned himself with everybody else and their problems—everyone except his own wife.

In her dreams that night, Rita Connally was sitting up in bed. She heard a loud rattling that was distinct from the wind under the eaves, and she put her robe on and went over to the window. Snow covered the ground, and standing under the patio light was a woman in a dark woolen coat and a smart '40s-style pillbox hat with a veil covering her face. Rita wondered if this might not be one of the Altar Guild ladies, one of the elderly members. The woman just stood there on the patio, her face turned upward to the bedroom window.

Then the woman lifted the veil from her face.

Rita did not immediately recognize Louise Gaston because most of Louise's face was just not there. But it was the voice that was unmistakable. Rita heard the woman speak as if she were in the room with her. "Love did this," Louise said, "and love will do this to you."

5.

Others in Town Who Could Not Have Been Dreaming Because They Were Not Asleep

Dr. Brian Cammack tapped softly on his walk-in closet door.

"Lily?" he asked. There was no response. He had dressed in his summer seersucker jacket and gray wool slacks. He opened the closet doors. Shoving aside several belts and ties that drooped across a coat hanger, he drew off a red and gray Scottish tartan bowtie. It had been a gift from his one good daughter. Lily loved seeing him in that tie, and the seersucker was Rose's favorite jacket of his. "My handsome cavalier," she would call him.

Dr. Cammack went to his dresser mirror and fiddled with the tie, trying to remember the right combination of moves to make it bloom at his throat the way Lily could. "That girl can't keep me in this prison forever—why I raised her from nothing, and now, she does this to me. Scares everyone away. She will be the death of me yet." Finally he gave up on getting the bowtie to bloom; he let it hang from the collar of his Oxford cloth shirt. "When I get to the party, Lily will make it bloom."

He spent a few moments brushing his silver-gray hair neatly to the side. He squinted at the mirror. "Good enough," he said. He turned about and picked up his blue woolen walking cap, the one that still made him feel rather young and jaunty.

Brian Cammack brought his gold watch out of his pocket. He held it up to his eyes.

11:45.

"She'll be here soon."

As he sat waiting for his one good daughter to come get him and escort him to the party at the old house, Dr. Cammack wondered if he was forgetting some rule of etiquette regarding guests at parties. Should he be bringing a bottle of wine? Some sort of gift? But then he felt relieved of this burden. "Rose will remember for me," he said and watched the closet.

Prescott Nagle looked out his window at quarter to twelve and thought he could see the storm coming from far off over the hills. Like a broom, the clouds swept down into the valley, and the distant trees bent in submission. The snow continued to come down, less delicately than it had earlier, in a miniature cyclone motion.

As the wind outside picked up, the barnhouse began its characteristic shuddering. He returned to his study. He sat in his overstuffed reading chair; the chair seemed to sigh as it accepted his weight. He lit his pipe, puffing on it steadily, and reached across the coffee table for the paperback copy of the Bible that lay upside down and open like a pup tent waiting for him to crawl inside. He set his spectacles on his nose.

Prescott was not a Bible-reader. He considered himself a nominal deist, believing that God had set the world up to spin and then abandoned it to its own devices. His late wife Cassie had read the Bible, was in fact buried with the Bible that was her confirmation gift at Christ Church.

But that evening he'd picked up this paperback King James Version because he felt the need for some comfort, a voice somewhere to tell him that he was not losing his mind.

Prescott read from Ezekiel, not knowing what he was looking for, hoping that somewhere there was a key to all this: the children of Nathaniel Carson, Giles, Olivia, Andrew, Thomas, Matthew, Anne and Nathaniel. The anagram that Worthy Houston had made of their names: GOATMAN. Those bones he unearthed. The bones that, in Worthy Houston's words, "sang."

And Teddy Amory, the girl who had come back from the dead, a girl who, damn her to hell, either did one killer imitation of Cassie Nagle, a woman who died years before that girl was even born, or had found an uneasy union with the taint that was upon Clear Lake and the goat dance. The way Virginia Houston, Worthy's sister, had in 1802 and had met with some end that remained a cloudy mystery along with the missing pages from that diary. The way a tent revival preacher had in 1926, and been hanged from a tree for it. The way the Kidd Sisters, Sara and Christine, had in 1875, and paid for it with their sanity. Who could be sure of how many others there had been? Prescott suspected one other case, closer to him; but if he thought about it he would fall apart just as he had in 1941. And now, how had this little girl paid for her gift: by burning to death in a housefire that the police investigators believed was set by her own brother?

Prescott doubted it. Her remains had not been found; there was the evidence of her bathrobe found intact but singed a half-mile from the house. She had escaped.

But to what?

* * *

Ezekiel, Chapter 37, from which Odessa Amory read before each séance with her daughter:

> *The hand of the Lord was upon me, and carried me out in the spirit of the Lord, and set me down in the midst of the valley which was full of bones. And caused me to pass by them round about: and behold, there were very many in the open valley: and, lo, they were very dry.*

And lo, Prescott would've added, *they were very restless, too, and angry as hell for being disturbed.*

Sheriff George Connally went home about two A.M. feeling he had accomplished nothing since finding Warren Whalen's corpse in the morning. The snow was blowing fiercely, and the windshield wipers of his black-and-white cruiser had a devil of a time keeping up with it. The streetlights were flashing yellow in town, and the streets were clean of people.

This man scratching himself to death seems like such a wild card—where does it fit? How does someone go about doing that? As George drove with one hand, he reached up and scratched his neck. *How the hell do you keep at it so that your blood spritzes out like soda water? Wouldn't you stop before you'd done that much damage? And Jesus, just what kind of allergic reaction would cause you to itch that badly?*

His cruiser skidded in a slush puddle as he turned off Main Street onto Lakeview Drive. The dirty water splashed up on his car, and it was as if someone had sprayed cold water on his face—he woke up. George had almost fallen asleep at the wheel.

Shocked into a second wind, George parked the car in his driveway.

The house was completely dark as he entered. He tried to be as quiet as possible—he took his shoes off as soon as he was inside. Carefully he edged the door shut; but a cord of Christmas jingle bells, a leftover from the holidays, dangled from the doorknob, sounding an alarm.

George sucked in air, as if this would keep Rita from having heard the tinkling bells.

When he got upstairs to their bedroom he felt a chilly draft. He turned on the light. The drapes were blowing into the room, and the window was shattered. Broken glass lay across the carpet.

Rita was not in bed.

When George walked across the room, the broken glass crunched beneath his shoes. With a clawing dread he had not felt since he'd opened that cabin door and found the Gastons' bodies, George followed a spotty trail of blood into the adjoining bathroom.

He found Rita crouched like a frightened child beneath the sink—a 38-year-old woman curled up on herself, shivering in her nightgown on the tile floor. Her hair a sweat-soaked tangle. Her eyes bulging and twitching. Staring at him blankly. A weak moan escaping her lips. Her mouth, smeared with blood, chewing. And when she opened her mouth, more blood sluiced across her teeth. Her hands, lacerated from the broken glass, holding onto something. And when he bent down to lift her out from under the basin, the thing which she'd held so tight in her hand dropped to the floor. It hit the tile with a wet slap. George barely missed stepping on it.

Her tongue.

"Jesus," the sound barely escaped his lips as he hugged her close to him, carrying her through the bathroom doorway, "who the hell did this to you?" He fought back tears as Rita, her face distorted in a frozen rictus of fear, stared at him—through him.

Her chin quivered.

Rita whimpered, "Oooweef, Oooweef . . ."

Clare Terry thought she was dreaming, but she was not. She heard the front door slam, and got up out of bed.

She went to her window and watched her father, in his seersucker jacket and woolen cap, walk across the snow-covered front lawn.

Clare waited at the window expectantly. She wondered when something was going to happen in this dream, and nothing ever did. Her father was brushing snow off his car, while more snow continued to fall. Finally, Clare returned to bed and closed her eyes.

When she opened them a few seconds later, it was with the question: *What's wrong with this dream?*

She knew the answer. *It isn't a dream.*

Clare threw a robe on over her flannel nightshirt, and ran out of her bedroom.

Outside, she managed to stop her father from getting into the old black Cadillac that he never drove anymore. He was fumbling with the keys at the car door, and Clare ran up from behind him and grabbed the keys out of his hand.

"You can't do this to me!" he shouted.

Clare, who was freezing, pulled his arm, leading him back to the house. He resisted at first, and for a moment she thought, *Well, just let him crash on some icy road and then you'll be done with him.* "Look, Daddy, you're coming back in this house whether you like it or not!"

"Little blind Clare," her father muttered contemptuously, but turned and began walking back to the house.

6.

The residents of Pontefract, Virginia, awoke the next morning, weary from dreaming, to what Cappie Hartstone with characteristic enthusiasm would refer to as a "winter wonderland." As the day progressed, some would wonder if they had yet awakened from their sleep.

7.

From *The Nightmare Book of Cup Coffey:*

TUESDAY MORNING, JANUARY 6, 1987

Of course I haven't slept a wink, and I see the sun is coming up which is a bit of a relief. I've spent the whole night poring over these articles, and skimming bits and pieces of the diary. Fascinating, but I don't know where it all leads. How does it go from children who may have been killed in the 18th century to a little girl who may have been killed in a recent fire, and finally to Bart Kinter's hand which may or may not have gripped my ankle on that footbridge? I don't know any of this, it's all supposition. That is perhaps what frightens me the most.

In spite of that hand on the bridge last night I still want to believe there's a nice tidy phenomenon involved, maybe a law of physics. But I know there's nothing that pleasant involved.

And those missing pages from Worthy Houston's diary that Dr. Nagle mentioned.

What is it he's looking for?

Now that the sun is up, I don't feel quite as scared as I did in the night. Maybe there's an explanation, a reason. Outside, it's all covered with snow. Again, so normal. Snow. Don't feel tired at all—guess I'm still living on the adrenaline rush from last night.

CHAPTER THIRTEEN

WHENEVER IT SNOWS, THIS TOWN IS A GODDAMN ZOO

Tuesday, January 6, 1987

1.

"Whenever it snows this town is a goddamn zoo," Gower Lowry said to his housekeeper as he lifted the window shade. He scraped the thin skin of ice that had formed overnight on the window and tried to focus his vision on the two men standing at the doorstep. All he saw were the tops of their heads, one hidden by the hood of his coat, and the other, by a red stocking cap. "Damn," Gower said, recognizing Prescott Nagle beneath the red cap.

2.

The white snow that had fallen the previous night became muddy by noon; the sanding truck had seen to that. Cars were dashed with a gray slush as drivers maneuvered the side streets during the lunch hour. Main Street was fairly clear of snow and ice because of the bulldozer and sander that had come through, the morning traffic, and the trucks that had passed through on their way to Route 64; but curbside Main Street resembled a traffic jam with no drivers. There was a Chevy Vega with one tire lifted as though it were about to urinate on the sidewalk. A red VW

Rabbit kissed the back bumper of a Pinto, but gingerly. A Ford station wagon was double parked next to a blue van. The owner of the van was out at lunchtime shouting up and down the street: "Move your fuckin' car, man!"

The external temperature remained at a cold twenty degrees, but internal temperatures seemed to be rising. You could hear bickering along the Main Street stores. If you were to take a walk through downtown Pontefract from West Downtown to East Downtown (a stroll that might take anywhere from five to ten minutes) you might be witness to:

A bag boy at the Hotchkiss Market telling his boss off. A bag of groceries had just split open, and an irate customer was waiting in her car trying to keep her kids quiet while the boy picked up the paper towels, peanut butter jars, Wonder Bread, Fruity Pebbles, Diet Dr Pepper cans, plastic milk jug, and an apparently endless selection of cold cuts that were spread out on the sidewalk in the snow. Old Man Hotchkiss walked out to scold the boy for his negligence. "Who the hell do you think you are, talkin' to me like that?" the bag boy said. "I'm gonna own this store some day, Fat Ass, and when I do . . ."

But walking past this management-trainee problem, you'd come to the customer in her car trying to keep her own children quiet in the back seat. Cappie Hartstone said, "I don't care if you think aliens are coming from another planet, Jennifer, I will not have you doing that to your brother—oh, don't give me that look, young lady—" and she reached back and whacked her daughter on the side of her head. Jennifer squealed, and in a moment they all began crying, even Cappie, who was moaning, "We just have to get out of here for a few days, that's all, that's all there is to it, I'll just have to tell him, we need to—"

Fisher's Drugstore attracted the same crowd year 'round to its front stoop—good old boys, in their eternal uniforms of flannel shirts and mackinaw coats, baseball caps and plaid hunting hats with the floppy earflaps. One of them pointed up at the clouds as if divining the future from their formations. "Just like '41," this guy said, and as if to emphasize his point, he stomped his Bean's Duck Hunting boots on the smoldering cigarette butt he'd just tossed from his lips.

"No it ain't, nothin' like '41—and how the hell would you remember what '41 was like anyway, wisenheimer? Your head was so full of suds back then you wouldn't know that crack in the sidewalk from your mama's—" another said.

"I tell ya," the first continued, not listening to his interrupter, "if anything comes down like '41, it's bound to mean trouble."

"Jenny's gallstones're givin' her trouble," said an older man in a blue baseball cap with the letters USA printed across the brim.

"Yeah?" someone asked.

"She says she didn't get a wink of sleep last night and she was dreamin' about her mama again, and whenever she dreams about the old cow it's her gallstones."

"Didn't get much sleep myself last night," the man trying to read the clouds said.

Tom MacKenzie, Sr., and his son Tommy were changing the plastic letters on the marquee down at the Key Theater —from Disney's SLEEPING BEAUTY ("Damn videocassettes have ruined my business," father grumbled to son) to NIGHTMARE ON ELM STREET, PART III. Tom, Sr., stood on the sidewalk with a mug of coffee in one hand while he gripped the ladder with the other. To help keep the aluminum ladder steady, he pressed his gut up against it, too.

"Not like that—shit!—now you got—all the letters—well, they're crooked, Tommy, can't you see—not like—" Tom, Sr.'s words whistled out of his mouth like a string of spit. "I don't know how you're ever going to make it in the world, son, unless you—"

Maude Dunwoody's Ham Biscuit Haven was practically empty at lunch hour; none of her regulars had come in. Maude, her grease-stained apron drawn tight across her broad hips like the top of a drum, stood in the doorway shivering from the cold, telling her cook, Billy Fine, about the scary dream she had the night before. The Columns restaurant didn't even open on Tuesday. A handscrawled sign on the door said, *Closed Due To Weather.*

All those folks on their way to lunch, or running errands while the sun was still shining, or just looking out their windows at the gritty snow, all had one thing in common. They looked tired, as if someone was robbing them of sleep.

3.

George Connally had spent the night at the Westbridge Medical Center in Newton. He sat in the lobby even after his wife had been given a painkiller and was asleep in her room. He had never been so frightened in his whole career as he was when he finally understood the word his wife repeated weakly over and over.

"Oooweef, Oooweef . . ."

And the only name George could come up with, no matter how he figured it, was "Louise."

4.

Lyle Holroyd was left in charge while George remained at the medical center, and it seemed like it was going to be a slow day as he looked out the window of the sheriff's office (imagining what it would be like when George retired or was fired, and Lyle was, himself, occupying this particular office) when someone came up behind him. The surprise attack made him spill his coffee on the front of his shirt.

"Say, Lyle," Detective Hank Firestone said, slapping Lyle on the shoulder so hard it almost stung, but in a friendly way, "let's you and me go and take a ride around town."

5.

Ten minutes later, Lyle Holroyd and Hank Firestone were sitting in Lyle's cruiser in front of the Marlowe-Houston House.

Firestone reached over and turned off the police radio.

"I'm very confused, Mr. Firestone," Lyle said, glancing from the radio up to Firestone's face.

"Call me Hank, Lyle." Firestone seemed sure of what he was doing. "I think we can talk here. I know what small towns are like. Why I'm from a small town, myself. Gossip travels like, well, like seeds on the wind, and where it lands, well, it takes root you see, and grows."

Lyle scratched his head beneath his deputy's hat. "I don't follow."

"Well, it all goes back to this missing little girl, Lyle. Do you know the one I mean?" Hank patted the dashboard in imitation of a drumroll. "The Amory girl, Teddy Amory. We have cause to believe she is somewhere in this very town, Lyle. Kidnapped. She has an illness, Lyle, a disease, and we need to help her. You'd be quite the hero rescuing a little girl from a kidnapper, wouldn't you?"

"Gawd, that's what George thought, too—kidnapped." Lyle said this last word in a pregnant whisper.

"Did he? Interesting. It's under investigation with the FBI. But there is a deviate in this town, Lyle, an aberrant personality who is keeping that poor little girl in agony. We think we know who."

"Why didn't George tell me any of this?"

"Let's just say your sheriff is considered a risk with regards to his mental state. He hasn't told you because we've chosen not to tell him of our . . . involvement. But we have chosen you, Lyle. And we need your help. You know this town, don't you, Lyle?"

"Yes, sir."

"We believe we can draw out the perpetrator of this crime

this very evening. Now, our main goal is to not endanger the little girl—we are well aware of who this man is, and we don't want to alarm him. He's a dangerous personality type. Our aim is to follow him, find out where he's keeping the girl, and when we've made sure he's clear of the place, we want you to go in and get her. And bring her out to us."

"What if—" Lyle interrupted.

"Leave the 'what ifs' to us, Lyle, we'll keep your back covered. You're a bright young man, Lyle, everyone I've interviewed has said it."

"They have?" Lyle raised his eyebrows.

"A go-getter." Hank Firestone grinned and patted Lyle on the shoulder. Firestone opened his car door. "Come on, some of the other undercover boys are inside, I want you to meet who you'll be working with tonight."

6.

On the wire:

Georgia Stetson called up Patsy Campbell as soon as she'd remembered where she'd heard that name: Coffey. "And Patsy," Georgia said, "I am truly surprised you didn't remember yourself . . . that boy . . . the one who was involved in that tragedy with your nephew Bart—that's right, dear, right under your own roof . . . I should say so, and I would do that right now if I were you . . ."

7.

When the housekeeper was not able to send Dr. Nagle and Cup away from Gower Lowry's door ("Mrs. Saunders," Prescott said, removing his red knit cap in deference to the lady, "we will pitch tent if we must."), Gower Lowry finally shouted from upstairs that he would be down momentarily to speak personally with the two callers. He came down several minutes later dressed in a heavy tweed overcoat, his shoulders hunched, clutching a cane, wearing galoshes. "I was just on my way out," he said, coming to the door and simultaneously shooing Mrs. Saunders away. "Saunders, to market, to market, I must have more fruit and vegetables with my meals . . ."

Looking confused, Mrs. Saunders took her coat from the rack by the front door and squeezed past Prescott and Cup as they entered the house.

Gower led them to what he referred to as his "chamber of horrors"; Cup glanced apprehensively at Prescott upon hearing this, but the "horrors" turned out to be nothing more than a series of floor-to-ceiling portraits of Lowrys and Houstons, going as far back as the late 1700s. As he glanced from portrait to portrait, Cup wondered which painting was of Worthy Houston, or his father, Stephen, or the sister, Virginia. "The only ones missing are over at the ancestral home," Gower said proudly, meaning the Marlowe-Houston House. He pointed out a portrait of himself as a young man on horseback.

"At eighteen. Quite the equestrian in those days," Gower said, and then paused, searching Prescott's face for some reaction.

There was none. Prescott nodded and said, "Yes, your father kept the finest stables in the county. I should know, I bought the barn didn't I?"

Gower's mood darkened. He looked over at Cup, who had just taken a seat near the window. "I remember you very well, Mr. Coffey. But what's past is past. We are all capable of mistakes . . . I am happy to see you've obviously made something of yourself."

Cup smiled pleasantly, ignoring the awkwardness of this ass backwards compliment. Gower Lowry hadn't changed a bit in twelve years. He still liked to stick it to people.

"We're here about the diary," Prescott said firmly.

"Yes," Gower said, "you are. I haven't for a moment entertained the notion that this is a social visit."

Prescott proceeded to explain about the bones and the dig, and the whole time he was talking, Cup watched

Gower's face for some expression. There was none forthcoming. Gower sat listening with a slightly bemused look, occasionally turning to Cup in sympathy. Cup burned with the implication of Gower's nods to him—that Cup, too, was thinking what Gower Lowry apparently thought: *Prescott Nagle is an old hack, an academic fuddy-duddy who has lost too many boxcars from his train of thought.*

"Ghosts?" Gower finally interrupted Prescott with a wave of his cane. "Is that what this is all about? Ghosts? Oh, dear, Prescott," his voice faded. He winked at Cup. "And you've been the willing accomplice through all this, have you, Mr. Coffey?"

Cup felt his embarrassment, his shame at not speaking up, but he remained silent. He felt as if he lay suspended in a block of ice, unable to break out. *What in God's name do I believe, anyway? In this room, it seems so far away, a dream I had last night. It's just a story I've been suckered into. A logical explanation, a physical reality. Got to be. Bart Kinter is dead. Lily Cammack is dead. I am not insane. This room has four walls, there is snow outside, Dr. Nagle is holding a red cap. That's reality. That's sense.*

Cup watched as Prescott's face went from one set in its determination to a face that was losing all its muscle tone—without saying it, Cup felt that sinking disappointment communicated from the older man to himself.

No, Cup thought, *this is real. He knows and I know, and whatever this is won't cease to exist just because I won't bear witness to it.*

Cup broke through the ice that had formed around his mind.

"No, Mr. Lowry," Cup said, feeling stronger than he had felt in years, finally telling the truth as he saw it, not as he thought other people would want to hear it. But as it was. "I don't know for sure what it is, but I believe there's a threat—just as Prescott says—to this town, and I believe I am involved somehow, and Prescott, also, and that somewhere in those missing pages is the key to what's going on, be it rational or irrational. And yes, even ghosts, sir, or maybe something worse."

8.

"Thank you, Cup, for coming through for me," Prescott said afterwards as they walked back to his car.

"Fat lot of good it did. What's his problem, anyway?"

"Couldn't you tell?"

"Other than just plain meanness?"

"Cup, over the years you learn how to read people the way you do books. And the book that Gower Lowry was scribbling in with all those nervous chuckles and asides to you about old men and their wild imaginations can only point to one thing. Himself. He was trying to use you as a sounding board, someone to reassure him that this is all some sort of elderly disease like Alzheimer's. Because he must have had his own encounter with . . ."

"The Eater of Souls," Cup said to himself quietly.

9.

Patsy Campbell, nursing an RC Cola, pushed the door to Cup's room open slowly. She wasn't entirely sure that he had not returned since the morning. "Hello? Mr. Coffey?"

She counted to twenty and then went inside the room. Patsy wandered around the room, scanning the surfaces of desk and dresser, daintily stepping over her empty RC Cola bottles trying to find something that would confirm her worst suspicions about this man.

She found it, tucked beneath one of the pillows on the bed.

A thick black notebook. She opened it.

"'The Nightmare Book, Volume Three,'" she said, and began reading.

Within ten minutes she was "on the wire," and this is how the news filtered down:

From Patsy Campbell to Georgia Stetson:

"The man is psychotic, I am telling you, Georgia, he possesses a messed-up brain from too much drink. Do you know that man who killed all those boys? Gacy, yes, well this man Coffey talks about him like they are best friends, and about butchering innocent children with lawn mowers—no, dear, I don't, the Miller boy brings his own mower when he cuts the lawn —you don't think he'd try something like that here, do you?"

From Georgia Stetson to Maude Dunwoody:

". . . And he is thought to have murdered several children in cold blood and he is staying right there at Patsy's . . . Yes, Maude, a cult of some kind, well, yes, he probably is at the bottom of the Whalen killing . . ."

From Maude Dunwoody to Cappie Hartstone:

"It's true, he's part of the Manson family, and you know they were all devil worshippers—well, goodness, Cappie, I don't believe in any of that, but that doesn't matter to a psycho, does it? All that's important is that he believes it . . ."

And, finally, to Bonnie Holroyd from Cappie Hartstone:

". . . I didn't want to bother you about this, but I'm a little worried about Mrs. Campbell, and if the sheriff could just go check on her to see how she's . . . Well, I understand there's a psycho boarding with her, and he's already wanted for murder and kidnapping. I understand he's a dead ringer for Ted Bundy. That's right. I thought you should know . . . Thank you so much, Bonnie."

Bonnie Holroyd radioed Officer Dave Petty, who was writing up a parking ticket for the station wagon that remained double parked next to the blue van on Main Street.

"Look, Dave, I can't get hold of Lyle, so could you head on over to Patsy Campbell's—she's got some kind of problem with—yeah, if you're real busy I think it can wait . . ."

CHAPTER FOURTEEN

THE BOY-EATING SPIDER

1.

Tommy MacKenzie, Jr., had been chewed out by his dad for abandoning his post at the Key Theater last Friday night when he'd walked Clare Terry home. That was what he'd told his friends, anyway. "It was only ten minutes," Tommy protested. Tommy told his friends that his dad had pounded a wall with his fist; his father had actually thrown Tommy up against the wall. "In that ten minutes, somebody could've robbed me blind!" Tommy, almost sixteen, was taller than his father by six inches. He could easily have pushed his dad away. But whenever his father got in one of his rages, Tommy still felt like a little kid. Tommy didn't know for sure that other fathers didn't behave this way; he rarely shared his feelings on the subject with anyone.

Tommy dreaded the three weeks of vacation around Christmastime more than any of the year. Not only did he have to put in a full day's work at the theater, but in the morning and early afternoon before the first matinee he usually just hung out in his room to avoid any confrontations with his dad.

But after Friday night his dad had grounded him to the house for his two nights off a week, Tuesday and Wednesday, when there wasn't much business at the theater. "You can just sit in your room, young man, and not waste your time playing videos or running around with your idiot friends." Tommy knew that his father wasn't angry so much at him for his leaving his post last Friday as he was trying to hang on to something in the family. Tommy's mother had gone to her sister's in Roanoke again, and Tom, Sr., was always on edge whenever she did. His mother took these little trips usually after his dad had hit her, too, and it was not untypical of her to stay away a week or more. Tommy didn't consider this very unusual, either: he figured most families probably did such things. Moms left their families when they got hit, Dads threw their kids against walls, and the kids themselves stayed in their rooms as often as possible.

And that was just what he was doing Tuesday night when somebody scared him half to death.

He was sitting at his desk doodling a caricature of just how he felt—the picture was of a boy whose brows pushed his eyes down almost to his mouth, and underneath it he scrawled: *Grrrrr.* He twisted his gold class ring on his hand—it was too loose for his finger, but he'd never complain to his dad about it. Tommy had bought the ring with money saved from his running the concession stand at the movie theater, but even so it had been drilled into him that it was essentially out of his father's pocket. Tommy had mislaid the ring around the house a few times since he'd gotten it in September, and his dad had hit the roof and given him a lecture on responsibility and the value of things. Tommy grew to dislike the ring because of that; but he tried to have it on him at all times lest Tom, Sr., notice that it was missing. But, in the relative safety of his own bedroom, Tommy took the ring off and set it down beside his sketch pad.

Occasionally he would look out his bedroom window. He couldn't see much in the dark; but there was the streetlamp shining down on Main Street through the alley behind their house, and sometimes he caught a glimpse of couples making out near the dumpster. Once he saw a guy beat another guy up. The streetlamp light was also a fairly good indicator of snowfall. Tommy was hoping for more.

As Tommy sat drawing, he thought he heard something

outside the window and looked up. There was a face pushed up against the glass on the other side, a piggish nose, bloated lips, eyes shut.

"Here comes the boy-eating spider!" it cried out, and for a moment Tommy thought it might just *be* the boy-eating spider.

"Jee-sus," Tommy gasped, realizing halfway into his terror that it was Rick Stetson. How could he not have recognized immediately that bozo red hair and toothy grin?

Rick pulled his face away from the glass and tapped on the window. "Knock, knock," he said.

Tommy reached over and lifted the window up so his friend could come in. "What the hell are you doing out there? I'm still pissed off at you for that shitty thing you did to that albino."

"I just thought I'd scare the shit out of you," Rick said, crawling across the sill, and then onto Tommy's desk, shoving books and papers onto the floor. He wriggled like a snake to get his legs in, while Tommy, finding it necessary to stand beside his desk so that Rick could have more room to get in, pulled on his arms to help. "Cold as a witch's tittie in a brass bra." Rick shivered as he swiveled around on the desk, more or less righting himself.

"Don't ever do that again," Tommy said crossly.

"Scare you, or make fun of the Crispy Critter? You weren't down at the arcade, so I figured something was up. Had a bitch of a time climbing up here—I started on the trash cans and almost broke my neck." Rick stood up and brushed himself off. As always, Rick was wearing his army surplus olive drab jacket over a Ratt T-shirt, and his jeans were torn and frayed around the knees. No matter how the temperature dropped outside, Rick always wore this uniform. Rick held up the palms of his hands for Tommy's inspection. They were covered with grime. "Tell your old man to wash down the wall sometime, will ya?"

"Yeah, right."

"Riddle me this, Batman, whyfor are you not at the arcade monopolizing Space Invaders?"

Tommy went over to his bed, sat down and brought his

knees up against his chest. Using his hand as an airplane, he buzzed it around and then crashed it into his left knee, accompanied by the appropriate sound effects. "Grounded."

Rick shrugged. "In this life, Tommyhawk, sometimes you crash and sometimes you crash and burn. But you, you don't crash, you don't burn, you just quit. Your old man's running some two-hour movie and you're acting like you can't get away with murder."

"I don't know—I guess I'm just not up for the arcade."

"Well, as it turns out, me, neither."

"You want to listen to some tapes?"

"Sure, you got any Ozzy Osbourne?"

"Funny. No Iron Maiden, either. I've got Kate Bush."

"You like those weird chicks, dontcha? No, Tombo, music just won't do it for me tonight. Not when I know what I know . . ."

"Yeah, like what do you know?"

"Just because I go to public school and not some faggy preppie institution for the criminally insane doesn't mean I am an ignoramus. You know about how one of your teachers bit the dust?"

"Yeah—Hardass Whalen. I heard my mom talking to someone on the phone. It was an accident at the M-H or something." M-H was the cool abbreviation for Marlowe-Houston House.

Rick smiled. "This, my friend," he said, pointing to his mouth, "is a shit-eating grin."

"I always say you eat shit," Tommy laughed.

". . . Because I know wha' happen."

"Okay."

"My mom gave me more information."

"Your mom gives everyone more information."

"Your teacher didn't just die in any old accident. He bit the big one over at the M-H, buckaroo, and they had a detective and everything. But the best part is that the place is supposed to be covered with blood and guts—all around the walls and everything. And they will have washed it away by tomorrow morning, so you know what that means?"

Tommy put his hands out as if blocking a pass. "Whoa, buddy, no way."

"Where's your sense of adventure? Did your old man cut off your balls, too? We got to go tonight—this is one of those things you wait your whole life to see!"

"No."

"What's it going to take to get your ass out of this house and over there?"

"Nothing. I don't want to go."

Rick leaned back on Tommy's desk. He picked up the sketch pad. "How about if I pissed on this."

Tommy shook his head. "It'll just improve the colors. I've got too much blue, a little yellow piss might give it some green."

Rick looked around the desk.

His gaze stopped on one shiny item.

Tommy saw this at the same time Rick did. "No, not my class ring."

Rick grabbed the ring and slipped it on the middle finger of his right hand. Then he flipped the bird at Tommy. "Your ring will not see the light of day unless you accompany me over to the M-H."

"No, seriously, give it here." Tommy got up off his bed and started walking over to where Rick was.

Rick leaned his head back, lifted his hand to his mouth as if he were about to swallow the ring. "I hear it's just like downing goldfish, only you'll have to dig through all my shit just to find it."

"This isn't funny."

"Look—all we're gonna do is go across the lake and look into that old museum. We're not doing anything illegal, and the place is probably all roped off anyway. Don't go into a hissy-fit. You'll get your ring back—you know your problem?"

"No, Stets, what's my problem?"

"You got no sense of adventure. Now, let's get a hanger from your closet and if you got a flashlight, that would be great, too."

2.

"God, I knew this was a dumb idea," Tommy said. He was wearing a hooded sweatshirt under his dad's old Navy pea jacket, and his Levi's, and he was still freezing.

It had taken them close to an hour to get from one side of town to the other. Rick had insisted they do nighttime maneuvers, "just like in the army," and so they had taken a roundabout route through town, down alleyways and over back fences. Rick would plaster himself up against a wall and whisper, "Douse your lights, men," and Tommy would mutter, "Jeez," but comply by turning his flashlight off.

They stood on the front porch of the Marlowe-Houston House and tried the door. "Of course, it's locked—what did you think, a guy dies here and the next day they have open house?" Tommy started clicking his flashlight on and off, aiming the beam in Rick's face. Rick swatted at the beam of light when it came on. "Just give me my ring, Stets."

"Willya hold the light up a little?" Rick bent down and kept turning the doorknob. When Tommy came closer with the flashlight, Rick reached over and tilted Tommy's hand down so the light would hit across the keyhole. Rick noticed that Tommy's hand was trembling. "Cold or scared?"

"Both. Will you hurry up?"

Rick pulled the wire coat hanger out from under his arm and twisted it until it was all straightened out with a little curl at the end. He began jiggling this in and out of the keyhole. "I don't know what I'm doing wrong," he said, "this always works on cars."

When they could not break in through the front door or the picture window, and when Rick almost broke his neck trying to scale the warped trelliswork, they went around back. "I thought for sure this place would be cordoned off," Rick said. There had been a single lawn spotlight in the front of the house, but in the back the only illumination was from the moon filtered through the cloud cover.

Carefully, feeling their way as much as seeing it in the flashlight's thin beam, the boys went up the back porch stairs. Rick kept putting his hand on Tommy's shoulder, which made him jump. When they approached the back door, Rick began whispering ominously, "What was that? Did you hear that? Did you feel that? Something touched me . . . someone—or something. Could it have been the boy-eating spider?"

"Cut it out," Tommy said. Rick was one of his few friends to whom he confided anything, and right now Tommy wished he'd never told him about the boy-eating spider. It was one of those tricks his father had used when he'd been little. "You tell anybody where you got that shiner," his father would say when he was five years old, "and the boy-eating spider's going to come out of your closet and eat you up. Boy-eating spiders go after bad boys, that's why only good boys grow up." Tommy had been terrified that the boy-eating spider would come out of his closet at night just because it knew what he was thinking. Sometimes his father would leave the closet door slightly open on purpose just to scare him. By the time Tommy was nine, he knew that the boy-eating spider had a lot in common with the Tooth Fairy and Santa Claus, but the image he'd had as a child stuck with him: a large daddy longlegs, with a man's face painted white, and a huge dripping maw for a mouth with mandibles shooting out from between its lips.

"You must have given me a retarded hanger, Tombo," Rick muttered, after going through the same routine with the back door as he had with the front. He tossed the coat hanger down the steps. It seemed to clatter endlessly as it hit the slate walkway.

The flashlight felt heavy in Tommy's hands. He switched it off and lowered it to hip-level. "Well, now what?"

"We could always break a window."

"No."

"Just kidding. Let's try the cellar."

"This was a dumb idea, and we're both looney tunes to ever come out here." Tommy lifted the flashlight back up and clicked it on, blinding Rick with the light.

"Shut that thing off."

The light clicked off. "I've got to go back soon. My dad's probably already home—what time is it?"

"Relax, relax, what's a couple of more minutes?"

"We're not going down there," Tommy protested. How many times had he said a variation on that theme in the past twenty minutes, and still, here he was. His eyes were just beginning to adjust to the darkness again now that he'd left the flashlight off for a few seconds. He scanned the campus, along the colonnade and down to the chapel. The place was dead empty, and he thought of Mr. Whalen, the Disciplinary Counselor. Dead. Found somewhere in the M-H.

The boxwood hedges surrounding the house seemed to be dark shadows crouching, waiting. It was so cold, Tommy wished he had just said to hell with this scheme, and stayed home in his warm room. Even if he didn't get his ring back.

"Yes," Rick said when he'd felt his way back down the veranda steps, "we are going down there. It might be fun. We might find something."

"If we find something," Tommy whispered, more to himself than to Rick, "it will *not* be *fun.*"

They stumbled in the darkness. Rick almost emasculated himself on the useless old pump that sat square between the porch steps and the door to the cellar. The cellar entrance was slanted at a 45-degree angle against the house.

Rick directed Tommy to shine his flashlight over on the Yale lock that kept the doors closed together. Tommy heard the metallic rattle as Rick tried the lock.

"Somebody's going to know if we break the lock."

"Somebody," Rick said like a smartass, "already beat us to it." Tommy watched as Rick held the broken lock into the beam of light. It was so rusty it practically crumbled in his fingers. "They don't make 'em like they used to."

Rick opened one of the double doors. Its hinges creaked. Both boys winced when they heard it. As he carefully laid the door back against the side of the house, Rick motioned for Tommy to come over to the doorway.

"We should go home," Tommy said. The dread that had overcome him was almost palpable. He did not want to see bloody walls, guts across the floor.

"You afraid?" Rick asked.

There was a moment when Tommy felt like a five-year-old, and wanted to scream: *Yes! I'm afraid! I'm afraid of the dark, I'm afraid of dead faculty members, I'm afraid my dad's going to throw a fit when he finds I'm not upstairs in my room, I'm afraid I'm going to freeze my balls off, I'm afraid we're going to be arrested for breaking and entering; but most of all, Stets, I'm afraid that the boy-eating spider is hibernating down there.*

But he shone the flashlight in Rick's eyes. Rick didn't flinch this time. Tommy asked, "Are *you?*"

But rather than answer this question, Rick stepped down into the darkness of the Marlowe-Houston House's cellar. "You coming?" was all the reply Tommy got.

Tommy moved forward reluctantly.

3.

"This is it," Rick said, grabbing the flashlight out of Tommy's hands and directing the beam to the chalk outline of a man in the middle of the concrete floor. "It must've been murder, 'cause I don't think they do that when somebody falls down the stairs or something."

"Look, this place gives me the creeps," Tommy said. He was sitting on the bottom cellar step, his chin resting on his fist. They were surrounded by what Tommy felt was an unearthly silence. It seemed colder in the cellar than it had outside, if that was possible, and it stank.

"What I don't get is, if this guy gets killed, why don't they have this place roped off or something?"

"Stets, you watch too much TV."

"No, really," Rick swung the light around the room, "and they've got to have a light in here someplace." He finally saw a dangling cord which ran up to a single light bulb. He went over, tugged on the cord, and an anemic light bled across the dusty gray cellar.

Once his eyes adjusted to the light, Tommy stood up and stretched. He looked around the room: dusty shelves, broken bottles piled up in a corner, several cardboard boxes stacked on top of each other. Rick in his olive drab jacket standing over the chalk outline where Mr. Whalen must've fallen. But no blood, no guts, no bones.

"A big fat zero," Tommy said, relieved. "Well, let's go."

"No, wait—don't you think this is weird? This chalk drawing?"

Tommy glanced down again at the outline.

It was weird. Extremely weird. Tommy hadn't noticed the detail on the drawing. It wasn't just an outline, roughly approximating a man's body. Someone had drawn in eyes, and a nose and mouth, and as Rick pointed out with his foot, even a penis. "You think he really had such a teeny pecker?"

"Cops wouldn't do that," Tommy said, moving over to where Rick stood. The man's eyes were cartoonishly evil, reminding Tommy of Wile E. Coyote's when he was scheming against the Road Runner. And his teeth were equally canine-sharp.

"Speaking of peckers," Rick sighed, bored by the lack of gore-splattered walls, "I got to take a leak."

Tommy made a move toward the steps.

"No, I'm gonna use the can over here," Rick said. Tommy turned around to see what Rick meant. "In eighth grade we went on a tour of the M-H, and they showed us this shitter." Rick arrived at the long shelf, and dusting part of it off, lifted a square lid. "An old-fashion can. Sort of a cross between a latrine and a wishing well for those Southern belles too delicate to walk across the field to the outhouse. I've always wanted to use it and now's my chance. P-U! It really stinks—musta built up a lot of methane in its time, all that ca-ca."

"Just hurry up," Tommy said.

"Relax, relax, if you talk I can't concentrate. Shy bladder, like my old man." Rick stood there and began humming. "I have to think of things like, you know, rain forests and waterfalls to get the old pump flowing."

"I think I hear someone coming," Tommy lied.

"That's my piss—it's kind of fizzling down there."

"Hurry up, I think I hear somebody."

"Okay, okay. I just got to tap it. They say if you tap more than twice you're playing with it. Just think, the shit of centuries down there," Rick said. He zipped up his fly and looked down through the dark opening. "Halloo, potatoes!"

"Come on."

"I wonder how far down that goes. I could barely hear my piss hitting."

"Jesus, let's just get out of here."

Rick picked up the flashlight from the shelf. He turned it on and waved it down into the opening.

"Gimme that." Tommy went over and grabbed the light from Rick's hand.

"Ooops," Rick said.

"What?"

"Umm . . . you'll never believe this, but guess what I accidentally dropped down there?"

"No."

"Yeah, your ring."

"What the hell did you— Jesus, my dad's going to kill me—"

"You can always reach down and get it."

"No, fuck you, forget it, let's just get out of here."

"Okay, look, I'll try and reach it."

Rick made a show of pulling his sleeve up, wiggling his fingers, like a magician about to pull a rabbit out of a hat. For a second it reminded Tommy of "The Rocky and Bullwinkle Show" when the moose thrust his hand in the black top hat and came up with various wild animals instead of a rabbit, and Tommy could practically hear his heart thumping against his ribs, because that smell of gas was getting to him, and he was sure that he heard someone, not just his imagination, not some lie to hurry Rick along; but something, coming closer and closer. He couldn't tell from what direction.

Rick stuck his hand down into the opening of the shelf. "Got it," he said, and even as he said it, thinking he'd really gotten hold of the ring by just plunging his arm down into that indoor latrine, he began screaming, and Tomm watched in horror as blood shot up from that opening in thin stream as if from a water pistol, spraying Rick in th face.

Before Tommy could even reach him, before anothe scream had escaped from his lips, Rick's entire body wa pulled down through the opening, his legs kicking like swimmer drowning. Then, sucking and chewing noises, bu no scream. No sound from Rick.

4.

Tommy did not remember much of anything after tha except running, running, running. He did not think, he di not contemplate what he should do, he did not find th nearest payphone and dial 911, he did not even scream Because whatever was down there in that shithole had calle out his name, "Tommy MacKenzie," even with its mout full. "The boy-eating spider eats bad boys."

His throat felt dry and numb as he ran across th footbridge, back to town and home. He was panting lik a dog, his hair flying wildly, the hood of his swea shirt slapping against his shoulders as it dropped fro his head, his pea jacket open, flapping with the co wind.

One thought burned in his mind: *Get help, get help, g help.*

In his panic he brushed against a couple strolling arm i arm down Lakeview Drive, and almost got hit by a car tha was turning off from Main Street; the driver honked th horn, the car's brakes squealing like frightened pigs, an almost took the vehicle up on the sidewalk to avoid th running boy.

When Tommy arrived at the Key Theater, he ran straig up the stairs to the projection booth. His father turne surprised, his plastic features melting to a look of anger an reproach. Tommy was aware that his dad was mad as hel and was trying to find his own voice so he could explain. H felt like the wind had been knocked out of him. "Get help," was all Tommy could say at first, but the other words came later.

Crying and gasping for breath, Tommy quickly told him that Rick was getting killed, was probably already dead and . . .

"Let me smell your breath, young man," his father said sternly. Tom, Sr., turned from the projector and marched over to his son. "If you've been drinking, by God, your ass is gonna be grass."

"No, Dad, you don't understand." Tommy grabbed his father by the arm.

Before Tommy could get another breath to speak with, his father whispered to him in his listen-up-and-listen-good tone of voice, "I don't know what you've been getting into when you're supposed to be in your room, but your friend Rick bought a ticket to the nine-thirty show and is down in that theater right now watching *Nightmare on Elm Street.*" His father wrenched himself free of Tommy's grasp. Then he grabbed Tommy by his right hand and held it up. "And just where may I ask is your one-hundred-and-fifty-dollar gold ring? You have got to take care of your things, how many times—" But before his father could finish, Tommy had shaken himself loose from his grip and was running again, out of the projection booth, down the stairs.

He ran into the darkened theater, looking through the rows of seats, praying his father was right, that something had happened back there at the M-H, that it wasn't anything like the boy-eating spider, it was some kind of gag, just another one of Rick's practical jokes. Tommy shone his flashlight over the passive faces turned up to the man on screen with the long, sharp fingernails.

5.

Torch Smells Something

Torch first noticed the smell as he was combing through the Dempsey Dumpster in the alley behind the Columns. The Columns restaurant threw out perfectly good baked potatoes, and sometimes even those square pats of butter were left in the baggie with the old french bread they tossed away. Torch could sniff out a good garbage can from a mile away.

But the other smell soon overpowered that of table scraps and soggy baked potatoes.

It was the smell that had been growing stronger in town. They were growing stronger, even while Teddy was weakening.

The odor was as palpable to Torch as a freight train would be bearing down on him; it was a crushing weight, making him feel all his human frailty against its evil stench.

The scent of the grave. Of bones long buried. Of nightmares made flesh.

Torch followed the smell out of the dark alley.

Torch stood, partially hidden by the wall that said MILLER'S FEED AND SUPPLY, watching as the dark-haired man in the white suit paid for his movie theater ticket. The man looked around the street as if expecting to see someone. But there was no one else on Main Street. Then the man went inside the Key Theater. He paused near the concession stand just inside the glass doors. The man turned and jogged up a stairway, out of Torch's sight.

Torch knew what he would have to do.

He reached beneath his raggedy outer clothes and felt around in his pocket.

When he'd located what he was after, he ran across the street to the theater, wondering if he was already too late.

6.

Tommy almost tripped on a popcorn box stuck in the middle of the aisle, and as he grabbed the edge of a seatback to balance himself, he heard Rick Stetson say, "I really scared the shit out of you back there, didn't I?" Tommy smelled that same gassy smell that Rick had made a joke about when he'd lifted the lid of the shelf in the cellar.

Tommy wheeled around and flashed the light upon Rick's face, only it wasn't all of Rick Stetson's face, it was only the parts that hadn't been ripped off. There was the mop of unruly carrot red hair, and the pale eyes, but most of his nose was gone, and his entire lower jaw. His face was streaked with blood.

Someone behind them yelled, "Sit down, bozo, and shut off the damn light!"

"You're dead," Tommy said, not trying to understand any of what had happened. He kept the light on what was left of Rick's face, hoping that it would become someone else's, that he was hallucinating, that there was some normal explanation for all this, like he was crazy, had gone off the deep end, went looney tunes.

Rick said, "It should've been you, Tombo, it was your ring." And Rick held up something into the beam of light, something that at first looked like a bone that had been torn into by dogs, with some meat still on it. It was Rick Stetson's hand, and in the center of it gleamed a gold ring. "The boy-eating spider only eats bad little boys, Tommy. Like you."

Tommy repeated, "You're dead."

He heard a gurgling sound come up from Rick's throat. Tommy assumed this was a laugh. "Part of the inevitability of things, buckaroo. You'll be dead, too, and soon. The door is opening and then we'll all be dead together. Why, old Hardass Whalen is upstairs introducing himself to your old man right now."

7.

The boy sitting in the ticket booth shouted after Torch, "It ain't a freebie, Mister!" But Torch ran past him, through the glass doors and into the lobby.

He gagged when he inhaled the air inside. The smell was so strong—it was as if the place was crawling with them. The stench made him sick to his stomach. There was no time. They might all be here. He had to act fast.

The boy from the ticket booth was approaching him, shouting, but the words didn't seem to have any meaning. "What are you, some kinda weirdo— Oh, I heard about you, you're the crazy guy who—"

Torch was already running up the stairs to the projection booth.

8.

Tommy dropped the flashlight; it rolled down the aisle. He felt paralyzed, rooted to where he stood in the semi-darkness of the Key Theater. Somebody yelled for him to sit down and shut up, and just then, someone else booed, but not at Tommy. More boos and hisses followed, and someone in one of the back rows started clapping slowly, rhythmically, beginning the chant: "Fix it, fix it, fix it . . ."

Tommy turned slowly to the movie screen.

The film had caught in the projector mid-frame, and the image was already melting, transforming into a celluloid bubble. Other kids in the theater were chanting, "Fix it, fix it." Tommy looked back in the darkness for Rick Stetson, but the seat was empty. "Itsy-bitsy spider climbed up to the projection booth," Tommy heard the voice buzzing around his ear like an angry hornet; he stood, terrified, waiting to be stung.

9.

When Torch rushed inside the projection booth, the odor was overpowering.

The man, who Torch did not know, but who was Warren Whalen, had Tom MacKenzie, Sr., literally by the balls.

The dead man in the white suit tightened his grip on Tom, Sr.'s crotch. The theater owner was standing, his back pressed against the small rectangular window that looked down on the theater. The loud chanting of "Fix it, fix it, fix it" seemed like a distant swarm of locusts.

Tom, Sr., was not saying a word, but as Warren Whalen tightened his grasp on the man's genitals, he emitted a sound like wind through rotted wood that seemed to come right out from between his ribs.

Warren Whalen smiled. His teeth were yellowed, and as he spoke he seemed to be experiencing difficulty in pulling his jaws apart. Thick mucus dripped from his mouth. "We were expecting you, Mr. Torch, for our little private screening."

Torch bleated at the dead man.

"As at home in the barnyard as in town, I see, Mr. Torch," Warren said. Tom, Sr., rolled his eyes in his head and passed out. A trickle of dark blood leaked down his pants where Warren was holding him. Warren let go. Tom, Sr., slid to the floor in a heap.

Warren brought his bloody fingers up to his mouth and licked each one. "Mmm—no, he's not dead yet, Mr. Torch, no need to be filled with human pity. We intend to feed on this one—nice and plump, don't you think? No, he'll live for a few more days. But you know, big fish eat little fish. It must be a bit of a disappointment to realize you the living are not at the top of the food chain, mustn't it?"

Torch clutched the thing in his hand. The thing he had taken from his pocket moments before entering the theater. The only weapon he knew of, the only thing he'd ever had against them. "Muuu," Torch snarled, feeling triumphant as he pulled his box of matches out from under the rags.

Warren's eyes filmed over for an instant, as if the sight of the matches made him remember something. "Yes, 'matches.' And you're a very smart man, Mr. Torch, but you must not let yourself burn the candle at both ends. You see, we know you pride yourself on your sense of smell, we know how you tracked us here. But there is one of you, and we are infinite. We have no beginning, and no end. And Mr. Torch, we have an ability similar to yours. We, too, can smell . . . things. For example, right now, your, shall we call it a suit? exudes a cool, delicate aroma, like our own. An eau de what—oil? Gasoline, perhaps? Old tires? What a delightful cologne. Every scent tells a story, does it not?"

Torch sniffed at the air; the stink of the grave seemed to be fading, receding, slipping under the door, even while the dead man spoke.

"And the musk that you anoint yourself with, Mr. Torch, has already told us all we need to know. A gas station. Close by. There is only one. And you are here, and she is there." Warren Whalen took a step toward Torch. "You believe that she is somehow protected from us, do you not? Hope among your kind certainly does spring eternal. But we have a member of the local police rescuing her even as you and I speak—one of your own, the living. Now, if you give me those matches, perhaps we will show some mercy. Death need not be painful, Mr. Torch, and we do appreciate your playing the guardian angel for our own anointed one . . ."

"Baaakkk," Torch said, and held a match in the air, ready to strike it against the wall of the projection booth.

Warren Whalen, his violet eyes gleaming in anticipated triumph, took another step forward. "There are innocent lives sitting in that theater. Fires are dangerous things—you of all people should know that." Warren reached his hand out. "Give me the matches, Mr. Torch, now."

Torch looked at the man's hand. Ants crawled across deep red gouges in the skin around his wrists. He glanced back at the dead man's face, which was oozing pus from its sores and cuts.

Torch struck the match against the side of the wall.

10.

Something bright caught Tommy's eye and drew his vision up to the projection booth. A ball of fire seemed to explode outward, through the plexiglass of the projection window. The flames spread quickly to the rippled red velvet curtains alongside the wall. Cries of panic filled the dark theater, but Tommy, frozen in the aisle, stared up at the projection booth where his father had been, only hearing the roar of the fire as it stretched its canopy around him. Then he was pushed aside by people running down to the emergency exits; he came to himself, and also ran down to the double doors. The rush of air that swept through the theater as patrons ran out into the alley fanned the fire, and as Tommy ran out the doors he heard glass exploding, and the screams of those who were not making it out in time.

Tommy now ran with a blind animal instinct, afraid that if he looked back he would see the flames licking at his neck with their rough tongues. If he stopped running, he thought, he would die.

11.

Lyle

Deputy Lyle Holroyd was convinced he was going to come out of this a hero. It was worth any minor confusion he might be experiencing: the memory lapse between this afternoon and this evening, as soon as he'd entered the Marlowe-Houston House with Hank Firestone, the detective from Roanoke. Lyle just could not for the life of him account for the time between the moment he'd crossed the threshold of that house and ten minutes ago. He thought he'd been talking with some of Firestone's state police friends, but he could not recall a single face. In fact, standing in the dark alley waiting for the signal over his walkie-talkie, Lyle could not even remember exactly what Firestone looked like.

Fire engines shrieked past him; he heard police sirens down Main Street, but Lyle could not be bothered. Detective Firestone had warned him th[illegible] might be some trouble when they got hold of the kidnapper. Lyle stood firm. When the signal came, giving him the precise location of the kidnapper's hideout, Lyle tried to stay in the shadows as he headed to the back entrance of the dilapidated Mobil Station across from the Henchman Lounge.

All the back windows were blackened over with paint, and when he kicked the back door of the deserted gas station open, the inside looked like it had been set up as a last stand. The front garage doors boarded from the inside. Tires were set up along the windows as reinforcements against break-ins. Several cans of gasoline lined up end-to-end along one wall.

And on the other wall, burning candles. Lyle gasped; this kidnapper was some fire freak.

"Hello?" Lyle called out. "Teddy? Where are you? It's all right now, you're safe—" *Don't let me find her dead. Don't let her be dead—you can't be a hero if you're lugging a corpse.*

"You're safe. It's all over," his words echoed back to him.

He glanced down into the pit. There were a bunch of old torn and wadded sheets piled up. A filthy mattress. A children's toy that Lyle himself had once owned when he was a kid: Etch A Sketch. Lyle continued talking as he walked back into the run-down office, "It's all right, Teddy, we'll take care of you, everything's going to be fine."

The dozens of candles burned in the office; Lyle wondered that this place hadn't gone up in flames.

A noise. A shuffling noise, and then the creaking shut of some door. Not far from where he stood.

She is in the washroom. Please God Almighty let her not be dead in that room, let her be tied up, even let her have been tortured to within an inch; but not dead.

He tried the door to the washroom; locked.

"Look, everything's okay, it's all right."

No answer.

"Honey, I know you're in there. My name's Lyle, I'm a policeman."

No answer.

"Now, honey, I know you're in there, so try to move as far away from that door as you can. You understand?" Lyle pushed against the washroom door.

He heard a noise from inside the bathroom. She was coming to the door. "Wait," the girl said, and she sounded weak.

He heard the metal click as she unlocked the door and opened it a crack. She thrust an oil lamp in his face. Her hand was trembling. The flame of the lamp wiggled. "Where is he?"

"It's all right, everything's going to be all right, you got nothing to worry about from here on in, Teddy, just let Deputy Lyle carry you out of here." He pushed the door open wider.

"You're not one of them," she said, and her voice was frail and uncertain. In the lamplight, he saw she looked like a living skeleton, she was so skinny and drawn. Dark rings around her eyes like a raccoon's mask. Her once frizzy hair had thinned and clung to her scalp.

"Honey, you're safe and sound now, ain't nothing gonna hurt you." He took the lamp from her hand and set it down on the concrete floor. He lifted her up. She seemed ridiculously light. Her entire body was greasy with sweat.

Lyle carried her out of the gas station, the way he'd come in. He walked through the alley, expecting the cruisers to be out on Main Street, and an ambulance waiting for the girl. But he never made it that far.

"We'll take her from here, Lyle." The voice was Hank Firestone's, but Lyle could not see anyone in the dark alley. He held Teddy Amory against his chest, her legs flopping over his arms, her own arms hugging around his neck.

Lyle looked around. "We?"

12.

Cassie

It had been at Prescott's suggestion that he and Cup drive over to Cabelsville for dinner. "Get our minds off this morbid stuff for a while," he said. They took the overpass to Route 64, and then followed it for about forty minutes before taking the Cabelsville exit. Cup observed that Cabelsville didn't look a whole lot different than Pontefract, just more brand-name places: a Safeway, a Baskin-Robbins, a Pizza Hut, and several fast food hamburger chains. They settled on McDonalds.

"Gee, this Mc-whatever looked really good when I ordered it, but I just don't feel all that hungry," Cup said.

"Need to keep your strength up," Prescott said, reaching over the table and picking at Cup's french fries.

"I think I'm more afraid of dying right now than at any other time in my life." Prescott looked out the side window, and Cup felt he could read his thoughts: the damn nerve of this world to go on with such normal things as Drive-Thru Windows and Big Macs. "I always thought that when you get to be up in years death looks like a friend. Bull, as they say."

"I thought we weren't going to get into this morbid stuff tonight."

"Well, we're geographically removed from it. In a McDonalds you could be anywhere in the world."

"I know what you mean though. Death just doesn't seem like the same obscure threat it was a week ago. God, Prescott, less than a week ago. I feel like I've been here months, but it's only been—what—five days?"

"But you've been preparing for this week for twelve years. And in my own way, I've been preparing for over forty years."

"I knew there was something you hadn't told me. It was

that little interchange between you and Lowry today. Something about that portrait of him on the horse."

"Yes," Prescott said, "and I suppose McDonalds is as safe a place as any to tell it."

13.

Prescott's Story

When I was one and twenty—do you know that poem by Housman? Well, that could've been me. In the golden olden days, the halcyon days, the salad days. But, Cup, my most cherished memories are not of my youth, but of you boys, my students, watching you discover what was exciting, and always seeing the world with your enthusiasm, newness. Teenage boys have few bad memories, their whole lives are something to look forward to. I suppose that was what I found in teaching, the ability to capture that contagion for the possibilities ahead, not those prisons of the past. Or if the past, then the distant past, the past that was far enough removed from my own situation that I could get lost in it.

And yes, that horse. The one in Gower's portrait was called Lady Day for Billie Holiday, and I suppose is as good a starting point as any for what I am about to tell you.

My wife Cassie loved horses. She and Gower were childhood friends—perhaps something like you and Lily Cammack. Except they had the extra bond of being first cousins. They were closer to each other than I was with her. Gower's father owned the only half-decent stables in town. My barn is the last remnant of what they were. I bought it from Gower's father when he was selling them off in the fifties. Gower was a much different man then—you can't imagine from seeing him now. He was, first, the richest young man in the county—they had been the only family in the area to prosper during the Depression, mainly because of the furniture factories his father had gotten hold of down in North Carolina. Also, Gower was one of the handsomest young men. He's about six years my junior, and I remember all manner of women between the ages of sixteen and thirty literally swooning over him. And yet, he was an affable fellow, and his heart belonged to one woman and one woman alone, so men didn't feel in the least threatened by him.

I was perhaps the only one who did.

Because it was my wife, Cassie, who would always be the object of his affections.

Cassie was a beautiful woman. It was a shock to me when she accepted my proposal in 1938—I was still an undergraduate at Washington and Lee University over in Lexington. I had no real prospects for the future. She and I got married three weeks before my graduation, and Gower's father, Stone Lowry, gave me a job as an accountant with one of his businesses in Newton. So Cassie and I set up house in Pontefract, and I commuted. I respected her friendship with Gower—he had always behaved honorably. My own family was telling me I was some kind of fool for closing my eyes to what was going on, but I paid them no mind.

I was in love, and I couldn't see what was coming.

There was something else, too. About my wife.

Something that none of us noticed at first. It occurred after a party at the Marlowe-Houston House—Gower's family still lived there, it wasn't turned over to the school until 1951—Dr. Cammack was the first and only headmaster to move into it. And it seems they moved out just as quickly, so it became the useless museum it is today.

Back to this party—it was in the summer. The Lowrys were always throwing summer parties, and all the socially prominent of the county turned out. Because of my marriage, I was counted among these. Cassie could never hold her liquor, and she'd had too much to drink that night. She suggested that we three—her, Gower and myself—take a stroll down by the lake. I can't speak for Gower, but for myself I can say I was flying three sheets to the wind, and was up for anything. Remember, I was about 24 when this happened, and Gower was 18, and Cassie had just turned

22. In spite of what young people think, free spirits were not invented with their own generation.

When Cassie started taking her dress off over her head, I wasn't all that shocked. We had gone skinny-dipping in one of the quarries outside town; she and Gower had grown up together practically like brother and sister. I was a bit of a free-thinker, I guess. And, I might add, it was very, very dark.

Soon we were all three naked and in the water, swimming around; and drunk, I swam over to Cassie, and said, "Do you love me?" She didn't answer immediately; I saw the reason. Gower was dog paddling nearby, and I knew she didn't want to admit that she loved me more than she did him. So she responded, "I love you both in your own ways," and she was giggling and Gower was giggling and I was giggling, and I pushed her down under the water's surface. What I didn't know was, at that precise moment, Cassie got a cramp in her leg, and when she came up, went down again.

I swam around, trying to find her, but I couldn't. Gower also was looking frantically for her, and it was he who pulled her out of the water and carried her to shore. As I came up on land, this was the scenario in the partial moonlight:

A naked man kneeling next to a lovely naked woman, his mouth against hers in an effort to revive her. She came to rather quickly, and gave him a kiss on the cheek, and by then I was standing over them both. Jealousy had sobered me.

Two things occurred this night. First, I forbade Cassie to ever see Gower Lowry again, and said we must sever all ties with the family. And second, the taint of Clear Lake had possessed her. She changed in her attitude toward me, but more importantly, she had acquired an ability. Yes, a psychic ability, but something that I chalked up to wishful thinking combined with a powerful woman's intuition.

Cassie began to predict things that would come to pass. Little things, like the weather, or if someone was going to be taken ill that week. I began to kid her and called her "my witch." "What does my witch see in her crystal ball today?" I'd ask. After a bit of this ribbing, she became secretive. I started working longer hours at the accounting firm (I didn't fulfill my promise to sever every connection with the Lowry family), and when I was home, my wife and I didn't discuss things the way I thought young couples should.

It was easy enough to find out why, but I was a young fool—I assumed that she had kept her word and did not see Gower Lowry at all.

Cup, are you done with your french fries?

14.

The reference to french fries had jolted Cup out of the trance he'd been in listening to Prescott's story. "Wha—oh, yeah, I guess." The two men were sitting in a booth with a cutout of Ronald McDonald staring at them from across the room; one of the girls from behind the counter had come out and was sweeping the floor.

"Maybe we should be going back now; it's getting late."

"So that's the connection with Teddy Amory? Your wife had caught the same thing from the lake that this Amory kid did?"

Prescott said, "I'll tell you the rest on the way home."

15.

The Rest of the Story, on the Way Home to Pontefract

I didn't have an inkling that my marriage was in any kind of trouble. I took it upon myself—I assumed that she did not seem very open to me anymore because I had come between a childhood friendship she valued greatly. So I gave her the go-ahead that December, 1940. She could resume speaking with Gower Lowry. In fact, I inaugurated this renewal with a cozy dinner, just the three of us.

And she and I did begin speaking more, what I assumed was fairly openly. And I became very afraid, Cup, for her sanity.

She began talking about voices she was hearing. She said they'd begun that night in Clear Lake, like a ringing in her ears. And these voices told her things, some of which she had never mentioned to anyone. People who would die, women in town who would miscarry, words that would be said. And all, she assured me, had come to pass.

I begged her to go to a doctor to make sure it wasn't some physical problem. She laughed and said, "I'd hardly call prophecy a problem." That Christmas I fell into a great depression—I was literally worrying myself sick. I kept to my bed with a psychosomatic flu from the 26th through the 1st of the year.

And on the day after New Year's Day, 1941, my own brother came by the house and dropped a grenade right in my lap.

He told me that I'd been the laughingstock of the whole town. That she had made me the laughingstock. Because everyone knew that, right under my nose, my wife was having an affair of the vilest sort with Gower Lowry.

This information cured me of the lingering effects of my flu virus, and I went immediately to the stables where they were saddling up Lady Day, the mare that Cassie adored. I accused them of everything under the sun, adultery, lying, and that ultimate betrayal among us Southern Gentlemen: dishonor. Cassie went into hysterics—she began crying, telling me that I was wrong, that she and Gower were like brother and sister, that nothing of the sort occurred. She got on Lady Day and rode off down the trail; leaving me there, confused and angry.

I pulled Gower back inside the stables. I was ready to kill him. Here was this teenaged rich boy who thought he could just steal my wife right out from under me.

But he told me something, and it was the way he said it that made me believe him. "You've got every right to hit me," he said, "because if anything, I'm guilty. But Cassie is quite innocent."

He told me that he had indeed been meeting secretly with my wife for the past year, and that their relationship was no longer platonic. If I'd had a gun just then I would've shot him full of lead. Lord, I was even eyeing a pitchfork in the stable as a potential weapon. But, Gower added, Cassie was innocent by reason of an instability of mind which Gower had taken advantage of in the past year. "You see," he said, "Cassie was never willing to consummate our relationship until fairly recently. And only then, when this other woman had taken hold." My blood was boiling, Cup, that word *consummate* had taken on a hideous meaning for me. But I promised myself as I stood there that I would not disfigure Lowry until after he'd had his say. I would be a gentleman about it.

"What other woman?" I asked him.

"Your wife calls her Virginia," Gower told me.

You see, Cup, my wife believed that she was possessed by this spirit, this dead woman. And in playing on this belief, Gower took advantage of her.

But, after reading bits of Worthy Houston's diary, you may recognize that name: Virginia. Virginia Houston, Worthy's sister. One of Gower's ancestors. In fact, an ancestor of several of us here in town.

Well, suffice it to say I thought my wife was positively insane and that Gower Lowry was the vilest creature on the face of this earth. I took the riding crop right out of his hands and thrashed him soundly.

Then I went off in search of my wife.

I would not find her for another seven days.

That winter, in fact that very day, January 2nd, the worst storm in the history of the Shenandoah Valley came through. The blizzard lasted from the 2nd through the 8th. We formed a search party on the second day of the storm, but came up empty-handed. I kept hoping that after Cassie had ridden off that morning, she had hidden in a nearby shack, or that she'd managed to make it to one of the empty hunting cabins that are spread out throughout the hills before the snow came down.

But on January 8th, we found the horse, Lady Day, practically frozen into the ground on the hill they call

Steeple Ridge. But not just frozen. Lady Day, one of the most beautiful mares you'd ever seen, had been mutilated, one of our search party said it looked like someone operated on the horse but forgot to put the vital organs back inside. It was a horrible sight, but gave us a strange kind of hope. We thought that the horse had died from cold and hunger, and Cassie had cut the animal open in order to eat. It was only a thin strand of hope, out of left field, but it was something.

But before nightfall, we found Cassie's body. Not far from where Lady Day had fallen.

One of the men in the search party had seen the scrap of red cloth—from Cassie's winter coat—caught on an ice-covered bush.

And, behind the bush, was a cave. Very small. To call it a cave conjures an image of a large space. But it was barely of a size large enough to accommodate an adult human being.

We . . . we found her in that tiny crevice in the rocks. She was frozen to death, of course—I had prepared myself for that. The blizzard had taken many lives with it when it came through the valley—hunters stranded in cabins, caught unprepared and not so wilderness-ready as they believed themselves to be—a woman and her children died and were not found until two weeks after the storm ended.

But it wasn't just that my wife had died.

She was naked, Cup—had taken all her clothes off and pushed them up into the far end of the cave.

She had a small pocketknife in one hand, its blade open and bloody. There was blood on the rocks.

Cup, my wife had frozen to death. But before that had happened, she tried to skin herself alive.

16.

They reached the exit to Pontefract, and both men wondered if they ought to just drive past it.

But Dr. Nagle turned onto the overpass and headed home. Neither had spoken a word since Prescott finished telling his story.

17.

Tommy MacKenzie spent that night in the empty sheriff's office of an equally empty courthouse. He huddled in the crawlspace beneath the sheriff's metal desk.

He did not sleep.

18.

Wednesday, January 7, 1987

IN THE A.M.

Cappie Hartstone, who decided she just hadn't been getting enough sleep lately, got up extra early to go jogging. Exercise always seemed to help with sleep at night. She'd been having one too many nightmares about Uncle Arthur, and the arguments with her husband, Bill, were on the rise. A bad winter all around with Arthur dying, that nice Mr. Whalen killing himself (although Georgia Stetson didn't think he did it by himself), then the news of the psychotic man over at Patsy Campbell's who she hoped the police had already picked up before he hurt anybody.

She'd been jogging three miles by 6:30 A.M. Clothed head to toe in fluorescent pink sweats that were just the cutest thing and had been on sale over at the Sweaterobic Sports Shop in Newton, Cappie barely felt the cold air. She slid once or twice on a patch of ice as she turned right onto the Old Carriage Road, but other than that, the bad weather was not stopping her from getting a good workout. Another mile or so wouldn't hurt her fanny.

The thing she absolutely loved about jogging was the way it allowed her to work off all her frustrations and anger.

Cappie realized she had become an unpleasant person to be around lately.

With every step she took, every time her New Balance running shoes came down on the road, she imagined her husband's face beneath the sole. *Bill, with his rash-giving beard, his smug hamster brown eyes, those Dopey Dwarf ears: pound him under your heel, into the gravel, yes, Cappie, grind that man right into the dirt like a roach.*

She'd awakened at five A.M., unable to sleep, and wrote in her Day Runner Book:

Bill yelled at me, and I thought he was going to hit me again, but he didn't. But I could see he wanted to. I know I haven't been the best wife for him, but do I deserve this?

I really would just like to get away for a while—from him, from the kids, just some down time for ME. But I can't leave. And I don't really want to leave him, do I? I want to kill him.

Pound! Her heel came down on the road, *tearing open Bill's face, smushing his features until you could not tell that it had been a human being under there—the ripped treads from her running shoes left their imprint across his eyes.*

No, she thought as she jogged, *I must not be so negative. You wrinkle faster when you are negative. Think positive. Think positive.*

She turned the volume up on her Sony Walkman. It was Olivia Newton-John singing "Physical," and Cappie felt cheery. *The sun would be up soon, this was a new day, things always turned out for the best, didn't they?*

It was still fairly dark out, although a purple haze filtered from over the eastern hills. As she jogged forward she saw a man walking up the road toward her—he seemed to recognize her, he waved, and the thought went through her mind while Olivia Newton-John sang in her ears: *why would a man in a tuxedo be walking along the Old Carriage Road before sunrise? Was he just coming from a party?*

But then Cappie recognized the man as he came closer, and he was opening something on his chest, it was like a medicine cabinet on his chest and he was opening the doors, pulling them back, but it was not a medicine cabinet, it was his skin, and Cappie stopped jogging, and Olivia Newton-John stopped singing.

And something came up behind her as she watched her Uncle Arthur show her the inside of his chest just like the little plastic Visible Man she'd given Jason for his science project, but Uncle Arthur's insides were steaming; and whoever came up behind her pulled the Walkman's headphone cord tightly around her neck.

Cappie Hartstone's throat was crushed ten minutes before the official sunrise. But she did not die. Yet. In another hour she would long for death while something in the pit of a dark cellar fed upon her.

19.

Somebody was knocking like crazy at Patsy's front door and it wasn't even eight yet. Patsy was watching "Good Morning, America" and alternating between a cup of coffee (she had run out of RCs) and a moonpie. Her only boarder, Cup Coffey, had not returned last night, *thank God, although this might be him at the door now.* Patsy hoped that the man had just fallen off the face of the earth or had been picked up by the police.

The knocking continued.

"Is that you, Mr. Coffey?" she shouted from the front hallway. If it was, she thought, she'd boil a gallon of Crisco and dump it on him. After what she'd read in that book of his, practically a horror story, she knew that man was crazy. A real sicko. All that evil stuff he'd written about her nephew Bart, poor, poor Bart who'd never meant anyone any harm.

And me being so hospitable and all!

If only she'd remembered that last name sooner: Coffey.

She glanced cautiously out the front window, but whoever was knocking stood directly behind the door and she could not see him.

That knocking—it just kept on like he was hammering something into the door.

"Enough, enough, I'm coming!" *Well, if this is the Coffey person I'll just call Sheriff Connally and have this pervert put away.*

Patsy piffled over to the front door, touched the knob and hesitated.

She took a deep breath, the aftertaste of chocolate moonpie going sour in her mouth, and turned the knob, swinging the door wide.

Before she got a clear look at the curious figure standing there grinning yellow teeth, Patsy noticed his handiwork: the screen door had melted down where the man's fingers touched it. She thought he was a black man at first (which put a double-dose of fear in her heart because she'd never had a black man at her door). She reached into the breast pocket of her robe and extracted her glasses. She held them up to her eyes.

She saw immediately it wasn't any black man. This man seemed . . . charred. As if he'd been barbecued. Exploded from the inside out, and his skin was blistered and falling onto the front porch floorboards even while he stood there.

She tried to scream, but felt the air rushing out of her lungs with no sound attached, and that sickly sweet-and-sour moonpie taste. Patsy was about to fall backwards in a genuine faint, but the burnt man reached through the melted screen door and grabbed the collar of her robe.

"Aunt Patsy," he giggled. Foam spat out from his mouth.

He wiped his free hand across his lips as if he were very, very hungry, and not for a moonpie and an RC.

20.

Neither Georgia Stetson nor her husband Ken would think it unusual if their son, Rick, did not emerge from his room until the afternoon. He always slept late during his breaks from school.

CHAPTER FIFTEEN

GEORGE

1.

The fire at the Key Theater had not spread to the adjoining buildings on Main Street—the fire department had seen to that. On Wednesday morning, the theater itself did not look that much different than it usually did. The top windows had broken outward, and the huge marquee was a mess of melted plastic. Part of the outside wall was blackened. The worst part of the fire had been inside the theater. When Sheriff George Connally returned from the medical center that morning, one of the firemen, Mike Scoby, was down at the courthouse filling out a report. George asked him what the probable cause was, and Mike had shrugged. Said something about film being flammable, and the whole conflagration having begun in the projection booth.

Nine people died in the fire, although only two had been positively identified so far. One guy they were sure of was Thomas MacKenzie, the theater's owner, and another name that came up was one George hadn't heard in years. Well, at least not the fellow's proper name, which was Dylan Houston, better known as Torch. The albino who had once been burned, and perhaps liked to burn. Allegedly, Pontefract's resident arsonist. George hadn't believed it when Lyle accused the man of torching the Amory house; but hell, maybe Lyle was right. Because the witnesses out on Main

Street had seen this guy Torch leap from one of the second-story windows of the Key Theater. Everybody knew Torch—he was the popular scapegoat. George would not even be surprised if parents used stories about Torch to scare their kids away from matches. "If you play with matches, Torch will come get you."

And when Torch made his dramatic, Errol Flynn exit from the theater, he landed on the pavement. "Splat!" Mike Scoby said, splaying his fingers out, "just like a bug on your goddamn windshield, only this bug was on fire."

"And he was dead?"

"Not quite—we got there just about that time, and I saw what happened to him. He was trying to stand up, you know it reminded me of that Mommy joke about 'Shut up or I'll nail your other foot to the floor' 'cause he kept going around in circles, all on fire." Mike realized what he was saying, and added softly, "'Course, it wasn't funny."

"Didn't anybody help him?"

But George didn't need that question answered. Mike's eyes said it all: it hadn't even occurred to any of the bystanders to help Torch, or put him out of his misery. He was a non-person to them, he was the invisible man. "So you . . . people . . . just let him burn."

Mike went back to writing his report and said, "That guy was a goner before I got there, Sheriff, and if you ask me, he's better off now than if he'd lived."

George got back in his cruiser and went to look at the wreckage, but by 10 A.M. a crowd of gawkers was milling around the building. *Jesus, he thought, no matter where the shit comes down, the flies are always there before you can clean it up. And speaking of clean-ups,* he thought as he smelled his own B.O. in the car.

He hadn't thought about himself since the night before, since that moment he had walked into the bedroom and found his wife, Rita, beneath the sink, her tongue cut out. Dr. Scott informed him that despite appearance, her blood loss had not been that great. It hadn't even been her whole tongue—just the last half-inch to the tip. "Isn't that enough?" George had asked, and Dr. Scott had patted him on the shoulder and said, "Well, let's say it could be worse . . . Tell me, Sheriff, has your wife been depressed lately?"

George had put his hands up in the air. "Hey, I know this line of questioning. But Rita says someone did this to her."

"She told this to you?" The way the doctor emphasized the word *told,* George recognized his mistake immediately.

"I mean—she tried to make sounds like—"

What Dr. Scott told him next chilled George to the bone.

"Your wife, Sheriff Connally, wrote on a pad to one of our nurses, just before she went to sleep, that she didn't mean to eat the glass. Which, I'm afraid, would indicate . . ."

I know what the fuck it would indicate, George thought as he drove down Main Street in the morning, *it would indicate that she either was taking her own life or awfully anxious to sink her teeth into something that might sink its own teeth into her. I'm going to go home and take a shower and clean this damn town off of me, wash all of it down the drain, and then I am going to be someone else, not sheriff, not even a cop, but just a someone who lives his own life and walks down the street and doesn't lift a goddamn finger when his fellow man bites the dust. Rita and I are going to live a normal life, albeit a quieter one now that she can't say much—Jesus, Jesus, Jesus, I'm losing it. Burnout, it's here, it's happening, it's burning, just like the Key Theater, just like Dylan Houston, a.k.a. Torch, Mommy-Mommy, why do I keep going around in circles? Shut up, or I'll nail your other foot to the floor—that's me, going around in circles, aimless goddamn circles.*

George Connally had not slept in two days. When he got home, he lay down on the couch for five minutes, setting his shoulder holster across the couch arm, and did not wake up again until someone standing over him said his name.

2.

Wednesday, January 7, 1987

IN THE P.M.

Cup had spent the night at Prescott's, after drinking too much of Prescott's beer. ("My way of coping, I guess," Cup said; Prescott raised his pipe. "This is my way—both methods have their hazards.") The beer helped Cup sleep, and he slept into the afternoon. When he awoke at 12:30, he shoveled Prescott's driveway for him. Anything to take his mind off what was going on. As the shadows grew longer, Prescott suggested he go collect his things at Patsy Campbell's and that he could borrow the car.

3.

"George," the man said, and George awoke, his back sore from the couch, his left arm asleep because he'd kept it behind his head for support while he napped on the couch. "It's okay, it's me, Lyle." George's eyes began to focus on the figure looming over him. The living room was prematurely dark; all the drapes were drawn on the windows. George did not at first notice the nervous quality in Lyle's voice.

George sat up on the couch. "What time is it?"

Lyle went over and peeked through the drapes that covered the sliding glass doors to the patio. "I dunno," he said, "it's getting late. And you know what happens when it gets dark."

George combed his fingers through his greasy hair, and tasted the scum residue of his own bad breath. "What are you doing here, anyway?"

"They're all out there, I needed someplace to go. Someplace they wouldn't look because they already looked here, so I know—"

"Lyle? You all right?"

"It's vampires, George, and it's werewolves, and it's ghouls. They got the girl and they almost got me, too, but Christ! I was smart! Christ! I brought this cross." Lyle pointed to the coffee table, and George focused his eyes on the outline of a crucifix about the height of his arm. "I stole it, actually, George, from Christ Church, I spent the night there, behind the altar, 'cause vampires can't go to church, and I know I'm taking a chance coming here, but I seen something I think you should know, and they already been here, so it's safe, and it's not dark yet, well, the sun hasn't gone down, so I think we're okay, brought this cross with me, I stole it, and—"

When Lyle took a breath, George interrupted him. "Lyle, will you just relax a little, now what the hell has happened to you?"

Lyle stood motionless, but silent.

George got up and turned on the overhead lights. He gestured for Lyle to take a seat on the couch. "Do you need a drink, boy?"

Lyle sat on the couch. He began bouncing up and down on the cushion nervously. He picked up George's holster off the arm of the couch. "I never even take mine off when I sleep," but somehow when he said this, even he was not sure what he meant. Lyle set the gun and holster down beside himself. He shook his head. "I smoked a little weed just a couple of hours ago, well, a shitload of weed, and I think a drink might not sit well with me right now."

George sat on the edge of the coffee table and tilted the brass crucifix back. He laughed. "You actually stole this from church?"

"Nothing to laugh about."

George brought his left hand up and clapped it against his forehead. "Lord, Lyle, I leave you in charge for a day and you're nothing but a fuck-up. And you're fucked up on top of that. You march in here high as a kite, you who swore to uphold the law, on marijuana, you steal this thing, and now you've got some Hunter Thompson syndrome—and I know he's an idol of yours, though God knows why—and you think devils are chasing you down. Your daddy must be spinning in his grave."

For a moment, Lyle reminded George of Tony Perkins in *Psycho.* He kept smoothing out the upholstery of the couch and glancing from side to side as if someone else was in the room speaking. George had never touched marijuana in his life, and he wondered if this was a side effect. "Well, come on, Lyle, talk to me, but slowly, okay?"

Lyle Holroyd half-grinned. "That's what he said, too, slowly, slowly, slowly, they eat you, very slowly, and you get to live awhile because they like especially to eat you alive."

"Lyle, make some sense, who said that?"

For a moment some semblance of his old self appeared in Lyle's face. But when he spoke, the words came out scraggly and torn, mutilated by a bad case of paranoia: "Jake Amory."

4.

"Daddy?" Clare asked the empty house.

She wanted to search it again, for a fifth time. Then a sixth time. Then a seventh time.

She did not want to think that her father had left earlier in the day. That he had taken a long stroll. Across town, across the footbridge, across the lake, to

The Marlowe-Houston House.

For the party that his favorite daughter, his wife, and his favorite son-in-law, *who were all, ha ha, as Lily would say, dead as you're feeling right now, Clare, although maybe* you *feel* deader, *if that's possible, little blind Clare with no i,* the party they were throwing.

Before she began crying, wondering how insane you have to be before it all seems rational, Clare decided to call the sheriff's office again.

5.

"The Amory kid?" George asked. He decided to play it cool with Lyle, let the man speak.

"Oh, but you never would recognize him, no, no, no, I didn't recognize him, George, and I used to whop him upside the head every other day when I used to catch him inside the Henchman—had a fake I.D. But down there, George, down there, he wasn't half the troublemaker he was before—that's pretty fucking hilarious, you know, him not being half the troublemaker, because all they'd left was his— Oh, Christ, George," Lyle said, and his face crumpled in on itself, becoming a mass of creases and wrinkles. Lyle began crying like a baby, "Christ, I was smart, I was so smart, I was so so so smart."

"It's all right, Lyle, whatever it is, you're here and you're safe," George said. He kept his voice at an even pitch.

"They got the Amory boy, he told me they eat you real slowly, slowly, they like to play with you like that, and that Amory boy, he only had one arm and no legs, no legs at all, none to speak of—ha-ha—only stumps and you can't run on stumps, so they didn't even have to tie him up or anything. They only tied up the arteries, George, they're pretty smart when it comes to keeping us alive, because they like to play with us, George, they like to play with us, and maybe not kill us right off the bat, that's what he told me, but I'm smarter than he is, I still have both legs, and both arms, and your Smith & Wesson," and Lyle reached into the holster that lay beside him on the couch and pulled the gun out. His hand trembled, and he had to hold on with both hands to keep it steady. He pointed it at George.

"Lyle," George said.

"Christ! I'm smart! George! Because they really want you! Not me! And I told them, I'll get him, yes, yes, yes, I'll get him, just like I got the girl, and wasn't that—oh dear sweet fucking Jesus H. Christ—wasn't that smart!" Lyle pulled back on the trigger.

6.

Patsy Campbell, wearing her foamy pink curlers, blue chenille robe and fluffy slippers, was watching TV when Cup came through the front door, and if there was one thing that struck him as: what's wrong with this picture, it was not only the absence of chocolate moonpie essence wafting in the air, but also that the house was very cold.

Involuntarily, Cup said aloud, "Brrr."

Patsy did not turn around, but seemed glued to the TV.

"Hello, Patsy," Cup said, but softly; for some reason he felt as if he'd entered a library and so could not speak above a low whisper.

Patsy Campbell turned and looked at him. Those hoot owl eyes magnified a million times by her glasses, a cursory glance, and then back to the "Oprah Winfrey Show." When she turned her head, one of the pink curlers fell to the floor, and rolled a few feet toward Cup. He went to pick it up, and then stopped. He felt like he'd done something horribly wrong, like an errant lover being punished with silence. Perhaps this is how she treats guests who spend their nights elsewhere.

Cup went up to his room.

Another what's wrong with this picture, only he knew almost immediately what was wrong with it.

His diary, *The Nightmare Book,* lay open on his bed.

7.

George Connally was hoping his face did not betray his true feelings. He wasn't half as scared as Lyle Holroyd evidently was. Even while Lyle pointed the gun at him, his eyes darted left and right as if at any moment someone would come in the room.

"Are they in the house?" George asked.

"George—if you knew what they could do—you wouldn't even ask, no way no how, 'cause they can be anywhere and anyone they want . . . he told me that, he still could talk, they hadn't eaten all of him, his nose, just his nose, he looked like a goddamn leper, George!" Lyle's voice had become high and shrill, and he was fighting to keep the tears back.

"But are they in the house, Lyle?" George repeated.

Lyle's breathing was rapid; he sounded like he'd just run a marathon and his heart was giving out. "I don't know, Christ! I'm safe, don't you get it, I'm safe, and I had to do this, George, because they want you more than me, and they promised me, promised, they'd kill you right away, so you know you won't suffer or anything, not like him— Oh, God, George, his face, you wouldn't—wouldn't—"

"This house, Lyle, are they here?"

"Cut that, stop that, out," Lyle said, hiccupping his words. George had trouble taking his eyes off the barrel of the Smith & Wesson. "No, I told you, I told you, they're not in this house, they got what they wanted, the girl, the girl—"

"If they got the girl, Lyle, why do they want me?" George tried to sound as calm as possible. He tore his gaze free of the wobbling gun Lyle held and glanced about the room wondering what he could grab that would be a good weapon: next to him was that brass crucifix, and he could throw it but (Lyle answered, "Sure, yeah, they got the girl, but you're part of it, too, they're friends of— Now—you won't believe this—") by the time he got hold of it a bullet could be plowing through his brain. If he rolled back on the coffee table, he could use it as a shield, and then try and get to the—

"You listening, George? What you looking at anyway?" Lyle was suspicious. "You trying to get away?"

"No, Lyle, I'll do whatever you want, honest."

"What were you looking at just then—you saw something."

"I just thought . . . I heard something in the house."

Lyle sniffed the air. "I don't smell nothing, 'cause they got a real strong smell, because—ghouls, you know, and vampires, they're all dead, George, so they're bound to smell, you should see the maggots, George, the white white white maggots . . ."

George sniffed. "I smell something, Lyle, are you telling me you don't smell it?" *This better work.*

"They can't be here, 'cause they've got the girl, they don't care—they don't really care—it's only an eye for an eye they want, and you, why, I'm gonna be a hero, yes! Christ Almighty!" But Lyle's voice was fading as if he'd been running on empty for the past half hour.

"Lyle, seriously, didn't you hear that? They must be here."

"Don't make me shoot you, George," Lyle said.

"Don't tell me you can't smell them, right now, it's as strong as . . ."

"Like gas?"

"Yeah, like a big ol' tanker just spilled across the highway."

"Well—I don't—you could be lying."

"I'm telling you."

"They won't hurt me if I have my cross." Lyle had come down from the heights of his screechiness. "Hand me my cross, George."

"I'll do it if you promise to let me go." George reached for the crucifix.

"I can't do—"

"Did you hear that?"

"For Christ sake, they'll tear me apart, and they don't even want me!"

George picked up the cross. It was heavy. *Good. Serves this bastard right.*

"H-H-Hand it to me." Lyle now held the gun with his right hand and turned his palm toward George. "Carefully."

George held the cross out, but it was too far from Lyle.

"I can smell them, Lyle," George said.

Lyle took a step forward.

George lunged at him, swinging the brass crucifix down as hard as he could against the side of Lyle's head; the gun went off, and George felt something like fire in his left shoulder and then a freezing numbness, but that was okay, he only needed his right arm to bludgeon Lyle into unconsciousness. Which was relatively easy. Lyle toppled over on the first blow, and George hoped the son-of-a-bitch was alive so he could kill him.

8.

"You say they're at the Marlowe-Houston House?" George asked as he secured Lyle's handcuffs. The bullet Lyle fired from the Smith & Wesson had only grazed George's left shoulder, but it felt like it had gone into his heart because Lyle had finally cracked, the son of Cal Holroyd, former sheriff of Pontefract, former mentor of George Connally, had lost it.

Lyle, who was drooling and moaning from getting hit on the head with the brass crucifix, muttered, "Yeah, bu-but it's g-g-getting dark, George, and you know v-v-vampires—"

George pushed Lyle into the back seat of the cruiser. "Yeah, Lyle, I do know vampires, don't I?"

George shut the door, and then went around the other side of the car and got in behind the wheel. He took the mike from his radio and said into it, "Bonnie? You there?"

"George?" She croaked the name. Her voice was laced with weariness, and fear.

"Well, I found your husband, and it isn't too pretty, but we're going to take a trip over to the Marlowe-Houston House right now—"

"You can't take me there!" Lyle bellowed from the back seat. "They're gonna kill me!"

9.

Cup turned around when he heard the bedroom door creak open. Patsy stood there grinning. Her teeth, normally black from moonpies, looked like they'd been smeared with some kind of strawberry jam. The foamy pink curlers were dropping out of her hair like petals from a dying rose. Her face seemed more bloated than usual, and in the harsh bedroom light had a bluish tint to it. "I read that nasty book of yours," she said, clutching her robe closed.

"That was none of your business," Cup said, and then noticed something else; she stank. He hadn't gotten a good whiff of her downstairs, but she didn't smell like moonpies or Lilac Vegetal. She smelled like an old outhouse on a hot summer day.

"Mowing lawns, Mr. Coffey, is that what you want to do? The Good Book says that all flesh is grass, isn't that right? And you'd like to mow that field over, but it's their flesh, don't you see, it's their flesh, you filthy, nasty man, you nasty man. Bringing your filth in here, pushing it on me, smearing my face in it, you nasty, nasty man, pushing it in me, that's what you want to do, isn't it? Nasty men like you, you're not even a man are you? You nasty little boy, you nasty, filthy, filthy—"

The whole time she was spitting the words out, raising her right hand in emphasis like a tent revival preacher calling for the Holy Spirit, she was moving slowly toward him. Her words were punctuated by the piffling sound of her slippers. Without realizing it, Cup was also moving, backwards, his back to the wall. He stumbled back against the carton of empty bottles that Patsy had been storing in the room. Gingerly, he stepped over them, moving backwards, more bottles, rows of bottles all the way back to the wall.

And when Patsy let go of her blue chenille robe, it fell open like a curtain just drawn apart, and he screamed.

10.

"We go there," Lyle said, leaning his head over next to George's shoulder, "they'll get both of us now, George, and they only want you—it's not fair! It's not fair!" When he shrieked, his voice sounded like someone was raking razors across his vocal cords.

"Will you shut up!" George shouted.

"No—please, please—no—they got what they wanted—the girl—the girl—Firestone—" Lyle whimpered.

"Firestone?" George asked, and almost ran down Betty Henderson as she jaywalked across Main Street. He pulled over abruptly to the side of the road, skidding into some slush. It sprayed crud all across the right-hand side of the windshield. George kept the car running, his foot on the brake. "What the hell does Firestone have to do with this bullshit, Lyle?"

"I'll tell you if you promise—not—not to take me back there—please, please!" Lyle began sobbing, dropping his head against the vinyl of the seatback.

"You're going to tell me, Lyle, or I'll take you to that house and leave you handcuffed to the goddamn banister!" George kept his eyes on the street as Lyle began relating the events of the previous day, from Firestone's discussion about the Amory girl to Lyle's carrying the girl into the alley behind the abandoned Mobil Station and being hit over the head.

". . . And I woke up, and all these bones, sticking up, it was like a cage, and I was tied up and that Jake Amory—and then those Gastons, saying they wanted you, you, George . . ."

When Lyle collapsed in the back seat, carrying on about werewolves and vampires, George let out a string of profanities he didn't even know existed within himself. When he'd recovered, feeling that the worst of what was inside him had been unleashed, he said: "Damn it, Lyle, I don't know if you're flipped out or I'm crazy, but we are going to that house before I put a bullet in somebody's head—yours or mine!"

George tapped his foot on the accelerator, and drove on down the street.

"George," Bonnie's voice came over the radio, sounding even more drained of spirit and energy, "I've been getting calls from East Campus about Campbell's Boarding House, and now we got a report somebody's screaming over there, I can't get ahold of any of the boys, and I think you should—Oh, God, I've got to get out of here, George, I've been in here all night, I hate this job, I hate it—"

11.

Inside Patsy Campbell's robe: her naked, bloated body, the sagging, pendulous breasts, shriveled like a scrotum, her belly elliptical, and beneath the great folds of flesh, between her legs, silver jaws embedded with needle-like teeth. Slick strands of pubic hair dangled over the lips as the jaws snapped open and shut, and Cup was not sure if the voice that was speaking came from Patsy's mouth or from this feral nether maw.

Patsy continued speaking, her robe open, moving toward Cup, slowly, slowly. "Inside me, Mr. Coffey, I want you inside me, in there, you'll find what you're looking for—you're looking for that slut, aren't you? Well, she's in there, just take a peek, she's there waiting for you, why, I've had whole armies inside me, Mr. Coffey, one more won't hurt, you filthy filthy—"

Cup pressed himself against the wall; he scratched at the flowered wallpaper with his fingers as if he could dig himself into it. His legs gave out like jelly and he crumpled down on the floor. An empty RC Cola bottle rolled around as he knocked a six-pack over. He began yelling at the top of his lungs, "Help! Help me! For the love of God—"

"Love," Patsy dribbled, spraying blood across Cup's face

as she spoke. "Love me, no one's ever loved me, it's awful to die and to never know love, true love—do you believe in true love, Cup?" Her voice had gone from Patsy's adenoidal Southernness into the smooth dulcet tones that Cup recognized as Lily's. "Mow it down, Cup, mow the field, all flesh is grass, Cup, all flesh, all flesh . . ."

Cup reached over and grabbed one of the empty RC bottles by its neck. He held it up like a shield.

But when he used that bottle, breaking it against the wall to give it a cutting edge, brandishing it against those gnashing silver teeth between Patsy Campbell's legs, he would use it as a weapon.

12.

George's head reeled when he entered Patsy Campbell's home. It stank to high heaven. He heard the shout for help coming from upstairs, and as he ran up the stairs he felt cold, invisible fingers holding him back. The stairway didn't seem to end. George felt like his feet were mired in a bog, could hear his shoes thudding on the carpet, but his movements seemed to be in slow motion.

The shouts from upstairs were drawn out, lasting for hours. The house was chilly, and the smell . . .

George felt as if he were undergoing hypnosis, regressing to a past event through this present one, and the other scene flickered in his head. The hunting cabin in the woods behind the lake, and in that scene he wasn't running up stairs, but across a muddy driveway, freezing, as if the ice had gotten under his skin and into his blood. This was his chance to do something nice for them, he knew he could, he knew that the phone call Frank Gaston had made down to the courthouse was a plea for help, a last chance . . .

He knew he could rescue them, and when George got to the top of the stairs, he clung with both hands to the banister. He was out of breath and it felt like a gas-soaked rag had been stuffed down his throat, gagging him. The stench was so repulsive and strong it knocked him backwards, reeling. George fell to his knees and began hawking phlegm up into the back of his throat, his stomach heaving convulsively. He leaned on all fours, hacking and vomiting a greenish yellow lumpy cud onto the carpeting.

When he recovered from vomiting, he covered his nose and mouth with a handkerchief. He was completely disoriented. George did not think that the hunting cabin Frank and Louise owned had a stairway up to a third story. He stood up and walked cautiously over to the bedroom door. A woman was speaking rapidly behind the door, but the shouts for help had ceased.

No pools of blood, no skull fragments, no words written on the wall, no death, no death, please, no death . . .

Then the flashback to the Gaston tragedy tore apart, and George remembered where he was: the third floor of Campbell's Boarding House.

George heard a loud thumping sound, and he pushed the door open.

Patsy Campbell lay face up on the floor, which was littered with pink curlers and pop bottles still rolling like felled bowling pins. Her robe was open. There was something shiny protruding from between her legs, at her pubic area. It was, George found out later, a broken RC Cola bottle. Cup Coffey, whom George had interviewed just two days before, was sitting against the wall, shivering as if he'd been sprayed with ice water. His eyes bulged from their sockets. He did not even seem to notice George.

The smell of decay and death like some just-sprayed room deodorizer lingered in the air.

"You have the right," George gasped, unsure of his own sanity but able to repeat these words even in his sleep, "to remain silent."

PART THREE

VALLEY OF THE SHADOW

. . . A large mirror,—so at first it seemed to me in my confusion—now it stood where none had been perceptible before; and as I stepped up to it in extremity of terror, mine own image, but with features all pale and dabbled with blood . . .

—Edgar Allan Poe,
"William Wilson"

CHAPTER SIXTEEN

IN THE FLESH

1.

In the Sheriff's Office, Clare Terry watched as Bonnie Holroyd took her car keys out of her purse, and then went over to the coat rack. Someone was calling on the radio, and Bonnie went over and disconnected the machine. She even tore apart some of the cables.

Then she returned to the coat rack and unhooked her down vest.

"I don't understand," Clare said helplessly, not able to hide the desperation in her voice. "You know my father, Bonnie, if you could just get one of the officers on the—"

As Bonnie put the vest on, buttoning it up, she said, "This town is falling apart, honey, I've gotten twenty-five emergency calls today from folks saying their dead friends and relatives are up and breathing, and we only have so many cops to go out on wild goose chases, and we had some burn victims from last night who aren't going to live to see tomorrow morning. Jesus, one boy lost his dad in that fire, and he's sitting in there, been there all damn night as far as I can tell," she pointed to the sheriff's private office, "and it makes me nervous 'cause he was talking ghosts, too. I hear my man Lyle is high as a kite and talking about vampires. And some joker keeps calling me up and telling me he's Lyle's Dad, who, if you don't know, bought the farm a while back but now he's paying off the loan, if you know what I mean, because this joker tells me he wanted to be back for Founders Day, and to tell his favorite son that they know what he did and are not terribly happy about it. And the crazy thing is, Clare, this joker sounds so much like the old guy I peed my panties when he called. And you're worried about your old man disappearing? Wandering off in the morning like a chicken with its head cut off? I tell you, don't you worry about it one bit, 'cause he'll be back, dead or alive, he'll be back." Bonnie's face seemed to have aged decades since Clare had last seen her; it could've been a middle-aged woman's rather than that of a girl more than ten years younger than herself.

"But, my father," Clare said, gesturing despair with her hands, "can't the sheriff do—"

"Stick around and you can find out what he can do, but Bonnie's got to say bye-bye." Bonnie picked up her purse and slung the strap over her shoulder. She wiped her eyes. "If you want that state detective, Mister Hank Firestone, I believe he's camped out in the john flushing his brains away for all the good he's done here. Oh, and give this message to George for me, and Lyle, too, if you see him. Tell 'em I said: fuck it. That's all, just fuck it." Her voice cracked, and she walked swiftly past Clare, out of the office.

From inside the sheriff's private office, Clare heard a familiar young boy's voice: "Is it safe to come out now?"

2.

"Hello, Tommy," Clare said. Tommy MacKenzie, his whole body trembling as if from cold, gently nudged the inner office door open. The hood was up on his gray sweatshirt, and he held the corners of his navy blue jacket together as if it was thirty below inside. His blue eyes were lined with red.

"Hi, Mrs. Terry. Did you see him, too?" Tommy spoke in a shaky tenor, and he kept glancing around to the corners of the room, hardly even looking at Clare.

Clare raised her eyebrows. "Who?"

"Rick Stetson. He's dead, and then I talked to him." He said this just as if there was nothing contradictory in the statement. Tommy's eyes were smudged with charcoal gray and he kept blinking like he was afraid Clare was making a move to hit him as she came closer to the open door. "I heard you talking in here with Mrs. Holroyd. The boy-eating spider got your father, too, didn't it?"

3.

"Goddamn dispatch is off!" George swung the cruiser in a sharp left onto Lakeview Drive off of East Campus. Cup was riding shotgun and had not said a word since he and George left the house. George had not asked any questions other than, "You all right?" Cup had nodded, and George told him to walk ahead of him down the staircase and out the front door. While George fiddled with the radio with one hand and drove with the other, Lyle, still handcuffed in the back seat, began sniffing the air.

"He might be one of them, one of them, vampires, ghouls—" Lyle wailed, and pushed himself up against the back of his seat, sliding toward the door behind George's seat.

Cup's voice was stoical. "I don't think they're anything as simple as vampires." Only his haggard, pale demeanor belied the calmness that came up from his throat.

"What the—?" George watched the road as he drove; in fact, he didn't even want to look at either of the other two men in the car.

"I wish they were. If we're dealing with vampires, it's just a matter of waiting the night out surrounded with garlic and then getting some wooden stakes. Then we could do the job in the morning." Cup looked out the car window, across the frozen lake.

George looked bewildered. "Well, this takes it, doesn't it?"

Lyle chimed in, "They are *too* vampires: they eat people."

"It's a thin distinction, I know," Cup said evenly, "but vampires are supposedly blood-suckers. Prescott Nagle believes they're part of some spirit. Maybe several spirits."

"You're wrong, what touched me was skin, you hear?" Lyle had also calmed down, and leaned his head against the window.

"Dr. *Nagle* said that?" George asked, incredulous.

"He's got some documentation to back up his theory."

"I can't wait to hear about it from him." They were approaching the courthouse on Main Street, and George parked the car illegally, *but,* he thought, *who the hell is going to notice?*

"Well, what do you think, Sheriff? That *I* did that to Mrs Campbell?"

"Look, buddy," George said as he unbuckled his seatbelt, "some psycho cut my wife's tongue out with glass, and I find a dead woman who just got it with a broken bottle up the kazoo and you want to tell me there aren't any similarities?"

Cup held his hands up for George's inspection. "If I'm such a psycho, what: are you all out of handcuffs?"

"What is that, a smartass comment?" George got out of the car and opened the back door. "Come on, Lyle," George said as he reached in and grabbed hold of Lyle's shoulder.

Cup got out of his side of the cruiser. His head hung down and when George glanced across the hood of the car at him Cup reminded him of himself at that age whenever he spoke with his own father (which had been rare if at all). "Look," George said to Cup. George was steadying Lyle, who'd almost slipped in the snow; when Cup looked at him, and George saw the shattered, uncertain look in the man's brown eyes, he was unable to remember what he was about to say. "Let's just go inside and figure this thing out."

4.

"Saunders?" Gower Lowry said as he went into the kitchen. He had been waiting in the dining room for fifteen minutes. She knew supper was promptly at six. His time was valuable. This may have been a vacation break for other teachers, but for the Acting Headmaster at Pontefract Prep there was no respite. He'd spent the entire afternoon reviewing administrative spending. After such a day he did not enjoy being kept waiting at table. He drummed his fingers against the oak table. "Saunders!"

He heard her customary shuffling in the kitchen. "Saunders, when you're quite ready . . ."

She came through the kitchen door. But that is not how Gower Lowry saw it. He saw someone come through the kitchen door. He thought he was hallucinating again. He hated being old. Because the woman standing before him looked like Saunders in every respect save one: the skin of her face had been turned inside out. That was the way Gower would've put it, although he knew it didn't do her justice. After his recent nightmares, this didn't seem all that surprising. He pretended not to notice. *I am just seeing things; this happens to old men sometimes. The trick is to not let on.* Gower did not want Saunders to think he was completely senile, so he said, "Saunders, I am ravenous, I hope the menu this evening is up to your usual standards."

The Saunders-thing didn't react to this. She went over to the dining room table and pulled out a chair for herself. She sat down. It was very odd to see this Saunders-thing with her bluish hair streaked with blood, her lacy collar coming up right to the point where her throat seemed to have been slit. Gower kept watching her, assuming that if he didn't turn away, she would become ordinary, homely Saunders again. He waited for this flicker of sanity. When she spoke, it was not with Saunders' voice, but Gower assumed this was simply another symptom he would never admit to a doctor.

"Gower," she said, and the flickering image Gower longed for came and went—the bloody inverted face of Saunders shimmered and became that of Cassie Nagle. Her auburn hair, the face smooth and lightly freckled, the small sad green eyes. Wearing the emerald green dress, just as she had that summer night long ago, the dress she shed like a constricting skin to dive in the dark waters of Clear Lake in the moonlight.

"Saunders?" Gower asked, but Cassie threw back her head and laughed. "Cassie, how . . ."

"It was always you, Gower, you were my first and only love," she said. "I told you we would be joined forever one day. I told you that, didn't I?"

The face flickered like a candle flame in the wind. For a moment he saw Saunders' bloodied face, but then it was Cassie again, beautiful as the day she died. Her eyes were like two fiery jewels. Gower felt himself being drawn into them.

"Cassie, what do you want?" his voice rose to a boyish tenor.

"I want you, Gower, all to myself, for eternity, just give yourself to me," Cassie said, her arms outstretched to him. She touched his hands, folded on the table, and it felt like icicles pressed against him. He wondered if this was the smell of the grave that he inhaled. Again, Cassie's face quivered, and he saw beneath it Saunders' mutilated features. The truth dawned on him then.

"You're going to kill me," he said, more as a statement of fact than as a question.

"Do you love me?" she asked, and as she brought her face closer to his he could smell the rotting skin of Saunders and when she kissed him, slipping her tongue between his lips, he tasted death.

Georgia Stetson's son Rick had come in around six in the evening and Georgia, who was putting birdseed out in the feeder by the back-porch light, dusting snow off its edges, heard an argument developing between her son and his father.

"Where have you been for the past twenty-four hours, young man? Your mother and I have been worried sick!" Ken Stetson yelled, and Georgia thought the windows would shatter with that booming voice of his. "What did you say, young man? What did you call me? I'll send you to Fork Union Military yet, and don't you go running to your mother! Come back here right this instant! Did you hear me?"

Georgia dreaded going back in the house with her husband in such a state. She sprinkled sunflower seeds around in the snow, and then looked up at the sky. The clouds across the distant hills were moving swiftly westward toward town, and Georgia wondered how bad the snowfall would be. The thing she disliked most about living on their street was that the sanding truck never seemed to hit their hill, and in the winter she felt stuck in the house if the roads were icy.

She went back inside when the yelling had stopped. The house was so silent Georgia assumed they were talking things out quietly in Rick's room.

Georgia sat on one of the stools at the kitchen counter and reached for the telephone. She didn't understand why none of her friends had been calling her with the latest.

She dialed Cappie Hartstone's number.

5.

Cappie did not answer the telephone.

She was just finishing up preparing dinner when her husband, Bill, arrived home from work. The kitchen fairly steamed with a heavy meaty aroma. Bill had always been a meat-and-potatoes man, and just that odor brought out a smile on his face. "Smells great, honeybunch," he said, taking his overcoat off and tossing it across one of the kitchen chairs.

It had been a rough day down at the Savings & Loan, absenteeism was at an all-time high. "People fall apart in this town with the first snowfall," he told her as he hugged her; she pulled away from him.

"William, please, I have to make the gravy now."

He went to the refrigerator for a beer. "I had six customers pull out practically their life savings today, who the hell can figure? Marty Aiken said that Janet thought somebody was living under their house, and so he just decided to up and put the place on the market because he said he didn't feel too good, either, and they were going to spend a few weeks at her mother's in Roanoke—now doesn't that just sound like he's been on the juice again?"

Cappie didn't respond. She kept checking under the lid of the frying pan.

Bill continued, "It's like some folks are getting cabin fever and we're not even into February." He sucked the beer out of the bottle.

Without turning around to face him, Cappie said, "You can either sit like a vulture and watch me cook this, Bill, or you can go relax in the living room, and when you're done with that beer I'll bring you a nice martini."

"Sounds great." Bill hadn't been treated like this in quite a while. Maybe years. Cappie was really starting to shape up again after being such a slouch in the wife department for so long.

"Go on, I'll be out in a tad," Cappie chirped.

Bill sat in the living room on the plastic-laminated couch. He realized he could stand up, walk over to the bar and make himself a drink, but he was looking forward to his wife doing that. Nobody would ever say William Hartstone was pussy-whipped.

When Cappie walked barefoot across the yellow carpet to the bar, he wanted to run over and kiss her so hard on the lips they'd bleed. The lousy day at work had raised his libido, and he wanted to take her right there beside the coffee table. He restrained himself. *Let her come to me.*

"I do love you, Cappie," he said enthusiastically, like a virgin about to get laid.

She blew him a kiss. "Feeling's mutual, sugarbuns," she

purred. She filled a highball glass almost to the top with gin, and then added a splash of vermouth.

"Oh," Bill said, "the kids." He was about to ask if they were upstairs or out playing in the snow.

"Honey, I thought, since we've been so tense lately, that you and me we could have a romantic evening alone. I hope you don't mind."

Bill scratched his beard and kept grinning. He couldn't believe his good luck.

Cappie brought the double martini over to him. "They're over at Mrs. Stanhope's down the street—you know that nice old lady? She's so sweet." Cappie sat down on his lap, wriggling her hips into his crotch. He held her with one arm, pulling her close to him, running his fingers up and down her stomach and breasts. "Roamin' hands and rushin' fingers," she said. Cappie was not wearing a bra for the first time in the twenty years he'd known her.

Bill Hartstone didn't fulfill his fantasy of making love to his wife on the yellow living room carpet. Instead, he carried Cappie up to the bedroom. They made love in the usual way: fifteen minutes of her lying very still while he mounted her and "inserted Tab A in Slot B," as he liked to tease her. Afterwards, she pressed her index finger against his lips, sliding it in between his front teeth. He bit down gently. "Is that what you been practicing in your aerobic classes?"

She kissed her way down from his lips to his toes, taking each toe in her mouth, nibbling like a fish on a line. He was in heaven. She popped her mouth off his big toe and said, "Well, we better get to dinner now, Billy Boy."

"Baby, we don't need dinner," he moaned, hoping she would lick the fleshy ridge between his toes again.

"I know," Cappie said, sitting up at the end of the bed, "you just stay like this, all stretched out on the bed with nothing on, you hear? Not a stitch. I'll bring your dinner up here."

Bill waited upstairs for another ten minutes, drinking his second martini. *Oh, wait 'til the boys at the bank hear about this!* He shouted, "You been reading *The Total Woman* again, love bunny?" Then, thinking that the shiny black book on the nightstand might have been her inspiration for this evening of sexual pleasure, he opened up her Day Runner to that day's entry:

1) *Cook the kids!*
2) *Scare Bill to death.*
3) *Stick to diet!*
4) *Hello, William, I know you're reading this, and I want to ask you while you're still alive how it feels to know you just did It to a dead woman? I hope it felt good, because now a dead woman is going to do It to you.*

Bill set the Day Runner down and roared with laughter. Cappie had a wicked sense of humor, she did. "Cook the kids!" he yapped gleefully.

"Love me, sweetie?" Cappie called up to him from the bottom of the stairs.

Bill kept chuckling to himself. He scratched his balls, and when he did, his fingers came away with something thick and slimy which he knew hadn't come out of him, and which he hoped hadn't slipped down out of his wife. Whatever it was wriggled in the palm of his hand.

Cappie came up the stairs with a tray of steaming, covered plates.

6.

On the wire:

Georgia Stetson to Maude Dunwoody:

"Me, too, Maude, it must be the weather. Yes, they say electrical activity from a storm disrupts the mental flow and causes nightmares. Well, it looks like it's coming in fast—no, I hadn't heard. Patsy? I thought the police were taking care of that young man . . . no, no . . . good lord, dead . . . I don't mean to be morbid, Maude, but somehow that doesn't surprise me. Not at all."

* * *

Off the wire:

When Georgia hung up the phone she was nearly in tears, but Rick was standing there in the kitchen in his old army surplus jacket and she tried not to let her emotions show. "You really shouldn't stay out so late, Ricky," she said, "with that fire last night your father and I were worried. Funny things are happening around town, and it's just as well if we know where you are."

Rick pouted, thrusting his hands into the pockets of the olive drab jacket. "Don't you trust me?"

"Of course we do." Georgia, overcome with a feeling of relief that her son was, after all, safely home, reached her arms out toward him. He went to her, and they embraced. Tears from her eyes soaked into his shoulders. "It's just that we were scared."

"And you're not scared now?"

"No, Ricky, but you're our one and only and we love you, of course we're not scared now," she said, hugging him tighter.

He drew back from her. "How about *now?*"

Georgia saw her son for what he truly was, and she screamed and screamed and screamed as any mother would in a similar situation. Until her son ripped her vocal cords right out, and then Georgia Stetson gushed.

7.

None of the good old boys in town stood on the front stoop at Fisher's Drugstore, and with the Key Theater empty, the Columns restaurant closed, Maude Dunwoody's closed, in fact, every store on Main Street shut completely up, Pontefract would've resembled a ghost town.

Were it not for the green neon light flashing at the Henchman Lounge, which began filling up with regulars, past and present, by seven o'clock.

And the party music that was coming from across Clear Lake. The water could carry sound better than anything, and Prescott, who had fallen asleep in front of his fireplace, was awakened by the music as much as he was by the sounds in the old stables outside.

8.

"Shit!" George Connally yelled, lifting the large radio transmitter. "Damn your wife, Lyle, she tore the cables apart!" He set the machine back down and played around with a few wires. Since his arrival with Lyle and Cup in tow, the outer office had been a cacophony of questions battered around between Tommy, Clare, Cup, Lyle and George. George finally said, "Enough!" and went over to the radio.

Tommy was about to say something and then stopped himself. But Clare, waving her cigarette around, said, "If you want help, Sheriff, your detective was last seen in the men's room down the hall. That's what Bonnie told me, anyway, before she blew out of here."

George looked up from the radio. "Firestone?"

"As in the tires," Clare said.

Upon hearing the name, Lyle, who George had handcuffed to the metal file cabinet, began rattling against it, crying out, "Don't let him come near me, George, don't let him—"

"This Firestone's the one Lyle was talking about?" Cup asked, and Lyle continued moaning and whining, but with less volume.

George nodded, opening the door. "This is police business, Coffey, I should go alone." He said this as if he didn't mean a word.

"If Firestone's one of *them*"—Cup opened the door in an "after you" gesture— "then the worst thing you can do is go alone. It wants you to be alone."

9.

"Toilets are interesting things," Firestone said, leaning against a stall door. "Don't you ever wonder where it all goes when you flush?"

"Let's plow through the bullshit, buddy," George said. He pointed his gun at Hank Firestone's stoical face.

"Very appropriate metaphor from a glorified meter maid, George." Firestone grinned. His mouth was black and toothless and seemed an endless chasm.

"Just shoot it, George," Cup said, standing behind the sheriff.

Hank laughed. "Not before the floorshow. You wouldn't shoot the piano player before the floorshow, would you? Don't you know the opera ain't over 'til the fat lady sings, Mr. Coffey? Of course, I don't suppose our resident fat lady, Patsy Campbell, could carry much of a tune. But she has had her uses, I should say. A diversionary tactic. Interference, Mr. Coffey, seems to be your bent, and we don't want you getting hurt just yet, not until we've weeded the garden." Hank Firestone began unknotting his tie. "Rather hot in here, don't you think?"

"What are you doing here? Who are you?" George kept his hand steady, but his heart felt like it would burst through his ribs.

"The Goatman," Cup said.

"Hardly. You must picture witches dancing around their Horned Master. Gods and devils, are those dreams the limits of your feeble tongues and imaginations? We are the flesh within the flesh and the blood within the blood. Perhaps the good deputy who provided us with the means for our ends has come the closest to knowing our nature—the vampire, how wonderfully romantic, the ghoul—our fictional cousins, perhaps. Warped and perverted by your culture's myopic vision. We are not strangers, Mr. Coffey, and we can't be found in diaries."

"You're a bunch of graverobbers," Cup said.

"You always were a man of spirit." Hank began undoing the buttons on his starched white shirt. His voice faltered a moment, seeming to blend with another. The only way George could've described it would be to compare it to a song on the radio ending with the DJ smoothly sequeing it into another. Hank's voice segued into that of a woman. Lily Cammack Whalen. "But love blinded you, didn't it? You live by a code, don't you, Cup? And when you break it, as you did at sixteen, that haunts you. It's your stain of guilt, Cup, your own taint that opened yourself up to us, Cup, and you have been a fine breeding ground. The question is not, *who are we?* the question is *what kind of monster are* you?"

"That's a lie," Cup said. "Shoot it, George, there are two of us. It likes to get people alone. It must be scared when it's confronted by more than one."

"You know what it feels like to burn from the inside out?" Lily's voice fell to a whisper, *"It's like maggots crawling under your skin, maggots with stingers and suckers boring through you, eating their way out, real slow at first . . ."*

"Shoot it," Cup repeated.

But George felt so bewildered he wondered if it wouldn't be better to just turn the gun on himself. Then he thought of Rita at the Westbridge Medical Center, and he knew there was something to live for. There were pieces to pick up.

Hank laughed, slipping out of his navy blazer and shirt. It was Lily laughing. "Only you, Cup, all to myself. You said you would love me forever, Cup, did you mean what you said?"

"But you're not Lily Cammack. You're somebody who calls himself Firestone."

Hank Firestone's own voice returned. "And there's the thing of it, who is Hank Firestone?" His chest was completely bare, white and hairless. He pressed his fingers into the middle of it over his sternum. George heard a rending sound like wet rubber being slit. He'd heard that sound many times before when he'd visited the county morgue and watched as the doctor's assistants cut into the dead bodies. It sounded like the man's chest was . . . *gasping.* George began withdrawing into himself. He felt like he was shrinking into a dark corner of his own body, someplace where this Hank Firestone *(who is, oh, God, sinking his fingers into his own chest, ripping himself down the middle, and the crimson cavity inside . . .)* could not touch him. Someplace safe. George didn't even feel he was there on his own surface, but suspended beneath the frozen water of a pond. *Safe.* But Hank Firestone's voice reached inside him and pulled him out, just as he was pulling out this other body beneath his skin. "George, I would've thought you'd figured me out by now, even checked with Roanoke to see if there ever *was* a Detective Hank Firestone. You were always a clever boy, but you never could get your facts straight, isn't that right? And you were never good at games—I doubt you'd even notice the anagram. Although to be fair—and we are always fair—it is a rather lopsided anagram. Oh, do I need to spell it out for you, George? Hank Firestone—what does it remind you of? Hank Firestone; think, boy, think—" The voice was dropping into a lower range, and out of the bloody mass of its torso, something else was emerging. "Think, boy, think, Hank Firestone, where have you heard that sound before—"

Hank Firestone—Hank Firestone—what does he mean, anagram? Another name within that name, just like someone else beneath the skin that is falling off him in clumps? Then George knew. *Hank Firestone, holy shit.* "Frank . . . Gaston."

And Frank Gaston's voice, the thing within Hank Firestone's skin said: "We did it for love, you know that don't you? And we love you, too, George, why you're just like a son to me and Louise, and we want you to come home—our home, George. Why, hell, boy, the whole dang town is in the house, just waiting for you Johnny-Come-Latelys to make it to the table in time for Founders Day . . ." Wobbling as if he were drunk, his blood-dripping arms extended toward George in a good-old-boy embrace, the thing that now spoke with Frank Gaston's voice made a move toward the two men.

Cup grabbed the Smith & Wesson from George's hand,

but before he could fire a shot, whatever was shedding Hank Firestone's skin fell to the floor. When George looked down at the thing now lying on the bathroom tile, it was the body of Ken Stetson looking as if he'd been chewed up and spat out.

10.

When Prescott Nagle awoke from his nap and looked out the window upon utter darkness, he was disoriented. He leaned forward in his cushiony reading chair and strained to hear the music again that seemed to be coming from outside, but could not. The creaking of the boards in the stable continued, and he called out for Cup, wondering if he was just getting in from parking the car. He waited for an answer, but none came.

He looked out the south window of his guest bedroom at the stable entrance, and saw a horse ambling from the stable out across the snow. It stopped at the edge of the gravel driveway and sniffed at the air. Sleet was coming down, and drove the shiny dark horse back into the stable.

"Lady Day," Prescott said aloud; his face felt like it was burning with blood as he watched. He felt like someone had gotten hold of everything he was ashamed of and had sent it all in the form of this horse. *If you were a smart man, you'd wait for your friend to return.*

And then the opposing thought whispered in his ear, and his skin tingled with a new awareness: *your friend might be dead. You've been waiting too long, Scotty, you've been waiting for all the pieces to come together, but it may be too late. You may have missed your golden opportunity, you old fool.*

They may all be dead.

He pulled a wool sweater over his head, slipped his rubbered loafers on and went outside.

11.

"What was it?" George asked as he leaned over Ken Stetson's lifeless body. "Was it just Ken? God, what happened to him?"

Cup looked unbelievingly at the gun in his hand. "It called me a breeding ground. Something else it said, about using Patsy Campbell—for what?" And then, it dawned on him. *A diversionary tactic, it had said. But what is it diverting our attention away from?* His face drained of all its color.

"Prescott, I completely forgot! Jesus, we've got to get up there, he's all alone!"

12.

Prescott could not see anything of the horse itself in the shadows that enveloped the inside of the stable. The floodlighting along the drive and the outside of the barnhouse cast only the thinnest of beams into the first few feet of the doorway. But in that feeble light, Prescott saw twin breathclouds from the horse's nostrils; he could hear its impatient whinnying as it kicked against one of the empty stalls.

As Prescott approached the doorless entrance to the stable, he heard the animal shy away, moving further into the shadows. When he got inside the stable, his feet clopping like a horse's on the concrete floor (he didn't wonder why the horse itself had not made this sound with its hooves), he switched on the string of lights he'd set up along his worktable. The sleek black mare stood silently against the far wall, watching him.

Prescott glanced at the tools he kept piled against the bench, finally picking up the pitchfork that leaned against the bench. It was so heavy he dragged it as he walked toward the horse.

The horse stamped the floor with its hooves. It snorted; Prescott saw no animal intelligence in its eyes. Its movements were not as fluid as the real Lady Day's had been. Prescott held the pitchfork up with both hands. He aimed the tines at the horse's neck. He continued to walk toward the mare.

One of the light bulbs on the overhead string popped out, and Prescott looked up for a moment, and when his eyes returned, quickly, to the horse, it was no longer a horse.

"Cassie," he said, and the pitchfork fell, clattering, to the floor.

13.

She was as young and beautiful as he remembered her being, her eyes still possessed that element of sadness which he found so attractive in a woman, and her auburn hair fell in a Rita Hayworthish wave to her shoulders. Wearing the green dress, what she called her "green folly." She bit her lower lip like a child hesitating to admit something to him. "It was stronger than me, Scotty, I thought I could escape it, but I was wrong. It was inside me, Scotty, it's inside us, all of us. It's not something that will ever go away."

Prescott tried to stay calm. "Cass, what is it?"

"I loved you both, you know that, and I've been to see Gower, and he agrees that you should leave, Scotty, it's too dangerous. You could never defeat it, not in a million years, and I don't want it to end for you as it did for me, Scotty, I was so cold and so alone, and it hurt—oh, the pain I went through." She clutched her left arm with her right hand and took a step toward him.

"But, Cassie, your skin, what you did . . ."

"I was wrong, Scotty, so wrong, to take my own life like that, to destroy the gift I had been given . . . the gift we'd been given . . ." He noticed her feet were bare, dirty, as she took another, more confident step. "I was to be the door, Scotty, but I squandered my gift, and now they've chosen another to take my place. What I did is unforgivable, but they've promised, if you would just go away that you won't be hurt, Scotty, and then I'll be free." She was close enough so that he could feel her feather-light breath upon him, and when he inhaled, imagining Shalimar and Ivory Soap, what he got was something rotten, something so foul that tears came to his eyes as much from the odor as from this vision of his late wife. She saw the change come over him, and clenched both hands in fists and beat the air between them. Cassie was sobbing, "Oh, don't you even love me? What I've gone through, and just for you, what I sacrificed . . ."

Prescott reached out and grabbed her small fists in his hands, just as he used to, and as he looked at them, they unfolded like a fast-motioned film of a flower blossoming. He kissed each one in the center of the palm, and he thought: *yes, death can be sweet. I am old, I am ready to die. If it means being with my wife, then surely I must do it.*

He glanced up and caught her off-guard. Something in her eyes. Something in those eyes, for a split-second before they glazed over with Cassie's eyes.

He had seen something there in those eyes, something fierce, and wild. A caged beast waiting to spring.

You know I saw you, for just a moment, Prescott thought, and let go of her hands. Her arms swung lifelessly to her sides. *You know something else? I almost had you fooled, I just about caught you at your own game. You thought you had me.*

Cassie's voice broke the silence. "I do have you," and then it was no longer Cassie's voice, or even Cassie's body, but Gower Lowry standing before him, leaning on his silver-tipped cane. "Prescott, I must warn you—you are treading on thin ice, just like that Amory girl did, and look how she ended up, will you? I know I kept my distance from you all these years, but I had my reasons. I was afraid—Lord, how afraid I was. Those missing pages you're so anxious to see, they can tell you nothing, Prescott, just the ravings of a lunatic. But you're up against something so powerful, Prescott, and good, too, a powerful, terrible good . . ."

"Why don't you just show yourself to me?" Prescott asked.

Prescott watched as the shape flickered. He was seeing through Gower Lowry, through his wife, through the mare, all superimposed one upon the other.

"I am beneath the skin, Prescott, come closer, see, taste—" The voice possessed no human quality, it rasped as if experiencing some difficulty in breathing.

"Like hell I will!" Prescott dropped to the floor and grabbed the pitchfork that lay between them, and with all his might drove it at an upward angle into the creature. Prescott lay on the concrete floor in a heap; his legs had given out when he fell, and his back felt like a ton of bricks had just been dropped on it. There was a pain in his ribs, shooting up to his head like an electric current; he saw flashes of light. But Prescott still clutched the wooden end of the pitchfork. It was vibrating wildly in his hands. He did not look up. He expected that at any moment, the pain of death would be upon him.

Prescott lay with his head against the cold concrete floor of the stable waiting to die. He wondered if the piercing siren sound and the howling wind through the storm would be the last things he'd ever hear.

But then there were other voices above him.

"We're too late, goddamn it," one man said, and Prescott recognized that one and lifted his head. *George Connally.*

"Better late than never," Prescott muttered, and it hurt just to make that feeble joke.

Cup stood over him and grinned. "Mister, you have got nine lives if you ask me."

14.

"Look at it come down," Tommy said. He stood with his back to Clare, looking out the window in the sheriff's office. The sleet was turning to clumps of snow as it fell down on Main Street. He wrote: TOMMY MACKENZIE WAS HERE on the windowpane with his finger.

Lyle Holroyd stopped whining so much after George and Cup had left. He whispered to himself, "Firestone got him, didn't he, yes, yes, he got him, he wanted him, and now *they* got him, too . . ."

Still facing the window, Tommy asked, "Who are *they?*"

No one had paid much attention to Lyle since George had handcuffed him to the file cabinet. Clare Terry kept calling people she knew on the office phone asking if they'd seen her father yet.

"You talking to me?" Lyle asked, nervously.

Tommy moved away from the window and went to the opposite end of the room from Lyle. He treated Lyle as if the man were a tethered lion.

"You want to know, don't you?" Lyle asked. Tommy hated to look at that face. The deputy looked the way Tommy felt inside: disheveled, deadly white, slick and shiny with sweat. His eyes were wild. The eyes of a man who would believe anything you told him. Angels, gods, devils, ghosts, vampires, werewolves, ghouls, aliens; an acceptance all there in those bloodshot eyes. Wanting to believe, just like Tommy did. *Because if they were up against the Devil, you just go to church and maybe confess your sins. And if they were just ghosts, well, what's to be scared of? After all, people are just ghosts waiting to happen. If it was God or gods, then they must walk happily to their fate. You get a werewolf with a silver bullet, a vampire with a stake, and for aliens you call in Sigourney Weaver.*

And if they were up against the boy-eating spider, you waited patiently for It to eat all the bad boys. Or maybe

It wraps you in Its web and saves you for an after-dinner mint.

Yeah, Tommy thought, *when you've got a name for what you're up against, it makes it easy. There are rules to every game, just like school. You go in the morning, you sit still for a few hours, you pretend you don't care when they pick you last for the team, and then you go home. Home, there were rules for home, too. You keep your room clean so your dad doesn't blow his stack and sock you in the jaw, and you try to stay out of the way most of the time. That was what life was all about.*

"I'll tell you, okay? If you promise not to take me there, okay?" Lyle said, jerking Tommy's mind back into the room.

"I don't want to know," Tommy said softly. *I already know where they live,* he wanted to say. *What I want to know is what they are, and you can't tell me that. Because nobody in this room or in this town knows what they are. What it is. What he is. What she is. Whatever the hell* It *is.*

Lyle began telling about the Marlowe-Houston House, the cage of bones, Jake Amory, *how they were eating Jake Amory piecemeal, heh-heh,* but Tommy wasn't really listening.

He heard Clare on the phone: "Well, I'd appreciate that, Shelly, but only if you're going there anyway, and be careful, no, not just the snow, you know, all the accidents—yeah, let me give you the number here . . ."

"They aren't accidents!" Tommy yelled, hoping whoever was on the other end of the phone heard him.

Clare cupped her hand over the phone and whispered something into the mouthpiece. Tommy heard his name mentioned. Then she hung up. "This must be awful for you, Tommy, but it'll be over."

But Tommy wasn't even listening to her. Tommy looked at Lyle Holroyd. "What do you call them?"

"They're vampires, you know, but they're all ghouls, yes, yes, ghouls . . . they eat people, I seen 'em. They got that little Amory girl down in that shithole, man, and I just know they're gonna eat her, too, 'cause they're all *hungry* sons-of-bitches."

"You saw a vampire," Tommy stated, waiting for Lyle's nod.

Lyle seemed to hesitate before grinning. "Got to be something like that. Big teeth. Hungry as the devil."

"And a ghoul."

"Well, they were dead people, the Gastons, eating people, isn't that kinda what ghouls do?"

Clare rolled her eyes. "Don't forget the big teeth."

Lyle scratched his head with his free hand.

"I don't believe in vampires," Tommy said. "Or ghouls."

"Thank God somebody is being normal," Clare said.

"I saw my friend Rick get killed, but I didn't see who did it. I just heard the—the boy-eating spider. What did you see?"

Clare sighed. "Nothing. Absolutely nothing."

"Nothing at all?" Tommy asked.

"I'm just here because my father has left home, although to be honest, he might be back there by now—I've wasted all this time waiting here for Sheriff Connally to get back."

"Heh-heh, yeah, but you're scared, too, huh? Huh?" Lyle sounded like a dog worrying the flesh off a bone. "I can see right under your skin, lady, heh, and they know about you, they *asked* about *you.*"

Clare gasped when she noticed that Lyle's mouth was foaming.

"And that other guy with the sheriff said he called it the Goatman, and Sheriff Connally . . ." Before Tommy could complete his line of thinking, the telephone rang and Clare picked it up.

Lyle, who leaned against the file cabinet, his face now turned to the wall, moaned, "It's them, huh? It's them, it's them . . ."

CHAPTER SEVENTEEN

THE HENCHMAN LOUNGE

1.

Clare was glad to be out of the courthouse, even if it meant braving the sleet and snow, and trudging the few blocks up to the Henchman Lounge. Tommy MacKenzie walked behind her several steps as if watching for something. He had refused to let her go alone. Back at the courthouse, Lyle had been crying, "You cain't leave me alone! Puh-leez, you just cain't!" But Clare actually felt safer out of the sheriff's office, away from that crazy deputy, and on the slippery winter street.

When Shelly called her at the sheriff's office, she'd said, "Well, you'd never believe who I found sitting all by his lonesome at the Hench, drinking Brandy Alexanders. Your dad, that's who. He seems really out of it, Clare, but none the worse for the weather. He keeps talking to people about Lily, you know, which is kind of creepy, but other than that—"

Clare felt like she was standing outside a brothel. The indistinct voices emanating from beyond the front door of the Henchman Lounge were wild and raucous; it sounded like a bacchanalian orgy inside.

She'd only been in the Henchman Lounge once, and that

was when she'd first made friends with Shelly Patterson and Debbie Randolph. Shelly loved to go there "to scope men," and Clare had gone in with her newly acquired friends thinking it might be fun. Nearly two years ago. Clare was only recently divorced from David, and was bored to tears by her hometown when compared with the vast choices that Manhattan had offered. Clare warned Shelly that she hated singles bars, and Debbie told her that to call the Henchman Lounge a singles bar was to give it too much credit. But Clare had felt cheap when some man she'd known from childhood had bought all three of them drinks and then suggested they take a drive together. She even felt cheaper when she accepted the drinks, thanked him politely, and then left feeling vaguely guilty for not having taken that ride with him. From that night on, Girls Night Out met at the Columns restaurant, which Clare felt had a more dignified ambience.

Clare closed her umbrella; she was freezing, and even the umbrella hadn't made her feel any less soaked to the skin. Tommy was still behind her; he was dripping wet, and had, in fact, refused to stand under the umbrella.

She hesitated only a moment at the door of the Henchman Lounge.

"I'm freezing," Tommy said. "We should've waited for the sheriff."

Clare pushed the door open, stepped inside, and then the inner Western saloon-style shutter doors swung open against her as a tall drunken man loped past her, tipping his hat as he went. Clare caught the swinging doors, held them open for Tommy, and entered the barroom.

The place was packed. The drone of conversation filled the air, replacing the usual smog layer of cigarette smoke. Their voices crescendoed and de-crescendoed, as if someone were playing with the volume knob.

Tommy MacKenzie sniffed at the air like an animal trying to locate danger. "We should go back and wait for the sheriff," he repeated.

A short fat barmaid with a blue beehive hairdo sailed past them with a full tray of beer pitchers. A young pretty blonde in tight jeans and a white frilly blouse leaned against the bar and raised her eyebrows at a couple of lawyerly types who were talking shop at the other end of the bar.

Groups of men in baseball caps and flannel shirts sucked in their guts as Clare passed them by; she kept looking over the sea of heads for Shelly's carrot red hair or her father's wool cap. Without realizing it, Clare had reached back and grabbed Tommy's hand. (She glanced back at him to make sure he was *with* her, and he was, soaked, tired, shivering, in the pea jacket and the red baseball cap he had had scrunched up in his back pocket, and Clare was thinking: *see? this is* normal, *I don't need Valium or a drink, my father's somewhere in this dive, it's snowing outside, somewhere someone is watching an "I Love Lucy" rerun, and here's a teenager who doesn't use bad language and wears a red baseball cap in winter. All is right with the world.)* Clare faced forward again, squeezing Tommy's hand, and he squeezed back as if in a vote of confidence and trust, only he was squeezing a little too hard, and it hurt just a little too much, his grip on her hand became like two rocks crushing together with her hand in the middle. She wanted to tell him to ease up, to let go, because it was hurting too much, but something inside her told her to not turn around suddenly, because maybe *just maybe* it wasn't Tommy back there at all. *But that's a silly, stupid, dumbshit thought.* On the jukebox was "I Fall to Pieces," and Clare began scanning the booths along the far wall. Trying to ignore the screaming pain in her hand. *I will not turn around, he's just squeezing it hard because he's scared, and that kid has been through the wringer, so who am I to tell him to lighten up?*

But Clare could stand the pain no longer, and she turned around and was about to say something like, "Please, Tommy, my hand—" but she saw it wasn't Tommy holding her hand at all.

2.

"You're still living, aren't you?" Prescott asked as Cup and George carried him out of the stable through the swirling snow. Cup bore most of Prescott's weight, for which he swore to his former teacher that he'd get even one day. They'd found him lying on the floor, barely able to move from his fall. When Prescott looked up to see what he had pitchforked, he looked away just as quickly. It was the body of Gower Lowry. His throat had been ripped out, and there was a deep gash running from the bloody opening just above his collarbone all the way down to his navel. The pitchfork stood up straight, its tines having sunk deep into the corpse's already open wound. A blood-stained scroll had fallen out of its vest pocket when the corpse had hit the cement.

Cup picked this up. He unrolled part of it, then quickly tied the string binding. "The missing pages of Worthy's diary," he said. "Practically handed to us. Why is everything so *easy?* It's like whatever is at that house is *playing* with us."

Prescott felt pain everywhere in his body as they lifted him; when they reached the cruiser, the two men propped Prescott temporarily against the front door. He saw the distant look upon George Connally's face and knew that the sheriff must have recently had his share of run-ins with the thing from the goat dance. "You know, there's a saying from antiquity . . ."

They loaded him into the back seat, and he lay down across the cold vinyl. Even with his back feeling like an army was marching across it, this felt good. Prescott heard the other two get in the front seat. The doors slammed. The motor started.

"What was that saying, Prescott?" Cup's face peered over the seat at him as the car backed down the gravel drive.

"Along the lines . . ." Prescott felt as if someone were

piling heavy stones upon his chest. His breathing was slow and heavy. He shut his eyes.

"Are you sure you're—" Cup began. "Maybe we should take him to—"

"Along the lines," and Prescott thought that the cold felt good, so good, "Do not despair, all men . . . all men . . . must die."

"Prescott!" Cup shouted, reaching into the back seat while George said, "Whoa, what now?"

Prescott opened his eyes slowly. "Oh, Cup, I'm not dying. I'm very tired. I was thinking . . . Gower, and seeing him even like . . . I am too tired, now, please let me sleep . . . not bleeding, just an old man fell down. Sore everywhere old men are . . . and sleepy." Prescott closed his eyes and did not open them until he became aware that the police car had stopped, and they were parked outside the front steps of the courthouse.

3.

It was Shelly Patterson squeezing Clare's hand, and Clare would not ordinarily have screamed so loud at seeing her friend (the oversized black sweater, the mountain of curly red hair, the pudgy, doll-like face, the jeans stretched like a tanning hide over her enormous thighs) were it not for the fact that Tommy MacKenzie was nowhere to be seen, and when she glanced at Shelly's face she realized it was not Shelly behind her, not really Shelly, just something wearing a Shelly mask, a skintight mask, but even so Clare could see beneath it. The face that stared out at her from beneath the skintight mask was just a blackness, an empty dive into the abyss.

There was a man at one of the red booths who said, "Clare, who loves ya," and his voice was a perfect imitation of Warren Whalen's. The man did not look up as the two women approached, but kept his head down contemplating the beer set before him. His hair was dark and shiny from grease; his white suit was comfortably rumpled.

While Clare heard her own scream dry up in her throat, the thing that was not Shelly Patterson whispered, "Oh, we *do* love screamers."

4.

"She what?" George Connally shouted more than asked when he ran into his office after parking the car.

Lyle, giggling, jumping up and down, his handcuffs jangling against the file cabinet, repeated what he'd said: "They went to the Henchman, get it? The Henchman? Heh-heh, Georgie-Porgey, I told 'em not to go, I told 'em, I was gonna put them under arrest, heh-heh, Christ, George, am I smart or what? 'Cause those ghoulies can eat them, I bet they taste real good, a pretty woman and a boy, I bet their skin's real fresh and tender—"

5.

"You look like you could use a drink, 'beam," Warren Whalen said when Clare caught her breath. His violet eyes were less intense than when he'd been alive; they seemed coated with a milky fluid. He held his beer bottle up for her inspection. "St. Pauli Girl. Do you remember your first girl? I remember my last one." He winked.

Shelly, standing behind Clare, was holding both of Clare's hands behind her back. Clare was silent.

Warren continued speaking. "You're thinking this is another one of your crazy visions, aren't you, Moonbeam? One of your neurotic episodes."

Clare could feel Shelly's putrid breath against her ear. "Gee, Clare, we're the real thing, you know? All that time you thought your daddy was out of his gourd, but he was all there, you know?"

"What did you do with Tommy?" Clare finally asked.

Shelly giggled. "Nothing we're not going to do with you."

"Your pulse is quickening, sweetie, you're sweating, and you have a funny feeling, am I right?" Warren took a swig from the bottle and slammed it down on the table. The music in the jukebox stopped. The Henchman Lounge fell silent for a moment, and then the chattering and giggling among the patrons picked up again. "This is a swell spot, I've always had a fondness for it. Lily never liked it. You remember Lily, don't you? She never liked a lot of things, but she's changed. We all change when we go through the door."

"It's just the Ultimate Diet, Clare, and it's great. I'm only hungry once in a blue moon. Like tonight," Shelly chimed in, and Clare felt the grip tighten on her wrists. Fingernails going into her flesh just as if she'd gotten tangled in barbed wire. "Dying isn't so bad. I mean, there're worse things, you know?"

"Why, people die every day," Warren said. He grinned boyishly, revealing canine teeth.

"They got me at the library, I went in to do some work just before dinner," Shelly said as if describing her first sexual encounter, "it was kind of scary at first, I mean, I've *never* been *dead* before, but once you get used to the idea . . ."

"The idea," Warren made a circling motion with the bottle, "of death, why the *pain* isn't so bad. Especially when you think of how little life really means when you compare it with what our Eater of Souls has got to offer. Immortality, power, and love, love, Clare, the kind you probably have never known . . ."

Clare struggled against the razor-sharp fingers on her wrists. She spat at Warren. The wad of spit landed across his forehead. He wiped it off with his hand, licking his fingers lasciviously.

"Why don't you scream some more?" Warren asked.

"We all love a screamer." Shelly twisted Clare's hands making her moan.

"Hey," Warren said cheerfully, "look who's coming back from the men's room."

Shelly, twisting Clare's right arm behind her back

dropped Clare's other hand. Clare felt pressure on her neck, and turned in the direction Shelly indicated.

"Hello, Doc," Warren said, "we're over here."

Dr. Cammack pushed his way through the crowd on the way over to the booth. He was wearing his seersucker jacket, his wool cap perched on his head.

Lowering his voice so that Dr. Cammack would not hear as he approached them, Warren said, "What Doc doesn't know is that we're going to open the old guy up and see what's kept him ticking all these years. There *are* worse things than death, 'beam, and you are about to witness one of them. You ever see a guy get turned inside out?"

6.

"How's our casualty in back?" George asked. He turned the key in the ignition.

"Alive and well and I refuse to go to an Emergency Room," Prescott said, almost cheerfully. He still lay across the back seat, apparently content to stare up at the car roof. "The way this blizzard's coming down, I don't think we'd make it halfway to the medical center anyway."

"This damn snow," Cup said. He pressed his hands across the dashboard. The windshield was entirely covered with melting snow.

"Bear with me for a few minutes," George said as he steered the car into the street and made a U-turn. The windshield wipers struggled against the beating storm.

On the way to the Henchman Lounge, a one-minute drive, none of the men spoke. Several cars passed the cruiser, on their way out of town, reckless and speeding through the icy streets with practically no visibility for driving, and George thought: *rats off a sinking ship.*

He envied the rats.

7.

Warren broke the bottom of the beer bottle on the edge of his table. The sound of the glass shattering distracted Clare from her screaming. She was out of breath and heaving. "Give yourself over to the fear, Clare, that's it," Warren wrinkled his nose, "let's go through this together shall we? Right now, it's dawning on you that maybe this isn't a dream. There's too much continuity. Am I right? You feel ice cold inside, and you're thinking maybe that's shock, or maybe, just maybe, you're dead. But you don't believe in life after death, do you? You think consciousness just stops, like a machine whose batteries have run out. But what if you could replace those batteries?" Amber liquid flowed out of the broken bottle onto Warren's vanilla suit. He held the jagged edge of the bottle up for Clare's inspection. "You don't know what to believe, do you? But they say seeing is believing, Clare."

Dr. Cammack had made it through the crowd, and sat down at the table. He looked at Clare nervously. "So you found me, did you?"

Tears were streaming down her face. "Daddy, you've got to—"

"Seeing is believing, 'beam," Warren said, and reached across the table with the broken end of the bottle pointed toward Dr. Cammack's face.

Dr. Cammack was glaring at his daughter. "Yes, listen to him, Clare. But how would you know? Little blind Clare, not like Lily, not at all like Lily. You will never see, will you?"

8.

When George and Cup entered the Henchman Lounge, they beheld this scene:

Francie Jarrett, the barmaid who gave George a free beer when he was off-duty, was digging her gold teeth into some guy's throat; his legs were kicking, his arms were at her throat trying to get her off him, but it did no good. Blood spurted sporadically from his neck and mouth, and his screams came out as watery choking sounds. Francie's blue beehive hairdo was speckled with blood. A man wearing a straw cowboy hat and a young girl were fighting like dogs over an unidentifiable person's body. It hardly even resembled a body, it looked more like a butcher shop's display case. George recognized a cluster of men as the boys who hung out at the drugstore shooting the breeze cheering the girl and the cowboy on. Three torn, disemboweled bodies lay sprawled across the blood-stained floor. Georgia Stetson was down on her hands and knees, pressing her face into the slit along one of the bodies, and then looking up to the ceiling, punctuating her feeding with howls and barks.

George felt something inside him reach into his guts and hose down his stomach and chest with fire, hitting the back of his throat with a sour acidity, and then he sprayed vomit across his shirt. His entire body was racked with the effort. He broke out in a sweat.

He felt someone's arms around his shoulders as he doubled over. George wriggled free of the arms, terrified of who they belonged to. He turned to the side and glanced back.

It was Cup, who looked as terrified and as brave as any man George had ever known on the force or in life.

Over the din of the feeding frenzy, Cup's voice was soothingly steady. "It's just a show, remember, like Patsy, a diversionary tactic. It's got to be for our benefit or we'd be dead by now. It would be easy for them to kill us." The corollary to what Cup was telling him slapped across George's face like cold water: *they're just buying time, because they must be* saving *us for something . . . special.* Cup helped George to stand up straight. He squeezed the sheriff's arm which held the gun in a vote of confidence.

George raised his Smith & Wesson, aimed for Francie Jarrett's blood-freckled forehead, and fired.

9.

Clare struggled with all her might to free herself of Shelly's iron grip. Warren was leaning over the table, holding Dr. Cammack's head by the back of his neck. Dr. Cammack seemed very confused but did not offer any sign of protest.

"We're going to try an old Indian trick, if my memory serves me correctly. Those Tenebro Indians used to do fun stuff like this, they knew how to have a good time," Warren said, raising the broken bottle over Dr. Cammack's head, "or maybe it was a French trick, I forget who taught who what. It's called scalping. You ever hear of it, 'beam?"

Shelly's fingernails dug into Clare's flesh; it felt like someone was hacking away at her wrists with a knife.

If I close my eyes, they'll go away, if I close my eyes, they'll go away.

Clare's head felt like it would explode with the pressure as she willed every part of her being to keep her eyes shut. She continued to writhe in Shelly's grip.

"Oh-ho," Warren laughed, his voice insinuating itself like a worm digging into her brain, "little blind Clare with no eye, is that it? Is that what you thought when Daddy touched you all over in the cellar? You close your eyes and it goes away? But Daddy did touch you all over, we were there, Clare, we were watching down below, in that dark place, we used to wait for you there, Clare, for you . . ." A growl came out of his throat. "Well, it's not going to happen this time, Clare, 'cause I'm just going to slice away at the old Doc like this," and Clare, pushing her eyelids down like a heavy blanket of darkness, heard her father scream.

I will not open my eyes, this isn't happening, this isn't real, if I just keep my eyes closed, it's just an episode, a dream, I'm crazy, if I don't open my eyes

Another scream, and it sounded less like her father this time than a bear caught in a trap.

"Oh, the blood!" Shelly squealed.

"You're really missing something by not looking, you know," Warren said, "but visuals aren't everything, are they?"

Clare felt her breath giving out, as if she were willing herself to *not breathe,* and inside the dark cave of her head she was a little girl sitting on the cold stone steps of a dark cellar and her father was touching her legs, and she was holding her breath pretending it wasn't happening, not at all, *let him do this to Lily, not her, not Clare not Clare, let it be happening to Lily,* and if she just held her breath for a minute, she would be *little blind Clare with no eye, no i, no eye, nowhy,* and just as she had done when she was a little girl on those cellar steps, Clare passed out at the Henchman Lounge. As Clare drifted off into a blissful unconsciousness, she heard what she thought was a cherry bomb exploding, or *was that the last sound you hear before you die?* It was the sound of George Connally's bullet ripping through a reanimated corpse called Francie Jarrett.

10.

Francie Jarrett fell when the bullet burst through her swollen belly, her teeth still digging in for one last bite at a man's throat; she flopped about on the floor like a fish out of water, but within a few seconds lay motionless. The other torn and dismembered corpses, who were feeding on the few barely living-and-paying customers, also dropped to the floor as if imitating Francie in some new dance craze. The Henchman Lounge was littered with bodies, all in their last moments of animation. A hand, with a thread of life, slapping against the cigarette machine as if trying to get matches out of the damn machine; someone's head jerking;

a girl, her body torn almost completely in two in a zigzag down her torso, seemed to be trying to put the two halves together. But then, complete motionlessness. As if the breath of life had just been sucked right out of the Henchman Lounge with that one intruding gunshot.

In the back of the Lounge, a man in a rumpled and bloody vanilla suit was carrying a dark-haired woman out the Emergency Exit doors.

George, who could not take his eyes off the bloody pulps of bodies, did not find the strength to move.

But Cup, tripping over the corpse-littered floor, ran after the man and the woman.

11.

"I know who you are, heh-heh, yassah, I do, you gonna eat me now? I don't taste no good, you wait, George'll be here, and I know he's the one you want? Why'n't you saying nothing? That other one, Coffey and the old man, you get them, too? Heh-heh, you get that lady and the boy? I bet they taste dee-licious, yassah, Kee-rist, puh-leeze, no, don't put it in my mouth, no, puh-leez."

12.

Cup ran out into the alley and was met with a luminous darkness; the darts of sleet jabbed against him as he ran out onto Main Street. The whole town shone with the white snow, and the slick streets echoed his desperate shouts of "Tommy! Clare!"

And then a scratching sound, like a rat scuttling among the dumpsters and trash cans that lined the alley behind the Henchman Lounge. And a voice.

"Coffeyshit, you know where they are. We're gonna eat 'em, Coffey, and eat 'em *raw.*"

And Cup, looking down beside the dumpster for the

origin of this voice, of Bart Kinter, saw what he at first thought was a giant salamander, wriggling with a last moment of life pulsing through its jelly-like skin, and then realized that he was looking at a man who had been turned around, inside out, so that his veins and organs were on the outside of his body—there was no skin at all. Beside this corpse was a blood-stained seersucker jacket and a blue wool cap.

CHAPTER EIGHTEEN

THE HYSTERICAL SOCIETY

1.

Thursday Morning

2 A.M.

Pontefract, Virginia:

The sky was white with the snow that continued to fall, but the town itself had gone dark. The fact that it was two in the morning didn't matter; it could've been two in the afternoon, it could've been six at night. The town had gone dark, like a light bulb that has been in that socket too long. It had just zapped itself out, it had been alive and now was dead. The snow was burying Pontefract in a white shroud, and the only people left to dig the hole in the frozen ground were a cop, an elderly prep school professor and a young man who was beginning to wonder what kind of monster they were up against.

The black-and-white police car was the only vehicle moving on the street; the last of the living, if you didn't count the three men in the car, had gotten the hell out of town by midnight. That was it, too: *the hell out of town. The town out of hell. A hell of a town.* It had been on everyone's lips like a contagious melody. Some of those living people *did* manage to escape from Pontefract—they smelled their long-dead relatives in the cold air, and before they saw them, they *knew* that something bad was happening. Betty

Henderson, whose love letters had so inspired Howie McCormick in his last night of life, thought she saw Howie, in his pith helmet and blue mailman's suit, scratching at her window in the night. Betty knew something was wrong with Howie the way she knew when a guy was drunk or coming on to her. Maybe it was the way he licked the window when she screamed. Maybe it was the way his head fell back when he laughed, revealing a gash so deep that for a second Betty thought she was looking right down into his throat. Maybe it was the fact that the window was on the third story of Betty's house, and Howie was clinging to the sill, not for *dear life,* but as if he were trying to pull the thing out of the damn wall. And Irene Rowe, Dr. Cammack's sitter, thought it was the retired headmaster of Pontefract Prep himself standing over her bedside when she awoke in the purple darkness of night. Irene reached over to turn on the bedside lamp because she was sure it was *not* Dr. Cammack, after all *what would that dear old man be doing in my bedroom in the middle of the night?* When the sixty-watt bulb light flooded her bedroom, Irene still didn't think it was Dr. Cammack, because the last time she'd seen him *he'd had skin covering his body.* Before Irene could reach for her glasses there by the cup of drinking water, the skinned man in the blue wool cap and seersucker jacket bent over and embraced her. But Irene and Betty had not been among the car caravans that skidded out of town on the boot tip of a snowstorm. Those who did make it to the cars had been worried by nightmares all week, they'd heard old friends talking out on the street, old friends who had caught the bus, bought the farm, pushed up daisies, slept with the fishes, all of them dead, buried, turned to dust. *The worms go in, the worms go out,* as the song went. So they packed up their troubles in their old kit bags and loaded up the kids and the dog, and drove the family wagon out onto the skidding highway, looking for the furthest Travelodge or Howard Johnson's where they'd pretend for at least one night that maybe there was just a power outage in Pontefract, or maybe it was just the phone lines being down, or maybe *(heh-heh,* as Lyle Holroyd would snigger) *just maybe, it was that face pressed up against the picture window that looked, shit, it looked just like Evvie Cavendar, the little girl who died in that bicycle accident two years ago, or was that just yesterday? Because, hell, it looked* just like *she'd had that accident just yesterday, now son, eat your fried clams and then you can have your Fudgeana, we didn't come to Howard Johnson's so you would look so goddamn* dee-*pressed*—

But there were those that stayed, the three in the police car (and don't let's forget the fourth, Lyle Holroyd, but he pretty much stayed because he was handcuffed to a file cabinet, and he was laughing and foaming at the mouth and figuring out how to outwit the vampires and the ghouls). Those three men in that chilly car—the heater wasn't working properly—driving through the snow, down Main Street, didn't even see a corpse. They saw no one.

What they *did* see:

Christ Church with its scaffolding frosted with snow. Its display board, the one that usually announced the upcoming sermon, something along the lines of: COMMUNION SERVICES, 7:30, 9, AND 11 A.M., REV. WM. UPTON, "SIN IN OUR LIVES: WHAT CHARLIE BROWN CAN TEACH US." That display board was lit up with floodlights, and some joker had rearranged the plastic white letters against the dark fabric beneath the glass to read: VALLEY OF THE SHADOW.

You could guess fairly correctly that come Sunday there would be no church services.

The police cruiser skidded, and George cursed his deputy Lyle *in absentia* for not having put the snow tires on in November like he was supposed to, and then he cursed himself for not making sure the heater had been fixed, and then George Connally laughed. Things like snow tires and non-functioning car heaters must seem funny when you think about it, and George was probably just thinking about *It* too much.

They passed two more churches, Gethsemane Baptist and St. Andrews Presbyterian. Both were dark, but on the Gethsemane Baptist marquee, where the words of comfort had read:

REPENT YOU SINNERS,
THE END IS AT HAND

this was replaced with:

SIN YOU REEPERS,
THE HAND IS EATN

The windows along Regency Row were all smashed in, and the awning at the Hotchkiss Market flapped in the howling winter wind like a flag of surrender. The Federal-style buildings, etched with snow, lined the street like giant tombstones.

The police car pulled alongside another police car, and the three men in the car entertained a *hope*—although none of the three would call it that. They had momentarily forgotten about *hope.*

But the town of Pontefract was still dark. The man inside the other police car was dead. Officer Dave Petty, just 25 years old. George didn't tell Cup or Prescott how Dave had been killed, because *dead is dead, even if it took a lot of blood spritzed around the upholstery of a car before the actual moment of dying had come, even if whatever had gotten to this cop, Dave Petty, whose usual tour of duty meant stopping a drunken fight or handing out parking tickets, even if what had gotten to him had probably* hopefully *not begun devouring the man until after his heart had stopped beating.*

Yes, the whole town had gone dark, just as the burnt-out hull of the Key Theater had, with that one marquee in town that had curiously enough restored the movies that it had stopped showing a week ago: SLEEPING BEAUTY, and beneath that, DAWN OF THE DEAD.

Pontefract, Virginia: 3 A.M., dark and white with snow, and who among the three in the police cruiser, now turned and heading back to the courthouse, knew if the sun would come up in a few hours?

2.

From *The Nightmare Book of Cup Coffey:*

We are all so *fucking* calm.

Thank God George Connally retrieved this diary for me. Who else can I talk to about what the hell is going on here in Pontefract? Am I really finally losing my grip on sanity? Is the whole world becoming a reflection of all these nightmares boiling around inside me?

It's 3 A.M.—so who can sleep? I keep going over things in my mind, ways of getting around going into that damn house across Clear Lake. I could just sneak out tonight and freeze to death. They say freezing has its advantages: you feel warm just before death comes on, and you fall asleep. Dying in your sleep seems like a good way to go—unless your dreams consist of mowing children's heads in gardens or having weedwhackers come for you. I am probably more afraid of dreaming than anything right now. What if I pull that nightmare right out from behind my eyes and smear it across this town? What if that is what has been happening all along here?

That house. The Marlowe-Houston, where my nightmares were born. Bart Kinter, that asshole, just had to fall down the stairs and die, didn't he? He couldn't have just gotten a concussion, or broken his legs. Or even become paralyzed. Nope. He had to die, and make me feel guilty. I am not denying my participation in his death—I could've left well enough alone, and allowed him to run screaming into Dr. Cammack's party. But I was sixteen, what did I know? Everything seemed bigger than life then, I just didn't know how much bigger it could get, I didn't know about how guilt eats away at you when the absolute worst thing happens to you: *your enemy dies, and maybe you killed him and maybe you didn't. Tell it to the Judge. Or the Eater of Souls.* And ily—dead. Everything I loved and hated in this world, ead. As if something was out to get me, to pull me back to . Hate and love and death.

Eater of Souls, the mother of my nightmares.

I am going fucking crazy. My ex-therapist would say I am irning against myself.

And even Clare, Lily's sister. Barely spoke two words to er, and yet, maybe *because* of Lily, I feel connected to her. he is my remnant of Lily. All other Cammacks are dead: ily, her mother, now her father. Maybe even Clare—but iere's hope, isn't there? Goddamn hope. Hate, love, death, nd hope. I will tear this Eater of Souls limb-from-limb ith my bare hands if It has killed Clare, or that boy, Tom-y. But what will I do if they've only been partially eaten?

While I am scribbling in this I hear Lyle giggling like a ourth-grader over some sick joke that he doesn't even nderstand. Although the sick joke Lyle just heard is not ne of the better ones—it loses something in translation. *top me if you've heard this one: a guy waits twelve years to eturn to the girl for whom he carried a torch, only to find she dead. But something has crawled inside her skin, you see, it walks, talks, looks and acts like her. Happens to a lot of ead people these days. The handy-dandy reanimated corpse, slices, it dices, it beats it, it eats it, you know it mistreats . . . Sort of like Orpheus, huh? I mean, maybe when rpheus was coming out of Hell, he looked back over his houlder* not *because he wanted to make sure she was llowing him, but to make sure it really* was *her, his one true ve, and not something foul and ancient dressed up in her kin, speaking with her voice. Heh-heh, as Lyle Holroyd ould say—and is, in fact, muttering right now.*

We are back at the sheriff's office—as safe a place as any I uess. Except for the thing that he put in Lyle Holroyd's outh, like a bit to keep him quiet. He being my best friend, a-ha, Bart Kinter. "Lyle," George said, halfway between iivering and laughing, "you look the way I *feel.*"

Lyle's eyes were wide with terror when we came back to ie office. George pulled the small square of paper out of his outh. It was soaked with Lyle's spit. For the first time since

I had seen him handcuffed to that file cabinet toward the back of the office, Lyle was silent. His teeth chattered like those joke plastic teeth that you wind up and then they hop across the tabletop.

"In blood, oh, sweet Jesus," George said, shaking his head. When he turned to look back at Prescott and me, I saw his eyes were red with tears. His skin was a pasty gray color and I guess we all look like that right about now, because he handed the piece of paper to Prescott and then to me.

Written in blood, done in the haphazard way that a child fingerpaints.

HE SAYS YOU CHEAT.

Of course, I recognized the message. I mean the last time saw it, it was scribbled in fluorescent blue chalk across a blackboard. Billy Bates—the little dickens! For a brief moment I entertained the notion that maybe that I'il imp Billy from Hardy Elementary School in Arlington was behind this elaborate charade, and at any moment he would jump out from behind something, the curtains, say, if there *were* any curtains, and everyone would say: SURPRISE! and THIS IS YOUR LIFE would flash in neon above my head.

Yeah, I am *that* far gone.

The Eater of Souls has a *wicked* sense of humor.

The equivalent, I suppose, of a sense of humor on the part of this Goatman. (God, I feel like there are a hundred names for It, but somehow they're all wrong—it's like the Mother of Nightmares more than anything because it seems to scare us with what we are already scared of—individually packaged nightmares.)

Who—or what—is the Mother of Nightmares? The Eater of Souls? The Goatman?

I got to tell you, I just don't believe in vampires like Lyle. And I don't know about the Devil, because if there's a Devil, what the fuck does he care about my worthless little soul? I'll hand it over to the Devil if he'd just make me an offer. I've always been that way.

I keep running the film reel in my head of my own nightmares, the worst being of the children, buried in the garden, all needing mowing. And Billy Bates at Hardy Elementary at the beginning of this waking nightmare—how had a fifth-grader been involved with this? He couldn't have been. Was it my imagination? But that kid had known to write in blue chalk: "He says you cheat," and of course, I had. When I was sixteen. During the chem test that finally got me booted from Pontefract Prep. Billy Bates believed that he spoke with Bart Kinter, and in that other cellar, that boiler room of Hardy Elementary, what did I see? Who was it speaking to me?

To keep going on this train of thought: was there something in me that came out and got hold of Billy Bates, if briefly, maybe because he was already bad, and he could soak up all my badness? Like a movie projector—was I sending out that image of Bart Kinter, projecting it right over Billy Bates? Is that the disease that Clare has accused me of bringing into this town?

And all these blood ties—Prescott says that in a town like Pontefract, the people that are still there (until tonight, that is) pretty much are all related to one another. But I am the foreigner among them. An outsider.

Although, what if, in this weird witch's brew of extraneous information (blood ties, guilt, death, love), you need an Outsider to give the final ingredient?

Why would anyone need an outsider when you have all these insiders from generations past, all linked to each other by blood?

I'm almost scared to write it down.

Scared, scared, scared. I wish I could just be scared to death and have this all done with.

Because what if the Mother of Nightmares needs
What if the Goatman needs
What if the Eater of Souls needs
New blood.

Looking back over these few pages, I see the kinds of thoughts a sleepless mind conjures up. Some of this seems silly; it just leads me in circles. My mind can't seem to discriminate between a good or bad idea anymore. I try to remember what life was like before this week, and I find i difficult to recall a world existing too far beyond my nightmares.

But I still don't understand my place in all of this, why there ever was that phone message from Lily Cammack, why Bart Kinter was there, even in the Washington suburbs That night Bart Kinter died, when I dreamed of a monste that was and was-not Bart Kinter simultaneously, the ange in the voice as it burned in that cellar . . . so confused, don't know what has been a dream and what has not.

I have been writing in this book for nearly an hour.

It is time to stop writing.

We've got to go over to that house.

And if it's me that the Eater of Souls wants

3.

"Cup—" George said after his fifth cup of coffee.

Cup set his pen down in mid-sentence. "Just writing ou some thoughts. If I'm going to lose my mind I wan documentation." Neither Prescott nor George seemed to ge the joke. Prescott was gazing out the window at the dar snowy landscape.

George unlocked the handcuff that kept Lyle chained t the file cabinet. "Now, Lyle, I'm taking you with us."

"Ain't gonna be your bait!" Lyle squealed in an almos female, high-pitched voice. He tugged at the cuffs whil George connected his wrists behind his back.

"Nobody said anything about 'bait,' Lyle. I just thin you'd be happier with *us* than back here. In case they com back for you."

"They wasn't gonna hurt me," Lyle drooled, and ther was a snarl to his voice, "'cause it's y'all they want. Yes, yes oh Kee-rist, yes."

George slapped him on the back, shoving him in th direction of the front door. "Well, then, you've got nothin to fear, Lyle, right?"

"But first a smoke for me—soothes the nerves," Prescott said, pressing his pipe between his lips and then patting each of his pockets (vest, jacket, pants), "if only I could find my darn whatchacallit, oh for goodness sake, I can never remember simple words like that, isn't that silly?" His voice caught, as if he'd snagged it on a lost memory. "I could tell you the maiden names of every married woman in this town, but not the simplest of objects, you know, a pipe thing—"

"Lighter," Cup volunteered.

"Quite right, Cup, good lord my memory—" Prescott plucked the silver lighter from an inside pocket of his gray suit jacket. Then he said sadly, "You know my wife gave this to me on my birthday, the year before she . . ."

"She's there, too," Lyle said from the doorway. His eyes seemed to have grown to the size of saucers, ready to burst from his head. His face had taken on a rat-like aspect, and Prescott found that he could not bring himself to look at the mad deputy beyond a quick glance. "In that house, and it's time for the feast, ain't it? Pull up a chair, folks," he growled, "plenty of room at the table, yassah, plenty to go around. The worms go in, the worms go out, heh-heh."

George pulled Lyle backwards by the handcuffs into the hallway, and Prescott did not, after all, light his pipe.

No one said a word again until all four men were in the police cruiser, and then it was Cup who said: "Anybody remember that golden oldie by Alice Cooper? 'Welcome to My Nightmare'? . . ."

4.

Clare had already crawled inside her own nightmare somewhere in the darkness of the Marlowe-Houston House.

"Now, Clare, stop that crying," Rose Cammack said, and her voice was like a hole in the fabric of the darkness surrounding Clare. She clung to cold stones with the icy water running across her numb fingers. Through that hole came a shot of vivid blue light, and Clare realized that she was not thirty-six years old, but nine, and being punished in the cellar again because she'd taken her scissors to Lily's party dress.

A thin slice of blue light grew from the hole her mother's voice made, and this grew larger to become a rectangle of light, until finally it was simply the cellar door being opened above her while she herself sat on the steps. Her mother appeared in the doorway, looking not quite like her mother: her hair was askew as if it had been put on Rose Cammack's head backwards, although perhaps it was her *head* that had been twisted on backwards, like a light bulb not quite in the socket. Rose's head wobbled as it adjusted to the high collar of the dress. Then she was all Clare's mother again, prim, proper, vaguely Country Victorian, the perfect wife for the perfect headmaster.

"Now you stop that, Clare," Rose repeated, "if you wrinkle your nose like that it will freeze that way and then won't you be sorry."

Clare managed to sniff back a sob. "I'm already sorry, Mama."

"You're just being *evil,* Clare, doing that to your sister, saying those things. Just like that awful white trash Amory girl."

"Please let me come back up, I hate this place."

"You hate every place, don't you? And those evil stories you told Lily, trying to frighten her about this house—why, you'll give her nightmares! Is that what you want? To give a little five-year-old girl nightmares?"

"But her baby," Clare said, "I saw it, cross my heart, and Lily, all that blood, and Warren . . ."

"I don't know who this imaginary friend of yours is, this Warren, but I can tell you I don't like this nonsense one bit, and those evil twisted things about your father . . ." When her mother spoke, gusts of foul warm air blew across Clare's face. The smell was like a backed-up garbage disposal. Clare realized the odor was her mother's breath.

"Please, I take it all back, let me up—"

"Not until you start acting like a little lady, do you understand?"

Clare began crawling on her elbows and knees up the steps while her mother spoke.

"Why, how dare you say those things. I've known your father a sight longer than you have, let me tell you, and I don't think he plays funny little games with his daughters, I can tell you that. Why, he's a member of the Society of the Cincinnati, and he's an Odd Fellow, you don't find Odd Fellows doing that, and yes, he has a Ph.D. in History from the University of Virginia, an institution, I can assure you, that does not turn out—" Clare's elbows hurt, but her hands were so numb they seemed absolutely useless, like mitted claws, as if there was some jelly-like concoction spread over them. The icy water poured down the stone steps across her knees; her skirt was soaked through.

"Please, Mama . . ."

"Don't you 'Please Mama' me, young lady, why if I had my way I would discipline you myself, but I am reserving that right for your father—"

"Mama, please, I love you, I won't do it again, please don't, not Daddy—"

Clare reached up with all her strength to the top step. Her face a bare inch away from her mother's ankle. She extended her arm into the smoky blue light to touch the hem of her mother's skirt. In the light, Clare saw for an instant what had gummed her fingers together.

Across the back of her hand, intertwined with her fingers, were dark leeches sucking greedily at the soft white flesh.

Clare screamed and slapped her hand down hard against the top step. *"Please, Mama, no, not Daddy . . ."* She grasped her mother's skirt as the slimy worms hung like mucus from her wrist, and then she looked up into her mother's face.

It was no longer Rose Cammack standing over her.

It was no longer a skirt. The material shifted, became slightly fuzzy; Clare thought her own tears were distorting her vision.

The creature that stood above her had no face.

But Clare recognized the gray flannel slacks and the seersucker jacket and the blue wool cap on the creature's head. And beneath that blue wool cap was a bloody tangle that the creature kept rubbing at with its hands as if trying to scrub the blood and pulp off the skull.

"Give Daddy a big kiss, little blind Clare, big kiss," the creature hissed. From between its pudgy, skinless fingers that were pressed against its mouth, something emerged. A pink tubular tongue shot out of its maw like a party favor, and then went flaccid as it drooled across its chin.

5.

It had all been an awful nightmare for Tommy, but that's all it was. He lay in his bed, staring up at the moonlit shadow of the window that pressed against the far wall of his bedroom. He'd awakened because he'd heard his mother coming in the front door, and then his father crying in the hall; Tommy imagined that his mom and dad were embracing as his father said, "Please forgive me, sweetheart, I didn't mean to do that, it was the beer that hit you, not me, I love you honey, I love our family, I don't want to drive you away . . ." And then Tommy, laying his head back into the familiar concave slump of his pillow, heard his mother's response, "I could never leave you and Tommy for very long, you know that . . ." And the words all blended together the way Tommy knew words did when you were still half-asleep and eavesdropping on a hallway conversation.

Just a nightmare—and what a nightmare! Tommy turned on his side, straining to hear the comforting sounds of his parents as they made up to each other and swore undying love in the hallway. There were no ghoulies and ghosties and long-leggedy beasties, nothing like a rotting corpse had grabbed him in the Henchman Lounge from behind Clare Terry, nothing had dragged him through the sewers to this dark cold place, it had all been a nightmare. And fire? There'd been no fire in the Key Theater—why, his dad must've just gotten off work an hour or so ago.

In the hallway, his father said: "Why, honey, I must've gotten off work an hour or so ago."

And Tommy's mom replied, passionately, "And there was

no fire in the Key Theater, was there, dear? Just another night of *Sleeping Beauty* and *Dawn of the Dead."*

Tommy was drifting off to sleep again, thinking how wonderful life was, after all, how you shouldn't let your nightmares scare you, they were just nightmares, like the Boy-Eating Spider—*it wasn't real, it was just something Dads tell their kids to keep them in line, to keep them out of dark alleys, and sewers, and old cellars in empty houses. "The Boy-Eating Spider only eats bad boys," Dad says.*

"Hey, Tommy," a voice whispered.

Tommy's eyes fluttered closed and then open again. "Huh?" he asked the darkness. He turned over on his other side, his arms sprawling over his head. "Wha?"

"Itsy-bitsy spider climbed up the water spout," the darkness murmured.

"Dad?" Tommy pushed himself up on his elbows. He shook the sleep groggily from his head.

"Tommy?" His father's voice, reassuring in the now-total darkness of Tommy's bedroom.

"Is everything all right now?" Tommy asked.

"Itsy-bitsy spider climbed up the water spout," his father repeated, and then again. The darkness around him became physical, stones pushing against Tommy's chest, pressing him into his mattress.

Tommy heard the closet door creak and rattle; something that sounded like claws scuttled across the floor out of the closet. *I don't believe in the Boy-Eating Spider. I don't believe in you. I don't believe.*

"All that matters," his father said, close enough for Tommy to feel his breath against his face, "is that I believe in you, you naughty, bad boy."

Tommy felt something long and spiny and bumpy stroke his chin *(Hey, Tommy),* and then Tommy screamed, trying to wake himself up, hoping that there was something to wake up to beyond this nightmare.

6.

In the dark pit.

Teddy Amory, her face pushed up out of the cesspool she lay suspended in, slept. Her arms and legs kicked out like a swimmer trying to escape drowning, and her eyes rolled around in their sockets. Her body trembled with the freezing water that she felt inside herself.

But still, she remained asleep.

7.

What kind of monster are you?

Lily, I love you.

What kind of monster are you?

Breeding ground.

What kind of monster are you?

He says you cheat.

He says you killed him. Down in the cellar.

Do you know what it feels like to burn from the inside?

Like maggots eating away at you.

Stingers.

Suckers.

You. You. You.

Welcome to My Nightmare.

"No!" Cup yelled, and was looking up into Prescott Nagle's face. He lay shivering, leaning against the older man's shoulder. Then Cup said, quietly: "You let me fall asleep." He sat up in the back seat of the police cruiser. George was in the front seat sipping a cup of steaming coffee from a styrofoam cup. His sixth cup. He did not turn around.

Lyle Holroyd, giggling, looked back over the front seat, resting his chin against the vinyl seatcover. "They're gonna have us for breakfast."

Prescott offered Cup his own cup of coffee. "You let *yourself* fall asleep. And anyway, it was just a couple of minutes."

"We have to destroy It," Cup murmured, almost as an afterthought to whatever dream he'd been having. The memory of it had already begun to dissolve. They were parked on Lakeview Drive, almost directly across the lake from the Marlowe-Houston House. The moon's light was scattered by the cloud-cover as snow continued to fall. Clear Lake shone like a bright coin, and the house was like the gaunt, hungry face of a miser waiting for an old debt to be repaid. Watching the town. Waiting.

Cup rubbed his eyes, but refused the coffee that Prescott offered. He yawned. "Why are we parked?"

George did not answer; he was apparently lost in his own private world as he gazed across the lake to the Marlowe-Houston House.

Prescott held up the dusty brown pages. "I've been reading this."

"Worthy Houston's famous missing diary pages." Cup nodded. "And . . . ?"

"Worthy found a way to temporarily destroy the Eater of Souls, and perhaps temporary destruction is enough. Even at the cost of our sanity."

"Ha!" George laughed. He reached over and patted Lyle on the head, who responded like a loyal dog, licking George's hand. "Sanity? What the hell is that? Where do you get it, do you know, Lyle?"

"Christ, I am so fucking smart, George," Lyle snarled, trying to bite George's hand. George slapped Lyle lightly across his stubbled face. Foam squirted out of Lyle's mouth onto the front seat of the car.

"Sorry, Lyle," George said. Lyle whimpered and pressed the palm of his free hand against his face, rattling the handcuff that connected his left wrist to the car door handle. "Just trying to prove a point is all."

"If we can stop this evil," Prescott said, "it will be worth our sanity."

"I'm insane, you're insane." George grinned into the

rearview mirror at Cup. "The Historical Society is now officially the Hysterical Society, isn't that right, Pres? So go ahead, read me the minutes of the last meeting. This Worthy Houston's last meeting, anyway."

8.

Prescott Nagle Quotes Worthy Houston

"Worthy Houston encountered this . . . *force* at the goat dance in the early years of the nineteenth century. His diary, George, basically relates the tale of his father, Stephen, digging up bones in the field and burying them beneath their newly built home. Cup and I have both read most of the diary Worthy kept. But there were these missing pages, which as it turns out are rather crucial to our understanding of the events at the goat dance. Cup and I visited Gower Lowry to get these pages, but he pretended we were crackpots.

"Only in death did Gower turn them over to us." Prescott said this last with a sigh. "Poor Gower."

"He practically handed them to us," Cup said.

"It seems like this Eater of Souls you keep mentioning is a damn nice adversary, 'cause he just helps y'all out an awful lot," George said, and then apologized for the flippancy in his voice. "I mean, it's just so fucking easy to keep these *things* from attacking *us*—like that one shot in the Henchman, and even old Hank Firestone . . ." George sounded exhausted; he paused mid-sentence. ". . . I mean, hell, it's like whatever's in that house *likes* us."

"They *like* to play with their food," Lyle sniggered. His teeth were yellow and scummy from froth. "That's what Jake Amory told me, what was left of Jake, what they were still *playing* with. He told me they played with him, oh, yes, just like a little kitty with a mouse. Play, play, play."

George, about to say something else, fell silent. He scratched the back of his head.

Prescott continued over Lyle's chanting of *play, play, play.* "Gower must've carried these pages near his heart, for who knows how long. He must've been afraid, but perhaps more afraid for his own sanity—" (*"Yeah,"* George huffed) "—a fear he might not be willing to admit to someone like me.

"But, George, this Eater of Souls isn't the brightest of adversaries, because sometimes it *is* frustrated, sometimes people like Worthy Houston slip through the cracks. And maybe it was Worthy's own insanity that saved him, maybe whatever is inside the Marlowe-Houston House can only wield its evil power over the sane or near-sane. Perhaps a touch of planned insanity would be useful. Because the Eater of Souls seems to be using the thing we fear most against us: the people we have loved and lost. My wife, Cassie, Cup's friend, Lily, and your friends, Frank and Louise. The images of love, to distract us, perhaps? To keep us in our individual cages of denial? Well, I am no good at psychoanalyzing my own self, let alone others. But let us turn now to Worthy, dear, crazy Worthy.

"He ended his days a drunk, in debt, believing himself doomed to Hell, a raving lunatic as many an observer remarked in his day.

"And *still* he was able to shut the door on the Eater of Souls." Prescott leaned over so that he was directly under the car's interior light. He held the diary pages almost against his nose as he began reading in the manner of someone exhausted, reading over a recipe to make sure he wasn't leaving out any ingredients:

"*'I have done it and am damned. I have looked into the heart of the heart, to find what manner of hellish creature lay there beating, and it has been my own corrupted heart in a prison of thorns.*

"*'I found my sister, sweet Virginia, in the crawling pit wherein our father laid the bones of the tormented Carson children. What could that madman have thought when he buried her amongst the foul water, her face barely risen from the filth as if she herself were come from the grave with the others? Oh, evil day that this house were built!*

"'*She was in her fever, and dying. Surrounded by the minions of Hell. When I came to her, the filth departed from her heavenly form. Virginia was more beautiful then, even close to death, but closer she looked to the angel than to eternal damnation. I felt the stirrings of untethered nature in my loins. The voice of Satan rose up in me and bade me to go to her as man does to his wife. My sister! Oh, weak mortal vessel! Virginia shuddered with a gentle violence as if she and the molten earth were one.*

"'*My body was possessed of a vicious animal nature, as if I had drunk wormwood and gall and now longed for the taste of blood. In my sister's eyes I saw the dark impetuous fury of carnal desire, and in her eyes, the reflection of my own.*'

"Suffice it to say," Prescott looked over the page, "Worthy proceeded to rape his unconscious sister. But he was repentant in the same hour. And he decided then that it was too late to save Virginia, so he must do something to end her torment. He used the only weapon available to him, and it was quite horrible although it does make for interesting reading, if you will indulge me:

"'*Born of the same Evil that led the savages to their winter bloodfeast, and so shall be snuffed out with a funeral pyre as were their demonic revels. I have buried her in kindling, like a bird in its overturned nest—AND STILL SHE BREATHES! I hear her beneath the dry wood, her soft moans and delicate sleeping motions betray her life. Oh, forgive me, Maker of All Things, Judge of All Men!*

"'*I have put her living in the tomb!*

"'*And now to seal that tomb, to drive out this evil plague from this house, from this abominable goat dance.*

"'*I bring the torch to my sweet sister's tenebrous pyre.*'"

"Like the Key Theater," George chuckled absently. "Oh, fuck a duck, Lyle, I'm getting to sound just like you!"

"Not just a fire, George," Prescott nodded, "a fire*bomb*. Whatever energy is behind this evil, it is highly combustible. Something like—"

"*Gas,*" Cup said, "I knew that's what I smelled. With Hank Firestone, and even at the Henchman Lounge."

"The gas," Prescott said, "that the dead give off."

"But Worthy lived to tell the tale—"

"Yes, Cup, he escaped his own fiery death by tunneling through the old sewage conduit, the same foul waters that have contaminated Clear Lake. He must've thought at first that the whole house would burn to the ground, and in his later diary, he expresses disappointment that it did not. Of course, some of it burned, but all was rebuilt, and Worthy never returned to the place of his birth."

Cup shivered involuntarily. "I hope we're as lucky as Worthy Houston."

George turned the key in the ignition; the cruiser sputtered, shaking off ice and snow. "We've waited too long, already. Seems I'm as much of a coward as you, Lyle."

"Heh-heh," Lyle said, because life itself had become a joke.

"You both saw the note: *he says you cheat,*" Cup said. "That was for me."

But none of the others was listening. George put the car in drive, and proceeded on the slick icy road, turning left onto Campus Drive, ignoring the stoplight that had frozen into a red orb.

George parked the car in front of the Marlowe-Houston House. "If it's just fire that'll do the trick here, I've got some flares in the back, and maybe a few bullets will slow this Eater of Souls down."

"You got *silver* bullets, George? They gonna eat you and your bullets, heh-heh," Lyle slobbered.

"Weapons?" Prescott asked. "You think we'll be able to defeat whatever is in that house with weapons? These reanimated corpses have just been puppets, George. Inside there," he pointed to the house, "is whatever is pulling the strings." But still, Prescott reached into his jacket pocket and felt for some object that he could not quite name.

George raised his eyebrows in the rearview mirror for Prescott's benefit. "What, then? I thought you said fire . . ."

"We must get Teddy Amory—and any other survivors—out of there, first. Then we can burn the evil out. I'm afraid for the time being the only real weapon we have is already in that house. A door which must be shut."

George handed a gun back to the older man. "You just take this anyway, Prescott. Consider it insurance in case we can't get that little girl, or anyone else, out of there."

Prescott accepted the gun reluctantly.

9.

Cup was the first up the front steps; the others lagged behind.

"Don't go in until we're all together!" Prescott shouted from his side of the car. "We must work as one unit, we can't separate—whatever is in that house can't get us alone!" He was having trouble getting out. "My joints aren't doing so well," he said.

Cup turned and glanced back at them. *Christ, what a crew: an old man, a cop, a certified lunatic deputy, and me. Helpless, defenseless, maybe marching right into our deaths.*

10.

From *The Nightmare Book of Cup Coffey:*

Twelve years before, I walked up those very same brick steps. Standing before the paneled door, peering through the warped dark sidelight panes into the front hallway. The night of Dr. Cammack's Christmas fete, before the party. Before the Tenebro Initiation, when I had hopes of becoming a Shaman with my offerings to the tribe of the bone and the bottle of bourbon Lily had promised to swipe for me. Lily was helping in the kitchen, and had seen me through the open kitchen door. She'd come to the front door and scolded me for being so obvious. "One of the guests will come early and see you. If anyone catches you here you've sealed your doom," she'd said.

"I'm already getting canned, what else can they do to me?"

But she told me to go around to the back entrance, to hang out in the shadows on the porch, and I did. It was dark. The cellar door had been open then, and I'd thought of going into the house from down there. But there had been something in that cellar, some wild animal lurking in its depths. I wondered if it was the janitor's dog that I'd stolen the bone from. It was so cold outside, and a warmth emanated from the cellar. I wanted to go down in that cellar, but I was afraid. And something spoke to me: *If not now, later.* That's all: if not now, later. It was just the wind from across campus, or it was just a ringing in my ears.

If not now, later.

And Founders Day, 1987, *later* had come for me.

Payment for stealing that bone, and substituting Bart Kinter as the sacrifice to the thing in the dark cellar. I closed my eyes, and wished that upon opening, none of this would be real. But I opened my eyes, and the white paneled front door of the Marlowe-Houston House was ajar.

I glanced back down the steps, and it was as if the entire landscape had shifted, actually jolted from one image to another, just like a slide being superimposed over another until it entirely blocks the former image. Behind me: the snow-covered lawn, the low brick wall that marked the boundary of the house before the street, then West Campus Drive, and across that, Clear Lake. But there was no black-and-white police car, no Prescott, no George, no crazy Lyle Holroyd. It was dark, and across the lake, streetlamps flecked the shore and lit Lakeview Drive as it twisted alongside Pontefract. From inside the house, the Morse code tapping of footsteps toward the door.

What was I thinking then? That it was my responsibility? That this Eater of Souls wanted me, and if I was all It wanted, well, *hell,* why waste an entire town, even of such dubious distinction as Pontefract, Home Of My Nightmares, just for a cup of coffey?

What terrified me at that moment as I stood on the

threshold, hearing the sound of approaching footsteps, was not *death,* or *pain,* but having to make a stand against *wrong* in favor of what I believed to be *right.*

I was terrified that I was not up to that.

"Cup," Lily said, opening the door wide enough for me to see her creamy face rising from the collar of Gower Lowry's tweed jacket, "you shouldn't be here yet, it's not time. The house isn't even ready."

11.

"Cup!" Prescott cried out. The older man was halfway out of the car; George, who was helping him out, looked up to see Cup stepping through the front door of the Marlowe-Houston House.

"They got him!" Lyle, his tongue wagging along his lips seemed to be cheering for the wrong side.

"Jesus!" George shouted, "nobody goes up those steps by themselves!"

Prescott looked at the gun in his hand as if he wouldn't know what to do with it. He looked up to the front of the house and wondered why Worthy had not destroyed that house completely when he had the chance. "One mind," Prescott muttered, "we should be of one mind entering this house. We can't let it divide us."

George dragged Lyle out of the shotgun seat. Lyle howled in pain but George felt like he was beyond caring: *thank God Rita just lost her tongue and not her whole brain like the rest of us.* He went around to the trunk of the cruiser for the flares.

"Don't make me, Christ! Don't make me!" Lyle screamed, but did not make a move to run away.

Prescott stood, silently staring at the Marlowe-Houston House. The world was dim and quiet. There was no wind.

"My God," Prescott finally said.

George began swearing because there was only one damn flare in the trunk. "Lyle Holroyd!" he shouted. "There's always supposed to be more of these in here."

"Dear lord," Prescott said. "I am afraid of death. I am an old man, all my old friends are gone, my wife is gone. And I am afraid to follow them." The Smith & Wesson burned in his hand.

None of the three wanted to move from the cruiser.

Finally, George came up behind Prescott and touched his shoulder briefly before moving away. "C'mon, Lyle," he whispered, and Lyle, whimpering, followed like a beaten dog too scared to go off on its own.

George went in first, kicking the door open, and pointing his gun directly at the portrait of Marjorie Houston-Lowry, who was Gower Lowry's mother, and the great-great-grandniece of Worthy Houston. She did not seem amused by the sheriff's presumption. The portrait had been slashed repeatedly, particularly across the woman's face. Prescott and Lyle stepped inside the open door.

Lyle said, "Play, play, play."

George didn't turn around when he said, "This is amazing."

The Marlowe-Houston House was in the process of changing. Like a Daliesque landscape, it melted and shifted. The drapes in the living room flowed like a slow mucus down across the carpeting; the ceiling dripped with water, and stalactites had formed as in a cavern. The baby grand was lopsided. Two of its legs had shrunk in size, and the yellowed ivory keys were like melting ice cream across the keyboard. The display cases, full of documents, Indian arrowheads, Civil War and Revolutionary War buttons and other memorabilia, were smashed and lay broken on the dark wood floor. The floor itself had experienced some upheaval as if there'd been a minor earthquake, for it had split in several places, boards jutting upwards, cutting through the already ragged and threadbare carpet.

The whole geometry of the house had changed on the inside. The doorjambs were pushed further into the walls, and the wall itself had given in to the jabbing doorframes like clay. The ceiling was bowed, and met the wall with a curve rather than a straight line. The living room, the hallway to the kitchen, and the stairs to the second floor all seemed twisted, gnarled.

As the Hysterical Society, minus Cup, trooped into the hallway, George said, "It's like it's alive." What he didn't add was: *and it's in the process of digesting.*

Prescott sensed that, too, what George was saying: because the house seemed to be breathing, inhaling and exhaling.

George turned around and grabbed Lyle by his arm. "Show me wherever the hell your ghouls are, Lyle." He shoved Lyle ahead of him, into the foyer.

Lyle stumbled in, falling to his knees. He looked back up at George, his eyes wild, and whimpered, "G-G-George, don't you make me do that, I ain't going back down to that cellar, don't you—"

George, feeling for his gun, whispered: "Lyle Holroyd, if you don't get off your goddamn knees right this second . . ."

Lyle did as he was told, glancing about the shifting room like an animal looking to break out of its cage.

"Front door's blocked, so get moving," George said.

"George—" Prescott was about to comment on something he'd just noticed, something he'd *sensed.* But before he could say anything, Lyle was bounding up the staircase to the house's second floor, crying out: "You ain't gettin' me down in that boneyard, they ain't eatin' me for breakfast!"

"Damn you, Lyle!" George shouted, running up the stairs after him, and realizing too late, just a few steps up the stairs, that the Eater of Souls had already managed to divide them into their own private hells.

CHAPTER NINETEEN
PRIVATE HELLS

1.

Cup

"I know you're dead," I told Lily. When I stepped inside the front door of the Marlowe-Houston House, everything was in order, and the whole house was set up for a party. There were already people milling around the party tables, the sound of clinking glasses, the gurgle of cocktails being poured. I even recognized a few faces: Patsy Campbell, stuffing her face with a moonpie, but blood dripped from her mouth as she bit down into its moist hollows; Gower Lowry flirting with a young curvaceous blonde. My guess was they were all First Families.

But Lily drew me away from the gathering in the living room, down the hallway. "Please, Cup, don't—don't mention *Death,"* Lily whispered this last word as if it were an obscenity. "You don't understand what they do to me here, Cup, it's like being in hell. They treat people like . . . *meat,* Cup, living or . . . We're all only food for them, Cup, we're their cattle, their sheep." She wore the royal blue dress under the tweed jacket, just as I remembered from the night of the Tenebro Initiation; her normally pale face burst with vibrant color like a brilliant leaf in autumn. Her eyes were that ethereal translucent blue I had always been so entranced with; her blond hair sparkled. But even behind this beauty was a terror-stricken creature, as if Lily, *her soul,* were being held in this nightmare world, beyond the boundaries of life or death, against her will. And I remembered the words that Bart Kinter had said to me beneath the footbridge: *I fuck her every night, Coffeybutt. We do it in the cellar doggystyle. She loves it. Your friend Lily's got the whitest ass I've ever seen.* And on some level between my own terror and the crack that was now running through my body like lightning, splintering my mind into fragments, I believed her as she spoke. "I called you down here from Washington, Cup, because I do need help, and you might be the only person in the world who can help me. They're holding me here, in this *house.* But it's not just *them."*

"Who are they?"

"Does it matter? Worthy Houston called them Goatman for the blood of the children spilled in sacrifice to them, and the Tenebro Indians, before the white man came, feared them as the Eater of Souls. You yourself have called them the Mother of Nightmares. But all I know is they have *power,* ungodly power. My own son was sacrificed that they should rise and find their way."

"And what about Teddy Amory?" I asked. Oh, have I mentioned that in the space of a few hours I could feel my sanity slipping away? Have I mentioned that fact? An insane logic seemed to rule now: I no longer looked at this nightmare around me as alien. This was the world that I was born to live in.

"She is the door through which they may pass and claim what is rightfully theirs." Even while Lily spoke, I detected the unnaturalness of her pronunciation, as if she were hypnotized, repeating rehearsed lines. I wanted to shake her awake. But there was that animal fear in her eyes, as if at any moment someone or something would crawl out of the shadows and tear her limb from limb. She said: "But now it's you I'm afraid for, Cup, because I was wrong to bring you here, dreadfully wrong. Cup, they get *inside* you, and it's like maggots—"

Boring their way out, suckers, stingers— I could've finished the sentence. I thrust my hands into my pockets; the place was becoming very cold, and a cold blue light began throbbing around Lily's form.

"I've been infested, too, and now I'm afraid . . ." She was speaking haltingly now, as if on the edge of tears. Lily took a deep breath and averted her gaze from mine. For just a moment I saw:

her body bloated and naked, scalp ripped partially off to reveal a bony crust, her face white, her eyes sunken into brown empty caves beneath her forehead, her lips peeled back away from gray teeth. Her ribcage jutted out from her sides. A jagged rip like lightning running from her navel down to her vagina, and the scar throbbing, giving birth to something inside her, something that could feed on corpses, and when it erupted it was a vast yellow pit crawling with thick worms and blood-bursting leeches, turning the skin outward with their sucking.

One of the maggots had grown enormous, five times the size of the others, as if it was their queen pushing its way out, its egg-sac full, wriggling out of Lily's lower abdomen, and it turned to stare at me.

The maggot that emerged from Lily's open wound had Bart Kinter's face.

I sucked air into the back of my throat in a feeble attempt to gasp, but I was looking at Lily again, beautiful young Lily.

She knew I had seen, and I felt she was pretending that to see her dead like that was a gift that she and I shared, that she would never show her dead self to anyone other than me.

When she spoke again, her voice was smooth. She had collected herself. There was no fear, only resignation. "You, Cup, are the key," and when she said "key," we were sitting in a dark movie theater, and the screen suddenly lit up with a blue light. A thin shaft of light shot over my head. A movie began projecting onto the screen.

I'm at the Key Theater; she said the word "key" and that triggered this image. The images are triggered by words, or thoughts. But whose thoughts: didn't I think of the word "key" a split second before she'd said it? Standing at the door to the Marlowe-Houston House, what was I thinking? My hands deep in my pockets, clutching stray coins, stray coins and the spare key to Patsy Campbell's Boarding House, that was it, my fingers felt that key and identified it, and the word in my mind, "key," triggered her word, gave birth to this image: the Key Theater.

"Watch the film," Lily said, resting her hand firmly on my wrist.

The movie image flickered, sputtering like a candle flame. It was out-of-focus, but what I could make out was myself in the boys' room at Hardy Elementary School, with Billy Bates crouched against the tile near the toilet, masturbating. "He says you cheat," Billy moaned as his small hand slid up and down on his penis, only, as the camera came in for a close-up, it wasn't a penis at all, but a shiny dark snout, like a lamprey's sucking maw, tiny sharp teeth along its edges.

In the movie, I took a step backwards, pressing myself against the shut stall door. The dark thing coming out from between Billy Bates' rapidly moving fist stretched, elongated, brought itself up to my face. I reached out and grabbed its neck, trying to wrestle it away, and it became the handle of a lawn mower. I was in an empty field mowing over the heads of children, who were screaming, crying out "Father! Father!"

I watched with fascination, thinking: *I was right, the Mother of Nightmares. If anyone's become infested with something it's me, it's all in me, these people are just players in my movie*

As I thought this, I felt something crawling around.

Inside me.

Maggots.

Stingers.

Suckers.

Under my skin.

And I was no longer in a movie theater, but was standing in the rear of the Marlowe-Houston House with Lily. It was freezing cold, and dark. She was wearing Gower Lowry's tweed jacket around her shoulders, and my eyes were fixed on the erect nipples which poked at the fabric of her dress. I found I had an erection straining against my trousers; Lily brought her face close to mine and kissed me. Her salty mouth stung my lips, and I brought my head back. Away from her face. She was too close, too out-of-focus. For a flickering second, I saw something other than the girl of my dreams licking Its lips as if It had just sucked something out of my mouth. I tasted blood on the rim of my lower lip. I did not want to see that . . . thing . . . again.

"Mother of Nightmares, Eater of Souls, all one and the same, Cup. With them, there is no male or female, Cup, there is only the one love which calls itself . . ." It was Lily again, happy, shining like a streak of sunlight through clouds. As she spoke, I felt curiously aroused by her voice, and I longed—yes, *longed*—to kiss her again. My erection was painful and enormous as it pushed against my trousers' rough fabric, and I felt the inside of the zipper slice against its thin skin. I reached down to adjust myself in my pants, and clutched something other than my crotch, something cold and hard and long that I had, twelve years ago, wrestled from one of the Jack Daniels Hounds.

A long, thick bone.

"Ask me," she said, and it was as if she'd read my thoughts, because accompanying the surge in my loins, the feeling that the graveyard bone belonged to me, my weapon, in a way that nothing made of flesh did, was that burning question.

I asked. The last question in the game we played. The last question in "Smoke." Not the first, which is, "What kind of smoke are you?" Because this insanity was beginning to taste delicious to me, I was at the Goat Dance and I could've danced all night. I felt my blood steam inside; I have never felt more alive.

Hell, no, I wanted to rip through that game to that last question, the one I had cowered from like a beaten dog.

"What kind of monster are you?"

She smiled and replied, "Only if you really want to know, Cup, only if you'll be my knight in shining armor. Then I'll show you. But if you lose at this game, Cup, if you lose—"

Maggots.
Under your skin.
Tearing.
Suckers.
Breeding ground.

Lily took my hand and led me to the cellar doors, which were flung open. "You have to come willingly, Cup." She grasped the bone that I now held in my hand; she tugged lightly on it. She glanced down into the dark entrance. "Down there, all your dreams will come true." She went gingerly to the edge of the top step: it was slick with a thin layer of ice, and she balanced herself both against me, clutching the edge of my jacket, and the bone for support. Again she tugged at the bone, taking another step down into the cellar—I noticed that she seemed to hesitate there, one foot still barely on the top step, waiting for me to follow her down.

"I . . . *can't.*"

As soon as the words were out of my mouth, Lily let go of the bone. In that moment I saw her face drain of color, and an emotion ranging from surprise, to uncertainty, to terror wash behind the blue of her eyes—I have no doubt that this was a mirror-image of my own face.

She fell.

I looked down in amazement at my left hand, gripping the bone.

In less than a second I saw the girl I had always loved fall down the steps of the Marlowe-Houston House just as Bart Kinter had done twelve years before.

Falling down into that darkness. The sound of a body hitting the floor.

I looked at my betraying hand; my reaction was slow because I was remembering that *other* winter, and I was waiting for the sound of the wet pop of bone as Bart Kinter's neck snapped.

But what I heard instead as my gaze went from my hand to the shadowy cellar was an adenoidal male voice taunting me: "Coffeybutt, you finally came back to face me, didja?"

Grasping that bone firmly in my left hand, I descended

the stairs. Without being conscious of it, I slapped the bone into the palm of my right hand like a schoolteacher with a ruler, preparing to punish a bad student.

2.

Prescott

The woman apparently came from nowhere, as if she'd just sliced herself into the air; Prescott last remembered looking at the living room, and had been about to remark something to George Connally, but he couldn't remember exactly what it was he intended to say, something about the smell, something about that smell. But George had run too quickly up the stairs after his deputy. Prescott wanted to stop him, knew that they should not separate, but that *smell.*

Not just the smell of gas, but the smell of . . . his late wife.

Oh, Cassie.

"You wanted to see into the heart of the heart, isn't that how Worthy Houston put it?" Her voice was low and throaty. Sexually exciting. She was just as she'd appeared in the barn, a young, beautiful girl, while age had run its course with him. Her small eyes were filled with a lively playfulness Prescott could not recall from their life together. Her auburn hair had grown wild like a forest, and flowed down her back and along her shoulders. Her skin possessed a healthy glow. It was as if she were more alive now than she'd ever been.

Prescott was not standing in the Marlowe-Houston House's hallway at all, but in an empty field, and it was summer. The yellow grass was high, the sky was clear and blue. He stood alongside the bank of a clear stream.

Cassie threw her arms around him and hugged him tight, and he felt differently, as if something were missing . . . something inside him, and then he knew. He was young again; he glanced at his clothes, his old man thrift shop suit was enormous on him. He felt his face, and it was smooth. Cassie drew back from his embrace and said, "Isn't it wonderful!"

"What is it?" Prescott asked.

Cassie grabbed hold of Prescott's hand and led him over to the edge of the stream. She pointed down into the stream. A small circle of stones had created a miniature bay, and in the still water Prescott saw his reflection.

He was indeed a young man. His hair, which had been speckled with white for nearly thirty years, was restored to its original dark black. No crow's-feet around his eyes, no veins erupted on his nose. His teeth, when he smiled, were white and perfect.

"You are a handsome devil," Cassie said, and he felt her hand as she slipped it beneath the thin material of his jacket, warm and alive as she touched where his sweat-soaked shirt clung to his ribs.

"Am I dead?" he asked, and heard his own voice: it was the voice of a young man, light, uncertain, barely free of an adolescent tenor. "Is this heaven?"

"Yes," she said, kissing him on the neck. "We're together in heaven now."

"But the others," Prescott said, absently; he could still not direct his gaze away from the reflection of this young man in the water.

"The natural order has been restored, Scotty. The others happily died, willingly sacrificed themselves to the ecstasy. Passage has been secured, Scotty, for the rebirth. Theodora Amory is the door, and your friend, Cup, the key. And with the key the door is opened, passage is secured, and the word is made flesh."

"You mean God?"

Cassie laughed. "Not your God who lives only in books and in feeble words, but a creature of such beauty and splendor."

"The Eater of Souls," he said.

"Beauty, Scotty, Death and Beauty in harmony, incomprehensible in our small human terms. Unspeakable beauty, Scotty. A man would be a fool not to yield himself up to It." She unbuckled his belt; his slacks were so loose on his thin frame that they almost slid off. He felt a moist heat there, where she stroked him, not entirely comfortable, as if he had no control over the feeling. He wanted to ask her why she was doing that to him; it was distracting him, because he was remembering other people, something about a little girl in a house. "It entered me once, too, I was to be the door. But I was foolish, Scotty, full of profane desires. I was unworthy of Its love."

He looked up into her eyes. "How did I die?"

She rolled her eyes, exasperated. "Is that so important . . . now?"

"Yes," he said, "it is important."

She pointed down into the stream, and he looked, and did not see his youthful reflection at all. Instead he saw:

Himself, an old, weary man, sitting at the bottom cellar steps of the Marlowe-Houston House, looking into the empty blackness. It is cold and he hugs himself, shivering. He reaches in his pocket and extracts a gun.

"That's the gun George gave me," Prescott said.

"Shhh . . ." Cassie pressed a cold finger to his lips.

He gazed at the reflection.

The old Prescott lifts the gun, putting the barrel to his mouth.

3.

Clare

The skinless thing in her father's clothes pushed her down onto her stomach against the rough edges of the cellar steps. It slid like a gelatinous lizard over her hair, and down her back. As soft and pliant as the creature seemed, it had incredible strength—*or is it my weakness?* the paralyzing fear overcame her. Moving further along her wool skirt, it left a snail trail of warm gum as it rubbed its head against her ankles. She could feel the buttons on its seersucker jacket pressing against the back of her thighs as it slithered, the wet leather smell of her father's brown loafers as the thing-that-could-not-be-her-father dug his toes into her scalp. She swallowed the cold water that flowed beneath her face, now pressed into the stones. The water tasted like someone else's vomit. Clare gagged and groaned, parting her lips again to expel the foul water from her mouth; she felt worms crawling just under her chin.

Please, don't let me die like this.

"Big kiss, baby, big kiss for Daddy," the serpentine voice hissed, and she felt that worm-like tongue, hot and dripping, coil around her left calf. Involuntarily, her legs kicked out against the face, and met with a quashing sound as her foot felt the oatmeal of the creature's cheek. The heel of her shoe seemed to sink *into* the face. To the hard bone of the skull.

Clare's stomach lurched.

But she had momentarily stopped the . . . *Thing. It's not Daddy, I know it's not Daddy.* And she knew what The Thing intended to do to her. *The gaping pink mouth with flashing silver teeth, the long tube of tongue winding like a copperhead up between her legs.*

"That's lovely, lovely," the thing said, making smacking noises with its mouth. Clare felt the tongue wrap sloppily around her ankle. "Lovely, lovely," the voice began breaking like a country singer's, sliding up a scale and then down. Clare tried to press her legs together to keep that tongue *away* from her, but she was quickly losing all feeling in her legs from the ice cold water and the weight of the thing that was pinning her to the steps. And yet, even going numb, she felt that tongue, like a warm-blooded creature twisting up her legs. The voice, changing, molting like a snake shedding its skin, becoming lower, deeper: "There's a saying that goes, I'll take a dip in the red river, but I won't take a drink from it, lovely, lovely, little blind Clare." As the freezing water ran across her face, her nose just pushed to the side so she could breathe, Clare realized that The Thing was going to bleed her *down there,* just as she had the last time she went to bed with Warren, just as she had when she'd dreamed in the bathtub, and then another memory tore itself out of her brain: *just as Lily bled to death,* down there, *in the cellar, blood running from between her legs.* And whatever lay on top of her. It wanted to drink her blood. That pink tongue. Breathing against her legs. Shoes digging into her hair. She felt the tongue, slithering up on the back of her thighs.

Clare once again opened her mouth to scream, and water flooded, cold and sour, against the back of her throat.

"Clare," he said, "my baby, give Daddy a big kiss."

4.

Tommy

"We need some light in here, son," Tom MacKenzie, Sr., said in the dark—his breath was hot and smelled like trash that hadn't been taken out for two weeks. Tommy gagged when his father spoke. He tried to see in the dark, but could make out nothing other than a dark shape looming over him. The spindly thing sliced across his throat like a long skinny finger. If Tommy, who was slowly going into shock, could've pictured that thing in his mind's eye he would've seen a detached spinal cord studded with tiny feathers and a thin serrated cutting edge caressing him just beneath his chin. It gave him the humiliating feeling of being slowly tickled to death with a fine razor and not being able to do anything about it. Once, when Tommy had just begun to shave, he cut a shallow red line down the side of his face and it had tickled and burned just like this thing seemed to be doing when it stroked him.

"We need some light in here, son," the voice that sounded like his father repeated, as if waiting for the meaning of the words to sink into Tommy's brain.

Which it did.

"Dad, no, no light, I don't—" Tommy gasped, sputtering as if he were drowning. He wanted to say: *I don't want to see.* A pincer-like claw wiped across his mouth, stinging him, and something warm and sticky brushed his lips. He was wrapped in tight fabric that clung to his skin; he began shivering even though he did not feel particularly cold.

"We need some more light in here, son. The Boy-Eating Spider wants you to believe in him like he believes in you."

Light flooded the room, and Tommy screamed inside himself. He felt like he was imploding.

Tommy was wrapped like a mummy in a spider's web, and the web was jiggling, not with his own struggles but with the thing that bounded across the web toward him. Not the Boy-Eating Spider, but his own father, his eyes wild with insanity, his tongue wagging from side to side, giggling and gibbering, chanting, "Naughty, naughty, naughty . . ."

5.

George

"Lyle? You damn fool, get back down here." George tried to sound like this was nothing, that this misshapen house itself was nothing, that they had all gone off the deep end, but no reason to make a big thing of it. He ran up the staircase thinking he'd just get to that landing, find Lyle, and then turn back around. *Just like Lyle Holroyd was sneaking a beer on the job, or had been riding a little too hard on a chronic violator of traffic rules, or was flirting too much with the teenage girls down at the Jump 'N' Save. This wasn't much more than that: hell, so what if my wife's been eating glass and is laying in a bed over at the Westbridge Medical Center, and so what if I've seen enough corpses in the past twenty-four hours to last me a—heh heh—lifetime, and so what if some of those corpses are moving around just like no one told 'em they were dead? Who am I to say that's not the way it should be? Why, shucks, ma'am, I'm just here to keep law 'n' order, keep the peace, I don't give a cat's asshole if this Eater of Souls goes about Its business in Its own special way in the privacy of Its own home.* Up the staircase, as he passed the tall Venetian window that now seemed to stretch up to nfinity before it reached the ceiling, George was momentar-ly blinded by the glare of the sun reflected off Clear Lake. *See? The sun still gets up in the morning just like the rest of us, and somewhere, yeah, somewhere, somebody's eating his Wheaties, someone's just gotten laid, someone is singing in his shower. Oh! What a beautiful morning!* George had not expected the sun; the light outside the window was still murky with the hangover of night, but that bright strip of light off the lake, like a brilliant fish flashing as it came to the surface, hit him hard with a fear he hadn't completely realized.

I will not wake up from this nightmare.

Dear God in Heaven, I will not wake up from this nightmare.

As he gripped the greasy banister that seemed to wriggle beneath his fingers, George glanced back down the stairs. The carpet rippled as if it were hanging on a clothesline in a strong wind, and the staircase, like the window, seemed to drop into an endless chasm, a staircase that twisted and turned and continued downward into a falling dark-ness.

No turning back no, nosireeebob, George laughed as he had been learning to laugh in the last few days, a laugh that started deep in his stomach and sounded like whimpering if you couldn't crawl inside George's mind and know that he really *was* laughing. *Something* is *crawling inside my mind, I can feel it*—George had once found a baby abandoned in the restroom of a coffee shop out by the overpass, and the baby was screaming mainly because a cockroach had crawled right into its ear. Those roaches aren't too good at just backing up, so here was this big old waterbug with its skinny legs wiggling and swiping at the kid's peach-colored earlobe, trying to dig its way through all that wax, and this baby just screaming not knowing what was causing all that pain, and that's how George felt right at the moment, like a cockroach was digging in his brain. *Cockroaches eat just about anything, and a mind* is *a terrible thing to waste. Oh, dear God, cut me a little slack, will you? I've always followed the rules, played fair, don't make me go like this.*

George let go of the snaky banister, and walked down the

hallway. He glanced in the bathroom as he passed, and there was some man in there wearing a pith helmet and what would've been a blue uniform (except for all the blood that was haphazardly shot across it). George just saw this guy through a large crack in the bathroom door. He knew it was someone who used to be called Howie McCormick, *my own goofy first cousin,* but George was not about to admit this even to himself. Barely visible, behind the bloody man was a woman lying dead in a bathtub full of blood, but a woman that George could not even in his wildest dreams have identified as Cappie Hartstone. Her face had been chewed off, and only a stubble of matted hair remained on her torn scalp. As if he were embarrassed to be caught in such an intimate act as chewing someone's face, Howie leaned over and nudged the bathroom door shut.

Folks have got to have their privacy.

George thought he heard someone call out his name from behind one of the bedroom doors. *You're going to have to do better than that,* he grinned. *If I am insane, and you're insane, whoever or whatever you are, you're going to have to do a damn sight better than that. This is the Sheriff you're talking to, the glorified meter maid, the man with the badge, the head honcho of Pontefract. You got my town, you got my marbles, but hell, you're not going to get my balls, too.*

George replied to the door: "Go play with yourself."

But he thought he heard another voice, a child's. "Dad, no light, no I don't—"

Tommy MacKenzie.

Inside that bedroom.

"Shit," George said, touching the gun in his shoulder holster for good luck. He walked toward the bedroom door.

6.

Cup

When I descended the steps, the only light in the cellar emanated from the wall to my left. It cast a bluish glow across the room, but most of what I could see was a torn shelf. I looked over the shadowy floor for any sign of Lily, expecting to see her twice-dead body in the same bent position as Bart Kinter's had been. Expecting to see Bart himself. *I KNOW WHAT KIND OF MONSTER YOU ARE!* My head throbbed with pain—I felt like something wanted to burst out of me. *NEXT TIME! NEXT TIME IT WON'T BE SOME HORNY COUNTRY MORON!*

I slapped the bone in my left hand down into the cup of my right palm; it stung. *STINGERS! SUCKERS! BURNING INSIDE YOU! BREEDING GROUND!* My ears ached with the thudding sounds, the whoosh of blood as it crashed against some inner shore.

YOU. YOU. YOU.

Slap! The bone hit the palm of my right hand, and I could no longer feel it. A wave of nausea overtook me as I moved toward that torn shelf. My eyes were not focusing; I saw insubstantial mosquitoes circling at the periphery of my vision. My tongue dried up in my mouth and felt withered and salty like a piece of dried meat hanging in a smokehouse too long.

I am insane.

I KNOW WHAT KIND OF MONSTER YOU ARE!

Insanity's okay. We've got doctors for that. Good doctors. I've been to a therapist before, no big deal. I told him my dream about the lawn mower running over kids in a garden and he told me it was my member.

I did not even realize that I was smacking the bone into the palm of my right hand.

MOW THEM DOWN, ALL FLESH IS GRASS!

Now my teeth—I can't feel my teeth—oh, God, did I lose my teeth? I flicked my beef jerky tongue across the upper ridge of my teeth, and they all fell out—well, my vision was bad, but I saw them all fall, all my teeth just like an old man about to die, and when my teeth hit the mushy floor, they shimmered and wriggled like ghostly maggots. *Oh, God, I'm dead, I'm already dead, my body, Jesus,*

MAGGOTS!

The bone whistled in the air. I watched my hand move of its own accord. My left hand, gripping the bone, whacking it into my right hand which was swollen like it had been pumped with

STINGERS! SUCKERS!

The worms go in, the worms go out

All right! I know what kind of monster I am! Just leave me the fuck alone! Drive me insane, just drive me somewhere, somewhere else!

Then, inside my head, the throbbing stopped.

I heard the white noise of a fan, eclipsing all other sounds.

And then Bart Kinter whispered in my ear: "*Well, asswipe, it's about time you came here. We're all monsters here, even your little debutante twat, Lily. I got her in the hole now, if you know what I mean . . .*"

I felt someone pull on the bone, leading me over to the ancient toilet and the long torn shelf.

I saw:

A gaping hole where the toilet shelf had been, with brick and wood blistering around its outer edges like venereal sores. The blue fumes were particularly strong there, curving and twisting, almost like a veil billowing upward from below. The dim light was coming from that pit, and as I went toward it, I stepped on what felt like several hundred jellyfish. The floor of the cellar crawled with worms. *The worms go in, and they do come out, oh, yes, they most certainly do—where you've got dead bodies, and this house must be a good gravestone to hundreds of 'em, where you've got dead bodies you got to have maggots.*

I gazed down into the opening.

A throbbing membrane was stretched like an animal hide from one end to another. Seepage from some stream running beneath the house slushed and gurgled across what was left of the muddy floor. Spiny tendrils had sprouted along the slick wet walls; a pink lip-like membrane hung like a canopy from the ceiling, dripping with a thick, cloudy mucus. The netherworld I gazed down upon pulsated as if the entire sewer was alive.

And a circle of human bones, dozens of them, ribcages, arms, legs, skulls, some half-in and -out of the mud, some stacked one atop the other. Within their circle, something moved.

I thought I saw many things at once, as if overlaid one atop the other. First some dark creature bending over another, reminding me of a lion feeding upon a fallen antelope. And then it was something closer to a Portuguese Man-Of-War, its many tentacles grabbing some small, pale creature beneath its translucent sac. Then a lover and his beloved, naked, lying in an undulating bed, the man, in a dominant position, bending over her, kissing her breasts. Then, for only a second, a little girl caught in a mudhole, surrounded by bones, but this flashed back to the lovers, and the man moved aside, giving me a better view.

And laying down on that slowly undulating floor was Lily Cammack, her royal blue dress torn, a look of terror in her eyes. Bart Kinter, naked, his backbone jutting out like a dinosaur ridge, pulled her knees apart with his hands. He turned to look up at me. That evil face, the stub of a nose wrinkling in lascivious glee, his green eyes becoming slits, his white hair blown by a static wind. "Hey, Coffeyshit, this old girlfriend of yours tastes pretty fucking good," and he licked his lips; but the tongue that emerged was blue and studded with warts as it slathered along his lips and down as far as his chin. "Through eternity, you know, we'll be banging her little brains out."

Weakly, Lily whimpered, "Help me, oh, God, help me, Cup," but then her head fell back and her eyes closed.

"You're a good corpsefucker, aren'tja, Coffeydick?" Bart

laughed. "Come on down and join the fun. We've all had her at least a hundred times, but she's good for another pop or two."

Just a show. Welcome to my nightmare, that's all. Bart Kinter is dead, and Lily Cammack is dead. Something coursed through my veins like Drano, burning and scarring as it went. The aches and pains returned, the feeling of being absurdly constructed of flesh and blood, vulnerable to constant attack. I felt a throbbing in my head like it would explode. I felt like I was sixteen years old.

As if someone else were doing this, and I was just watching the event, completely disconnected: I saw myself smack the bone against my swollen right hand.

I wanted to kill Kinter all over again. It was like a call in my blood. *Just kill him. If he's already dead, well, so what. You know what kind of monster you are, you've always known. Just get down in there, in that pit, and tear that motherfucker apart. All those years that guilt you carried. And he was always just waiting for you, back here, waiting for you to see this, to see him do this to Lily. Can't you just see yourself clawing into his flesh, hear his screams, look what he's doing to her now, he's God, Jesus, he's raping her, and you're going to let him get away with it. You said you loved her, and you did, and you still do, so get that perverted creature, rip his throat out.*

I heard a woman screaming from somewhere close by. I looked away from Bart (whose back was arched and whose buttocks beat like a tom-tom as he pumped away into Lily, her hands spreading out to clutch the earth—but it wasn't really earth—it was moving, like a thick liquid), but all that was behind me was a blue fog. For the barest instant I thought I saw Prescott Nagle through the haze, holding a gun, and then, the cellar steps running up to the kitchen, and a woman struggling against a man on a staircase, and in between these visions, layers of rippling blue fog—none of these visions seemed connected to me.

Something like mud was sucking at my shoes. My knees buckled.

And just before I fell down into what I thought might be

hell I saw a naked nine-year-old girl in the center of that pit of human bones, excrement and filth. She was unconscious, but trembling like a seismographic needle.

7.

Tommy

As Tommy MacKenzie's bed seemed to wrap around him, his father's spindly arms and legs stroked his cheeks, and he smelled mud and feces. And gas. His father's proboscis tongue shot out of his mouth and into Tommy's neck. Tommy felt warmth spread from his jugular vein outward. His father made horrible sucking noises, and his face became puffy and bloated; his father fattened, engorged on his own son's blood, and Tommy knew this thing above him was no longer *really* his father, but the Boy-Eating Spider Incarnate, like having a giant tick sitting on his chest, stroking him with sharp needle-like feelers, drawing his life essence out. When Tommy finally thought he could scream through the silver webbing, all that came up from his throat was a bubbling gurgle.

8.

George

George stepped into what he *knew* to be one of the old upstairs bedrooms, but what looked to him like a poorly lit chink-walled cabin. Written in blood across the wall: LOVE DID THIS. He was standing in the center of the cabin which seemed to grow and surround him as he breathed. The blood dripped down the wall slowly. George thought for one second that, *hey, I'm just going to leave this room, shut the door behind me—if I can find the fucking door—it was here just a second ago—and I'll just wait this thing out in the hall,*

I don't need to open any more doors, no way, Jose, but when he tried to move, his feet seemed to be mired in some kind of thick gum, like flypaper. He knew *he* was the fly.

Hearing the creak of floorboards, he raised his Smith & Wesson up to the level of his chest, pointing into the flickering darkness. There was a gasping sound, and George whispered, "Tommy? Are you—"

Frank Gaston's Southern Gentleman's voice interrupted him. "We saw it coming, George, we saw the turn of the tide while we were staying here." Emerging from the drapery of shadows: Frank and his wife, Louise. They seemed connected as they walked, leaning shoulder-to-shoulder as if comforting each other in some great tragedy.

Frank looked healthier than he had in the years before his death; his wrinkled skin had smoothed across his face like a hide that is stretched in the tanning process. He was wearing a Sunday Best suit, and his hair was thick and ash-blond. Louise wore a dark purple pillbox hat with a veil, which was pulled up to reveal a peaches-and-cream complexion. Her dress was black formal. They looked like they'd just come from a funeral and were celebrating the death.

George held his gun in his hand, but pointed it at the floor. His eyes became blurry with tears. "Oh, God, what's happening to me . . ."

"They're beautiful," Louise piped up. "George, you can't begin to imagine their beauty. I was in terrible pain, George, and Frank decided that it would be best if we ended our lives here, but look," she brought her hands up to her face, lovely and years younger than George ever remembered it being, "what they've done for us. The wages of sin, George. They can confer immortality and some beauty."

"As much as mortals can stand. Because, George, you see, most folks are just mortal, aren't they? You live sixty, seventy, eighty years, and then," Frank snapped his fingers, and it sounded like a bone cracking, "it's over. But these creatures, when properly worshipped and fed, why, just being near them, among them, you live forever."

"But you're both dead," George said, and Louise's face rippled with anger.

"Death is just a word," she spat. "After all we've done for you, and you treat us like this." She turned her face into her husband's neck and licked his throat around the curve of his jiggling Adam's apple.

Frank's eyes brightened. "Now, we know it must be quite frightening at first, to realize how empty your life is when faced with their omnipotence. Why, we're just shadows when you think about it. We're less than nothing. The best we can hope for is to be sacrificed or to be chosen. You got to think about how empty life is when you see how full they are."

Louise nodded, nuzzling against her husband like she wanted to crawl inside him. "How full they are."

"Then tell me, who are 'They'?" George asked.

"They are many, and they are one. Imagine a being so powerful, so strong that It would be worshipped as a god, sacrificed to, so omnipotent It could raise the dead, George, do you understand? Raise the dead. It must be a god, mustn't It, for It to do all that? We live in a godless world, and so It must be our only god."

"It might be a demon," George said.

Frank laughed. "Oh, that's how narrow our minds are, George, that's where our blinders come into play. We can only imagine in terms of our cultural limitations: demons, devils. But try to get beyond that, George, take it further. Put yourself in Its shoes: what if you were a god, were sacrificed to, could speak in the tongues of nightmares and dreams, and then were buried by blind ignorance? Made to feel small and puny, by creatures as absurd as man, whom you could easily rule? Wouldn't vengeance be on your mind?"

"Well, maybe. But if this thing is so powerful, why would it even deal with us?" *I am only speaking to these corpses because it is the polite thing to do.* George had to repress the mad chuckle that wanted to burst out of his gut.

"Because, George," Frank said, "sometimes It gets hungry. *Everybody's* got to eat." Frank took a step toward George, but George was momentarily distracted by Louise. There she was, looking so middle-aged smart in a pillbox and veil, her dark gloves, her shiny dress, but something was coming out of her mouth. Something small and slippery, and George wondered if she were vomiting an oyster.

George could feel the stench of Frank Gaston's breath as he moved closer and said, "Just put down that gun, George, those things are dangerous, you should've seen what it did to Louise when I pressed it against her temple."

Louise said, "Yef, you foulda feen, Gee-oo." Her words were garbled by the flicking membraneous thing that slid down her chin.

George remembered Rita's tongue. What they had done to his wife. "Oo-weef," Rita had moaned, and here Oo-weef stood as big as life with her own tongue problems.

George pointed his gun at Louise's mouth.

"I want Tommy MacKenzie," he said.

"You foulda feen, Gee-oo," Louise repeated, "da bwud, da wovewey bwud."

Frank Gaston snarled, "You want Tommy MacKenzie, do you? Well, we aim to please, George, that we do, and our aim is rarely off the mark. Louise, honey, George wants Tommy MacKenzie."

George could not take his eyes off Louise, whose entire form seemed to shimmer like gas heat above a radiator.

"How do you *want* him, George?" Frank growled. "Rare, medium, or well-done? I think the lad's down a few pints at this point."

Louise's entire face seemed to change with the slick dark thing that now flapped across her neck, her eyes began leaking a yellow milky fluid, while her jaw stretched outwards becoming a set of mandibles; her dress and pillbox hat melted against her skin. Her body crackled and became segmented, her hips expanded like a hot air balloon. Her arms reached out to him as he stood there, his own hand trembling, the gun bobbing up and down in his hand. Louise's arms turned into long crab-like pincers. The room itself was transforming around her; Frank Gaston seemed to bleed his skin, his suit, his ash-blond hair, right into what was quickly becoming his wife's arachnid abdomen, and the chinked walls dribbled across each other, leaving streaks and crosshatches until George realized that he was standing in the center of a spider's web.

George saw what looked like Tommy MacKenzie suspended in the web, wrapped as if in a cocoon. He seemed to be sleeping. Dozens of thin red scratches were etched across the teenager's face. *Shit! They're giving me what I want, Tommy MacKenzie, they put me right in his own fucking nightmare—*

"Tommy! Hey!" George shouted.

Then he heard the snap of the Louise-spider's mandibles as she moved closer to him.

9.

Tommy

The Boy-Eating Spider had moved from Tommy's chest. He gasped for air, breathing through the dark webbing that encircled him. Tommy couldn't focus his eyes in the dim room, but thought for a moment he heard his name mentioned.

But Tommy felt peaceful, warm, tired, like he just wanted to sleep forever in that feathery web.

Then something pulled him back, out of the warmth of unconsciousness.

Someone was shouting his name.

10.

Clare

The skinless creature pushing her down onto the stones let up for a second. Like a dog letting up so it can get a better grip on a bone.

Clare, with a renewal of strength, pushed up against its

heavy body, trying to turn over, fighting the father-thing. "Oh, lovely, lovely Clare," It made more smacking sounds, "Big Kiss." She would not be able to hold The Thing off much longer, and she longed for death to take her before all her strength gave out. She kicked out at The Thing, and with each kick, the long pink tongue wrapped itself tighter around her left leg.

She prayed the end would come quickly.

Clare thought the end was finally coming. *The light at the end of the tunnel, right? Except everything's getting dark, it's growing dark, dark and heavy.*

"Little blind Clare," The Thing cooed, its tongue releasing her for a moment. "Little blind Clare with no eye."

Clare felt worms crawling across her face, coming from the water, and covering her eyes.

11.

Tommy

A tear ran down the side of the spiderweb. Tommy opened his eyes, trying to focus on the room. Struggling against the web. He heard someone yelling at him, someone he was afraid was his father, but whoever it was wanted him to try to get out.

12.

George

George could not move his feet; it felt as if a thousand hands were pulling him down, trying to get him to fall on his knees. *WORSHIP THE EATER OF SOULS!*

He looked down to the floor, and the gummy web was tugging at his ankles. A tingling sensation began at his toes, and was slowly moving up to his calves. *DRAIN YOUR BLOOD, METER MAID!*

"Drain *this!*" George shouted, raising his gun up to Louise's snapping jaws. As he pulled the trigger, his legs went cold, and he felt himself *withering.*

The bullet he fired sliced off half of the Louise-spider's head, and the remaining right side of her arachnid face seemed to grin as she lisped, "Wove did thith."

George fell to his knees, and began crawling across the sticky floor toward Tommy MacKenzie. He felt something grasp him at the knee.

Turning, he saw that Louise was wrapping him in her silver cord.

13.

"What are you doing in my nightmare?" Tommy asked groggily. He did not know if he was still dreaming. Sheriff Connally was hunkered down on his hands and knees. Behind the sheriff, the Boy-Eating Spider was busily spinning a new web across his legs.

"Get *out,*" George gasped.

Tommy struggled against the web; he twisted his body to the side, but it held him fast.

"Pretend you're strong," George whispered, "believe in your own strength the way you believe in this nightmare. Pretend that you are stronger than this thing." George reached across the web. The Boy-Eating Spider was sewing a gray-white shroud around his hips now. Stretching his arm out, he ripped his hands down the webbing that held Tommy down. His fingers came back, bleeding, the nails torn back to the roots. George's face creased in agony. His hands, bloody, but free of the web, reached inside his coat pocket. He brought out a flare.

"Look," George gasped, then laughed. "I fucking forgot about the flare!"

Tommy managed to wriggle into the slit that George had made in the web's fabric.

George turned back to the spider. He held the flare up.

The Boy-Eating Spider paused in its wrapping. George was immobilized from the waist down. The spider reached one of its pincers out, pausing in mid-air near the flare that George held.

"Go! Run! Get the hell out of the house!" George shouted with all his remaining strength. He did not turn back to Tommy, but remained staring at the spider, keeping it at bay with this new threat.

14.

Tommy slipped his shoulder through the slit.

15.

"Hey, Louise, I *know* what fire does to you."

Inside his head, a voice cried: *THE EATER OF SOULS WILL SUCK THE MARROW FROM YOUR BONES, METER MAID!*

"Well, hell, let's just have a barbecue," George laughed. His face shone with sweat.

Tommy pushed his upper body through the web.

The Boy-Eating Spider remained still.

"You got about ten seconds to get outta here, Tommy, so give it all you got," George said. He did not take his eyes off the spider. "You can't feed on nightmares anymore."

"That flare," the Louise-spider wobbled her remaining mandible, "you don't really want to set it off, do you? Let me tell you, if even the smallest spark erupts from that flare, well, take a deep breath, you are surrounded by it."

"Gas," George said. *That sweet foul odor; not the smothering smell of your everyday fill-'er-up gasoline, but something more obscenely seductive. Sweet,* that's all he could associate with the smell that hung in the air, *sweet and deadly.*

"Yes, it *is* sweet," Hank Firestone said; he had his hand

out in front of him, palm turned upward. *GIVE ME THE FLARE, GEORGE, YOU DON'T WANT TO BLOW ALL THIS TO KINGDOM COME, DO YOU?* he was shouting inside George's brain.

They crawled inside me, they got me already.

We got you, George, yes, that's good, now, please, the flare, you're being very tiresome, and besides it's over for you, don't make this difficult for us.

16.

Tommy flexed his entire body as hard as he could. The gummy strands across his legs gave a little. It was like fighting off quicksand. His feet made a spitting sound as he brought them out of the cocoon-like thing he'd been wrapped in.

Behind him, there was a rattling at the door. He glanced back for one second and saw the door slide open. He stretched his leg out and pivoted toward the doorway. Someone was here to rescue them. Tommy leaned toward the opening door. Someone would be out there to help. He plucked his other foot out of the web. It was like his feet were nailed to the floor, rusty nails, ripping into him as he brought the foot up. He wanted to lay down and give up—the pain was too much, he wanted to lay down and cry and let the Boy-Eating Spider get him.

But the door—opening.

Slowly.

Uncertainly.

The pain, *the pain, the pain, it's like spikes in my feet, I'm so sleepy, just want to rest.*

The door opened further. Tommy touched the edge of the door with his hand. Someone—

Something was out there. Waiting.

YOU CAN'T WAKE UP FROM THIS NIGHTMARE

17.

"The gas that the dead give off, as Pres Nagle told you." Frank Gaston was undressing from Hank Firestone's skin just like it was a zipper-suit. The old man was naked, wrinkled skin hanging from the bone. Frank's head was half blown away. George had seen Frank that way before. He was prepared for it. He didn't scream. George did not want to give this thing that pleasure. "This house reeks of gas. You're thinking now of its hallucinatory qualities—quite right. The stuff that dreams are made of. And, just like dreams, quite explosive I assure you. But when the door is open wide, tonight, we will be invulnerable even to your flares and firesticks. Nightmare will become flesh and our long sleep, like your Sleeping Beauty, will be at an end. I could show you all your companions as they burn, George, before you've even rubbed your pathetic magic lantern." Frank's half-face seemed to be smiling, the half with the upper jaw that dripped like crimson buttermilk, and for a moment George did see *Prescott screaming as he burst into flames, Clare trapped in a room as the fire spread across the drapes, Tommy just undressing from the spider's web exploding like a human fireball, Cup Coffey rolling around in the dirt trying to stop his shoulders from burning.*

No. George ground his teeth together.

"I've always thought of you like a son, George," Frank said, stepping completely out of Hank Firestone's discarded skin. "But this corruption has always been with us—all of us—in this town, the sins of the fathers and all that *rot,* we need a clean sweep, fathers and sons, George. But *flares,* honestly. Would you do this to your old man? Your daddy?"

No.

"Give Daddy a big kiss," the thing said, sounding like a record that had been too long in the sun.

What the hell? George clutched the flare as the corpse shuffled toward him.

18.

Tommy watched the door as it opened.

A hand held desperately to the doorknob.

The hand was not attached to an arm.

Hanging from the shorn wrist of that disembodied hand was a handcuff that had not quite slipped off over the knob of bone.

"Heh-heh," a low voice sputtered from the hallway. "Christ! I was smart, George, I got them to take the 'cuffs off me! And they OBLIGED! THEY SET ME FREE, GEORGE! LIMB-BY-FUCKING-LIMB!"

Tommy MacKenzie did not scream. He had seen too much in the past week. He was beyond screaming.

He just wanted out.

19.

"Big kiss," The Thing repeated.

George managed a desperate grin. "You want a big kiss? Suck on *this!*"

He snapped the flare, thrusting it forward, almost touching the monster that was reaching a feeler toward him.

20.

Tommy tugged his foot again from the sucking web, and fell onto his stomach into the hallway. The hand that had been holding the doorknob dropped like a full tick into his hair and slid down the back of his shirt. Tommy brought himself to his elbows. He barely felt the fingers gliding down his back dragging the handcuffs with them.

Two inches from his face was another face.

Deputy Lyle Holroyd's head lay, battered and bloody, on the carpet. His eyes had been gouged out, and when he grinned at Tommy, blood sluiced from between his lips.

Tommy reached up and batted the head down the hallway.

Lyle howled as his head thudded against the carpet, and rolled to the edge of the stairs. It tottered there for an interminable second, and then went over.

Tommy heard the whump-whump-whump as the head hit every step going downstairs.

From behind him, in *that* room, Tommy heard Sheriff Connally yell: "Run, Tommy!"

Then the door slammed shut behind him. Tommy pushed himself up. The crawling hand pinched at his back; Tommy felt the ice cold handcuffs swinging beneath his shirt.

Tommy ran for the stairs.

21.

George snapped the flare a second time.

Nothing happened.

No light, no spark, no explosion.

Frank Gaston hissed like butter in a frying pan. He plucked the flare from George's hand. George did not put up a struggle.

What the fuck? George moaned. *Shit, Lyle Holroyd, goddamn you to hell for not replacing those damn flares like you were supposed to last summer. Goddamn you to hell, Lyle.* Gauze-like webbing reached his waist. He felt Frank's razorsharp pincers resin his face with something warm and sticky: his own blood.

"Feel free to scream, George," Frank said, "the Eater of Souls would like that very much. Loud enough for everyone to hear."

Sorry, George shook his head, in the middle of a prayer, *no last requests.* What could've been a large spider, or perhaps just an old man with his face mostly torn off, or maybe an old lady in a shiny black dress and a pillbox hat, laid its hand just beneath George Connally's chin.

The last thing George heard was a grinding, slicing sound, the way a garbage disposal hawks and spits when you put in too many old eggshells and grease and you forget to turn the water on.

The sound was coming from George's throat.

22.

Tommy was running down the staircase. He could feel Lyle Holroyd's hand hanging on to his back, trying to crawl back up to his shirt collar, pinching the skin, but Tommy did not stop running to pull the thing out of his shirt. The stairs descended into a twisting vortex, what Tommy imagined was like being in the eye of a tornado. He heard a woman screaming from down there, and saw that the stairs shifted in response to the scream, curving and wriggling like a snake as he ran down them, and Tommy realized too late that he was headed straight for the bowels of the house, the cellar, the place where Hardass Whalen had bitten the dust, and where Rick had been devoured and then spat out. *Heh-heh,* he thought he heard Lyle Holroyd's head laughing as it rolled *whump-whump-whump* into the dark pit ahead of him.

The stairs had uprooted themselves from the house, and were forcing him into the cellar.

Tommy could not stop running. The hand dug its fingernails into his shoulder as it shimmied up his spine. Tommy clutched the banister as the pain from the burrowing fingers became too intense—it felt like five hypodermic needles were injecting air into his blood. He arched his back, and dropped down onto his side with the pain.

He had reached the bottom of the stairs.

He was staring through an open doorway.

More stairs. Those leading from the kitchen down to the cellar.

Lying there in a blue smoky darkness was Clare Terry,

looking up at him with wild eyes, reaching a hand out to him for help. Her hand was covered with what looked like smushed maggots. And on top of her was something that Tommy knew was a creature from her worst nightmare, nothing more. The skinless man in the seersucker jacket was crouched over Clare, his head to her ankles, his knees crushing down on her chest. The thing swiveled its face around—*as if it's* looking *at me*—and Tommy realized he was no longer frightened of *anything* if he could look straight on at this monster without puking.

"Please," Clare whimpered. Her eyes were now blank and staring. Tommy wasn't even sure that she recognized him.

Tommy heard a noise that sounded like a vacuum cleaner being turned on full blast. He noticed that the creature pushing Clare against the cellar stairs had some kind of long pink tube running from its mouth along her legs.

"Join me for a drink from the red river?" The Thing sniggered, drool slopping from the side of its mouth.

Got to help her, but shit! How?

The Thing withdrew the tube back into its mouth.

Still holding Clare down, It turned to face Tommy.

ITSY-BITSY SPIDER CLIMBED UP THE WATER SPOUT, a voice that sounded like his father screamed in Tommy's ear.

Then Tommy felt Lyle Holroyd's fingers encircle his throat.

23.

Prescott

Young Prescott asked, "I killed myself?" Cassie's finger remained on his lips, so he found speech difficult. Her finger was cold, like steel, and when he moved his face away from his wife's pressing digit, it was the barrel of a Smith & Wesson for a flickering moment before becoming his wife's finger again.

"You saw clearly how little your life meant in the face of such unearthly Love and Beauty," she murmured, pressing her face against his neck, kissing him with her moist lips.

Then she looked deep into his eyes, and he felt drawn to hers: green orbs of light, turning to blue, like the cold heart of a gas flame suddenly turned up: then he struggled briefly *(no, I don't want this, I have to resist this, I want life, I don't want to die,* but her voice was already inside his head in a perfect union, twisting his thoughts. *Give in to this, you were an old man, now you are young, let it go, the battle is over, now the warrior must surrender),* caught in an undertow, being pulled further away from shore, down, down, down: the others were dead, there were no others, only he and his wife. He let her kiss him, slipping her rubbery tongue that tasted of sour vomit in between his lips, sour vomit and cold steel, her tongue became a cold steel rod stroking his tonsils.

He gagged, and it was the gag reflex that brought his teeth down on the barrel of the gun, and there was a pain in one of his molars from biting it. For a brief moment he knew that it was a trick, that they wanted him to pull the trigger, that he was in the cellar of the Marlowe-Houston House, but then he saw her again, *her face pressed against his and he reached up to stroke the side of his wife's beautiful face one last time. His thumb pressed into a cold hollow of her cheek, but it came down on a trigger.*

Quickly, Prescott pulled the gun out of his mouth.

Cassie exploded into a shower of cool blue radiance.

24.

Tommy

The hand was crushing his windpipe; he tried not to gasp for air: *Hold your breath, that's all, just like you're swimming, hold your breath, this hand's got to get a better grip, and when it lets go for that split second, you can get it.*

"Oh, God," Clare was moaning, "oh, please, please."

Itsy-bitsy spider! his father shouted from some empty room in Tommy's mind.

"Give Daddy a Big Kiss, Clare, lovely, lovely," the skinless thing sputtered.

Tommy thought: *Just another second, c'mon, you can do it, MacKenzie, you can feel those fingers just getting ready to—*

He felt the fingers relax. He exhaled.

Tommy grabbed the hand with both of his and wrenched it from his throat.

Lyle's fingers wriggled violently; it was like he was holding a horseshoe crab upside down and it was mad as hell. The handcuffs swung from side to side.

Clare began to make watery gasping noises that began deep in her throat.

Lyle's hand clenched its fist and beat at the air.

You want to strangle somebody, Mr. Hand? You want to really do a number? Tommy stepped onto the stairs. Carefully, he went around Clare who gazed up at him with unseeing eyes.

The creature that lay upon her growled at Tommy.

It opened its mouth: Tommy saw tiny silver teeth embedded in the purple gums.

NAUGHTY BOY! NAUGHTY, NAUGHTY! his father screamed from deep within the skinless thing's bowels.

Tommy slapped Lyle Holroyd's hand against the creature's neck. As if by instinct, the hand snapped like a bear trap around the exposed sagging muscles beneath the chin. Yellow froth began pouring out of the monster's mouth; Its own pulpy hands went to Its throat, tugging at Lyle's fingers.

While the monster was distracted, Tommy reached down and with all his might—*pretend you're strong, that's what the sheriff said, believe in your strength the way you believe in the nightmare*—pushed the monster off the woman.

It went over the edge of the stairs, falling into the deep blue cellar below.

Tommy heard a mushy thud as it hit the unseen floor.

CHAPTER TWENTY

THE GHOST DANCE

1.

Cup

The fall was no more than two yards, and I was cushioned by the writhing mud that splashed around me as I came down. It smelled like shit. I vomited into it. I landed beside Teddy Amory, who seemed to be asleep, dreaming. And I knew: The Eater of Souls, the Mother of Nightmares, needed this little girl to sleep, to dream. Awake she was just that ordinary little girl from the newspaper pictures: a blank canvas. An empty field. But asleep, in her trance, she was the door, she was the gift, she was the passage from the nightmare world to this. The house, above me, inhaled and exhaled with each of her breaths. And she did look beautiful, an otherworldly beauty, her skin smooth and glowing, vibrant.

They were keeping her in a constant state of arousal, of seizure. Attached to her arms, legs, chest, neck, along her ears, her forehead, matted in her hair, were the crawling minions of the Eater of Souls: the worms, the maggots, the leeches of corruption. They clung to her, but did not invade her body. All they were doing was keeping the door open for as long as possible. That meant for as long as the girl could survive. Their power increased with her in this state of flux; with the door kept open, the Eater of Souls was still on the verge of coming. The dead would rise, but not really the dead, just images of the dead, images to manipulate, to cheat, to use Its twin weapons of fear and revenge upon what the Eater of Souls, the Mother of Nightmares, was most jealous of:

Those who lived and breathed in the flesh, who possessed free will to worship as they chose, to love whom they would, who lived a limited span of years, and whose souls could not be eaten, could not be destroyed, but were beyond the reach and grasp of this sewer-rat god—even the Tenebro Indians had abandoned this spirit to Its underworld prison.

"You're mad because you *can't* live!" I shouted on my knees to the translucent blue smoke that drifted about the pit. "You're nothing but a graverobber and a molester! Come on, you fucking Nightmare Breeder, why don't you take me on!"

Sound of sniggering, and then like wind through a long twisting tunnel, "We have taken you on, we are a part of you, and you are a part of us," and the voice seemed not a voice at all, but words drifting through my bloodstream like the beginnings of a fever, blood cells fighting this new strain within me, fighting for their survival.

The voice I recognized finally: *my own.*

"I am not part of you, you, you—" Then an image from my past shot through me like a bullet: *Billy Bates on the jungle gym, saying 'You, you, you,' and seeing Bart Kinter in the gauze darkness of the school's boiler room, and Bart's hand clutching my ankle at the footbridge as he said, 'It's you, Coffeybreath, I'm in your blood,' and Clare slapping me at the courthouse, crying, saying, 'What kind of disease did you bring with you!' You—you—you.*

Inside me, the voice ate away at my strength. *The Mother of Nightmares is your mother, Cup. You are the key, and the door waits for a turn of the key. Do you understand?*

I was to feed upon Teddy Amory. I saw myself tearing her apart while her small white legs flutter-kicked out at me, spilling her steaming entrails across the slime and filth before the life went out of her, drinking the warm blood, gobbling down her heart while it was beating, sucking the eyes from her orbital ridge.

Like the Tenebro Indian Initiation, the test for Shaman, if I could survive it, if I could resist it . . . *(Why, Cup? Why resist such power, such glory, such beauty?) Teddy has the taint, she has the gift, oh, God, she is the door, but not from the world of the spirits, but the doorway to this particular spirit, this Ghoulmaker, and she is dying,* I knew that, because a human being could not live long with *that* inside them, that fit. *That dance. (That ecstasy, Cup, notice the gentle crescent of her lips, happy, pleasured, she longs for the key to bring her to the heights, to the pinnacle, oh, sweet Cup.)*

The goat dance within her, the empty field of her soul.

Mow it, mow that field. Get down on all fours like a bull, tear at the flesh and the grass, all flesh is all flesh is all flesh is . . .

To wear her skin and shave the thin epidermal layer of her face and wear it over my own as a mask. Because the birth of the Eater of Souls, the Spirit made Flesh, would come from within me.

Twelve years. It was you who took up the bone and who sacrificed Bart Kinter to us, when Bart himself had been Our Chosen. But your blood, new and fresh. Our corruption is coursing through your veins, taking you over. You have survived the years well; you have tried to resist, but that is done. You heard our call, and you came. Now, deliver yourself unto us. You are the key to unlock the door. It shall be closed no more forever.

I bent over the girl, her breath was like the sweetest perfume, and when I looked at her, she was Lily Cammack, naked, white, her hair licking the tips of her tumescent breasts; her legs were carelessly drawn apart, one knee bent, her body trembling as if from a slight chill. She gazed languidly up at me, and her petal lips drooped into a pout as she said: "To you shall be all love, all love, come to me, feel how my flesh desires you," and she reached out, grabbing my right hand, guiding it down her slightly distended belly, to the soft thatch of hair below. "Rip me, Cup," Lily said, forcing my swollen right hand against her moist labia, "there."

"No!" I screamed, and my cry echoed, bouncing and crashing through the throbbing chamber. I tore my hand away from her grip just as if I'd stuck it into a hornet's nest. Below her stomach, where her vagina should've been, was a small mouth, flashing silvery sharp teeth, grinning, and Lily also was grinning at me. It was no longer Lily, but Bart Kinter, laughing, and the mouth between his legs became an uncircumcised penis. It flopped to one side, and out of it poured blood, at first just dripping steadily, but suddenly it was spraying. Kinter began sobbing, "Jesus, man, it's bleeding, what did you make me do, man? You made me bleed, oh, man . . ." Beneath his face was Lily's face begging him "Give it to me, rip me to shreds, yes, oh, dear God, yes," and below her face, another, *some anonymous girl who might even be dead so what did it really matter if you were to tear into her flesh?*

"Just shut up, just shut up!" I cried out, and drawing myself back on my knees, I raised the bone high above my head and hit Kinter across the nose with it.

Like snow dissolving to rain, all the faces united for a moment and then separated. I saw Teddy Amory beneath the bone as I hit her. Her eyes opened with the contact, her nose was bleeding. It had brought her out of the low boil they'd been keeping her on.

Dozens of tiny dark snouts vacuumed at the blood when it splashed down on the filthy ground. Crawling maggots.

The blood, Cup, you will like her blood. You are hungry for her. You want her inside you.

"Fuck you!" I shouted at myself. The pull within my muscles, as if every cell cried out for the food this girl's body could provide.

2.

Teddy

Teddy screamed as if she were just being born, her eyelids fluttering as she tried to resist the constant seizure that was upon her. A pain shot across her eyes and her nose clogged; she gasped through her mouth for breath.

She awoke.

3.

Cup

I KNOW WHAT KIND OF MONSTER I AM.

MY NAME IS CUP COFFEY, AND THEY ARE INSIDE ME

MY NAME IS THE EATER OF SOULS

GIVE ME A BIG KISS, TEDDY, KISS OF THE POCKET LIPS

WE ARE GONNA BREED MONSTERS, TEDDY, YOU AND ME

YOU LOOK LIKE YOU BEEN GROWING IN THIS GARDEN TOO LONG

TIME TO MOW YOU DOWN, GIRL, TAKE MY MEMBER AND JUST PLOW

ALL FLESH IS GRASS.

4.

Tommy

"I—I can't see, please, help me," Clare gasped as Tommy lifted her up to a sitting position. "It made me—oh, God, it made me blind—blind—no eye—"

"It's all right now," Tommy said.

"So weak, I'm so—so sleepy," Clare gasped, and Tommy tried to bring her to her feet. He glanced down into the gaseous pit of the cellar and saw the floor writhing with maggots and leeches.

The hideous slick and shiny creatures foamed and rippled like a slow, viscous waterfall toward a gaping hole along the wall. Blue gaslight like steam hissed and boiled from the depths of that hole. Moans and muted shrieks seemed to be coming from that aperture, nothing that Tommy could say was recognizably human, although it did sound at times like a far-off chanting of several voices superimposed one upon the other. Images like slides were pressed one on top of another as Tommy gazed across the edge of that pit, and thought for a moment he saw *Prescott speaking with a young woman in a green dress, and there were dark formless things crawling across his face as he held a gun to his lips—*

But that moving-picture image flickered and was gone, and Tommy saw *an old man named Frank Gaston putting a gun to his wife Louise's head, just to the bottom of her pillbox hat, and pulling the trigger—*

—But that image melted like wax into a great valley of bones, ribcages, skulls, then separating into gray fat maggots, hungrily devouring the skinless creature that had once been Dr. Brian Cammack—

Tommy knew he was seeing only the hallucinatory vision caused by that gas that billowed from that pit. For a moment he thought he saw *Prescott again, the old man reaching down into his pocket—*

He shouted out for him, and he thought, for one split second, that Prescott looked at him, but out of the corner of his eyes, stealthily, as if he didn't want it known that *they* could see each other for that tenth of a second.

Then suddenly, through the fog of noise and blue came the tremendous wailing of a young child.

5.

Teddy

Teddy Amory awoke from her deep sleep. Her nose was bleeding where Cup had hit her. She looked up into the face of a human monster, sores bursting across his face, his hair slicked back, thick drool dripping from between his lips. He held a bone in the air. The end knob of the bone was red.

Red with Teddy's blood.

"I know what kind of monster I am!" the man shouted.

6.

Prescott

"Show me who you are," Prescott said. There were moments when he saw the others: Clare at the top of the cellar stairs, George Connally drained of blood in a tangled spider's web in an upstairs bedroom, Tommy staring deep into the cellar. Teddy Amory shrinking from Cup Coffey as he waved a long bone in front of her face, dripping blood-stained maggots into the festering mud; then his surroundings became that endless yellow field alongside the stream. When he had managed to remove the Smith & Wesson from his lips, and point it at his wife, she had disappeared, exploding into a million colors; he looked down into that stream and saw in the misty blue darkness Cup bending over the Amory girl and he was about to tell him to get her and get out as quickly as possible, but there was something about Cup that shimmered and was something else, something unspeakably monstrous there, something that was inside Cup, devouring him. But the vision melted into a stream again and his own reflection.

The mirror of our souls, he thought. Prescott even felt them crawling on him, along his arms, on the back of his neck.

You see, the voices hissed.

"I see you keep us looking into ourselves so much and showing us the fear in our own hearts, but I don't see you." Prescott realized that they were speaking to him inside himself. He was becoming infested, just as he was certain that Cup was also becoming infested.

The voices screeched in unison: *We are unspeakably beautiful. We are already inside you, Scotty, we are burrowing beneath your skin we will lay our eggs in the gray matter of your brain our children will suck the marrow from your bones—*

Prescott felt something squirming in his hand and looked down. The gun in his right hand became a mass of leeches, attaching themselves to his palm. He shuddered, plucking them from the skin. "You carrion-eaters!" And he realized too late that he had just tossed his only weapon away—*If there was any weapon.* Another illusion, another hallucinatory vision.

No, this is real, this is the world as it is, Scotty, the voices coursed through his bloodstream, *our world, the world of the Eater of Souls, the breeding ground of Nightmares, it is what all men come to, what you, too, shall call home, and very soon. We were worshipped and feared by men for centuries before your kind's history was even born. And now, through this door and with this key,* and for a brief flickering moment, Prescott saw below him again, Cup raising a bone against Teddy Amory, who lay naked amongst the filth and slime of that underworld. But the image became molten lava, and then Prescott was again surrounded by the blue fog.

"Then show me, show me who you are," Prescott repeated. He reached into his pocket, and hesitated.

What are you do—

"I was just thinking—"

We know your thoughts—we are *your thoughts.*

"Really? But an old man like me, my memory, so bad, sometimes I don't even know what I'm thinking—" Prescott knew he would have to act quickly, he would have to juggle several thoughts at once, *don't let your left hand know what your right hand is up to—is that the quote? My memory, so bad . . .* He would have to distract—

Distract? It was the chorus of voices sifting his blood, his memory.

"'When I was one and twenty,'" Prescott began, and he fished in his jacket pocket for that *thing—keep thinking* thing.

Thing? Their searching voice inside his head, like a blood disease taking over, like another being crawling beneath his skin, with his body fighting it.

Prescott was sweating, trembling. "'When I was one and twenty, I heard a wise man say . . .'" His hand clutched the thing in his pocket. Prescott thought: *thing. Just a thing.*

What thing?

"Poem, by Housman," Prescott gasped, and he felt suddenly weak as if someone had just punched him in the stomach, and he lost control of his bladder. "Oh, Lord help me," he cried.

7.

Cup

Like strings of spit, the jawless sucking mouths of worms clung tenaciously to Teddy Amory's body, holding her in the damp filth in which they lived. Teddy moaned as Cup ran the edge of the bone over her stomach; her white naked body was soaked in a viscous slime smelling of human excrement and rotting meat. The chilling water seemed to be rising gradually, soaking through his skin.

Cup looked up above him to the entrance to this ancient toilet. For a brief moment, he thought he saw Prescott Nagle. Cup did not recognize him as someone he knew.

I KNOW WHAT KIND OF MONSTER I AM

The smell of the girl, so delicious, irresistible.

HUNGRY—UNDER THE SKIN, SKIN OF THE WORLD, PEEL BACK, YELLOW FAT, INSIDE HER, UNLOCK, DOOR, MAGGOTS, EAT

8.

Clare

Clare cried out: "Prescott!"

Later she would be convinced she saw him standing before her in the cellar—but how could she when she could no longer see anything? It felt like another episode coming on. *One mind,* she thought, *we are all one mind now. We've been separated in our nightmares, but we've come together again. We're still one mind.* The pain from the blindness had been swift, but it was gone now. Her fear was still enormous, but she felt comforted with this . . . *communion.*

She felt that Prescott was speaking directly to her, although she knew he wasn't. He was reciting some poem, and the thought: *whatchacallit, pipe thing,* ran through her brain. In the dark night that she now was surrounded by, she heard his mind sifting through its own memory. *"My whatchacallit, oh, for goodness sake, I can never remember simple words like that, isn't that silly? I could tell you the maiden name of every married woman in this town, but not the simplest of objects—"*

Clare saw it: the pipe thing. It was silver, and had "To Scotty, Love, C." on one side, and when he opened it in the movie in her head it had a wheel, like a ferris wheel spinning faster, but not a ferris wheel, a spinning wheel—and then something else flashed with a lightning brightness:

"She shall prick her finger on the spindle of a spinning wheel and die . . ." and Clare knew that was from *Sleeping Beauty,* but could not figure out what that meant, it had something to do with the memory of having seen Lily in front of the Key Theater, and Clare didn't understand . . .

But the wheel continued spinning at a faster rate, and the silver pipe thing in Prescott's hand—

Without imagining the exact word, the precise image, Clare *knew.*

"We," she whispered to Tommy as he lifted her up, "have to—out—get out—now—out."

9.

NO!

All flesh is grass, mow the field, we know what kind of monster you are, Cup, you are us, we are in you, and in HER, Cup, the power, you will rule the living and the dead—

NO!

The Eater of Souls has conquered Death, Cup, life and death, one and the same, there is no life, only death, sweet death, we eat the dead, Cup, we eat the living, and you are us and we are you.

10.

Prescott

We are your Lord now, old man, show us what thing you have in your hand. The voice was at once inside and outside his head. It was as if something had crawled right in his ear and was speaking to him.

"'Give crowns and pounds and guineas, but not your heart . . . Not your heart . . .'" Prescott fumbled with the lines, trying to remember, and at the same time trying to forget something else, trying to not think about it, what his hand was curled about. He could feel his body going, losing functions: even his hand trembled, but he worked hard to embed that thing in his palm. That thing. Prescott thought: *whatchacallit. You know, pipe thing.*

He felt them rippling beneath the skin of his ankles, and he knew in moments he would be dead. *Moments,* the thought fluttered like some blood-sucking winged insect landing upon him, finding entry into his bloodstream, and Prescott didn't know if it was his own voice or *their* voices, because he was beginning to sound more and more like *them.*

Dead, yes, you will be dead, you will be food for us, you are food for us, Scotty—but like an alarm going off, the voices broke off and were searching through his blood, sifting this thought from his organism, trying to translate those words: *whatchacallit, pipe thing,* images swept before his face like a swirling cyclone. *His beautiful Cassie, Gower Lowry, Jake Amory, Lily Cammack, all blending into each other, the burning children at the goat dance, the Ghost Dance, visions of Tenebro Indian winter bloodfeasts, Virginia Houston sleeping beneath a bundle of kindling, burning, burning and screaming, burning, burning . . .*

And his blood cried out against him: *PIPETHING!*

It had an image now, *brilliant fire,* it had a picture from Prescott's own brain, and he knew that he would have to move fast, he would have to do it, just do it, *thank God for my bad memory, for not remembering whatchacallit, my pipe thing.*

Prescott shuddered as he lifted the silver lighter up high and pressed his thumb against the metal wheel. He sent out a prayer to the others. Through the filter of blue gas, he'd felt Clare there with him for just an instant. He hoped she could escape, that Tommy would run free, but he had no hope for Cup and Teddy in the sewer beneath the house: it was too late for them, Cup had already been taken over and the girl, the door, was in his grasp, awaiting the turning of a key. *The Eater of Souls must be destroyed, its carrion eaters must be buried in their catacombs for good.*

But their thought was eating its way out of his body: *destroy.* The skin along his legs was ripping open like rice paper, he would crumble in a moment. He felt his entire body begin to pull apart as if he were just a rag doll. Blood began pouring from his nose.

11.

Teddy

"NO!" the man cried as he towered over Teddy, waving the bone above her head.

Teddy smelled the gas station smell, the one in her dreams, the one that reminded her of Torch, and of that night when Jake came after her.

Do dreams smell?

"I know!" the man cried out. His face glowed as if inside him an electric current had been switched on and was making him twitch. "I know! What! Kind! Of! Monster! I! Am!"

Then Teddy knew:

It was in him just as it was in her. And what was in them was not Good or Evil, but was powerful, and whatever was keeping them here in this mire was Evil, and wanted their power.

"No!" the man cried, and his eyes were rolling up into the back of his head, until all she could see were the whites. "All Flesh!"

The bone came whistling down toward Teddy's face.

12.

Tommy

Tommy had felt it, too, what would happen, what Prescott was planning, and that thought went through his brain as he helped Clare to her feet, *One mind, we are whatchacallit, we are one, pipe thing, mind.* When Clare grasped his arm to bring herself up, it was just as if she'd said those words to him. Those words through her mouth, but with Prescott Nagle's voice.

13.

Teddy

The bone came whistling through the air; Teddy flinched, turning her head to the side. It missed her jaw by a fraction of an inch. The bone slurped as it sank into the steamy wastes.

Teddy looked up at the man standing over her.

He fell to his knees in front of her.

He was gagging, trying to vomit something out of himself. He twitched spastically; his tongue flagged out of his mouth, dripping with a yellow-green cud.

14.

Cup

Something had distracted the screaming voice inside Cup; something had sucked the corrupt blood right out of him.

PIPETHING! It cried.

Pipething! the voice got smaller.

pipething!

Drenched in sweat, gasping, Cup tried to spit the voice out of the back of his throat. He drooled maggots from the sides of his mouth. He coughed violently, expelling the evil that screamed like a tiny creature caught in his windpipe, *pipething.*

15.

Prescott

With the last of his energy, Prescott Nagle spun the metal wheel of the lighter his wife Cassie had given him, and a tiny flame erupted from its heart.

In his leaking brain, he shouted: *ONE MIND!*

16.

Cup

Cup looked above him, and the top edge of the pit seemed to be shrinking like the aperture of a camera when it is flooded with light. Maggots fell into his hair as the entrance began closing; he shook them off, holding Teddy closer to him. Water gurgled across the boggy floor.

Shit! We're going to be buried alive with these things in this septic—

Then Cup remembered. The taint of Clear Lake, what Dr. Nagle had guessed was "sepsis." A poisoning of the lake by the occasional emptying into it of human waste—*Jesus, and here I am up to my neck in the shit. But it had a way . . .*

A way out, there must be another way out. When Worthy Houston set his sister on fire, he escaped burning himself through the underground tunnel his own father had dug—the septic conduit, it was large enough for Worthy Houston, and if it hasn't collapsed over the years, maybe we can make it, maybe . . .

Cup heard a roar, as if a lion had been let loose upon the world above him, and he glanced back up at the now-tiny entrance to his fecal hell, and there was a bright blaze of yellow and searing white cutting through the opaque blue of the gas, and Cup knew:

Fire.

Holding Teddy Amory, who kept her face pressed in his shoulder, Cup hunched over, crawling along the slim trickle of water like Ariadne's thread down one of the tunnels of the underground. He began digging with his one free hand, carving his way through the yielding muck, and that trickle became a creek, and as he kept digging out the tunnel, the creek became a stream and Cup wondered if he wasn't digging his own grave.

He heard a hissing sound behind him, like steam on a hot burning coal. He recognized that sound just as if it were a distinct voice. Cup had heard it before, when he was sixteen and dreamed of fire and watched a million suns burst across Bart Kinter's dancing electrical corpse. *"I know what kind of monster you are!" that thing inside Bart had cried out, and then: "Do you know what it feels like to burn from the inside out? It's like maggots crawling under your skin, maggots with stingers and suckers boring through you, eating their way out, slow at first, real slow . . ."*

Cup's hand came through to the other side, numbed by the water that poured across his fingers, washing them of the filth; he turned and looked back over his shoulder to the source of that menacing sound. *If I could just get Teddy out there, on the other side of this, into the water, maybe she would be safe, maybe she'd find her way out, if I block this up so the Eater can't get to her.*

Cup knew in the instant before he glanced back that now, at last, he would meet the Mother of Nightmares, the Eater of Souls, what Worthy Houston had called the Goatman.

The Evil that existed outside himself.

Incarnate.

It would probably kill him.

And still, he turned to face It.

17.

Clare

The Marlowe-Houston House was melting back to its former shapes, as Tommy and Clare rushed out the back kitchen door, to the veranda, stumbling. In Clare's mind's eye (*one mind,* she thought) she saw the innocence that the Marlowe-Houston House had never possessed, that it never could possess wholly, because its foundations were on this field, this graveyard birthplace of the Eater of Souls. *This goat dance, the empty field that was not really empty. It was full of crawling evil things, of plagues waiting to be born.*

The Marlowe-Houston House was just an old house now, but it would be a house no more.

As Tommy pushed her through the open back door, and Clare stumbled across the veranda, bumping her head against what she assumed was a wooden column, she heard an explosion and was suddenly and inexplicably flying through the air.

Behind her, the Marlowe-Houston House exploded like a giant blood-engorged leech against the brilliant sunrise that had finally emerged.

EPILOGUE

WHAT KIND OF SMOKE ARE YOU?

Survivors

1.

They found Cup clutching the girl to him as if in his last moments he had cracked the ice and pushed her above the surface of the lake.

Clare knew where he would come out before the others; she *saw* in her head and directed Tommy where to go to find Cup and Teddy. She clutched Tommy's hand, and although the boy had sprained his ankle when the house burst into flames and knocked them all across the snow-covered backyard, he limped along (clinging to Clare as much as she was to him) ignoring the pain. Later Clare would make the excuse that she had practically grown up in the Marlowe-Houston House and knew every inch of the grounds, but this didn't explain completely how she knew to step over the bricks and splintered wood that lay in the snow like the aftermath of some violent battle.

The house itself had exploded outward in its first convulsions of death; the gas from the decomposing bodies and the vermin in the dark pit beneath the house was spent quickly, and the fire seemed to die away after that initial blast. Billows of gray smoke steamed up, blocking the sun.

When the Last of the Hysterical Society came around to the front yard facing the lake, Tommy saw the girl and the man he knew to be Teddy Amory and Cup Coffey, entwined like they were each halves of some design, trying to pull together. Neither of them moved.

Tommy let go of Clare and ran along the shoreline to the bodies.

Cup was lying face down, soaked to the skin with an icy glow of water, and when Tommy turned him over, he barely recognized his features: the young man had burns all over his face.

The naked girl lay shivering in the snow beside him *(alive,* Tommy sighed, *some of us are ALIVE),* still hanging on to him with her arms. Her hair was stringy and filled with tiny ice particles that twinkled like diamonds. Tommy, his eyes blurry with tears, tried to pull her away from Cup, but she would not let him go.

"Good—" she gasped, "I—can—good—it—can—bring—make—strong . . . " She stuttered, her teeth chattering from the cold, "B-b-blue—b-b-blue," and she found the blue that she was looking for in Tommy's eyes, and he felt as if he were being sucked out through those eyes as the little girl stared transfixed into them.

Teddy Amory saw blue, dreamed blue water, dreamed a never-ending sky of clear blue, and she felt her dance coming on.

2.

Clare knelt down in the melting snow, exhausted and shivering. She saw in her mind's eye what Teddy Amory herself was experiencing:

Behind Teddy Amory's eyes, the world became blue, and she crashed back through the frozen ice, but not that of the lake tonight, but that lake before, when she'd almost drowned beneath that chilling water. Her mind flexed like an atrophied muscle, and she was no longer a little girl, but an entity, something outside herself, something good, *invading her very being, through the pores of her skin, through her mouth and nostrils, she breathed in that* Pure Good. *The power that the bad thing in its jealous rage had tried to steal from her, had tried to turn into something bad. Because she had let it. But Torch had taught her:* IT CAN B GOOD, IT CAN B GOOD. MAKE U STRONG.

Teddy breathed better beneath the water than she ever had before.

But she was there for a purpose.

She'd done this for a rat her brother had killed.

She'd done this for a dead cat that her friend Torch had brought home for her.

And now she must—must do it for this man who awakened her from the endless night, who had brought her out of her living grave.

She saw the man burning beneath the water. She sliced her hand through the heavy water and reached out to him.

Burning, he began to split into two different men, each looking alike, each burning, and each man stretched an arm out to her.

One of them was that Bad Thing, the thing that had gotten into Jake, the thing that had brought her to the house and buried her in that slimy place with the creepy-crawlies.

She grabbed the hand of that man who seemed to be burning most, who seemed to not understand why she reached for his hand, who almost flinched. I AM A MONSTER! he cried.

She hoped she was making the right choice.

She did not want to deliver the Bad Thing into the world of the living.

As she touched the man, flames sprouted along her arms as though his burning were contagious. Teddy felt that Power inside her flow like water to him in exchange for his fire. The fire itself did not burn her, but extinguished itself in a blue aura surrounding her body.

Clare screamed, falling into the snow as if she had just been struck down by this shared vision between her and Teddy.

3.

Teddy was coming down from her seizure. Tommy wiped her forehead with his hand—he was sure she would die of pneumonia after coming out of that freezing lake. The girl no longer clung tenaciously to Cup. Tommy pulled off his sweatshirt and wrapped the girl in it. He lifted her up. She was very light.

Then he heard the noise gurgling like boiling water from the dead man's throat.

Cup Coffey opened his eyes and looked up into Tommy's face, and before the pain of his burns, before he vomited up the water he had drowned in, he saw Teddy Amory's face and knew that she had brought him back.

"Shit," Tommy said, his voice tinged with a weariness as if aware that some task was still not finished, "he's one of *them* now." Tommy lifted a brick from the rubble that had showered the area. He raised it, prepared to bring it down on the man's face. He wondered when it would end. When the evil that had drunk the lifeblood from this town would truly be destroyed. He saw brief flashes of *the Boy-Eating Spider, his father whispering in the dark, saw Rick Stetson in the Key Theater, his face torn.*

Something in Tommy's mind snapped like a boot coming down on a dry twig in a silent wood. *Enough!*

Teddy Amory cried out, "No!" She shivered beneath the sweatshirt Tommy had covered her with.

Tommy looked back to Clare who was kneeling as if in prayer. She seemed to be looking directly at him with uncertainty.

"But he's one of *them* now," Tommy whispered, not wanting to hit the man with the brick. *But I have to, he was dead, and now he's alive.* Beneath the shadow of the brick,

Cup was trying to say something, trying to move, but he was too weak.

Clare held her hand out in a halting gesture. "No, Tommy," she said, "I think—I *know* he's one of *us.*"

4.

March, 1987

From *The Nightmare Book of Cup Coffey:*

SPRING!

So it is over.

I've been in this hospital in Newton for what is it—nine weeks? But my strength is back, my skin seems to have healed quite a bit from the burns. Only my memory of this past winter continues to scrape back the scars inside me that have yet to fully heal. And all the pain of these treatments. Still, pain is never bad when it means you're healing. It passes more quickly than you'd think.

The pieces of what happened in those last few moments beneath the burning Marlowe-Houston House have been drifting in and out of my mind like a dream that can only be remembered in fragments. Fragments of pieces—I remember very little of the feeling that accompanied it. Fear, outrage, terror, wonder, awe, repulsion? Any and all of those perhaps.

I remember crawling along, holding the Amory girl as if she were my lifeline and I, hers. Trying to dig out through the muddy tunnel to the source of trickling water, and then hearing that noise behind me. And knowing that back there was the Eater of Souls.

And turning. Turning around to face something I would rather not have faced, I would rather have left buried.

When I turned around in that small dark tunnel, I pushed Teddy Amory ahead—if I was the key and she was the door, then what was most important was not whether I survive or whether she survive, but that *one* of us survive. If the Eater of Souls had both of us, I was positive It would be able to open the door wide and in Its own words, "be closed no more forever."

What I saw when I turned around in that well of human excrement was a young man of about 28, who had spent the last twelve years of his life underground, his hair matted with feces, his skin blanched worm-white, clothed only in the filth from which he came. His face running with sores, his mouth flapping dumbly.

His brown eyes glowing with a feral intensity—a need for freedom from this sewer prison.

I saw myself, my corrupted self, my brooding, nightmare cousin, what had been festering in the bowels of this miasmic earth since the night Bart Kinter had died. The evil I had disturbed then had taken hold of that part of me that was open to corruption and planted that seed into its fertile heart. Neither a ghost nor the worm of corruption, the Eater of Souls in its shape-shifting splendor had taken on the aspect of my own mirror-image.

I don't remember my feelings then: horror, disgust, fear. But I knew that this thing must be destroyed once and for all. This thing that was not me but in its jealousy and anger had wanted to be the distorted mirror of my soul.

Behind this creature, burning maggots crawled in feeble attempts to escape from the inferno that raged above us. They were Its own children, those worms, catching fire that brought destruction down upon the Eater of Souls, for they crawled to their Master and surrounded him, surrounded us both, with a ring of fire.

But Teddy Amory was out of that ring—she was pushing her way through the mud, to the cold stream, into the sewer that bled to Clear Lake.

I have heard that a scorpion, when encircled by fire, will sting itself to death. Watching this warped image of myself —this young man whose very existence seemed smudged with nightmares and vengeance—was like watching a scorpion's own stinger come down against itself.

This Eater of Souls tore into Itself as fire from Its crawling minions burst across Its overgrown greasy hair; It swatted at leeches that attached themselves to Its feet.

I watched my corrupted self die. Burning, Its jaws gaping in a soundless scream of fury and agony.

I let It die, and that, I suppose, is what It did not expect. It had no power to re-create those images of love and hate (Lily Cammack and Bart Kinter) which had for so long haunted me, and so I watched this Eater of Souls scratch at Its fiery open wounds, even as I felt the first tickle of fire across my own hands and face.

But I knew Teddy Amory would be safe—that whatever enormous evil power this cursed spirit wielded would not be fulfilled through any butchering of innocent children.

The last thing I remember, other than that mindless demon devouring Its own skin in an effort to rejuvenate Itself, was the heat of fire and then the clean, cool wash of icy water across my back.

And I knew: *I am not afraid to die.*

Then, waking upon the shore of Clear Lake, a boy I barely recognized holding a brick over my head. But I knew something in my blood: that Teddy Amory had brought me out of that fiery underworld through the freezing water of the lake, and breathed life back into me.

Through whatever "taint" that little girl possesses, my soul was restored.

Did I ever see the true Eater of Souls? Did I ever tear the mask off the creature, and see the nature of the Evil buried there at the Goat Dance?

Where Evil is buried, one should not go digging.

You may ask: What kind of smoke are you?

And I will tell you: It is enough that there is smoke. Nobody needs to look into the hellish pit where the smoke comes from. Some doors are meant to remain closed. Forever.

I see the others now: the survivors of what the newspapers are evidently calling an event of "Mass Hysteria" and "Spontaneous Combustion." The nurses here try to keep the papers and the reporters away. I suppose they are more interested in the story about the fictitious plague that was going around Pontefract—and I understand that some of the residents returned less than a week after they'd left, which I guess is okay. But not all the residents have returned. Some are missing, some are not even missed. People who live in towns like Pontefract become tied to the land; it is their lifeblood, and they live within a stone's throw of their great-grandfather's original homestead, they visit the graves of men and women who died before the Civil War. In a town like Pontefract, history is alive. And now the Dead only walk in dreams. Pontefract Prep is back in session, although it is advertising for a new headmaster and a few teachers. I miss Prescott, and George—I cannot begin to fathom those tragedies. I dreamed last night of them, and Prescott reminded me, *"Do not despair, for all men must die."*

A nurse escorts Clare in here, and then leaves us alone for a while.

Clare brought Teddy in a few times—although I guess I should say that Teddy brought Clare in. Clare is blind now—also suffered burns around her face, although not as bad as mine. All four of us—Teddy, Tommy, Clare and I—*know* about that power Teddy has. But she will have to learn to be careful with it—The Edgar Cayce Foundation in Virginia Beach has accepted her for a long-term study.

Tommy doesn't visit much—maybe he has once or twice. I don't blame him. He and his mother live in Roanoke now, just over the hills, and the last time he called to ask how I was, he said: "I don't have the nightmares anymore, I just want you to know that. I'm not great, but I'm breathing. Do you know? *Breathing."* And I told him I did know, because I wasn't great, either, just *breathing.*

That's better than the alternative.

When Clare comes to the hospital we haven't been able to laugh too much together, but when we do, it is a good laugh and I am left with a glow for days from her visits. She is still staying in Pontefract, with Teddy, at Prescott's barnhouse—who knows for how long. I don't blame her for not wanting to return to her father's house. I asked her why she was even staying in Pontefract at all—why any of us would want to—and she replied, "Because there's really nowhere else now."

Yesterday Teddy told me a joke, and although it was dumb and I'd heard it before, I laughed because of the way she told it.

It feels good when I can laugh, it is like the pain of healing.

5.

April 4, 1987

Cup held Teddy's hand as they walked together through the burnt foundations of the Marlowe-Houston House. They did not speak as they observed the vines tangling across the old stone and brick. The indentation that had once been the cellar was now covered with thick, caked earth and wild grass that had sprouted in the early spring.

Finally, Cup broke the silence. "You're going to enjoy Virginia Beach," he said.

Teddy nodded, but her eyes watched the ground carefully. When she saw a dragonfly alight on a brick, she smashed her foot down on it, but the insect flew away.

"You saved my life, Teddy, I want to—"

"You saved my life, too," she interrupted him.

"Do you still have nightmares? About the Eater of Souls?"

She nodded. "But they can't hurt me. Your scars are all healed."

He shrugged and laughed. "Same old Cup."

"Can we go?" She shivered as if from cold, and for a moment he was afraid she would go into a fit. She hadn't had a seizure in two months.

"You all right?" For a moment he thought he smelled a light jasmine perfume brought up by the cool slap of a breeze.

"Mmm," she murmured, and pulled his hand so they were stepping over the rubble, toward the yellow field, high with

grass. Into the Goat Dance. "Will you wait for me to grow up?"

"Anything for you, Teddy."

"No you won't. You're gonna marry Clare."

Cup raised his eyebrows. "But maybe you won't marry me when you grow up."

Teddy let go of his hand and punched him playfully in the arm. She didn't answer him. Then she grew very serious. "We should've burned all of this," and the little girl who had recently turned ten raised her hand to indicate the entire field. "Just to be sure."

Cup nodded. He felt the hairs on the back of his neck rising slightly. He squeezed Teddy Amory's hand.

"We will," he said. Time to mow this old field down the only way I know how.

Cup reached into his pocket and pulled out a pack of matches. He flipped the book open and plucked a match out. He struck it. He set the match down on the ground.

The man and the girl watched the grass curl and wither beneath the touch of the flame.